Black Shapes

in a Darkened Room

OTHER REBEL SATORI BOOKS BY MARSHALL MOORE

Novels

An Ideal for Living

The Concrete Sky

Bitter Orange

Story Collections

Love Is a Poisonous Color

A Garden Fed by Lightning

The Infernal Republic

Non-Fiction

I Wouldn't Normally Do This Kind of Thing: A Memoir

Sunset House: Selected Essays

BLACK SHAPES IN A DARKENED ROOM

Stories by

Marshall Moore

REBEL SATORI PRESS
New Orleans & New York

Published in the United States of America by
Rebel Satori Press
www.rebelsatoripress.com

Book design: Sven Davisson

Paperback ISBN: 978-1-60864-373-8

Black Shapes in a Darkened Room
Is dedicated to Jason Luciano

CONTENTS

If you're in pitch blackness, all you can do
is sit tight until your eyes get used to the dark.
Haruki Murakami, from *Norwegian Wood*
Translated from the Japanese by Jay Rubin

BLACK SHAPES IN A DARKENED ROOM

The siege has been on for weeks. I won't be able to leave my apartment again. Imagine the desperate claustrophobia of a Belfast, Beirut, or Banja Luka: an acrid veil of smoke overhead, bombs and gunfire in the background, Molotov cocktails crashing through every intact pane of glass, rooftop snipers on the lookout for pedestrian targets. Impossible to venture out. My circumstances are different, but the result is the same. I can't leave. And I'm in Berkeley. Apart from the occasional earthquake or student protest, this is supposed to be a place where nothing bad ever happens.

Edward, I write in my journal. It's exquisite, this journal. Hand-tooled leather the color of chocolate, heavy grey paper. I bought it in Florence. *I'm sorry. I will spend the rest of eternity telling you that. Will you ever listen? I'm so sorry.*

I used to be a flight attendant. Home is this old apartment a few blocks from the university: old furniture I picked up from consignment shops and flea markets, candles everywhere, cobalt-glass vases I filled with fragrant clusters of the white jasmine that grows semi-wild outside. Now I'm overdosing on my own hipness. I want to be above the clouds again, but work hasn't been an option for weeks. I had to call in, feign an illness, and quit. Too dangerous to do anything else.

Based out of United's hub at the San Francisco airport, I'd spend a week or two smiling and serving cocktails five miles above the world. One night I'd sleep in a hotel room in Sydney. Sometime later, Paris. Taipei. Never much time to acquaint myself with these cities, to be honest. It's not as glamorous as it sounds. I might have a couple of hours to stumble down some foreign street in search of a café or restaurant worth a second visit, maybe a friendly stranger to wake up with. After a period aloft, I'd fly home to California and sleep for a couple of days. From Shanghai, Madrid, or Toronto I'd have e-mailed friends to let them know when I'd be home, and soon enough the phone would start to ring. It was a life.

Now I can't go outside. The attack comes before the door swings shut behind me, invisible hands ripping at my hair, my clothes, my skin. The walls in the vestibule beyond my apartment cracked last time I tried to leave; clouds of plaster dust drifted down from the ceiling. The beams in the walls seemed to groan as some immense weight or force bore down on them. The light overhead flickered once, twice, went out. In the intangible distance, screams I couldn't hear so much as feel. Palpable rage. I slammed the door shut behind me and stayed home, praying the talisman would hold.

Last time I left this place was when… (*Be honest, Noel*) a month ago? Six weeks?

I write this knowing it will be my suicide note. Even if I'm not the one who does myself in, my death will be seen as the sad, solitary opt-out by a young man who lost his grip on the real world. The problem is, the real world is slippery. Your grip is never as tight as you think.

I don't want to die.

I don't.

But I don't think I'm going to get any choice in the matter.

When I met Edward Wright, we both lived in Baltimore. I had just finished college: U of Maryland at College Park, BA in psychology, useful for nothing but retail or a future of huge student loan payments for the advanced degrees I'd need if I actually wanted to work in that field. I wasn't sure what to do with myself next. My bookstore job turned into a full-time assistant manager gig, a professional cul de sac in the outer suburbs of hell. And in the romance department, when I met Edward, I arrived with more than my full baggage allowance. I opted to turn away at the check-in counter instead of trying to board.

I met Mr Wright while he was living with Mr Wrong. Edward's gorgeous Trinidadian boyfriend Nathaniel had lost several jobs in a row and about to lose his visa. The INS hung overhead like the paper-slicer of Damocles. Edward, the sweet naïve fool, had been sucked into supporting the guy: apparently he gave legendary head. I have to say, although Nathaniel made me a little weak in the knees, Edward was the one I wanted. Couldn't get him out of my mind. He worked 14-hour days as a personal trainer to keep Nathaniel in good clothes and good weed. Nathaniel, an elegant six-foot-three panther of a man with sexy shoulder-length dreads, got by on the occasional modeling gig. He'd pose nude for sculptors or slink down a runway to debut some department store's new collection. By contrast, Edward's looks revealed themselves on the second look: a lean and well-developed body beneath his dark clothes, fair freckled skin prone to sunburn, overcast blue-grey eyes, handsome in an offbeat way but devastating when he broke into a grin.

I influenced Edward's decision to get rid of Nathaniel. *You're addicted,* I told him. *And you feel sorry for the guy.* When I said nobody could blame him for loving to swab his tonsils with Nathaniel's cock, Edward socked me. Gave me a black eye. I'll remember the look of mixed shame and horror on his face long after I'm dead. Edward threw his arms around me, sobbing too hard to ask me to forgive him. He dumped Nathaniel the next day.

That same week, Edward threw Nathaniel out of their apartment and changed the locks. *Solve your own problems,* he told his newly-minted ex, who bawled like he had, in fact, cared once. *Go down on the goons from the INS when they come to deport you. It's not my goddamn problem anymore.*

I cheered. The bruise faded. What the hell, we've all had our outbursts. You can never predict what someone's going to do next, no matter how well you think you know him. Thing was, I sort of had it coming. I led him on. But I shouldn't have forgotten he did that.

When the attack comes, it's like someone is trying to drive an invisible car through the wall. The geometry of the house seems about to fail, as if a massive pair of shoulders are forcing their way into a child's sweater. The first time this happened, I called Henry, the condo association's manager. He stopped by my apartment the next day, surveyed the damage with widening eyes.

"We must have had an earthquake," he said. "Would you mind logging onto the Internet? We can confirm it."

"Earthquake," I said. The idea made sense, I guess, if you didn't know what was going on. "Sure. I've got a fast connection. Go crazy."

Of course there hadn't been one.

"I'll call the maintenance guys and get those walls re-plastered," Henry said.

One more attempt at leaving my apartment was enough to convince me to stay in. The hallway window imploded. Shards of glass peppered my face and arms. I'm lucky I wasn't blinded. Audible roars that time, deafening, the enraged bellows of a minotaur whose virgin sacrifice lacked a hymen.

Ever taken a really long flight, say San Francisco to Sydney or London? New York to Johannesburg? By the time you arrive, the cabin is fetid from all the farts and armpits, bits of food dropped on the floor, crotches in need of a wash. The same bad smells, exhaled over and over, assault you until you want to disinfect your tingling sinuses with a Q-tip you've dipped in peroxide. My apartment smells like the lavatory in a 777 that has just crossed an ocean. I live on the shady side of the building, and I keep the blinds closed, the curtains drawn. I'd open the window for fresh air but I'm afraid of what I'd let in.

Last week I parted the curtains and looked outside. Something struck my window hard enough to crack the glass. In my mind's eye I saw a corpse hurtling toward me, something dead and putrid, a dog flattened on the freeway, then snatched up and flung for the occasion. *Noel, you're seeing things.* For a second, I saw lurid purple-red smears across the crazed glass, clumps of fur, a pointed tooth wedged in one of the cracks. The stench of sun-baked rot underlay the armpit atmosphere of my apartment, evanescent like the cigarette aroma wafting off the clothes of a smoker you pass on the sidewalk. Now you smell it, now you don't. When I blinked, the vision passed. The roadkill stink subsided, and I saw nothing but a run-of-the-mill broken window. One more thing for Henry to take care of.

Edward, you're not going to forgive me, are you?

I tried to keep my head down for the two months between accepting the flight attendant job and moving to Dallas for training at American's headquarters – Barbie Boot Camp, my colleagues called it. (I wouldn't transfer to United for another year, when I decided I wanted to live in the Bay Area.) My excuse, I told Edward when he called: I needed to work overtime at the bookstore to pay off my credit card debt before I left. I needed some money in the bank to finance the move. Please understand, I begged him. You know I really like you. But I have to do this. Was it manipulative of me? That's a question for history, not for me; I thought I was doing what I had to do, putting the issue of this putative relationship with him on the back burner until I had put my own life together, until he had more time apart from Nathaniel, until until until…

OK, so I ran away and went looking for justifications after the fact. I had to whistle in the dark. The easy way out tempted me every time I saw the bastard. On one level, I wanted to press myself closer to him when we hugged each other hello, to turn the friendly dry kiss on the lips into something hot, wet, and horizontal. Any idiot could see how much he wanted that. His emotions hung out all raw and naked for everyone to see. When he didn't think I was looking, he'd look at me as if he couldn't believe I liked him at all. Even in conversation, his eyes would light up, letting me know there was no other place he wanted to be.

I didn't think I deserved that kind of adoration.

I see that now, Edward. How many times do I have to tell you I fucked up? That I should never have run away? It's not enough to say I thought you deserved better, is it? You made up your mind I was the one you wanted, and that was that. You stubborn son of a bitch.

In retrospect, I should have treated Edward like the miracle he was. The odds of finding a man like that… how can I describe it? It was like winning the lottery.

I fucking ran away and stayed gone for a long time. Did I want to punish Edward for loving me? As I said, I had baggage of my own. It's the classic pathology: you care about me; therefore, there must be something wrong with you, so I must make you suffer. I didn't call him. Well, that's not true. I did, sporadically. I weakened. I couldn't get him out of my head, goddamn it. I needed to hear his voice. I needed to know he was OK. I wanted him to hope I'd come to my senses and find my way back to him. And the hell of it is, I always believed I would. Just not like this.

I didn't kill him. That's how it sounds, I know, but I didn't kill him. Not exactly.

Edward, I write in desperation, as if an answer will appear on the page like invisible ink unvanishing. *Call them off. This isn't how our story is supposed to end.*

It's growing dark outside. This is the fogged-in time of year, here in the Bay Area. The sun gives up on the day rather late in the afternoon, 4.30 or so, suggesting winter even in July. Some primitive part of me panics at the coming of night. I used to enjoy lying on my sofa and watching the sky deepen with sunset; now I'm too scared. The furniture becomes a menagerie of dangerous black shapes in the darkened room. Sounds outside take on a terrifying quality. Has something evil hunkered down on the doorstep? What are those voices? Everything rational in me collapses.

Edward and I bumped into each other in Miami three months ago, after a year and a half apart. I'd barely written, e-mailed sporadically, never called once. The usual. I had no idea he'd be there… or where he'd be, to be honest. He used to e-mail me whether I replied or not, and I loved that about him. I hated it, too, and felt guilty. He deserved better. When I noticed his e-mails were coming less and less often, I felt a shameful flush of relief. Part of me wanted him to move on. The other part wouldn't let go.

After a hard month of too many overtime hours, too many cities, too many languages, my hands had started to shake from fatigue. I kept myself functioning with caffeine and twenty-minute cat naps. My circadian rhythms were as misaligned as trailer trash from Biloxi trying to tango. Exhausted to the point of incoherence, for some reason I couldn't fall asleep. I left my South Beach hotel for a few drinks, to dull the clamor in my head. In the club, there was Edward, talking with a cute Asian guy he introduced as a colleague. They were in town for a conference.

"But you're supposed to be in Baltimore!" I steadied myself against the edge of the bar.

"I moved to San Diego two months ago."

I couldn't look at him without welling up. Every few minutes I'd hug him again, then turn aside to knuckle tears away from the corners of my eyes.

I called in sick, persuaded a doctor friend back in California to fax a note to my boss, and spent three days in bed with Edward. He blew off the conference. We only got out of bed to let the room service cart in, shower, and use the bathroom. We went for walks through South Beach when we were drained dry, to drink in the sun, the warmth that made us want to tug each other's clothes off again and roll like puppies in the sweaty sheets of our hotel bed, the nouveau-deco-retro architecture, the acres of browning flesh.

"I could almost live here," I told him.

He shuddered. "Too muggy. Let's stay in California."

Our time in Florida felt like the first chapter of happily-ever-after, but we both had to return to the real world. We parted with kisses at the airport and made promises to be in touch, passionately determined in the moment to see where things could go. My old habits kicked in within a month: I stopped replying to Edward's e-mails and got slack about returning calls. True, it's hard to be in constant touch with someone when you're on an airplane most of the time. No matter how much you love him, the constraints on time and communication technology are real. I drifted away again. I took comfort in the familiar sensation of denying myself what I wanted most.

Three weeks ago, I got home from my last full-length work-related odyssey – Vancouver, Osaka, Singapore – and found a livid Edward on the landing. My legs almost gave out when I saw him. He wore a grey sweater the color of the sky, and his nose glowed red from the midsummer chill.

I fumbled in my pocket for my keys. My overstuffed carry-on suitcases toppled over backward. (Try not shopping when you're in Singapore.)

"Where have you been?" he asked me after an awkward hug.

I couldn't answer. With effort, I unlocked the front door and motioned for him to come in. I dropped my bags on the floor and collapsed on the sofa, then let Edward move me like a big rag doll so that my head rested in his lap. He stroked my hair. I hated myself.

"I got sick of waiting," he said. "I drove up."

Edward's fingers, while slender, were stronger than they looked. He massaged the knots out of my neck and shoulders.

"Noel, I thought we had started something," Edward said after a long silence.

I tensed up again.

"We did," I said quickly. "No, wait, that came out wrong. We have." My face burned. "I'm sorry."

He stopped the massage.

"Why do you keep doing this? I know you want me as much as I want you, but you keep running away. I don't understand that."

I sat up.

"Edward," I began.

He closed his eyes and shook his head.

"Don't," he said. "Please don't say anything that sounds like your old excuses. I don't want to hear it."

"I don't have an excuse," I told him. "If I did, that would be a step up from where I am now. You deserve better than me."

His face turned hibiscus red, as it did the time he hit me. He closed his eyes.

"Edward," I tell the air in my apartment. The journal pages feel like skin. I caress them like Edward's back after the first time we made love. "I know you can hear me. I know you're out there."

When mediums channel spirits, a state of deep calm must be attained. I have meditated. I have attempted to clear my mind. I've lit every candle I own. The stick of champa incense burning in the kitchen has rendered the air almost too sweet to breathe. Fear clouds my thoughts, but I have done the best I can.

The talisman won't hold forever.

An eye has opened inside my mind. Something has awakened, something that can *see*. When I recognize Edward's backward-slanted chickenscratch on the Florentine paper, I gasp as if I've been stabbed in the face with a length of piano wire. The psychic pain almost throws me out of my trance. The tiny window of vision threatens to close.

The voodooienne diluted the recipe to make sure you'd need a new charm from her. Its power is going to wear out in a few hours. Otherwise I wouldn't be able to write through your hands like this. That woman thought you were a fool. She thought you were another stupid white boy who had read too many New Age books.

"This is Berkeley. People here aren't supposed to do things like that," I said to the paper as if I'd drawn an ear on it, wondering if I'd ever in this life or the next stop feeling so stupid. The pen in my hand feels as if someone else is holding it, and describing the sensation by whispering to me.

I love you but you're kind of an idiot.

"We've established that."

You shouldn't have played with me for so long, Noel. You attracted attention, and once I was dead and the story got around, it pissed a lot of people off. Haven't you figured that out by now?

"What was there to figure out, Edward?"

On this side, there's nothing that infuriates people more than someone like you who could have had it so good and kept running away. You were too much of a pussy to grab the brass ring when you had the chance. AIDS and hate crimes sent a lot of gay guys to the grave with loose ends still untied. Couples who had been together for years were separated in their prime. A lot of relationships were never reconciled. Your behavior has been a major affront to those people. They're not impressed.

My hand ached from being forced to write someone else's words. My wrists felt as taut as guitar strings. If I were to thump them, they would twang.

It's like going to prison when you're guilty of raping kids, Noel. Before the cell door even slides shut behind you, you're already done for. Your inability to deal with our romance left me at the foot of your stairs with a broken neck, and I entered the afterlife screaming. People noticed. They were insulted, and they decided to do something about it. Pretty soon we're going to be together on this side, whether you're ready or not. I'm sorry it has to be like this.

"You hit me once. I should have known you'd do something like this to me in retaliation."

It's not me, Noel. It's not about retaliation, or my temper. There's nothing I can do. I've tried, and it's like trying to change the course of a hurricane by shouting into the gale. Look at it this way: I'll be there when they're finished with you. Be brave. It won't hurt for long.

I snapped out of my trance and slammed the journal shut, wracked with cold chills, shaking.

"You're never going to pull your head out of your ass, are you?" Edward had pulled away from me. At the other end of my sofa, he hugged himself like a six-year-old boy in adult guise. "You're going to keep doing this until… what? Until you get tired of the game and find someone else to torture?"

"No, it's not like that!" I tried to put my arms around him, exhaustion making me feel like a statue brought only halfway to life. "I just… I…"

"What?" He glared at me. "Finish the sentence. I dare you."

"I can't."

"That's the long and short of it, isn't it, Noel? You can't. For the last few years, you haven't been able to, and you still can't. I'm leaving now, and when I go, it's the last time you're going to see me. I'm done."

I ran after him and tried to hold on. I stumbled, lost my balance, fell against him at the top of the stairs. We teetered on the brink for a terrible two seconds; I fell backward on the floor and Edward pitched forward, crashing down the stairs headfirst. The amplified cereal crunch of his breaking bones will stay with me until the sun cools and God forgets he ever invented the universe.

"Edward, how long do I have?"

A wind has picked up outside. The talisman, contained in one of those tall red *bodega* prayer candles, has burnt itself out. Inside, its glass container is smudged black with smoke from the special wick the *voodooienne* had prepared for me and inserted ever so carefully while I watched, doubting and hoping in equal measure, wondering if I'd make it home without being run over by a car veering out of control or eaten by someone's rabid mastiff.

They're in here…

No answer comes, but the dozens of candles I've lit start to wink out one by one. Shadows are eating the room.

"Edward!" I scream. "Stop them!"

No answer comes. It's hard to breathe, my heart is beating so fast. My belly is full of rocks. I can't swallow. I have to wait and watch these little flames snuffed one after another.

Wait, Noel.

Of course I'll wait. It's out of my hands now.

I kept Edward waiting, didn't I? What choice do I have?

Fair's fair.

THE RIGHT WAY
TO EAT A BAGEL

A gust of cold early-March air buffeted George, distracting him from his crossword puzzle. He looked up to see if Angela had arrived. She'd said to expect a short black woman with shoulder-length braids and a brown leather jacket, glasses, but not wearing make-up, no way, not at this time of night. The diner door swung shut behind a chunky young white guy with acne. George turned his attention back to his half-empty pint of Guinness and the smudged newsprint on the table in front of him.

George hated crossword puzzles and wouldn't have been working this one if he hadn't been in a hurry to get out of his apartment. Meeting Angela like this, in the middle of the night, had to be the most impulsive thing he'd done in recent memory. On the other hand, why not? It had been her idea, and what exactly did he have to lose? He was desperate for a change of scene, some fresh air, a different perspective. A conversation with someone who had no vested interest in talking him into anything or out of it, either. He'd been a little stir-crazy, and not quite ready to close his eyes. Now here he was. A previous someone had left a dishevelled copy of today's *Post* on the table; George had read the articles that interested him while draining his first pint, waiting. That left him two choices: staring out the window like a lost soul in an Edward Hopper painting, or attempting the crossword puzzle.

Why did the puzzles he worked call for words like *ennui* and *narthex* and *cedilla*? Case in point: this one featured celebrity trivia. George knew a bit about literature and film, yes, but he tuned out the gossipy media as much as possible. Especially now, during Oscar season. Off the top of his head, he could name the actor who had played the reporter in Fellini's 8½, but could he name the seven-figure hunk who had played opposite Nicole Kidman in her last two films, and was there a reason why he should care?

The waitress stopped by.

"You want some chips or fries or a sandwich or somethin'?"

George shook his head.

"Just another one of these when I'm done," he said. "And a crossword puzzle dictionary if you've got one."

"Oh sure, no problem," the waitress, a cute but Q-tip skinny redhead named Elyce, said through her mouthful of gum. Her cinnamon-scented breath seemed to cling to him. "We keep two or three around for customers. They're by the cash register. I'll bring one right over."

"You're kidding," George said.

"Of course I am. This is a diner. I'll bring you some chips, though. You look like you could use a bowl of chips."

George shrugged. He clicked his fingernails on the tabletop, which was smeary from the moist bits of food and beverage splashes Elyce had no doubt been wiping away all day with an increasingly grimy hand towel: pale grey streaks over pink Formica gloss.

"I'm waiting for someone," he said.

"Who isn't?"

Elyce the waitress walked away and George studied the white squares on the crossword puzzle again, waiting for either Angela or some flash of verbal insight to arrive like a *deus ex machina* in an ancient Greek tragedy.

+

George: *i don't really understand why you're online… you know, in a chat room. you don't sound like someone who does this all the time.*

Angela: *I'm not, this is my first time, my husband is away on business and I just turned on the computer and here I am*

George: *had to talk to someone? had to make a connection? =)*

Angela: *I'm not sure what I'm looking for, just to talk with somebody I suppose. What's that thing you did, with the equals sign?*

George: *this? =)? look at it sideways, it's a smiley face. see?*

Angela: *That's cute. You're cute. Thank you.*

+

This is a bad idea. This whole thing has BAD IDEA written all over it in big red letters. I should pay for my beer and go home and just forget about Angela.

George's grip on the base of his beer mug would have strangled the glass if it had been alive. He twitched, from nerves he guessed, and his hand slipped on condensation. The glass pitched to one side and sloshed Guinness across the crossword puzzle. *Affleck hometown* (*Boston*, number 29 Across) and *Fred and* (*Ginger*, number 18 Down) and the empty stack of squares where Nicole Kidman's hot new romantic lead should have gone were all reduced to a Rorschach blotch of carbonated, alcoholic ink.

This did not make George entirely unhappy.

At least now I don't have to finish filling the goddamn thing out, not with two thirds of it soaked.

Another burst of cold air signalled the arrival of someone new, and when George looked up from the soggy mess of newspaper in front of him, he knew he'd lost his chance to slip away. A guilty blush warmed his face as Angela closed the distance between the door and his booth.

When she slid onto the bench opposite and extended a hand to shake, George's first thought was *She's prettier than I expected.*

George classified female attractiveness along three axes: Pretty, Cute, and Hot. Pretty women were the even-featured ones who had been the girls next door growing up, the ones his mother wanted him to take out on dates and marry and impregnate. They had clear skin and symmetrical faces and an air of steadiness about them. Cute women tended to be the shorter ones who seemed younger than they perhaps really were. The facial topology could be more varied but they smiled a lot and were easy to like. And the Hot women, well, they were the ones who smouldered like runway models with no panties on under their Prada. He would expect a Hot woman to snarl "Say my name, bitch!" in bed but not a Pretty one, for example.

Julia, George's ex-wife, had been a stunning amalgam of all three. She still was, he assumed. And she was gone now, wasn't she? George refused to let himself dwell on her. Enough damage had already been done.

And Angela? Pretty, yes, actually, somewhat to his surprise. Not for the first time, George suspected his rating system fell short when he tried to use it on non-white women. Black women, for example, could be Regal in a way that no white woman ever could. The towering cheekbones and the imperious bearing gave these women an air of being mistresses of all they surveyed.

This was probably the worst idea of my life, agreeing to come out on a night like this, tonight of all nights.

She's going to think I'm a loser.

By any objective standard, she wouldn't be wrong.

"Firm handshake," George said.

"I'm in upper management," Angela said. "I didn't get there by batting my eyelashes at people."

"Break many bones with that grip?"

"More balls than bones," Angela said. "Is the coffee here any good or should I just order a beer?"

"I guess it depends on the outcome you want," George said. "Caffeine or alcohol. Do you want to wake up or go to sleep?"

"Yes," Angela said.

This took George a second. "Right," he said. "*Yes.* That would be why we're here."

Angela stared at him. "I know why *I'm* here," she said. She turned and looked around for the waitress, apparently saw her, raised her eyebrows, and nodded in a *Come over here* way. "Are you sure *you* do?"

A darkness smiled in the center of George, and he filled it with his remaining two inches of Guinness.

"I don't want you to talk me into or out of anything," he said. He wiped his mouth with the back of his hand. "I'm clear on that much."

"Oh you sounded pretty clear on what you wanted," Angela said. "I guess that's the real reason I'm here."

"You wanted to see my clarity for yourself?"

"You could say that."

"First time anyone's ever wanted me for my *clarity*," George said.

Elyce returned to take their orders, two beers and a basket of fries to supplement the stale chips George hadn't touched, and left an oily kitchen smell lingering in her wake. George knew he and Angela would leave this diner reeking of grease. Soon enough, they'd bundle up in their coats and leave, with the waxy stink of the griddle in their hair, their clothes, their pores. Despite the cold temperature and the blustery wind, their noses would still pick up the odor. In the grand scheme of things, he supposed it mattered very little. George had other things on his mind, and Angela could go back to her family and her life smelling like an artery-hardening midnight snack.

Number Eighteen Across: *lox*. George hadn't filled that one in (*smoked and orange*) but an idle glance down at the dry half of the crossword brought the word to mind.

"What am I supposed to talk to you about, then?" asked Angela after a silence.

Their beers came.

"We should talk about normal things," George said. "Tell me the right way to eat a bagel. Do you toast yours and coat them with cream cheese? Do you like lox?"

"You're nervous," Angela said. "I don't think you're committed to seeing this through."

George knew his hands were shaking, and he couldn't warm up no matter how much beer he poured down his throat.

"I've come this far," he said, meeting her gaze.

She studied him a moment, then sipped her beer.

"I'm probably old enough to be your mother," Angela said.

"Don't say that," George said. "That's impossible."

Angela smiled and took another sip. Someone fed the jukebox, and an old Pink Floyd dirge filled the diner: *Set the controls for the heart of the sun…*

"OK, I won't say that. Maybe it's true and maybe it's not. Maybe I'm trying to shake you up a little. Is that such a bad thing?"

"I'm nervous." George looked down.

Angela reached across the table and took his hand.

"I hate lox," she said. "But garlic bagels are a weakness of mine. Lots of cream cheese. The kind with chives in it. We're going to be just fine, OK?"

+

Angela: *I've never done this before. Is it OK for me to ask what you look like?*

George: *that's fine, you can ask me whatever you want*

Angela: *Oh no, anything? I don't think I want to go that far... besides, if you sent me a picture I wouldn't know what to do with it.*

George: *it's kind of funny*

Angela: *What's funny about it?*

George: *my expectations, maybe. i just didn't have this in mind when i signed on*

Angela: *So are you going to tell me what you look like? I want to know who I'm talking to.*

George: *late 20's. red hair. freckles. kind of handsome i guess, depending on what you're into*

Angela: *You know I'm married, don't you? With kids. And I'm an African American.*

George: *great, good, cool. i had a wife once, for a few minutes.*

Angela: *What happened?*

George: *i'm still trying to figure that out but i guess it doesn't matter anymore, she's still gone*

+

"You loved your wife very much," Angela said, releasing George's hand.

"What makes you say that?"

"That lost look on your face. I think that's the real reason you wanted me to meet you here. I've been married a long time. Maybe you wanted my perspective as much as I wanted yours."

"Are you sure that's what this is about? Perspective?"

Angela nodded.

"All right then. Yes. I loved her."

"And that's why you're doing this?"

"No. I mean, maybe that's part of it, but there's so much…" George stopped to think. "It's not for just one reason. So my business failed and I'm bankrupt and my wife left me. For a woman, if you want to know."

Angela nodded again and sipped more beer. "Another woman. How about that. That's happened in my family too. Is she happier now?"

"She hasn't called to let me know. I'd like to know. I have to hope she is, after what she put me through."

"And where do I come in?" Angela asked.

"The door over there?" George smiled. "I think that's where you came in. Although I might have been hallucinating."

"Grief'll do that to you."

"I just want to feel *better*," George said. "I mean, I haven't been expecting to be on top of the world, but *better*? It's not unreasonable. It keeps not happening."

"You're trying to talk yourself out of it," Angela said softly. "Would it make you feel any better if I said I understood?"

"How could you?"

"I have a husband and great kids and a nice home, so my life must be perfect," Angela said. "That's why I came out on a night like this. Didn't it occur to you to ask where my kids were?"

George had to admit the thought had never crossed his mind. He had wanted to start a family with Julia. Once upon a time. Perhaps this proved he had never been cut out for paternity, that he didn't think to ask about her kids straight away? Did that indicate some deficit in his priorities, some inherent unsuitability? Or were kids something you had to get used to? If it was such a complicated thing, having a family, why did so many people do it? And how?

"With their aunt. Who would have me locked up if she knew I was out in the middle of the night like this. With a white guy at least 15 years younger than me." She smiled at him as if she'd made a very small joke.

"So your life is not perfect," George said. "Forgive me for assuming it was."

"It's not perfect," Angela whispered.

They looked at each other. Elyce broke the spell by asking if they were OK, did they need anything else, some coffee, a sandwich, some chicken nuggets? More chips?

Strychnine, George thought. *Something very old-fashioned like that. Arsenic.*

"We're just great, honey," Angela said.

She turned her head to watch Elyce walked away.

"How do you want to do it?" Angela asked.

"What?"

"You know what I mean. I want you to tell me what you have in mind."

George opened his mouth and closed it. A sourness crept up the back of his throat.

"You really want me to tell you. Right now. You actually want me to describe it."

"Yes," Angela said. "I do."

"What if I just wanted you to have a normal conversation with me?" George asked. This felt like treading water in a whirlpool: dark currents dragged him down. His palms filmed, and he wiped them against his jeans. The stickiness lingered.

"I already told you how I like my bagels."

"What's your husband's name? Your kids? How old are they? What grades are they in?"

Angela shook her head. "I don't know what to say."

22

"You don't know the names of your husband and kids?"

"Of course I do. But this is the last conversation you're ever going to have with another living human being, and you want to talk about bagels and my kids?"

"Yes. No. I don't know," George said. He drained his glass. Might as well optimize his alcohol intake. Look at it as getting things underway.

"Tell me how you're going to do it."

"I can't."

"You're not going to go through with it, then?" Angela asked. "You're going to lose your nerve?"

George shook his head. Tears stung the corners of his eyes.

"I just wanted to talk to someone," he said. "Someone *real*. Julia's gone. My family... I can't do that to them, call in the middle of the night like this, knowing what it'll be like for them afterward."

Angela took a deep breath. "Maybe I came here to meet you for inspiration," she said. "Maybe I'm braver than I knew."

"What do you mean?"

"There's a reason I asked how you were going to do it," she said.

"What do you mean?" George asked. Then it hit him. "Oh. *You?*"

She nodded. She started to speak and seemed to get choked up, as if there were a word she couldn't force out of her mouth. She grabbed the pen and wrote something in the dry corner of the crossword puzzle, a terrible word that when he saw it, didn't fit with any of the clues he'd been given so far: CANCER.

+

Angela: *So why is it such a surprise, you're talking to me?*
George: *i guess this makes it real*

Angela: *Makes what real?*

George: *last night on earth*

Angela: *I'm sorry?*

Angela: *Hello? Are you there?*

Angela: *George? Hey, be nice to me, I'm new at this, remember?*

George: *never mind, i'm being cryptic. i shouldn't have dragged you into this*

George: *look, this is the last conversation i'll ever have with anyone, as far as i know*

Angela: *Because?*

George: *think about it*

George: *you haven't typed anything for a few minutes, does that mean you're thinking?*

Angela: *I think I've figured it out. But why?*

George: *i should leave you alone. you have your own life. you don't need this*

Angela: *Well, now that you've done it, you can't back out now... We ought to talk.*

+

"I got the idea from an old girlfriend," George said. He surveyed the beer left in his glass. "I've nicknamed it combo therapy. I bought a tank of carbon dioxide from a science supply store. When I get home, I'm going to seal up my bathroom to make it airtight, duct tape around the doorframe, and then I'm going to drink and take pills until I pass out. I won't wake up."

"Very elaborate," Angela said.

"How are you guys doing?" Elyce asked, from out of nowhere.

George jumped. Nerves, he supposed.

24

"Fine," Angela said.

"Another beer," George spoke up a bit as Elyce turned away. Then, to Angela, he asked, "You're going to?"

She looked down. Nodded.

"My church teaches that it's a sin. But what's right about putting my family through hell? There's no treatment for… what I have. The bills will ruin them. How is that the right thing to do?" Her voice hitched at the end. "Both choices are terrifying."

"I envy you in a way," George said.

Angela looked up sharply. "Why is that?"

"You have a family. You have the comfort of a church. Religion. I'm kind of flying solo, here."

"That's one way of looking at it," Angela said. "I'm not sure if that makes me feel better, but it's something to think about."

"I completely underestimated you," George said. A truck rumbled past, rattling the windows. He looked back at Angela.

"It wouldn't be the first time I've been underestimated," she said.

Were there bags under her eyes or was it the light? George scrutinized her face for signs of illness. How impolite would it be to ask what kind of cancer she had, where it was, why it couldn't be treated? Was she in pain? Could she feel the diseased cells crowding out the healthy ones? Weren't they kind of off the edge of the world now, where most rules and conventions no longer applied? Of course he could ask those questions, he concluded after a moment's thought. Those and many others. The thing was, did he really want to know? He'd come here to have a conversation about nothing, after all, before going home to his pills and his gas tank.

"I read about a medieval form of torture," Angela said. "The victim would be immobilized, tied to a chair or something. A rat would be put in a metal urn, with the mouth of the urn against the victim's belly. They'd heat up the urn until the rat freaked out. It would be so desperate to escape it would burrow into the only soft surface it could find..."

"Oh God stop," George said. His gorge rose.

"Cancer took my mother," Angela said. "It seems to run in our family, this particular kind. I know what I'm in for, and it's a lot like what I just described to you. I'm..." She trailed off, shaking her head. "I'm not going through that. I'm not going to do that to my husband and my kids."

George stared out the window again. He couldn't meet her gaze. The corners of his eyes stung. Outside, the corona of mist around the streetlight was the color of a candle about to gutter out. A truck rumbled by.

"I have no idea what to say," George said. "This almost makes me feel selfish. Petty."

"Maybe you don't have to say a word," Angela said.

"I don't have cancer."

"I didn't come here to talk you out of it," she said. "Nobody holds the exclusive rights to pain. It's not an absolute. You make your choices."

"But..."

Angela looked away from him and shrugged her shoulders. A certain tension seemed to leave her face, a certain heaviness. George couldn't be sure. She underwent some subtle shift, as if she'd made a decision, satisfied herself somehow. He looked around the diner: two college students in sparkly club-wear were staring into mugs of coffee; several men around a table by the door were having a loud conversation with their mouths full; one girl who looked too young to be out at this time of night was eating a sandwich and picking her nose as if she were alone – a bruise purpled one side of her face.

"Maybe we've said everything we need to say to each other," Angela said.

She stood abruptly, murmured something that sounded like *Good night*, and strode toward the door. For a second or two, George watched her walk away, her braids bouncing, without the reality of her departure sinking in.

"Wait a minute," he said.

But Angela was already out of earshot.

"Wait a minute!"

Heads turned. The bruised girl withdrew the finger from her nose and stared at her nail as if she'd extracted a diamond instead of a moist crust of snot. The raucous discussion by the door stopped. George jumped to his feet, dashed across the diner, skidded in the slippery place by the front door.

"Hey!" He recognized Elyce's voice, calling after him.

"Just a minute," he said to her, flinging the door open.

Without his coat, the wind was a cold polar bear slap across the face. It had claws. A gust of wet rain stung his cheeks and forehead. His clothes were instantly soaked.

"Angela!"

She stood on the curb with her face in her hands, as if oblivious to the weather. Her shoulders were hunched up. She seemed to be crying.

"Angela!"

And, a second too late, he saw what she was about to do.

I didn't come here to talk you out of anything, Angela had said.

She stepped off the curb.

The words reverberated in George's head as a horn blared and screams erupted through the night. With a screech of brakes and an horrific thud, Angela disappeared beneath a speeding pickup truck. He had a split-second image of her body being dragged, of a tire crossing her chest, sinking into her as if it were no more substantial than a heap of newspaper, and then both the truck and the night were still.

27

Maybe I'm trying to shake you up a little, Angela had said. *Maybe I came here to meet you for inspiration. Both choices are terrifying.*

George ignored the screams and the cries of *Sir!* — he recognized the voice as Elyce's in some dim and unconcerned region of his brain — and set off at a brisk walk down the street in the direction of his apartment. He hunched forward to keep the drizzle out of his face.

Only a few hours left until sunrise. Better not to think about this too much.

Maybe I'm stronger than I knew, Angela had said.

"Maybe so, maybe not," George said to himself, mostly to drown out the terrible soundtrack in his head: truck colliding with body, horns, screams. He took a deep breath, thrust his hands into his jacket pockets, and walked a little faster.

Don't think about it, George, he ordered himself. *Just go home and do it.*

SEX AND DRAGONS

That forest fire a few weeks ago? The one that incinerated a substantial patch of forest along the Trans-Canada Highway? Blame Harry Potter for it, if you have to blame anyone.

I was reading the fourth book in the series at a sidewalk café in the West End, enjoying one of Vancouver's rare warm and dry fall days. It would probably be the last such day we'd have until spring. The weather forecast called for clouds and rain starting that same night, clamminess that would go unrelieved by much sun for the next few months. I couldn't pass up a last chance to bask in ultraviolet radiation. The waiter kept my mug coffee cup full and my ashtray empty. I got little read, with as much of my attention spent on passersby as the story in front of me.

All the coffee had made me kind of jittery. It's possible none of this would have happened if I'd been drinking wine.

This guy came up to my table and asked if I would mind him sitting down.

Because I am not Canadian in the sense of growing up here and knowing what to expect from the natives, his boldness surprised me. In a good way. When someone who looks like that comes up to your table and asks if you would mind him sitting down, unless you are terminally stupid you answer with something along the lines of "Sure, go ahead." If you're bolder, you ask, "That chair or my face?" I'm not that bold, but fortunately I am also not terminally stupid. Terminally single, maybe.

"Sure, go ahead."

I grew up in a small town in Minnesota. Nothing but white people.

Pale ones. Everywhere you looked, skin with the same luminous quality as the glow-in-the-dark stars children stick to their ceilings. So when somebody as deliciously brown as this strolls by, I have to bite my tongue to keep it from lolling out like a spaniel's. Whether I like it or not, my first reaction is to wonder, *Where is he from?* With the almond eyes, he could have been Asian, but with that snub nose and curly hair, there could have been some black or Latino in the mix. For a few seconds after he sat across from me I just let myself look. *Nice.* I imagined his skin would taste of cinnamon and allspice. Trite, I know, but that's what I imagined.

"You like Harry Potter?" he asked, eyeing my book.

"No, I'm reading it because this man in a black mask broke into my house last night, held a gun to my head, and said I was under surveillance. If I don't read the entire thing today, he's going to come back tonight with accomplices. They're going to take me off to a remote cabin and torture me for days, using techniques perfected in the Inquisition and patented by the Catholic Church."

He blinked, opened his mouth, made a sound that sort of resembled "ack" if it had to be spelled out, and closed his mouth again.

"Are you going to introduce yourself?"

"I shouldn't cut into your reading time. If that man comes back tonight and takes you away, it would be all my fault. I couldn't live with myself, knowing I had contributed to your demise."

I'm terrible with accents, so I could only identify the presence of one, not pinpoint its origin.

"You'd only be partially to blame. I chose a bad place to read. This is a nice day, and I don't have to work. So I'm enjoying the weather. Besides, for all you know, I have a death wish. I *want* to be slowly disassembled, a gob of flesh at a time. Red hot pokers and electric probes turn me on."

"And you're reading a Harry Potter story. What a fascinating

30

combination," he said. "I'm Mark."

He extended a hand. The skin on the back was darker than the skin on his palm. A handsome line separated the two areas of pigment: light sand on a tourist beach, dark sea calm against it.

"Erik," I told him. "With a K."

"If you're reading those books, then you must have at least a superficial belief in the unknown," Mark said.

"Of course I believe in the unknown. Without the unknown, most of the world wouldn't exist. I've never been to South Africa and don't know anything about it, but I know it's there. Existence is not predicated upon my perception and experience."

Mark smiled. "That was as subtle as a sledgehammer, but it made me laugh a little, on the inside, where you couldn't see. Let me try again. You must have some passing belief in the supernatural. Yes?"

I nodded. After a second's hesitation, I closed the book and gestured to him in invitation. He doffed his leather jacket (brown) then took a seat in the wrought-iron chair opposite mine. I savored little aromas in the air he displaced when he sat down, that new-leather smell mostly drowning out subtler tones like cedar and vanilla and something floral. Roses. *This is almost obscene*, I thought. *I want to taste his skin like a Cabernet, and name all the notes he leaves on my tongue. Is he wearing cologne, or is this just how he smells?*

Mark asked, "If I were to tell you that dragons exist, what are the chances of you believing me?"

"I suppose you'll have to tell me, and see for yourself. Outcomes like that are hard to predict, because one never knows whether the question is actually going to be asked." I finished the half-inch of cool coffee left in my mug. Out of the corner of my eye, I spotted the waiter and lifted the mug at him as a signal to bring a refill. I popped a couple of Tums from the roll in my pocket to keep my piss from turning into battery acid after all the coffee, then said, "It could be you expect the *possibility* of the question to function as a surrogate, as a means of leaving me hanging."

"You must believe very strange things about people, if that's how your mind works." Mark looked grave. "Either that, or you're a very strange person yourself."

I wanted to do something a bit vulgar, but for an instant couldn't figure out just the right gesture. Maybe scratching my ear and inspecting the flakes of wax beneath my nail. Or staring straight at him, without blinking, until he began to squirm. I was raised by immigrant Swedes, who have practiced cultural eugenics on such behavior for centuries. Being nasty took effort. I licked the rim of the coffee mug at Mark, never breaking eye contact, not too brazen, but just suggestive enough.

"I promise, I'm hopelessly bizarre," I assured him. "Despite the fact I look like the nice blond boy next door, I'm a goofball on the inside."

"Which would suggest you believe that dragons might, in fact, exist."

"Would you like for me to believe in them? If I clasp my hands together and say, *I believe!*, then will they magically commence to exist? Would that make your day complete?"

Mark took advantage of the arrival of the waiter to ask for a coffee. For quite a long time, he said nothing. The waiter, a handsome South Asian, made the mug-retrieval trip in mere seconds, travelling faster than the laws of physics ought to have allowed, white ceramic mug in one hand, coffeepot steaming in the other.

"I'm not asking you whether you masturbate with your right hand or your left," Mark said. "That would be rude. But you're reading Harry Potter. It didn't seem like a bad idea, to ask whether you believe dragons exist, because I have one of my own. Perhaps you would like to see it."

I blew across the surface of my coffee after I emptied four packets of sugar into it and leaned close to hear the tiny tearing-paper sound the crystals made, plunging.

"I think you're trying to pick me up," I said.

"You would object?" came the wide-eyed response.

"Of course not. I may be odd but I'm not stupid."

Mark insisted on leaving a five on the table to cover the coffee I'd drunk and he hadn't. He told me he lived in North Vancouver, not far from the ferry terminal, but he had to keep the dragon at his uncle's house out in the woods east of the city. We walked side by side up the sidewalk, parting to let other pedestrians through, shoulders sometimes touching. Mark lit a cigarette for himself, and as an afterthought, offered one to me. When I accepted, he surprised me by lighting one in his own mouth and handing it over. Think of Claude Rains in *Now, Voyager*. Even the trace of moisture from his lips struck me as erotic, and I had to play a quick game of pocket-pool to avoid public embarrassment.

"Where are we going?" I asked.

"My uncle's house."

"You want me to accompany you all the way out there." I stopped dead.

Mark took another couple of steps, realized he had left me behind, and turned around, eyes wide.

"Well, yes," he said. "Don't you want to see it?"

"You're sure there is a dragon. We're not going to get to your father's house, or your uncle's house, whoever it belongs to, and the only dragon will turn out to be a tattoo on your inner thigh?"

"You would object?" he asked again.

"No, but if that's what I'm in for, don't you think you should just tell me now, so there won't be any disappointments later? It would be criminal to build up my hopes of seeing this great, fire-breathing beast, then discover that the reality exists only in ink? Or, worse, is an exotic species of lizard you keep someplace both dramatic and faintly ridiculous, like a barbeque brazier?"

He closed the distance between us in one large step, leaned close, and whispered five things in my ear:

I have a beautiful uncircumcised cock.

I have a large, colorful dragon tattooed across my back, between my shoulderblades.

And I have a real dragon in the woods behind my uncle's house.

How many of these things you get to see is entirely up to you.

Do you have a car, or do you want me to drive?

I drove. No matter how bright the sparks flying between us got, I couldn't lose sight of how stupid riding out into the middle of hilly suburban nowhere with a complete stranger would be. I drove with a sense of urgency, slaloming in and out of traffic, photo radar be damned. I wanted to maintain some sense of control, and to keep the trip as short as possible.

"I like your car," Mark said.

I have a newish Mercedes roadster. It's red. I drive it fast.

"Thank you."

He put his hand on my knee and adjusted his seat slightly, leaning back, spreading his legs a little. When he closed his eyes, he looked like a young boy.

I struggled to keep my eyes on the road.

"Don't fall asleep," I told him. "I don't know where we're going. I'd have no choice but to drive home and take you with me."

"You would object?"

Mark's uncle lived in a wooden A-frame house in the middle of nowhere. This wasn't even the suburbs. Vancouver and its satellites had long since petered out. After almost an hour on the highway, I began to think we really would cross the mountains and end up somewhere remote, like the Okanogan, before he told me to exit. As the last of my patience ebbed, he directed me to take this exit, then that road, then that unmarked gravel path leading into a forest.

"This is a good climate for dragons," Mark said as my car crunched along.

"I should have driven the Pathfinder today," I said. "Something told me to, and I didn't listen. Why is this a good climate for dragons?"

"Because we get so much rain here. If the dragons set the trees on fire, odds are, we would get rain before much damage is done."

"Now you're saying dragonS with an S instead of dragon_ with no S. Had you noticed? Do you have more than one dragon? Will this be frightening for me?"

"There's only one, now. The others are no longer here." Mark looked out the window. I imagined a pensive look on his face. "As they grew, they were setting things on fire, so we were forced to move them to other quarters. The novelty of having them was offset by gruesome practicalities. We had to take steps. You understand."

I parked near the house. The place looked deserted. If anyone still lived there, I couldn't tell.

"My uncle is in Toronto on business," Mark explained. "He should be back in a couple of weeks. I'm keeping the house for him."

"I see."

"He travels constantly. Follow me."

Mark led me behind the house, down a trail into the trees. I followed and watched his ass, perfectly round and framed by his jeans. What would it be like to pull down his pants and bite his buttocks down low, not too hard, just enough to make him writhe and gasp? Then to turn him around and…

"He must have taken it with him," Mark said, disappointment in his voice.

We had reached a clearing. Light filtered green through the leaves overhead. A strong smell of earth and forest surrounded us, rich soil underfoot, a very clean smell. Birds squawked. Scuffmarks in the carpet of leaves underfoot were the only sign anyone or anything had been here before us.

"Isn't that the sort of thing you would have known? Didn't your uncle say, *Mark, I'm taking the dragon to Toronto with me, wish me luck because I want to carry it on instead of checking it. Do you think it will fit in an overhead bin?*"

"You're such a mean guy," Mark said.

"I think you like it. So is there really a dragon? Honest?"

He nodded. "Of course there is. I wouldn't have brought you here just for the sex. We could have done that closer to home."

"You seem to think it's *fait accompli* that we're going to get naked. I think you dreamt up the bit about the dragon just to lure me out into the middle of nowhere, to molest me in this jungle."

"So what if I did?" Mark began to unbutton his shirt. He exposed a widening V of hairless, lightly developed brown chest. "You would object?"

For the next two weeks I couldn't get him out of my head. I didn't hear from him, not a word, not a phone call, nothing. This surprised me. He had seemed determined to prove a point. The encounter didn't feel like a pick-up with kinky supernatural overtones. As delicious as Mark turned out to be, I assumed I'd hear from him, and when I didn't, I went a bit stir-crazy. Nobody really noticed, and I didn't talk about the encounter with the friends who had convinced me to move up here. I'd have sounded obsessive. Like a movie playing on a screen behind my eyes, I kept seeing him leading me by the hand down the trail out of those woods. In the house, we spent hours doing everything we could think of to try. Later, spent, we raided his uncle's refrigerator, then returned to feasting on each other once our stomachs were full. I got home at 4.00 in the morning.

Finally, an e-mail:

I have the dragon. Meet me at the pagoda in the Dr. Sun Yat-Sen Classical Chinese Garden. Not the public park. I assume you have been here long enough to know which is which. The pagoda is off-limits to most visitors, so we will have to time this carefully. Tell me when you can be there. Mark

This was Sunday. I could meet him no earlier than Tuesday.

His response came right away:

Terrific. Can you arrive late in the day, when the park is about to close, and hide until everyone is gone?

This sounded criminal. I loved it.

You bet, I typed. *Be sure to bring the dragon this time.*

The Garden, a tiny gem tucked away in a corner of Vancouver's Chinatown, made no sense whatsoever as a place to meet Mark, but I showered and drove across town to the rendezvous, chanting *Suspension of Disbelief, Suspension of Disbelief* as a mantra.

Little traffic, synchronized traffic lights, a parking spot next to the entrance to the Garden… all the signs portended a good afternoon, or evening, or whatever they call it here. Growing up in Minnesota, I'm used to long summer days, or rather, I used to be. I lived in San Diego for years before leaving the US. It gets dark there. North of the border, the sun continues to shine at 9.30 pm. What's the line of demarcation between afternoon and evening? I puzzled over this as I bought my admission ticket and entered the garden.

It's small. According to a brochure I picked up, a gang of artisans from Suzhou, a city in China, spent a year constructing it. *The materials, tools, and techniques used in the construction were almost identical to those used centuries ago in the building of the famous Suzhou gardens. Most of the elements were shipped from China in more than 950 crates containing the architectural components – hand-fired roof tiles, carved woodwork, lattice windows, limestone rocks, and even the courtyard pebbles.* Perhaps I was a clod for not having heard of the famous Suzhou gardens. I had only seen this garden mentioned in lists of Vancouver tourist attractions, along with the aquarium and a couple of suspension bridges in the mountains north of the city.

I liked the place. If it truly counted as one of Vancouver's top attractions, I wondered what that signified for the local tourism industry. The tourists must have finished their tours and retired to one of the nearby restaurants for dim sum, because I had the place to myself. I wandered the gardens, white pebbles crunching underfoot, bonsai jasmine treelets perfuming the air just enough to notice.

"Sir, we're about to close," said the woman from the Entrance Court.

"I'll just be a moment, thank you."

My brochure identified the only pagoda-like structure in sight as Ting. A ting? A Ting? The ting? To capitalize, or not to capitalize; that was the question. And which article to use? Shakespeare never faced that dilemma, to my knowledge, when confronted with a small but ornate Asian-esque building in which he hoped to view a real live dragon and then perhaps get laid.

To get to it I had to step over a rope, descend a few stone steps, and make my way into what looked like a cave. Water gurgled to my right, its source a small waterfall up ahead. I hoped I hadn't been seen. Being tossed out of the Garden would leave me feeling like the king of fools.

I climbed up.

"You're here," Mark said, looking surprised. I had caught him reading. John Grisham, of all things. I'd have expected something New Age, full of crystals and mysterious symbols. Kahlil Gibran, or maybe Shirley MacLaine. Mark had on jeans faded almost white, and a bulky grey McGill University sweatshirt.

Next to him, a metal mesh pet carrier. Empty.

"I am. It's nice to see you again. Show me the dragon."

"You frightened it," Mark said. "It's not here, exactly."

He took something out of his pocket. I envied his hand. The object he retrieved glinted when he held it up for me to see.

"This is a scale," he said. "The dragon is molting."

"Where is it?" I stopped to rethink my approach. "Jesus. Listen to me. It's nice to see you again – don't get me wrong. Even if the dragon is a fictional creature, I'm still glad to see you. I do have manners, really."

He nodded at me and looked pleased.

"Here." He gave me the scale.

It had the same iridescent quality as a circle of mother-of-pearl. When I looked at it more closely, other colors appeared: blues, purples, reds. When I scratched it with a fingernail, it felt like bone.

"How did the dragon become frightened of me? I'm not a frightening guy."

Mark shrugged, and gestured for me to sit beside him.

"Dragons are unpredictable, especially when they're young. You never know what to expect from them. I think this one couldn't figure out what to make of you, so he decided not to stay and find out for himself."

"Him?"

Mark nodded. He put his hand over mine. Despite the chill in the air, he felt warm.

39

"So where did he go?"

"He rotated. Have you ever read the book *Stranger in a Strange Land*, by Robert Heinlein?" When I shook my head No, Mark explained: "Heinlein knew a few things before his time, or he guessed well. The main character in that book had an ability to get rid of people and things: he didn't make them disappear, exactly, but he *rotated* them. My uncle explained this to me. The physics involved goes over my head. I still doubt I understand it fully, but the idea is, the universe is a mathematical construct, and objects can be rotated in relation to their current position, and they leave this plane for another one, which is both very close and very distant, and we have no access to them."

"Sounds like Heathrow," I said, lost.

"Something like that. In any case, the dragon can rotate himself and come back. Sooner or later he'll make up his mind to return to me, and then I'll have to find some hens for him to eat." Mark shrugged again. "He often stays away for days on end."

I sensed a game being played with me.

"Are you at least glad to see me?" I asked, trying not to sound as petulant as I felt.

He leaned over and kissed me, his tongue slipping between my teeth. His mouth tasted like electricity and peppermint. After a breathless minute, he pulled away.

"Of course I am."

"We're going to get caught, you know."

"No. I bribed the admissions lady. What will it take to get you out of those clothes?"

"The magic word," I said with a grin. "That's what you brought me here for, isn't it? There's no dragon." I couldn't help grinning at the silliness of it all: my own, for believing I might see a dragon, and his, for thinking I

40

would believe it, and for choosing this place for a tryst. Layers upon layers of quivering, gelatinous silliness. "You just want to ravage me."

"So what if I do?" Mark asked, unbuttoning my pants without first saying Please. "You would object?"

This time Mark accompanied me to dinner after we had enjoyed each other in various ways, as the sun set. We toweled off as best we could with Handi-Wipes I kept in my backpack, then drove to a Spanish place in the West End near my apartment. Drunk on sangria, he told me his mother was Puerto Rican and his father, a Straits Chinese from Malaysia. He had grown up in Montréal. Typical Canadian, in his way: he spoke French because of his Québec origins, Spanish because of his mother, Cantonese because of his father, and English because... well, that part's obvious. Degrees in English literature and French. He had moved to Vancouver for grad school, realized he hated his program, and dropped out to travel. Money didn't seem to be a problem. I didn't ask why.

I told him my own strange tale: the tightly wrapped Swedish childhood in Minnesoooooota, college in the Twin Cities, the job in San Diego I took only because I needed to experience warmth in January.

"Why Canada, though?" Mark helped himself to seconds from the vat of paella we had ordered. "If you want to experience warmth in January, there are many other countries where you're more likely to find it."

"My parents were killed last year on a flight to visit me. I lived near the airport. The plane crash-landed into a building down the street. I had ended a relationship not long before that, and all my friends were people I'd met through him. I lost my appetite for San Diego. Taxes would have eaten up a lot of the estate if I had stayed in the US, but I talked to a couple of immigration lawyers, got a couple of foreign passports, and left. Now I'm here." I shrugged. It no longer hurt to talk about this. I hoped I wasn't giving him the impression that I might be about to succumb to grief and leap from the Lions Gate Bridge. "No particular reason. I'd heard it was beautiful. I have a couple of friends here, and they invited me to stay with them until I either got my own place or moved to another city."

"Are you going to move to another city?"

"I doubt it."

"But if I fail to show you the dragon, then you might get the wrong idea about us Canadians. I might end up driving you away. That would be most unpatriotic of me."

"Then I guess you owe it to your country to make sure I see the dragon as soon as possible. Many things are hanging in the balance."

"I will have to put extra effort into it, definitely. Have you finished eating? Unless you want to drive me home, we should get going: it's almost midnight, and the ride home will take all night."

"You're staying at my place tonight," I told him. "Unless you have to be somewhere first thing in the morning."

I woke up to an empty apartment: no Mark. His half of the bed still felt warm, and smelled like him. I rolled over and pressed my nose into his pillow.

In the kitchen, a note:

I have an appointment today at noon. Call me later, and we can get together again. I will try to convince our mutual friend not to disappear this time. XO, Mark.

Questions surfaced:

Had he really taken a pet cage containing a dragon across the water from North Vancouver on the ferry, transferred to the SkyTrain, then walked the three or four blocks through Chinatown with it, to meet me?

Hadn't anyone noticed? Or could the thing turn invisible, in addition to *rotating* conveniently out of view just before I arrived?

Did the dragon, in fact, exist? And if so, how had he acquired it? Why? Of what use was a baby dragon, anyway?

Had I picked up a lunatic? Was I becoming one?

Was this an elaborate seduction or a complete crock of shit?

No answers revealed themselves. I spent the day in a stew, trying to piece together a puzzle with no clue what the final picture ought to look like.

Three days later, another e-mail came, as oddly formal as its predecessors, and as sweet in its off-center way:

Hi Erik… if you can be persuaded to drive out to my uncle's house again, then I will finally be able to show you the dragon. Not just the one on my back, either. I think we will be forced to turn the real one over to other caretakers, since it is growing rapidly. We would rather not be roasted. So come while you can. Let me know if this weekend will be a good time. Looking forward, Mark.

Dragon or no dragon, I decided I'd be a fool to miss this. Boys like Mark only come along every so often. It is important to pounce on them when they do.

The column of smoke above the horizon announced disaster, even from a distance. This could not be good. I remembered seeing no other homes or buildings in the area, as we had approached.

As I crunched up the track leading to the property, sirens wailed and lights flashed. Flames roared around Mark's uncle's house, and a firefighter standing guard waved for me to pull over. Amid the panic at the sight of the house ablaze, my mind went down stranger pathways. What is it about Canadian men in public service positions? Are they genetically engineered to be square-jawed and handsome?

43

"You ought to turn around and leave," he advised. A bead of sweat dripped off a towering, smoke-smudged cheekbone. Through my open window, the stench from the fire pummeled my face. The roar of the flames sounded like a giant machine eating the landscape. "We think we've got this contained but just in case we don't, you'd be safer somewhere else. You're surrounded by trees, up here."

"Thanks," I told him, amazed that he had stopped to talk. In the States, someone would have angrily waved me away, maybe shouted. Further proof I'm living on the more civilized side of the border.

One week, two weeks, three weeks: nothing. No word from or about Mark. What to feel? I hadn't been in love with him. Strange cocktails of emotions made me drunk: Concern with undertones of curiosity and dark notes of self-doubt. A double-shot of disappointment with a small bitter garnish of embarrassment. Brooding, neat.

Two months passed, then three.

I haunted the café where I met Mark – nothing new in that, though, since I'd haunted the place *before* I met him. The servers and both hostesses knew my name. I chose a table by the window and typed ramblings into my laptop, drinking cup after cup of coffee and sometimes staring out at the constant pall of dark rain.

One dry-ish afternoon, he showed up.

"What happened to Harry Potter?" He slid into the other side of my booth.

"J. K. Rowling is deciding that, as we speak. Ask *her*."

"She's in Scotland."

"My mobile phone is equipped to make international calls. But I doubt she's listed. It was worth a try. How was Toronto?"

"Pleasant. I always enjoy myself there."

"I'll have to go sometime. Never been there. What kind of Canadian has never visited Toronto?"

"The American kind with a Canadian passport," Mark said. "I was hoping you'd be here."

"You were?"

Mark's face seemed distorted for a second, and he clamped a hand over his mouth and nose. I noticed a sheen of sweat on his forehead.

"Almost sneezed," he said. "That would have been somewhat inauspicious of me."

"Look into the sunlight if you can find any," I said with a gesture out the window. "Sneeze and get it out of your system."

"No, really."

"Go ahead!"

Mark looked outside. That scrunching-up facial expression came back: his nose quivered, he shut his eyes tight, and his mouth puckered as the urge overtook him. He took a deep sharp breath and sneezed.

Several sparks shot out of his nose.

The landed on the tablecloth, which commenced to smoulder.

For a second I didn't believe what I was seeing, but Mark poured water over the burning spot, then concealed it beneath the salt and pepper shakers.

"Fuck," he said, wiping his nose. "That wasn't supposed to happen. I really do need to leave, and you should come with me, or at least leave, yourself, if you don't want questions. I can't assume nobody saw that."

The decision took two whole seconds. I turned off my laptop, thankful it hadn't been scorched, and hurried out of the café behind him. Heads turned. Who had seen?

We walked down the sidewalk.

"You did that on purpose, you fucker," I told him.

45

"Doesn't seem to bother you."

"Never slept with someone I knew was a dragon."

Mark shrugged.

"You did that to pick me up again, didn't you?"

"You would object?"

FOR YOUR OWN GOOD

May 5.

I can't tear my gaze away from my building manager's missing tooth. It's the second incisor on the top left and it isn't completely gone. A plain black gap would be more attractive. Instead, the front layer of enamel and the inner pulpy material seem to have rotted away, leaving a yellow-black shell in the back. This reminds me of a vacant locust husk. And Henry tends to grin widely at the slightest provocation. Has he no shame? No mirror? Doesn't he know his breath smells like swamp gas?

He means well. I know he means well. He's a gin-swilling relic from San Francisco's pre-epidemic heyday, he survived for some reason, and he's got the morbid *joie de vivre* of the Londoners who lit their cigarettes off burning chunks of rubble after World War II air raids. Every couple of weeks he finds some pretext to knock on my door, and he always wants to talk. And talk. And talk.

What I told him when I moved in: *I work from home. I don't like to go out much. I prefer my peace and quiet.*

The unspoken message: *Leave me alone.*

"It's a beautiful day, isn't it?" he asks. He slurs just enough for me to notice. His slushy sibilants tell me he hasn't fully sobered up after last night's binge. His lopsided grin unnerves me. Light from the overhead fixture reflects off his yellow incisors, the fetor of boozy sweat pours off him, and inhaling makes me feel ill. He sways. I want to chew a dozen Rolaids. *How many bottles did you drink last night, Henry? Nineteen? Twenty?*

In the six months I've lived in this building, he has ballooned out by at least ten pounds, and I'm convinced it's all liver.

"I haven't been outside in three months," I reply.

He shakes his head and clucks his tongue, a typical California reaction to my lack of interest in the outdoors. Sure the weather is lovely here, and we have the Sierras and the Pacific and the redwoods and the Wine Country and Lake Tahoe all within driving distance; great, good, so shut the fuck up and get in your car and drive there and leave me alone.

"Matthew, a nice young man like you should be out with friends on a day like this."

"I ate them," I said.

"You hate them?" Henry frowns. "You hate your friends?"

"No, I *ate* them," I said. "*With fava beans and a nice Chianti.* May I get back to work now? It's been nice talking with you."

The company of other people isn't for everyone. Nature abhors a vacuum but not as intensely as I abhor the vacuous.

I smile at him and close the door, in hopes he won't see the sweat that beads my forehead. I'd worry about him smelling the anxious reek of my armpits but I doubt anything less pungent than raw sewage could penetrate the cirrhotic miasma around him. Poor soul. Why doesn't he find other tenants to bludgeon with kindness? I must worry him. I'm recently 35, reasonably handsome, and compulsively reclusive. An old Mercedes roadster would be gathering dust in my parking bay if there weren't a tarpaulin over it. I never drive the thing because that would require going outside. I order books and groceries online. How hard does it have to be, Henry? If I want to go somewhere, then I will. If I want you to drag me out of my apartment, then you'll be the first person to know.

After I bought this place, I added three extra deadbolts to the front door and reinforced the hinges. All my windows are barred. Two HEPA air purifiers the size of end tables whirr all day and night. I'm not one of those obsessive Howard Hughes types who washes his hands 300 times a day; this isn't about germs. I just don't want to go out, don't want to be bothered, and don't want to explain myself whenever someone's curiosity is aroused.

Why is that so hard to understand?

Just as entertainment industry types down south in Silicone Valley understand facelifts and boob jobs, here in Greater Silicon Valley, real estate types understand nontraditional work-from-home jobs: plenty of people telecommute and earn six figures. Even after the dotcom implosion, there are still lots of virtual Volvos on the information superhighway. For all Henry knows, I'm one of those young bazillionaires who sold off his start-up stock before the market collapsed, or I'm a junior executive hanging on at one of the few companies that still has a pulse. I've hinted that I'm a day trader. Other times, I've hinted that I'm a writer with a connection to Hollywood. I've dropped vague references about moneyed family in Europe. If Henry's sense of smell weren't so pickled he'd detect the scent of red herring. Maybe in time, I'll feel like sharing my story with him, but on the other hand, it's been six months, and those urges haven't hit me yet.

I can't say I expect them to.

May 21.

There's a knock at the door. I'm not expecting anyone.

How ominous, I think as I cross the room to see who it is. *Maybe Henry's come back to belch swamp gas in my face.*

Through the peephole: a black man. A handsome one.

This is an improvement. At least it's not Henry.

49

I open the door a crack to say Hi and find out what he wants. Whoever this guy is, he hasn't caught me on my most sociable day, but then, I never have sociable days, so that's to be expected. I haven't seen him before – he's about my height and his skin is the color of an expensive creamy Starbucks beverage; his hair is buzzed neatly down to his scalp and his nose is pierced. Inasmuch as I have a type (*Diego was my type but he's gone now isn't he, Matthew?*), he's it.

Maybe he's an axe murderer. That would be about my luck.

I open the door wider to get a better look.

He extends a hand to shake.

"My name's Keith," he says. "I just moved in downstairs. Do you have any vodka?"

"Gallons of it," I reply. "Finlandia. It's a great preservative. Want to see my collection of human eyeballs?"

"Some other time." Keith doesn't miss a beat. Good for him. "I'm expecting my sister any minute and if I don't have a vodka martini waiting when she gets here, she'll kill me. Sorry about the vodka. Umm – she doesn't like olives, so I kind of doubt she'll want to see an eyeball in her glass."

"I doubt the eyeball would want to see her, either," I offer.

"Right. This is the strangest conversation I've ever had," Keith says. "I'll catch you later. Guess I have to go to Safeway after all."

He leaves without offering to shake hands again, and he backs away. I imagine he's worried about turning his back to me. But there's a half-smile on his face, as if in the middle of an excruciating conference call, he's just reminded himself he doesn't have underwear on. I don't understand why he should be amused. I want him to suspect I might chuck an ice pick down the hall after him. I want him to conclude I'm not the guy whose door he wants to knock on, the next time he runs out of something. That's why we make *shopping lists*.

Only I'm not sure how much I want these things, am I?

I lied to Henry about having work to do. These days I mostly lie on the sofa under a couple of blankets, reading. I have enough throw-pillows to pad the floors of three whorehouses and enough tea to give the population of Japan caffeine jitters. One of the great lies of our culture is that the major works of literature are interesting, so I've given up on Dickens, Tolstoy, Austen, and Toni Morrison. I want to turn off my brain. Since alcohol does awful things to my stomach and procuring drugs would require me to leave my apartment and talk to the sort of people I'd rather run over in my car, I read Dean Koontz's interchangeable thrillers and Danielle Steel's bodice-rippers instead. Give me Grisham or give me death. I read the weightless gayboy books with cartoon cover art depicting muscular clones smiling at each other; these are like taking deep breaths of pink air. I've devoured at least a dozen old John D. MacDonald paperback mysteries, the ones with colors in the titles and big-breasted women on the jackets. The alternative to suicide is to consume immense volumes of trash. Or perhaps it's just a slower means to the same end.

For intellectual protein, I sometimes read the BBC and the Financial Times online. Just a few articles. Afterward, invariably, I check out a few porno websites, have a wank, and fix myself a sandwich and more Earl Grey. Then it's back to my literary Rice Krispie treats. I'm cultivating mental flab and that's OK.

I know: It's not a life, it's the imitation of one. But it's mine.

June 1.

Henry's eyes cross slightly today. They're bloodshot. It's Saturday, late morning, and from the fumes, I suspect he drank a few gallons of jet fuel last night. I'd think twice before striking a match in his presence. The only safe thing to do is to take a step backward. God forbid he should ever decide to hug me.

I could just tell him to drop off my packages and leave, but I'm not that assertive. I know this about myself and admit it freely. The reason behind ordering essentials online is to avoid human contact and he's defeating the purpose. On the other hand, I've noticed a passive-aggressive streak in Henry. Not so long ago, he dispatched a yowling tomcat with a bowl of poisoned Friskies. He keeps D-Con around to deal with rats, which he calls urban bunnies, and I have to admit, I appreciated the quiet afterward. The homeless guy who persisted in rummaging through our Dumpster stopped coming around after Henry dropped a few urine-filled condoms on his head. It's not that I'm afraid of Henry himself, but if I were to say the wrong thing, how do I know he wouldn't *forget* to bring me my groceries when the delivery guy drops them off downstairs?

Why didn't I choose a building without a front desk?

"Keith told me he met you," Henry says.

Why doesn't he just hand me the box—a couple of sweaters from the Gap's online store if I'm not mistaken—and go back to his copy of the *Weekly World News?* Two-headed monsters from Mars that abduct and rape Topeka trailer trash are far more interesting than I am, honest.

Henry jabbers on: "He seemed like a nice guy, somehow I thought you might like him. Did you get to check out his backside? He may be a doctor but he looks like a go-go boy. I'd put a dollar in his G-string. Hell, I'd slip him a five. That day, when I sent him up to knock on your door, I was fresh out of vodka myself, you know, one or two extra martinis that night, and I stopped him on the way out and asked him to pick up an extra bottle for me. It's a lovely day, isn't it? No fog, not a cloud in the sky. There's a kite festival over in the city; maybe you should go."

"I'm in the middle of a huge project right now," I say. "I've got a deadline."

"Deadline schmedline," Henry says.

"Can I have my sweaters now?"

"I should hold them hostage," Henry says. "You have to go to the kite festival and talk to at least three handsome strangers today. Then you can have your sweaters."

"This is real life, not a Britney Spears video." I grab the box. "Thanks for the thought, but I have a ton of work to do."

I shut the door in his face and turn my back to it, sliding/sinking to the floor with the box cradled in my arms like an awkward cardboard baby. Sweat pours off me. There's an ugly heaviness in my gut, portending an emergency dash to the bathroom. The kite festival? Conversations with handsome strangers? Those things are about as likely to happen as the Vatican selling fluorescent Christ-shaped vibrators in its souvenir shops. When I can stand up again, and when the nausea passes, I close all the curtains. I wouldn't be surprised if he watches me from the sidewalk across the street; he must be dying to know what I get up to all day.

Will the condo association give me crap if I have the windows tinted and bars installed over them?

June 6.

When I hear the knock, I hurry to open it. I've ordered in – *chow fun* and potstickers from my favorite Chinese place, as well as groceries. At the door is a schoolmarmish woman of a certain age, narrow eyeglasses on a gold chain around her neck. She bears an unsettling resemblance to my seventh-grade French teacher, Madame Lebeaupin. I doubt she lives in this building. I'd remember. Mme. Lebeaupin was never satisfied with my pronunciation, and gave me lower marks than any other instructor of

French before or since. I always thought she looked like a Tonka truck in pumps. In any case, the woman smiling (in a tight-lipped, businesslike way) on my welcome mat (which actually reads GO AWAY) is not Zhe-Yuan, the Chinese delivery guy. Nor is she the uniformed grocery guy sweating with the three or four paper not plastic bags of junk food and toilet paper I ordered.

"Matthew Jaraschow?" She breaks into my amazement.

My first impulse is to respond with, "*Oui, Madame... qu'est-ce que c'est?*"

"My name is Betty Royalton, and I live in the brown shingle house down the block, on the corner. I'm sure you've seen it? The one with the jasmine vines and the lemon tree in the front yard?"

I shook my head *no*. "I don't get out much."

"Well, I'm here with the perfect opportunity." She consults a little notebook she has produced from a voluminous brown shoulder bag. "I'm on the committee to organize this year's Fourth of July block party. It's an annual tradition here in the neighborhood, and we're looking for volunteers to help coordinate the food and entertainment. Your building manager Henry gave us your name and suggested you might be available and interested..."

My thoughts gum up with horror. Entertainment?

"Henry thought you might be able to help write skits for the children..."

"*Children?*"

"Why yes, of course! I was thinking, perhaps you know someone who can get in touch with some clowns on fairly short notice?"

"Henry seems to know how."

"Shall I put you down as a definite for the committee?" Without stopping long enough to breathe—or let me get a word in edgewise—she steamrollers on: "So which shall it be, food or entertainment? If you want to do food, don't worry about the clean-up job, we have a separate committee for that. How do you feel about making a couple hundred pigs-in-a-blanket? Of course we'd supply you with the veggie hot dogs and organic tofu cheese." She giggles. Her eyeglasses bounce. "This is Berkeley, you know."

"I'm sorry, but I'm allergic to sunlight," I tell her.

Her eyes widen.

"It's a terrible problem. Indirect illumination is OK, like through the curtains, but if I were to go outside for that long, I'd be covered with gigantic bloody red welts within 20 minutes."

"Oh." She takes a half-step back. Then: "Is it contagious?"

I shake my head *no* again, wondering what she's going to ask me next. Perhaps if one is easily turned away, one does not tend to serve on neighborhood organizing committees. One would not last long, knocking on doors. I should have said *Very*. Or *Airborne*.

"Is there some problem? I have a little trouble believing your story about your ... condition."

Oh God it's Madame Lebeaupin all over again.

"I'm going to France," I tell her. "Sorry about the welts story. I like to be provocative. I'm working on that in therapy. I'm going to be in Paris for a couple of weeks. I'm afraid there's really nothing I can do. In fact, you caught me right in the middle of packing—"

Zhe-Yuan saves me by appearing with a bag of fragrant food, and his usual handsome smile. I like Zhe-Yuan because he is the only person who ever comes to my door and has almost nothing to say. It's possible he doesn't speak much English, and that's just fine. It's refreshing. It's just *dandy*. In a heavy accent, he says *Here's your food*; I say *Thanks Zhe-Yuan*; and he says *Enjoy your meal, see you next time*. I always tip him well.

"Hm. Well, enjoy Paris then."

Madame Royalton flounces away, and I tip Zhe-Yuan twice as much as usual this time.

"You make a mistake, maybe?" he asks.

"No, please. Keep the change. You just did me a big favor."

After I shut the door, I revive myself by taking deep breaths of delicious garlicky noodles and dumplings.

July 4.

As much as possible, I ignore holidays.

July 6.

I haven't ordered anything, so when there's a knock at the door, the spasm of panic stuns me for a second or two. Maybe I shouldn't answer the door. I haven't taken a shower this morning, nor shaved. For that matter, I haven't shaved in five days. My beard has grown out enough that it no longer itches. Whoever it is, let them knock until their knuckles bleed. On the other hand, I can't get away with pretending not to be home. Where else would I be?

What the hell, I'm not paying attention to the book I'm reading, anyway. Plus, it's dinnertime and I have to pee. I've been ignoring both needs as long as possible, and the weight presses me deeper into my sofa cushions.

Maybe it's Keith again. That wouldn't be so bad, would it? Maybe he'll come inside and take off his clothes.

The thought sneaks across my mind as if someone were whispering it in my ear. I can picture Keith stretched out on my sofa, unbuttoning his shirt. When was the last time I got laid? Not since Diego, and even then…

Don't think about it.

But I'm standing in front of the door. The knocking continues, and my knees are wobbly. The weight of my bladder intensifies. I flash back on the last night I spent with Diego, before the commitment ceremony that never happened: *Diego falling asleep in his seat at the cinema during the newest* Star Wars *installment, then waking up in the final action sequence and resting a hand in my lap. I was hard when the film ended and had to wait through half of the credits until I could stand up and walk outside. At home, we undressed and fell asleep straight away, both of us having had a long day. We didn't live together, but we planned for him to move in after the ceremony. Sometime later—I never looked at the clock--Diego woke me. "I want you inside me," he whispered. "Wake up, Matthew. Wake up." He had wrapped his hand around my cock and massaged it awake before the rest of me could catch up. Then he took me in his mouth and, finally, straddled me. I never spoke. I hadn't been sure I was awake, and still wonder. Afterward, he whispered to me again, "You will never know how much I love you." I drifted off to sleep again, and when I woke the next morning, he was gone.*

Through the peephole: someone I don't recognize, but he's young and male and hot. He's tan and blond, and he has that annoying Castro duck's ass hairstyle, but I wouldn't hold that against him. This can't be another neighbor wanting to borrow a cup of vodka.

"Yes?" I ask.

"Is your last name Jaraschow?" He doesn't mangle my name too badly.

"Yes, how did you know?"

"It's on the list by the door. Look, I came to visit my friend down the hall, but his door buzzer didn't work. Can I use your phone?"

I'm going to hyperventilate. This is how helium balloons must feel.

"I'm sorry…" There's no air in my lungs to form words. This isn't speech, it's deflation.

He cuts me off: "It'll only take a minute."

The door has hardly swung shut behind him, and he's already unbuttoning his shirt.

"You're hot," he says, spearing me with a porn-star leer.

"No, I'm frigid."

"I don't believe you."

We stand there eyeing each other.

I ask, "You didn't really come here to visit your friend down the hall, did you?"

The shirt falls to the floor. His abdomen is cobbled like the streets of old Amsterdam. I'm intrigued: he is neither tattooed nor pierced. He has retained his body hair. That makes him unique, as far as I know. Hell, I'll admit I trim my chest hair, and I have a little *om* tattooed on my left deltoid.

"Of course I did," he says. "Well, to be honest, the friend lives downstairs."

He doesn't meet my eyes. I suspect someone is up to something and when he unbuttons his jeans I find that I don't care.

"Bedroom's through there, right?"

I can only follow. I stop off at the bathroom and when I enter the bedroom I find him sprawled across the comforter in a lewd pose. Normally I am not passive in bed, but in this case, shock overtakes me. I go where I'm led. I do what he wants, because the fact that it's happening at all is enough to content me. I had forgotten: flesh is a drug, and sex is amnesia. I forget myself for a couple of sweaty, straining hours, and afterward, he showers, returns to the bedroom, and helps himself to a pair of my clean underwear.

I ask him, "Who's the friend?"

"Henry. Your building manager. I owed him a favor."

He finishes dressing. He never tells me his name, and I don't ask. I can't get the words out.

July 7.

In a daze, I'm deleting e-mail from friends. When I lift my cup to sip Earl Grey, I'm surprised to find it empty; I don't remember making tea, or drinking it. I haven't checked my mail in weeks because I don't want to hear from anyone. No-one has anything new to say: *Where are you?* (Right where I want to be.) *We're worried.* (There's no reason to be.) *Why did you drop off the face of the earth like that?* (I think you already know the answer.) *You have to move on with your life.* (Who said I'm not doing just that?) *Please call/ e-mail/ send a smoke signal!* (Don't hold your breath because blue's not your color.)

Whenever I shift in my chair, little morning-after pains lance my guts. But the pain has a pleasurable component. It's been a while, and my nameless visitor didn't want to waste time on preliminaries.

Nothing is so urgent as to require a response. I read through a few messages from friends, just to get an idea of what's going on in their lives, but… that's for later. They don't know about this apartment. The new phone number is unlisted. I'm so disconnected, in fact, that a few months ago I unplugged the phone from the jack. There's neither voice mail nor an answering machine to take messages. I cut off my mobile phone service. My e-mail address hasn't changed, but I rarely bother to check it. I've disappeared as thoroughly as possible without moving out of the country.

The encounter last night disturbs me: I didn't mean to let him in (in either sense). I didn't mean to give myself away so quickly. Human interaction is the thing I'm trying hardest to avoid, after all.

(Or is it?)

OK, there can always be exceptions that prove the rules.

Bright darts of pain pierce my gut when I stand and return to the kitchen for more tea. Penetration: better in theory than practice. What would it have been like with Keith? Hell, what would it have been like if Diego hadn't left me standing in front of a crowd of our friends with a scared but hopeful look on my face, praying he'd change his mind and show up?

He didn't even leave a note.

I decide I need to do two things: take a shower and talk to Henry.

This interference has to stop.

July 8 (late in the day).

First thing I do is plug in the phone. This requires a game of hide-and-seek. I have a new phone, almost new, but I'm not the most organized guy in the world and I have to sift through heaps and stacks of apartment detritus to find it. The dial tone shocks me a little; although I've paid the bill every month, I expect dry clicks when I hold the handset to my ear, like when a dead battery keeps the car engine from turning over. I listen until the dial tone expires, giving way to that horrible loud *hang up the phone, dipshit* beep.

This is how computers sound when they're angry. The thought floats through my mind like a dead goldfish in a pet store aquarium. I hang up the phone and dial Henry's number.

Naturally no one answers it. The answering machine picks up: *Thank you for calling Liberal Arms. You have reached the office of Henry Jessup, the building manager. I am presently unavailable to take your call at this time. Please leave a message and I will return your call at my earliest convenience.*

"Hi Henry, this is Matthew Jaraschow, from upstairs. Look, I was hoping we could talk about these little favors, right?…"

With an electronic shriek, the recording is interrupted: Henry has answered.

"Matthew! I didn't think you used your telephone except in the most… the direst emergencies. Extenuating circumstances and all that. To what do I owe this great privilege?"

"It's about the guy who came to my apartment yesterday evening—"

"Oh, right. Kurt. Wasn't he a dish? I thought you might like him."

"You went too far, Henry. I really don't need—"

"To get laid? You didn't need to get laid? Matthew, you're blowing this way out of proportion. Kurt owed me a favor, none of your business why, and I said he should stop by your place and see if you needed a little company."

"What, are you trying to say I needed to get laid? What the fuck is that about?"

"Did you turn him away? I happen to know that you didn't, young man, because I saw him leave. You look me in the eye and tell me you didn't enjoy it. I bet you can't."

By this point I am ready to choke him until his head falls off.

"Henry, if I wanted Anna Madrigal I could either reread *Tales of the City* or watch it on DVD—"

"It's for your own good, Matthew. You'll thank me for it someday."

Hands trembling, I press the OFF button on the handset and return the phone to its recharging cradle.

The decision to leave my apartment is not something I think about consciously; the need to coat Henry's face with spittle as I scream in his face overcomes the need to stay behind a locked door. I figure I've read enough crappy fiction in the last six months to have absorbed a few satisfying lines. Hell, Diego ruined my life when he dumped me; if I actually do succumb to my capering id and choke Henry with my bare hands, I can still read in

San Quentin, right? And I'll probably get laid more often.

I never stop to lock my front door behind me.

Henry opens his door before I'm finished pounding on it, and I almost sock him in the nose by accident. Not that I'd mind giving him a shiner.

"I've been expecting you," he says.

"What the hell is this, Henry? You look like you just laid an egg, you're so smug. I hate being manipulated. I wanted to be left alone. How hard is that to understand? *I wanted to be left alone.*"

"Have a drink."

He turns his back to me and pours one. Something amber. I can't see the label, just the base of the bottle. There's a forest-for-the-trees issue operating here, only in reverse: Henry has too much booze in his liquor cabinet for me to tell which libation he's picked out. In this state of mind, I'd happily accept two fingers of sheep urine, neat, if I thought it would calm me down a bit.

"So you were just about to tell me how much you resent my intrusions into your precious privacy." Henry gestures to offer me a seat on an overstuffed sofa.

The upholstery is the same color as a circle of red wine on a countertop, and velvet; his coffee table has this black lacquered Shanghai brothel look about it. Garish silk flowers overflow from chunky crystal vases on every flat surface, and the room reeks of cigarette smoke and alcohol sweat. Instant sensory overload. He refills my glass as soon as I set it on the table. I swallow the bourbon (that must have been it), and he refills my glass a third time. I drink that too.

"What the hell were you thinking, sending that neighborhood block party woman to knock on my door?"

"You need to get out more," Henry says mildly. He seats himself in a rattan fan chair opposite me and crosses his legs.

62

"Henry, I want to be left alone. It's that simple."

"Matthew, I've been around the block a time or two. There's a time to stay in, feeling sorry for yourself, and then you just have to get out and do something and be around people. I'm sorry, but that's just what I believe."

"It isn't mutual."

"You may own the condo but it's my building. Have another drink."

"Oh for fuck's sake." The alcohol is taking the edge off, though. I knock back my fourth shot and, when Henry hands me the bottle, I accept it without a word.

"If you were really so hell-bent on staying put, you wouldn't have come down here to yell at me, now would you?"

"I…" I stopped. He has a point. I take another swallow.

Don't ask me how, but the whole story comes cascading out of me at that point. The alcohol has finally kicked in. I spill my guts to Henry about Diego decamping just before the ceremony. How I couldn't get him on his land line or his mobile phone. How several of my closest friends admitted that same day, while I was catatonic on my sofa, that they'd never liked him in the first place, and anyway, Latinos are notorious for being unfaithful, so who had I been kidding? Had I really thought it would last? In the immediate aftermath of Diego's Disappearance, his e-mail address stopped working, and his phone numbers were cut off. His roommate said he'd packed up and left in a hurry. *I hate what happened to you guys*, he'd asked. *That sucks. I totally didn't see it coming. Man. I'm sorry. So, hey, do you want to, you know, like, smoke a bowl and fool around a little? I always thought you were kind of hot.* The same postmortem proposition had come in from a couple of other inappropriate people, and that was when I decided to hibernate until I could be around my fellow man without wanting to take a shotgun to the nearest shopping mall.

And then, with the whole thing out and on the table, raw and bleeding like a pile of entrails after human sacrifice, I slump over and, according to Henry, fall asleep for a while

Why I don't throw up, I have no idea. Perhaps because I've already done enough puking.

Henry, being Henry, calls Keith the handsome doctor for help getting me upstairs. *Take him to your own place so you can keep an eye on him,* Henry must have said, because I wake up in bed next to Keith at 8.00 this morning, strangely clear-headed.

"Good morning, sleepyhead," Keith says.

"Sorry about the eyeballs thing," I tell him.

"Henry told me you were kind of prickly but worth getting to know."

"He's so full of shit he smells like a—" But Keith puts two fingers in my mouth to shut me up.

NOTES ON A
DISAPPEARANCE

When the plane touched down at Heathrow, at last, after ten hours airborne, a few of the passengers applauded. I grinned like a lunatic even though it hurt the wound on my left cheek.

As we taxied toward the terminal, the dapper flight attendant in the jump seat across from mine suggested I take the train into the city, rather than wasting an hour on the Tube. Just follow the signs, he told me. It's called the Heathrow Express. You can't get lost. There are arrows. Once you're through Customs, you're practically there. What a smile he had, and what a face, handsome in that well-proportioned English way. I wanted to know if he had on underwear beneath that uniform. Aren't there cabins upstairs on these British Airways jumbo jets? Even if I couldn't bag him I'd have been content to squeeze into one of those awkward little restroom cubicles and unzip his pants, just to take a look, just to satisfy my curiosity.

We hiked miles it seemed into the main part of the terminal.

I looked back a few times along the way, hoping to catch a glimpse of that flight attendant, as if they ever deplane right behind the passengers. Trevor, read the badge on his neatly pressed uniform jacket. Trevor. Of course that would be his name. All Englishmen have names like Trevor and Nigel. No sign of handsome brown-haired, fair-skinned Trevor with the great grin. Nice welcome to England, though.

Not so appealing the bloke at Immigration.

"How long will you be staying in the UK?" he asked me. I couldn't get his accent. After he repeated himself three times, more irate with each attempt, I realized what his question was and answered it. I didn't fare much better with, "So what brings you to the UK? Are you here on business, or as a tourist?"

I nodded. *Fear*, I thought. "I'm a tourist. I'll be staying in Brixton…"

"Thank you." He stamped my passport. "That way to Baggage Reclaim."

Minutes later – just a few minutes instead of the half hour baggage claim at SFO tends to take – my suitcase arrived. Dragging it behind me, I set off to find the train.

As trains go, the Heathrow Express is sexy. It's fairly new. They set it up in the last few years. You take the elevator down to the train station beneath Terminal 4 and wait for it to roar into the tunnel. It's very sleek, the Porsche of commuter trains. Ergonomically correct seats are upholstered in soothing purples and blues. Certain trains are designated Entertainment Free: to enhance the soothing effect, mobile phone use is discouraged and the TV monitors are deactivated. Are fussy babies permitted? I've been wondering about that.

Twenty minutes later I reached Paddington Station, and switched to the Underground. Lucky I was traveling light. I only took what I could cram into a small suitcase. Seven stops on the Circle Line (yellow), then I changed at Victoria Station, then four stops south along the Victoria Line (sky blue) to Brixton. Round tunnels, cute toy trains with round roofs and unexpectedly comfortable seats. *What does this say about Londoners*, I wondered. *Toy trains for public transport.*

If you have to disappear in London, Brixton's not a bad place to start.

Brixton is gritty and funky and vital. Brixton feels much like the neighborhood Adams Morgan in Washington, DC, and San Francisco's Mission District – both places where I have lived, a couple of years each. In

Brixton, boatloads of black Caribbean immigrants have created a pleasing contrast with otherwise chalk-white London. Artists and club kids are drawn to the cheap rents and roomy old houses. (Cheap and spacious for London, that is.) Outdoor markets wind their way down narrow streets; in case you absolutely positively have to buy jackfruit, guava nectar, or a bunch of plantains at 10.00 on a Saturday morning, you can. Unlike Central London, the nightlife in Brixton is propelled by people who actually live there, not tourists thronging to spots like Piccadilly Circus, or Old Compton Street in Soho. Walking down Brixton Hill Road, music from the clubs pounds against your bones. I never ventured inside any of them, though. I always shrugged myself deeper into my heavy wool coat and hurried back to my room.

My name is James and I ran away to London because it was either that or die. I used to be a model. That came about because I dropped out of community college when some guy with the right connections saw me eating at a sidewalk café in Washington and liked the way I looked putting a baguette sandwich into my mouth. I did that for a few years: Banana Republic, Abercrombie… if you've seen the ads for stores like those, then you've probably seen me in boxer briefs.

Then I met Anthony. Older than me by 15 years, handsome in that swarthy Italian way, and a lawyer – the rich and corrupt kind. And a drunk – the cruel and angry kind. *Stay at home*, he told me. *There's more than enough money for us both. Go back to school. You're not anybody until you've got a couple of degrees under your belt. You're wasted on those photographers and those stupid fucking models. How many of them have brains enough to come in out of the rain?*

So I stayed home and tried going back to school. When he wasn't drinking he was… well, he was Anthony, and I lived with him, and it worked pretty well until he remembered he liked Jack Daniels more than he liked me. This took less than a year. Stupid of me, I know.

My friend Michael told me, "He *needs* the booze. He *wants* you. It's not the same kind of relationship." Michael used to be one of those circuit party guys: up all night on weekends, meth crystallizing in his bloodstream, brain cells gummed with THC, liver three shots of Stoli away from cirrhosis. He quit, detoxed, started going to meetings. He told me, "Get the hell away from Anthony before he comes home one night and kills you. He's the type."

I ignored his advice as long as I could.

You can't model underwear with bruises on your arms and upper body.

You can't limp down a runway.

But you can leave.

Home to the parents? No, not an option, they'd been dead several years. Back to the hometown, to fall in with old friends and forget what it was like to live too fast, even when everything was crawling along in slow motion as I spent my nights trying to smile and look handsome and not scared at his friends' dinner parties when his grip around my arm was so tight it hurt and I knew when we got home he was going to fuck me without enough lube, before my ass was ready, to make it hurt more? Because he liked it that way? Right. Anyway, nobody back in South Carolina knew who I was. Not anymore. And why would I want to return to Anderson? Some places are meant to be left behind. Others are meant to be destinations. Like London.

How to be inconspicuous? London's a crowded place, but I picked up a few things within my first 24 hours: don't talk. Accents raise eyebrows. Brits mind their own business, but they don't miss much. Also, don't wear jeans and trainers. I ditched mine, bought corduroy trousers and a pair of Doc Martins, picked up a secondhand leather jacket at the Saturday morning outdoor market on Portobello Road. It's perfectly acceptable not to be outgoing here. Unlike their counterparts in the States, everyday Brits don't necessarily expect you to be make small talk.

The room at the B&B was costing a fair amount of money but I could handle it. I stopped at Wells Fargo on the way to the airport and got cash. Lots of it. Unless Anthony got to my accounts somehow, there was enough to last; I have always been pretty good about saving.

How to disappear? I didn't think there was much to it. You just live. You get through each moment, one and then the next and then the next. Before I left, I talked to Michael, who said it's like getting sober after you've spent years fucked up: an act of will and an act of surrender at the same time.

Minute by minute.

In London, where the air coats the insides of your nostrils with soot, I finally started to breathe. My shoulders disconnected themselves from my earlobes. I joined a gym and started to exercise again. I saw a massage therapist and got the kinks in my muscles undone. The bruises Anthony left on me that last night faded to yellow-green shadows, and the scabbed-over cuts on the side of my face and back healed, peeled, receded to the place all my other injuries went.

You're wondering, What the hell did the man do? What was the breaking point? A fractured bone, a blinded eye, a trip to the emergency room? No, the moment was notable for the absence of drama. Anthony's friend Marcus bought a Glock and brought it over for dinner to show it off, just like he showed off Tran, his 20-year-old Vietnamese plaything, just like Marcus showed off his Corvette and his Chagalls and his cocaine and his dungeon and the suits he bought at Emporio Armani where all the cute little sperm-spittoon retail queens as he called them knew him by name.

"Hey, James, check out my new toy." Glock aimed straight at Tran, whose handsome almond eyes widened to the size of saucers, Marcus shouted, "FREEZE, MOTHERFUCKER!" and pulled the trigger.

It wasn't loaded.

Tran downed a glass of Chardonnay in one gulp, refilled his glass, and downed that in one gulp, too.

Later that night, at home:

"I should get a firearm, myself, don't you think? I think Marcus is onto something, there. We got lucky with the Y2K thing a few years ago. Nothing happened. But still. Can't assume we're safe, even for a moment. There's always something else coming down the pike."

"Yes, there is."

Anthony gripped my shoulder. Marcus had also bragged that Tran couldn't come without a fist up his ass (I knew this not to be the truth, but Marcus and Anthony could never be allowed to know how I had acquired this knowledge, nor how many times), but at least Anthony didn't feel the need to keep up with the Joneses in bed. Yet.

I couldn't assume I was safe, not with a gun in the house. It was that simple. That night Anthony was more rough than usual. He slapped me around. He unbent a metal coat hanger and left stripes. Shot his load on the cuts to make the stinging worse.

The next morning, I left.

Just like that.

London: what's not to like, other than the outrageous prices, the crowds, and the cold weather? I went to the theatres in the West End and shopped for clothes to replace the ones I'd left behind, then had to buy another suitcase to contain them. I wrote some. Read in pubs.

It took Anthony a week to track me down.

Back in the lobby of my B&B, after an afternoon at the Tate Modern:

"James, I can't believe you would just run like this, for no reason. You couldn't imagine how much you hurt me." Apparently not, but from the fumes on his breath, he had administered plenty of anesthesia on the flight over, and maybe more in the cab from his hotel. Wherever he'd just come from. I didn't want to know.

One of the proprietors looked at me apologetically and mouthed, *I'm sorry, I'm sorry.* I think they had figured out what things between Anthony and me were really like. I checked in looking like I'd lost a boxing match. You didn't have to be Sherlock Holmes to make that leap of logic.

"You don't know how much you hurt me when you left like that." Anthony tended to repeat himself when he was livid, not hurt. "I want you to come back to California with me."

When I found my voice, I said, "Let's not talk about this here. We need privacy."

"We could go up to your room and talk there."

I thought my knees would buckle, and hoped the broad-wale corduroy pants I had on were baggy enough to conceal the trembling. Did I really honestly think I could slip away without pursuit, or that he lacked the resources to track me down, regardless of where I went? Never. But I figured I'd have more time than this. At least enough time to figure out where I'd go next.

"Come on," he said, gripping my arm. "We need to talk."

He already knew which room was mine, and practically dragged me upstairs. Right to my door. I unlocked it with trembling hands. He shoved me inside and threw me across the bed. My head smacked the bedside table. I saw stars, planets, comets, entire goddamn constellations.

Anthony didn't have much to say, when it came down to it. He was already unbuckling his belt as the door swung shut behind him, and as he locked the bolt with one hand, he was undoing his Brooks Brothers trousers (I had bought them for him) with the other.

"Don't fucking talk. You're coming back with me on the plane tomorrow," he said, shoving me into the mattress.

I thought he was going to hit me but he kissed me and shredded my lips with his razor stubble. I gagged on his tongue, rank from alcohol.

"You want me to treat you like you're just a piece of ass? Fine, I'll give you what you want," Anthony said.

He broke the button on my pants, trying to get them off. He couldn't do it lying on top of me, so he wrapped one big hand around my throat and said *Strip.*

After I got my clothes off, he shoved my head down. I knew the drill. Suck his dick. Get it wet. He'd roll me over. I'd shut my eyes and take a deep breath and relax as much as I could. But he'd be rough. He'd do some damage. Because he loved me and I had it coming.

I picked at the cuticle of my left thumb while he fucked me. By the time he pounded his way to a gasping orgasm, I had pulled the hangnail down to the quick. It hurt. Anthony pulled out of me, ejaculated across my ass, and immediately went to wash up in my bathroom. After a few minutes he emerged.

"I'm staying here tonight with you, and we're leaving from here in the morning," he said.

"What about your luggage?" I tensed as a wave of cramps rolled through my gut. Felt like he'd ruptured something in there with that enormous cock of his. Then the feeling passed.

He shrugged. "What do you care?" After a moment, he told me he'd get the concierge at his hotel to put his suitcase in a cab.

"I need something to eat after that," he said.

"There's a good vegetarian restaurant up the street a short distance. We can go there. It's early enough not to be too raucous. I'm starving, anyway." All true but for the bit about starving: the thought of food turned

72

my stomach, but I didn't dare admit how terrified I still was.

"I'm surprised you're not staying up in Soho, or over in Kensington. Someplace more in keeping with the lifestyle I've afforded you." Anthony cast disdainful looks around the room. "This place is very cute, but very… *Damron's Guide*. I'm surprised they don't have rainbow flags hanging over the windows instead of blinds. Let's go."

We walked in silence. He noticed me crossing my arms over my stomach but did not comment. From his body language, I could see he was pleased with himself. He'd reminded me who called the shots. Marked his territory. And he was telling himself how much he loved me, what a shit I was for betraying him. In his mind, he was revising what had just happened. By the time we got back to the States, if he had his way, he'd tell Marcus I'd broken down and begged for a fuck the second the door had swung shut.

If I were to take off running, I could get back to my room, lock myself in, and call the police. Perhaps the embassy. And commence doing battle with Goliath. If he wanted me, he had resources to make things tough until I gave in. When he was done with me, the remains would be kicked aside without ceremony, unmissed.

He was well on his way to being drunk.

"I have a better idea. We're right around the corner from the Brixton tube stop. I found a great Thai place near Covent Garden." Not far from the Thames.

"Whatever, James. Whatever. I don't give a fuck. Bottom line is, you're coming back to the States with me tomorrow. I've already bought the tickets."

I nodded.

The restaurant I selected, a tiny place called Thai Pin on a tiny street south of the Strand, could hold maybe 25 people in its dining room. Even

Anthony would have a hard time raising hell in an establishment the size of a postcard. Drunk or not, he needed to believe he had class. And I drew a certain delicate satisfaction from knowing he'd end his meal reeking of curry, no matter what else happened.

Tense mutters from Anthony, over pad thai, between gulps of Riesling: "How much I've given you…"

"I've never loved anyone like this…"

"… so taken advantage of…"

And finally, inevitably: "Just you wait 'til I get you home."

I kept my eye on the waiter and kept the wine flowing.

I had a few, myself, to steel myself for the walk along the windy Thames. London in early December: not as horrible as the climate would later get, I'm sure, but gusty and much colder than the Bay Area.

Portions in British restaurants tend to be meal-sized. You are served about as much food as you're likely to eat, unlike in American restaurants, where one entrée is usually enough to feed five or six starving cowboys.

"Let's walk off some of this food before we go back to the hotel," I told him.

Approaching the line between belligerence and coma, Anthony raised token objections but went where I led him. He bitched about the wind and the cold, but we kept walking. Some of Anthony's anger faded at the sight of all those lights reflecting on the frigid black water of the Thames. We stopped on a bridge to take in the view. I leaned against him and tried to exude happiness and contentment, in case there were witnesses. I planted my feet firmly on the cobbled pavement.

The guardrail – stone, and slick from a light rain – only came up to about waist-high.

Did I mention Anthony couldn't swim?

The US Embassy and the London police investigated, but their efforts

74

were perfunctory: the autopsy revealed a blood alcohol level of 0.22%. I acted aggrieved. One thing I love about the English is their sense of boundaries. If the proprietors of the B&B suspected anything, they kept their opinions to themselves. Case closed. Within the week, Anthony's body was flown home to the States on a military plane; I opted not to return. I could afford to let lawyers deal with his estate.

For now, I'll travel: Scotland, Spain, Morocco. The South of France. Amsterdam. Lisbon. Florence.

In time, I'll come back to London. I'll take walks along the banks of the River Thames in my spare time. I'll touch the scar he left on my cheek. I can't see the ones on my back but I know they're there. Sometime soon, I'll call Tran and ask if he wants a one-way plane ticket. And, whether or not there is anyone around to hear me, I'll probably mutter things like "Should have taken swimming lessons, you bastard" when I come to the spot where his body washed ashore.

ENOUGH OXYGEN

People say the humidity pushed me over the edge. Things down South are different, a little crazier, a little more corrupt, a little closer to coming undone, because of the constant choking humidity. That sweltering heat. Indoors, you shiver in Antarctic air conditioning, the machines perched on your windowsills spitting out ice cubes and penguins, but you steam in your own juices like a lobster in a microwave the instant you walk outside. Everybody from the South is naturally a few steps closer to a psychotic meltdown than, say, people from Minnesota or the Pacific Northwest. After years of having all the oxygen sucked out of your brain every time you step out your front door, something bad happens between your ears.

It couldn't happen here. You wouldn't think so, to look at where we lived: a nice suburban ranch house outside of Raleigh in a nice suburban neighborhood, quiet, sane, two cars in every garage, dogs named Fido and cats named Fluffy. Station wagon moms drive kids to soccer and Little League, ballet and tap classes. Dads work as accountants and junior attorneys, teachers at the local colleges, nice sane respectable jobs. With nice sane respectable kids.

My parents weren't your average Ralph and Gloria, and as Justins go, I was maybe just a little bit too tightly-wrapped.

In gym class my first day back at school after Elizabeth's funeral, this boy named Curtis Vernon saw blood on the back of my underwear. We were both running late, detained by the teacher in our previous class. We were the only ones in the locker room.

"You been takin' dick up yo' ass, Justin?" he said, flicking me with his towel.

"What the fuck are you talking about?" I'd had a difficult night. My energy and patience were about gone. My internal organs shrank three sizes just then, leaving terrible empty places inside of me, increasing the void already there.

"Man, you got blood on yo' ass. Somebody been stickin' it to you, or you sick, or what?"

I didn't have a *Daddy Fucks Me* tattoo across my forehead, and I wouldn't have minded one if that's all that had been going on. I couldn't have been the only kid in school with an elastic asshole because Daddy had decided that Mommy's vagina was, as he said one time when he greased his dick with Jergens hand lotion and shoved it in, *like throwing a garden hose down a well*. There was more going on than that, but Curtis Vernon didn't need to know what we'd been eating for dinner all week. I'd just found out, myself.

"I don't feel so good," I said. "I think I'm sick." This wasn't too far from the truth.

"No, man, you been takin' it up the ass, don't bullshit me."

"You would know." According to rumor, Curtis had been seen loitering in public restrooms and even a truck stop outside of town. To his credit, he *was* kind of cute. The truckers probably loved him. "You wish you'd been the one doing it, right? Is that it?"

I grabbed my abdomen as if I'd been hit with an attack of cramps, dashed to the nearest toilet stall, and slammed the door shut. *Thank God this isn't one of those schools where the stalls don't have doors*, I was thinking. I pulled off my jockey shorts and sure enough, there was a patch of blood the size of a dime. With a wad of toilet paper, I dabbed at my ass. The paper stuck and tore. I guessed the blood was drying. There wasn't that much of it, you know, I wasn't gushing like a vampire on a rotisserie, but... blood.

Coming out of my ass. Not the best way to start off what was already a crappy morning. At least now I knew what was going on. I *had* been kind of achey back there. It had been a long night.

"You got the shits, butthole boy?" Curtis taunted from the other side of the stall door. He pounded on it and laughed, probably hoping for a few splattery farts to prove his point. "That big sloppy hole o' yours cain't keep the poop in?"

Sometimes, when you've had enough, it's not like a neon sign switches on and flashes red all night. No. It's more like the pop of a soap bubble in the breeze. A still, small voice at the back of your mind says, *Well, that was the cherry on the cake of my day.* After that, you give up. All bets are off.

I pulled on my underwear (after wedging a clean wad of toilet paper between my butt-cheeks) and opened the door without flushing the toilet.

"Curtis, it's awful," I moaned. I leaned against the side of the stall. "I just… all this blood! *Fuck!* Go tell Coach Galveston I'm going to be late."

Curtis hovered outside the stall door and alternated between making fart noises and laughing.

"GO!" I screamed.

He went. I fastened my pants and bolted out of the locker room. Supposedly the closest door was a fire exit but the alarm had been disabled as long as anyone could remember. I dashed through it, sprinted across the parking lot beyond, and hiked far enough away from school to jump on a city bus without the driver immediately turning me in.

I got home and found Mom in a strange green hat. She was dancing around the kitchen with no music on, waving her arms about and yowling. She had been watching belly-dancer videos lately, and must have thought she'd learned something. Her rhythmic wailing was probably meant to sound exotic and mystical. It wasn't working. The hat, when I looked closer, contained a live plant. I poured myself a Pepsi, plunked a couple of ice cubes in, licked the cola that ran down the side of the glass, and asked what in the world she was doing. Being up and around beat lying in bed with the curtains drawn and the pillows over her head, arms and torso weeping blood into yards of bandages, but that plant. On her head. I wasn't sure it was an improvement.

She did the hootchie-cootchie dance around the island in the kitchen, and undulated before me like one of those Indian blood goddesses with a dozen arms. One of her bandages came loose, and she slapped it back into place. A hunk of flesh was missing from her left bicep. She ought to have gone to the doctor for stitches, but she refused to leave the house.

"I'm trying to get the plant's roots to grow through my skull and into my brain. We'll become symbiotic," Mom said, between wails.

"Why would you want a plant growing in your brain?"

A long time ago, I read in one of my grandmother's scandal-sheets that a woman in some Midwestern state had gotten an apple seed stuck in her throat. It germinated and grew there. According to the article, she lived out her days with an apple tree growing out of her head, unless she found a doctor to remove the thing – either the tree or her head, whichever she needed less, I don't know.

"Plants produce oxygen. It will aerate my brain, and I'll think better," Mom said, dancing back to the sink and waving her arms over it.

She stopped her dance all at once, and turned to face me. She had a sharp critical stare, as if I were someone else's kid and had just spilled something. She didn't usually look so *there*.

"I should have named you Oxygen," she said.

"I like Justin better," I said.

I left the room.

I'm going to date myself by revealing this, but I grew up with a father who had napalmed one Vietnamese villager too many. My earliest memory was of Mom rocking me and crying because Dad was in Da Nang or Hue or wherever, blowing things up, bayonetting babies, pressing his face into rice paddy mud, and trying to look dead in order to stay alive. Entire paragraphs of his infrequent letters were blacked out by government censors. Mom didn't know whether the next time she saw him, he'd be a charred, bloody mess in a long pine box covered majestically with the Stars and Stripes. When he got home, Mom told me later, he had turned into somebody else.

He no longer allowed Mom to leave the house. Nor to wear makeup, unless it was to cover a black eye. No clothes that were too revealing. He read her letters and had to be in the room when she talked to her parents on the phone. Her friends drifted away. She held me in her arms, mashed my head against her breasts, and cried most of the time. She kept me nearby as much as possible, because she said she didn't like being "messed on," her word for sex. With me around, she explained, he wouldn't try to do anything to her with his *thing*. I was her little saving angel.

My father started visiting my room then, late at night.

I suppose you have to find your comfort somewhere, when your wife has run screaming into the night, in hysterics, and occasionally has to be taken to Dorothea Dix Hospital and given strong drugs and electroshock therapy because she won't stop making this combination giggle-sob noise that makes your hair stand on end. You can't have relations with a woman who's being kept an hour away. Even if you feel like making the drive when the urge strikes, there would be the straitjacket to remove, and the presence of bulky Nurse Ratched types who won't give you a moment's privacy. You can't be sure she won't take a bite out of your shoulder or pee on you when you try to fuck her. And there aren't exactly whores on every street corner in North Carolina cities.

In retrospect, I guess he acquired his taste for boy ass overseas. Sounds like the sort of thing GIs get up to during wartime, right? Smoke a few bowls of weed and/or opium, suck down a few bottles of beer, and if your dick can still get hard, you won't care what kind of hole you sink it into and how it smells when you pull it out.

I can see how it happened.

Does it sound like I'm excusing him? If so, let me put things in a different perspective. After a while, after I got used to it, it felt good.

Now? Well, everything is different. I'm…, technically I'm safe. That counts for something. How sane? That's debatable. Besides: *safe* and *sane*? The words mean different things to different people.

Canada, unlike the United States, has always seemed to be a bastion of sanity. Uncle Sam, a scowling retirement-aged monster whose mouth dripped with the blood of all the 19-year-old boys he'd sent off to die in Vietnamese jungles, scared me to death. My family would watch the evening news as we ate dinner, and I'd single-handedly keep the conversation going: "The body count's up to… how many thousand is that? I can't see the TV from here, Mommy. Why don't you make rice anymore? I'm tired of potatoes." My father would make a face and tell me never to join the military. Nothing could be worth getting your ass blown up or dying in a ditch thousands of miles from home, and Uncle Sam would only screw you over, even as he expected you to salute and thank him for the opportunity to serve your country. The conscientious objectors – the ones who had the most sense, in my grammar-school opinion – were treacherous but sort of heroic at the same time. To me it was simple logic. Stay in America and Uncle Sam will ship you off to die. Move up to Canada with the other dissenters, and you'll be safe.

I'm not in Canada, but I tell myself I will be soon enough. Everything else will fall into place, once I'm there.

When I was 13, Mom got pregnant somehow. I say *somehow* not because I don't understand the process, but because I couldn't figure out how it happened. If my father hadn't fucked her, then who had?

To hear my father tell it, he didn't have anything to do with Elizabeth's conception. Babies just look like babies — apart from skin color, I don't see why people say they look like their parents, because all they look like is other babies — but my father rampaged through the house while Mom was pregnant, shouting at her every other minute. It's a miracle she didn't miscarry.

"Who was it? You fucking whore, who did you let into the house while I was away?"

He'd lock me in my room unless I told him who came and went. *Nobody* didn't seem to be the correct answer, even if it was the only one I knew.

When Mom gave birth, he couldn't be bothered to show up. He went out drinking with a couple of his Vietnam buddies, these scarred and tattooed guys who drove pickup trucks and lived on beer and cigarettes. Didn't come home for two days. When he did, he stank of smoke and alcohol sweat, and his hair showed more streaks of grey than before. Mom's own parents had to drive her home from the hospital. She alternated between sobbing "I'm so sorry! I'm so sorry!" and cooing at baby Elizabeth.

"It wasn't mine," my father sniffed, when someone asked how things were going. "I'd divorce her if she wasn't a fucking lunatic. Don't ask me how she got pregnant, because I was the last person to know."

He never beat me up much when I got in trouble because he didn't like to fuck a black and blue ass. Elizabeth, on the other hand, got backhanded if she so much as looked at him funny. Which of us had it worse? Since I've never met a masochistic toddler, I guess it depends on your fondness for getting plowed, and how much you're into pain.

I ran away from school my first day back after the funeral. Elizabeth's funeral. The day she died, I got home from school and found Mom in one corner of the kitchen, turning around and around with her eyes shut. If she heard me come in, she gave no sign. The noise she was making confused me at first and scared me second. The sound resolved itself into words: "I'm a propeller I'm a propeller I'm a propeller." She lost her balance once, slumped against the wall, then pushed herself upright again, resumed spinning, wobbled. It was all she could do not to fall down.

"I'm a propeller I'm a propeller I'm a propeller."

"Mom?"

She came to with a little scream. "Justin!"

"Are you OK?" This was a standard question of mine in those days. She had never been OK and never would be, but I had to ask. "Is something wrong?"

"Oxygen," she said. "Not enough oxygen. She's going around and around. It's all my fault. I'm trying to understand what she went through."

"I don't understand." I had come into the kitchen for some potato chips and a Pepsi, but my appetite evaporated.

"She didn't get enough oxygen," Mom said. "Like the crops, when the farmers till the soil. They do it to let in the oxygen. That's why legumes are an essential component of crop rotation. They aerate the soil."

"Mom, who didn't get enough oxygen?"

"What they ought to do is have a big propeller churning through the earth, like the blades on an outboard motor. Only in slow motion, so the dirt wouldn't fly through the air. The blades could churn slowly through the earth. They'd be dozens of yards long. You'd be walking above them, on the surface of the earth, while they were spinning away in the ground under your feet. FWOOMP! FWOOMP!" She thrust out her arms and turned in a circle, to imitate the big machines she was talking about.

"You make it sound like a Cuisinart. Who didn't get enough oxygen?"

She kept spinning and making the FWOOMP noises. When she faced toward me, I could see tears streaming down her cheeks.

The house was too quiet.

"Elizabeth!"

I left Mom to churn the air in the kitchen. "Elizabeth!" When I dashed upstairs to her bedroom, she was not there. The flotsam of her toys across the floor suggested recent occupancy. Had she gotten outside somehow? Toddled down the street? Had she gotten herself lost in the overgrown azaleas and hydrangeas behind the house? Those shrubs were gigantic. If she'd wandered off the property, we'd never find her. She could waddle out in front of a car. "Elizabeth!" Black suspicions bloomed in my head.

"Elizabeth!"

No answer. Normally she'd babble.

I sprinted into the back yard, passing my mother (now chanting *round and round and round and* as she spun), stopping on the back steps to survey the yard. Nothing. No rustle of bushes, no toddler jabber.

"Elizabeth!" I yelled, with my hands cupped to my mouth. "Elizabeth! Where are you?"

Nothing.

Back into the kitchen.

"Where is she?" I screamed.

Mom covered her face with her hands.

Then it hit me. I knew exactly where I would find her.

When the ambulance guys came, I told them Elizabeth liked to play in the dryer. This wasn't even a lie. She sometimes slept among the warm clothes in there. It was her hiding place, a womb she could still fit into. Why Mom would turn the dryer on when the clothes were already dry, I'm not sure, but there are some questions you're not ready to ask, much less have answered. Maybe Mom forgot the dryer was full, threw a load of wet clothes in with the dry ones, overlooked her daughter, and left the laundry room. Or maybe Mom knew and did it just to see what would happen. I can't say. Beyond that, there was no talking to her. Elizabeth asphyxiated among the clothes in the dryer. If she screamed, any noise she made must have been muffled by the clothes and the noise from the motor.

And ever since I've been in here, where the walls are beige and the beds are single and the pills come in a small paper cup each morning with breakfast, I've been trying to recreate Mom's mental state. How she could look the other way as her daughter suffocated. I stretch out my arms like the crucified Christ, shut my eyes, and spin around: *I'm a propeller I'm a propeller I'm a propeller.* Still, I don't get it. I'll never quite know what made her tick. I tell myself it's a wasted effort. Yet I keep trying.

Dad refused to let Mom go to Elizabeth's funeral until she promised she'd be quiet. Her parents drove in from Greensboro and made sure she took her pills, strong sedatives Dad sometimes crumbled up and sprinkled into her food when she wasn't looking.

Mom started wailing and didn't stop until late that night. A series of loud crashes from the bedroom left me trembling, wondering who else was dying in there, but I didn't leave my own room to find out. I locked the door and hid under the covers. Even when the air grew hot and stale, I stayed beneath the sheets.

Next morning, when I went downstairs for breakfast, Mom started crying again. She was mixing pancake batter. Mucus dripped from her nose into the bowl. I wondered if anyone else noticed, and whether anyone would yell at me for not eating the pancakes.

No point in mentioning it to Mom. She'd just say, *But you came out of my body, so what difference does it make?* As if, with that in mind, I should then ask for a glass of her urine to go with my pancakes.

Birds were singing outside and I wanted to shoot them.

When we left for the church, Dad and Grandpa had to help Mom walk. Drugs and grief had left her limp, a big crazy Raggedy Ann doll who wouldn't stop crying. I hung behind and didn't say anything for the rest of the day.

That night, I asked Mom about the big bandage over her upper arm.

"Expiation," she said.

Mom looked more pallid than usual. Definitely kind of ill. I didn't know what the fuck she was talking about and didn't care to ask. It sounded like more of her psychobabble. Best to keep my distance in case she forgot to aerate her brain with one of her strange rituals and did me in by mistake.

I couldn't be in the same room with my mother after Elizabeth died. Couldn't stand to look at Mom, couldn't stand the sound of her voice, couldn't stand her insane fucking gibberish. Walls grew around the perimeter of my brain, to block off all thoughts of her. Hadrian's Wall. The Great Wall of China. Hell, the one from the Pink Floyd movie would have done just fine, as long as it established a boundary she couldn't cross.

"I'm trying to make it up to you, Justin!" Mom cried two days after the funeral. Dad was forcing us to eat meals at the same table. I wouldn't look up. "I'm putting my body and blood into making things right again! I'm trying with my entire *being*! Don't you understand how sorry I am?"

I stared into the melted circles in the veneer of our tabletop. Mom tended to take pots off the burner or bowls out of the microwave and set them, still blazing hot, directly on the table. Drinking glasses damp with condensation left round footprints in the waxy finish. I didn't look up, didn't open my mouth.

She killed Elizabeth. Crazy or not, she killed Elizabeth, and we might have covered up for her.

All the oxygen seemed to be sucked out of the room whenever I allowed that thought to enter my brain. My mind ground to a halt.

I finished my omelet (she'd put salsa in it) but did not ask to be excused from the table. My grandmother was softly crying.

Mom clapped her hands (both bandaged here and there) to the sides of her head.

"I can't breathe with you doing this to me!" she screamed. She flung herself away from the table and ran up the stairs.

"Now see what you've made her do," my father said, glowering into his omelet.

The night before I was to return to school, that's when things fell apart, when they broke past the point of repair.

I hid from Dad but he found me and beat the crap out of me, then burst into tears and held me close as sobs wracked his large, solid body.

"What's wrong?" I asked him, stroking his hair and wondering who was in charge here. I was sixteen. This wasn't how parents were supposed to act. "Why are you crying? I know it's not because you're sad about Elizabeth?"

After a few minutes he exhausted his supply of tears. He pulled away and looked me in the eye.

"I'm sorry for putting you through that," he said.

He turned around to look at the door, then rose to shut and lock it. I unbuttoned my belt.

"No, Justin, that's not why I'm here," he said, wiping his nose on the back of his hand. The look on his face made me wonder whether he'd had second thoughts about his late-night visits to my bedroom. "I guess I loved her too, in spite of everything."

"Then what's the matter?"

"Your mother. I'm sorry to tell you this, son, because it puts you in the middle of something you're not old enough to handle. I've thought about it, and there's no other way. It's something you need to hear from me.

"I know you're... you know, what boys do, when they're your age." Now he was blushing. "It's natural. To, you know, experiment."

Experiment? With what? What could I be experimenting with when I already knew the positions from which I could best be penetrated? I shut the fuck up and let him keep talking. No sense aggravating him. Grief might make his temper worse.

"I don't understand. What am I doing?" I backed up on the bed, to put some space between us. Just in case a word came out wrong, he'd have to reach farther to slap me. If I couldn't duck away from the blow, at least it wouldn't hurt as much when it connected.

"It's normal," Dad said, his face as pained as I'd ever seen it. After a couple more moments of this, he spat the word out: *masturbating*.

"Oh, that. Uh, yeah?"

"Your mother admitted something to me in the hospital, when they took Elizabeth's body." He took a deep breath. He wouldn't look at me. He looked at the sheets on my bed, which I hadn't made up. He looked at the decals on my lamp, at the book on my bedside table. He looked out the window for a long while, then fortified himself with another deep breath. "She wouldn't say how she did it. I couldn't get her to tell me, whether it was from your bed sheets, or some tissue in your garbage can, or what. I just don't know. She must have been spying on you, to know when it was still fresh. Jesus Christ, I'm not old enough for this. Fuck! Justin, Elizabeth was my granddaughter."

The farther toward the Arctic region you travel on the North American continent, past the Great Lakes and into Canada, north to where the land flattens out and becomes tundra, the more you feel you're on another planet. Overhead, the Aurora Borealis flickers like the dying breath of some distant star. The farther north you go, the less everything down here in the sweltering South seems to matter. It's all a malaria dream someone else had.

In my mind's eye I have a black pickup truck fitted with a camper shell. I'm driving hours and hours straight, stopping only to piss or refill my tank with gas. No special hurry, but I'm not taking needless breaks, either. Beyond Edmonton, things just peter out. Little towns come and go. I keep driving inexorably north, as far as I can go until the road ends, the land ends, or I end.

I can't leave this wing of the hospital but if I could, I know where I'd go.

In my dreams, sometimes a man is with me, the boyfriend husband partner lover I have never had, only imagined I might meet someday. Other times, I'm travelling alone.

The farther north you go, into the perfect white sterility of the Arctic ice, the cleaner everything becomes. Safer? No, because those extremes of climate are never safe, but the white purity of the ice goes a long way to compensate for that. If I drive far enough north, past the Great Slave Lake, into the frozen wild wastelands of the Northwest Territories or Nunavut, everything will be different. I'll be a different person. None of this will have happened.

It was almost time for dinner. Mom was downstairs cooking. She'd been doing this Italian thing all week, ever since the funeral. Because she was a North Carolina ethnic mutt with no grief traditions to speak of, she had to borrow from Catholicism to mourn with a satisfying degree of drama. The Baptist Church left her bereft of the consolation of black veils and ashes.

Walking downstairs to eat was unpleasant: invisible rubber bands held my arms and legs back. I didn't want to go near her but the alternative was starvation and she'd already killed one kid.

She held her left hand over a pot of bubbling tomato sauce and lopped off the pinky with one swift, sure slice of a gigantic knife. The scream came out of my mouth, not hers. I ran. She tried to follow me out of the house. When I looked back, I saw blood leaking from beneath her right hand, which she'd clapped over the hole where her pinky had been. Her face had gone chalk-white and waxy. I stopped as she sank to her knees.

"I'm trying to make it right, don't you see that? I'm trying to do penance! And you don't even care, you fucking ungrateful shit!"

Grandma came outside knelt next to her, whispering into her ear. The look on Grandma's face mirrored Mom's anguish. What I'd done for it to be directed at me, I had no idea. I wanted to ask, *Aren't you overlooking a few basic facts, here?* But I couldn't say anything, because I couldn't go back. I couldn't turn back. I couldn't face them.

I ran down the street and caught a bus into the center of Raleigh, ate at McDonald's, and wandered the streets until midnight. A man in a public restroom looked at me a certain way and I followed him into a stall. His cock slid right in. It was so long I thought it was going to poke out through my navel, and later, his come was a hot seepage I had to dam up with a crumpled handful of toilet paper. I walked all the way home bowlegged, crawled into bed without a shower, and nobody in the house seemed to notice I'd been gone.

Next morning, there was no trace of Mom's blood in the kitchen.

I got home from school that day and I'd had enough. There was no chorus line of Vegas showgirls holding up glittery placards that spelled out FUCK THIS, nothing dramatic at all. Just a quiet switching-off of the part of my brain that cared.

Downstairs, Mom gyrated around the kitchen, hands waving in the air like kelp from the Sargasso Sea. The plant kept threatening to fall off her head. It would list to one side, and she'd clap a bandage-plastered hand down to hold it in place. Most of the plant's leaves were broken.

Dad kept all his guns in an armoire I called the arsenal. I chose one of the longest and aerated Mom's brain with a blast to the back of her head when she wasn't looking. Not enough oxygen in there before? There was now. Dad got home half an hour later and I nailed him the second the front door swung shut behind him.

I took off for the border in his car and didn't make it, obviously. I didn't even get out of North Carolina. Note to anyone with parricidal aspirations: don't take the family car once you've done the deed, and don't speed. It's a really bad idea.

So here I am. Getting well. Every minute of every hour of every day, I am recuperating. I am approaching a state of mental health as pristine as the ice in Arctic Canada. When my brain has turned into a sparkling white glacier of sanity, I will leave this place and drive north.

I'll tell you one last thing. Do you want to know why I *really* did it? Not because of Elizabeth, no. When Mom cut off little bits of herself out of guilt, and feeding us minced bits of her flesh and blood, a sacrifice of atonement, I thought the meals tasted good. Delicious, actually. Just like what Dad was doing to me. Delicious. Evil and horrible, yes, those too. But that's still not it. I had to shoot them both because I *liked* what they were doing, and it couldn't continue. It couldn't last. So it was either them or me, and I wasn't in the mood to die that afternoon.

IT'LL KILL YOU IF YOU LET IT

Kate drummed the fingertips of her left hand against her cheek. Supporting her head by resting her head in her palm wouldn't do either her tendonitis or her posture any good at all, as her chiropractor kept insisting, but Kate did it anyway. One had to choose one's bad habits carefully. She'd recently broken the habit of clicking her nails on her desk – or any other hard surface within reach – under strict orders from her manicurist. On days like this, she had to bleed off the tension somehow. She had to do something. Eating wasn't an option because she had a clinic to run and staff to intimidate and a size 4 wardrobe to maintain; likewise, leaning out the window to scream into the wind until she was hoarse would only blur the boundary between herself and the few patients to whom she still provided direct services. On the best of days, she sometimes wondered how thin that line was, and today, she doubted there really was one.

In the low gloom of midafternoon, when lunch was a distant memory and her blood sugar was dropping like thermometer mercury in midwinter, it took a keen concentration of will to stay awake. One more client after this one, and she could leave. Her secretary Louise could field any incoming calls. Yes. Being the director had its perks. Deciding when she was done for the day ranked high among them. Her only real remaining decision would be how to drink the cup of coffee her body was screaming for: hot or iced. She'd have enough time between sessions, she kept her own grinder and French press in her desk, and three kinds of beans. Everything boiled down to a question of temperature.

Frank Franklin, the day's penultimate client, presented well enough, all things considered: for starters, Kate couldn't smell him today. Frank was there mostly for maintenance. She had to see him every three weeks to make sure he didn't revert to daily panic attacks and missing work. Despite her years of training not to judge clients, he couldn't avoid discomfort around Frank. She thought, *This is not the reason I got a PhD,* then suffered through the spasms of righteous guilt unique to health care professionals secretly appalled by certain aspects of their duties.

Frank's nest of dyed chestnut hair stuck out in all directions as if he'd glued tufts of barbershop detritus to his scalp. He had dandruff in his mustache. He owned at most two changes of clothes, ill-fitting jeans he cinched at the waist with a fraying belt and secondhand college sweatshirts that strained to conceal his dome of a belly. Either he neglected to do laundry or he neglected to use detergent. Most days, a rank odor trailed after him like the Peanuts character Pig Pen's dust cloud.

"But I do wash my clothes!" Frank insisted, the last time Kate had brought it up. "Once a week, with Tide! Whether I've worn 'em or not!"

Kate supposed weekly was better than not at all and only brought it up again when he came in smelling like Gorgonzola.

"I believe you, Frank. Your mother says you've been doing well. How about showers? Do you take showers every day?"

Frank nodded so fast and hard, Kate's neck vertebrae hurt in sympathy.

What Kate really wanted to think about was her date tonight. Austin had settled on his choice of restaurants, a terminally hip sushi place in Belltown with a live jazz combo. He told her they could arrive late, knock back a couple of drinks, listen to the music, and slurp exquisite morsels of raw fish until well after midnight, if they so desired. He seemed excited about the restaurant because the menu featured geoduck, although Kate couldn't see eating a crunchy mollusk that tasted like sperm as cause for enthusiasm. Parking posed the only possible problem because in central Seattle it was always a bit of a problem. Even during the dreariest weeks of February when the sky had been a constant pall of drizzle for as long as anyone could remember, people still flocked downtown. Kate resolved to look at the bright side. She plastered her best expression of professional concern across her face and nodded at whatever Frank had just said.

I'll pick you up at eight thirty, Austin said in his last text message.

She e-mailed her reply back to his mobile phone at once: *I'm not wearing panties tonight.*

Five minutes later, the session with Frank began.

To Frank's credit, he wasn't picking his nose today. He tended to do that. Absently he'd start working on his nose about halfway into a session. He'd tug at his little mustache as if he meant to extract the hairs one by one. Kate had pointed this out to him more than once. Frank would respond by shifting his weight from one buttock to the other, causing the faux red leather of his seat to emit rumbly noises like loose flatulence, and returning his hand to his lap. He'd pluck and pull at the inseam of his trousers. He'd smooth wrinkles and pinch creases. He'd trace the outlines of stains Kate had, to her chagrin and mild disgust, memorized. Then the hand would wander north again and, on encountering Frank's nose, plunge in like an explorer probing a glacial crevasse. First he'd fiddle with the scaly patches on the nostrils. He'd tug at any hairs he could grasp, plucking them out on occasion with a teary wince. For his finale, he'd root around until he found…

Kate snapped back to the present.

Frank didn't appear to have noticed the lapse. He stared out the window, a glazed look over his eyes, and droned on in his medicated monotone. That was the thing with Frank: get him talking and you almost had to throw a paperweight at him to make him stop. At first, he'd articulate clearly. Kate had no trouble understanding his speech. After a few sentences, all the words would begin to leak sounds into their neighbors, creating an incoherent linguistic puddle.

"Spiders in my head," Frank said.

"What?" Kate returned to the moment.

She'd been thinking about spider rolls and decadent slabs of *sashimi* and warm sake. She'd been thinking about drinking until she reached a rosy state of disinhibition. She'd been thinking about tantalizing Austin with glimpses up her skirt. In fact, in the car on the way home, she meant to move his hand from the gearstick to her inner thigh. She desperately wanted this day to be over.

"I'm tired of all the spiders in my head," Frank said.

Paranoid delusions, Kate thought. *Hallucinations. He'll need a referral to – who's his psychiatrist again?* She shuffled the papers in his chart, idly looking for the name of Frank's new provider.

"What kind of spiders are they?" Kate asked. "Do they have voices?"

Frank shook his head. He scratched his ear. His finger went farther into the canal than Kate would have thought possible, almost up to the first knuckle. None of Frank's long yellowish fingernail could be seen. All thoughts of *maguro* fled from Kate's head. Frank snapped out of his trance and withdrew the finger, looking guilty and a bit scared.

"I shouldn't do that," Frank said. "One of the spiders might bite me."

Kate took a deep breath. "Remember how we talked about delusions?"

Frank nodded.

Kate longed for the days before budget cuts when she could just run her agency and leave the crazies to her staff. Again, she felt the lance of professional guilt run through her. She thought, *I'd be better off in private practice.*

96

"Like if you start hearing voices again," Kate continued. "Remember that? Before you were on the blue pills? The voices used to tell you to walk down the street when there were cars coming. You caused a few people to have accidents. You remember that, right?"

"I know," Frank said. He inspected the matter he'd scooped out of his ear, then used the back of his thumbnail to flick the waxy stuff onto the carpet.

"Could I ask you to stop picking at yourself until after the session?" Kate asked. "I don't appreciate having to watch you pick your nose and your ears every time I see you."

Frank blushed. The flush of red to his face brought the white scales of dandruff caking the skin under his mustache into sharp relief. Kate made a mental note to get a facial next week. Maybe the agency's clients would benefit from facials. Exfoliation couldn't be any less effective than the medication most of them were taking.

"Sorry," he mumbled, looking down at his stomach.

Kate asked, "Do the spiders have voices?"

"No. I didn't notice them until last week. I don't know where they came from. They just, you know, showed up. Like, they were just there. I was meeting with my worker at her office, you know, Susan, and then the spiders were there."

"They were just there?"

Frank nodded. He raised a hand then stopped himself, as if aware he was about to pick his nose again. He looked at his fingertip, then looked up at Kate.

"Thank you," Kate said. "So about those spiders…"

Frank shrugged. His mouth opened and closed. Such yellow teeth, with bits of food littering the spaces between them. Kate squinted to see if there were any cobwebs in Frank's mouth.

"I don't know," Frank said.

"No voices?"

"No."

"Do you see things?"

"When I open my eyes? Or shut them?"

"Whichever," Kate said.

"Just the spiders. They're always there," Frank whimpered. He clutched at the side of his head, as if he meant to pull off his ears like decals. "Whenever I shut my eyes, I see them running around in there..."

"In where?"

"My head, where else?" Frank shot Kate a look that said *how stupid*, a clearer and more focused expression than Kate had ever seen on the man's face. Where else, indeed? "Running around in there. Reproducing."

Kate thought of egg sacs and felt ill. Queasy biological blobs of scuttling life. Spiders are horrible because they look alien. They have too many legs and their fat, segmented bodies look like nothing that is meant to be alive. Kate thought of clumps of egg sacs stuck to the inside of Frank's skull, throbbing brown knots the size of pencil erasers, pulsating with hideous babies. The number of spiders would increase inside Frank's cranium until finally there were so many of them, his head would explode. Rivers of spiders would fountain out of Frank's corpse. They'd eat the world.

"Reproducing," Kate repeated Frank to pull herself out of this awful fantasy. "It's the stress," she went on. "You've been through a lot of change in your life lately, right? Your housing situation? And didn't you change medications a couple of months back?" Almost to herself, and without waiting for Frank to answer, Kate murmured, "Stress. Too much stress is a bad thing, Frank. It'll kill you if you let it."

"I know." Frank rocked back and forth, then side to side. He winced. Sweat shone on his brow. "I don't feel so well."

He clutched at his stomach and leaned forward, then awkwardly stood. Swaying a moment, he steadied himself on the armrest of the red chair, took a step forward, two. The greenish tinge of his face alarmed Kate.

"Do you need to go to the restroom?"

"I… URP." Frank's mouth stretched impossibly wide and he coughed up what first looked like a mass of foam, which turned out to be a solid silvery object, and which landed on Kate's rug with an awful organic splat. As Kate stared in horror at the object Frank had disgorged, Frank – still clutching his swollen belly – waddled out of the room. "I don't feel so good," was the last thing Kate heard him say before the door swung shut.

The thing on the floor bulged. Now it was the size of a potato wrapped in foil; now it was the size of a grapefruit.

Kate spoke out loud, barely aware there was no one around to hear: "I don't think I feel so good either."

Before she could open the door to escape, before she could scream for Louise to bring a can of bug spray, the pulsating silver object Frank had orally birthed split open. Rivers of tiny spiders poured forth. The last thing Kate had time to think was, *But I wasn't going to wear panties tonight*, and then the spiders engulfed her. They ate her up, bones and all. Even her jewelry. They ate her office from the inside out. They ate Seattle. Then they ate the world.

Kate blinked again.

There were no spiders, no throbbing silvery object, no Frank.

"Boundary issues," she murmured.

She wondered again where the line was.

EVERYBODY LOVES THE MUSÉE D'ORSAY

Three hours into my mother's first visit to Malaysia, she was already scratching her fingernails across the blackboard in my head. She had called from London two weeks before: she'd bought a ticket to Kuala Lumpur. Would I mind a visit. She'd asked in the tone of voice that lacked a question mark, and I hadn't put up much resistance. In retrospect, I wish I had. Now I had to keep her occupied for the better part of a week.

Too strange, that she was here, this woman who until retirement had rarely ventured farther from North Carolina than one or two trips to Maryland and DC. Retirement seemed to be agreeing with her: once she untangled herself from the work force, she wasted no time travelling to the UK to research family history.

I should have flown up to meet her, I thought. *If she wanted to see me that badly. Haven't been to England lately. Or France. That's close. What was I thinking?*

"You just can't get good iced tea outside of the South." My mother's face wrinkled in disapproval. She sipped the drink I ordered for her again, then shook her head and pushed it away just far enough to show she'd stick with her ice water, thank you very much.

"I believed that until I visited Malaysia the first time," I said. "Ice lemon tea – I mean, it's not the Luzianne we grew up drinking, but it's really refreshing."

Ice (not *iced*) lemon tea is a Southeast Asian beverage: part limeade (although it's called lemon, go figure), part brewed black tea. Not too tart, not too sweet, perfect for the torrid weather here next to the Equator. Which, when you think about it, is not much different to those swampy summers on the North Carolina coastal plain.

A handsome Chinese waiter brought our appetizers. He caught my eye and offered the subtlest smile as he placed the platter of spring rolls on the carved wooden table between my mother and me. As Mom leaned forward to peer at the spring rolls as if she expected them to be writhing on their plate, I sent a look the waiter's way: *Parents!* His smile widened by a millimeter or two – hadn't I seen him out dancing at Liquid? – and he moved on to the next table, to attend to the patrons there. I let my eyes linger on the rear view as he walked away.

"The crust on these things looks like foreskin," my mother said.

"Mom, this is one of the best Thai restaurants in Kuala Lumpur," I said. *Deep breath, Quentin. Don't let her bait you.* "They're too hot to eat right now. Give them a few minutes to cool or you'll wish you hadn't."

I could already tell it was going to be a long week. Mom had a favorite story about me, and she dragged it out for company whenever she had the chance: when I was a baby, I was too pretty to be a boy. In grocery stores and other public places, she often felt called upon to pull down my diaper to establish my sex. *Isn't that funny?* As if I ought to laugh along with her and her mortified audience, which of course I never did. And she used to have a picture of me as a little boy, maybe three years of age, naked in a wading pool. She kept it in her wallet until I was 16. If she tried these stories on anyone she met here, I decided I'd hang an *I Hate Muslims* sign around her neck and drop her off next to a mosque.

The restaurant, Chakri Palace, anchored a series of exorbitant-by-local-standards Asian eateries along the top floor of the shopping mall at the base of the Petronas Towers. (Mom made awed sounds and craned her neck to look up, as we parked.) The décor, a sort of international Tasteful Thai I'd seen in restaurants on four continents, smoothed my frayed edges: deep purples and greens, wooden screens, a profusion of white and yellow orchids. I had chosen this place to make a nice first impression. The penis-like appetizers seemed to have stolen my thunder.

I took the day off (no easy task sometimes, even for the self-employed), to meet her at the airport and get her checked into her rooms. I had thought after a month in the UK, Mom would have been used to driving on the left side of the road. She wasn't. On the way into KL from the airport, she clutched the Oh-Jesus bar on the A-pillar and stomped an imaginary brake several times. She emitted dramatic gasps whenever someone cut me off or I had to swerve. This being Southeast Asia, that happened every three or four minutes.

"And I thought traffic in Raleigh had gotten bad! Lordy!"

She came in on a red-eye, she has jet lag, and that does tend to diminish one's social skills, I reminded myself. *Go easy on her.*

She had a suite in a guest house at the edge of Bangsar, a fashionable district with enough bars, cafés, clubs, and funky shops to make the local expats believe they weren't really so far from Soho after all. The guest house itself, a sprawling old colonial memsahib skirted with broad verandahs, featured ceiling fans in every room, hardwood floors, and charming pewter fixtures. It looked Old South enough to make Mom feel right at home, or so I thought when I arranged for her to stay there.

"Looks like this place your father took me to, in New Orleans, not long after we got married," Mom had said, depositing her purse on the bed. "Don't try to explain how the phone works, or anything. I'm too damn tired. Just take me somewhere for lunch, and then let me come back here for a nap. I'll be fine in time for dinner, I promise."

"Do you like it?"

She looked around, dubious. I think she was waiting for a cockroach to scuttle across the floor.

"Yes," she said, at last. "It looks like the plantation house in *Indochine*, only smaller."

She had actually seen a film with subtitles. The last film I could remember her going to the cinema to see was *Dirty Dancing*. Possibly one of the more recent *Star Wars* sequels. It was going to be a week of surprises.

"Honey, what's that little sticker on the ceiling?" she asked, pointing up at a discreet red arrow in one corner of the room.

"It points to Mecca, for Muslim guests," I answered. "You're in a Muslim country now."

"As long as I don't get caned," she said. "Where are you taking me for lunch?

Our entrees arrived: prawns with asparagus, a mild chicken curry, and a stir-fried vegetable dish. I waited for Mom to serve herself – she took tinier portions than I remembered her liking – then experienced a moment of cultural schizophrenia as I tried to decide whether to eat like a Westerner or an Asian.

"Well, you've said several times how Kuala Lumpur [she pronounced it *queue-walla-lumper*] doesn't have much in terms of tourist destinations, and the National Gallery here doesn't have works by anybody I'd recognize, so I thought I'd just spend the time with you. It'll be so nice to catch up. I've gotten so much work done in England, you just wouldn't believe it. The people there are so nice. And to think – we're related to them, something like 600 years back!"

It had begun. Mom, true to form, launched into an extended ramble about the genealogical research project that had taken her to Britain. Without charts in front of me, nothing she said made a glimmer of sense.

And she wouldn't slow up, nor leave me room to get a word in edgewise, until my eardrums felt like the homecoming queen's hymen the day after the prom. I dumped a spoonful of the curry over my bowl of steamed rice and, as I was going to spear some potato with my chopsticks...

"Aren't you going to use your plate?"

I sagged with relief. Something other than ancestral babble was rolling out of her mouth. "It's funny," I said. "People here serve themselves a little bit of this over their rice, then a little bit of that. They keep going back to the serving bowls and platters rather than dumping everything across a big plate. It's kind of nice."

As a Westerner, I was raised to fill my plate, then to clean it. Serving myself from a communal bowl with my own utensils would have been considered uncouth at Mom's table. Germs! She had brought me up on a meat-and-potatoes diet, pork chops and lima beans, casseroles wide and deep enough to do the backstroke in, and she kept after me to eat second helpings. "You're a growing boy!" "You're on the track team, so you need something that'll stick to your ribs!" "Have another glass of milk!" When I didn't gain weight or fill out, she shoveled more food onto my plate. "Dive in!" "You've got a hiney like two biscuits on a plate!"

"But isn't it...." The question hung unasked. She collected herself. "Never mind." After looking around the restaurant, she asked, "Won't everybody *notice* if I eat the regular way?"

"You'll be fine," I assured her. "People here are very reserved, but very accommodating. You'll enjoy yourself."

She answered with an immense yawn.

"Gee," she said. "That's good to know." Another yawn. I felt for her. "I believe I'm going to fall asleep in your car on the way back to my little hotel!"

Two structures dominate the Kuala Lumpur skyline: the Petronas Towers, also known as the Twin Towers, which held the honor of being the world's tallest buildings for a decade or so, and the KL Tower, a combination broadcasting tower/ high-rise restaurant/ tourist trap along the lines of the Space Needle in Seattle and the CN Tower in Toronto. The queues to get into the Towers are formidable. Or rather, the queues for the 46th-floor observation deck are formidable; the only people privileged to see the view from on high are, I assume, the petrochemical zillionaires who built the place. Show up an hour before one of the two daily tours and you still won't get in. Waiting out in that jungle-metropolis weather for God knows how long the day after a gruesome flight from London would have been torture for Mom. I couldn't put her through that. The KL Tower is a more accessible spot. You can get in. You can park. You zoom up the escalator to an observation deck almost 600 meters above ground, swallowing to equalize the pressure in your ears as you would in a plane after take-off, and marvel at what of the surrounding cityscape you can see through the haze.

"I don't think I've ever been this high up, except on an airplane," Mom said, staring out a window that faced south. "Maybe one time on our honeymoon, when we were in Hawaii, we went up the side of a mountain in a Jeep. I think it was higher than this. We were in the clouds."

She stared off into space. My father left her for another woman 15 years before, but I don't believe Mom had ever gotten her head around the idea.

"What do you think of the view?" I asked.

We strolled around the observation deck to look at the Towers. From here, they resembled two immense silver ears of corn planted in the earth. Behind us, a book-end pair of strapping blond guys murmured in German. Brothers? Lovers? Friends? Some combination of the above? I couldn't tell.

Mom squinted at the top of the Towers, gauging how tall they were relative to our position, then asked how much the admission charge was in US dollars.

"At the currency exchange, I just said I wanted to convert a hundred English pounds to Malaysian money, and I got all these little colorful bank notes back. I never even thought to look at the exchange rate first! Isn't that funny?"

"The exchange rate is fixed at 3.8 on the dollar. Has been for years. A ringgit is worth a smidge more than an American quarter."

"So we paid a couple of bucks to get in and see this." Mom looked smug for having done the math in her head. When I nodded, she asked, "You don't really care about my research, do you?"

Four or five responses drowned each other out. As I stood, jaw opening to form one word and then a different one, unconsciously backing up to give the German wonder twins a better view of the Towers.

Mom went on to say, "I can see your eyes glaze over every time I bring it up. It's your own family, too, Quentin. Isn't that important to you?"

How to explain that I loved my family but if I wanted or needed them nearby I wouldn't live in Malaysia? On the other side of the planet from North Carolina? So some queer magazine or other has proclaimed Durham one of the most livable US cities for gay men and lesbians. Break out the Moët. The Tar Heel State has come a long way, then. I still don't want to live there.

"You started this project what was it, five years ago? Yes? And since then, how many times have we had this conversation?" The idea that bystanders might overhear this made my skin crawl. "I don't know either. I'm glad you're doing this, I appreciate it, I encourage it, and I'm grateful you want to share it with me, but it's not something I want to take up. And without the big picture, when I hear that John Henry Bumblefuck begat five children by a German émigré princess named Brunhilde von Thunderwald, I don't know who they are, how I'm related to them, and why I should care. I'm sorry, but that's the truth."

I stopped cold. The Germans were watching us, not the skyline. Mom was looking at me with a sideways smile, Mona Lisa of the Magnolias. She had gotten exactly what she wanted. She had poked a hole in my composure.

"Great view," she said, walking toward the elevator. "It's like this building was put here to give those two bigger ones [she flipped a hand behind her without looking back] the finger. Can we go now? I'm ready to do some shopping."

Kuala Lumpur's streets are anything but logical. To get the basic idea, imagine someone dropped Atlanta and it broke. I drove preoccupied through KL's spaghetti-tangle infrastructure to Bintang Walk, choosing that district over several others on the assumption, perhaps naïve, that nobody in her right mind or even her left one could possibly badmouth the place. We ended up passing the UK and French Embassies. Lost. I had to turn around in another embassy parking lot – Italy's, I think – and double back. Lost. Great. Something else for her arsenal, to be dropped into a conversation with a third party later in the visit, apropos of nothing, to elicit a giggle at my expense.

Bintang Walk, to continue the Atlanta analogy, is KL's Buckhead, only more so, and with nastier summer weather. Chic shops, unique restaurants, fashionable people, and suffocating humidity. I chose Lot 10, my favorite of the malls in the area, as a starting point. The façade of the mall itself is an incandescent shade of lime green. Isetan, Japan's answer to Macy's, is the anchor store. Dôme, which bills itself as having "The World's Finest Coffees," tempts you with liquid refreshments mostly too hot for the local climate… at least until you walk inside and the layer of sweat you're covered with breeds squawking flocks of goose bumps.

"Oh my Lord," Mom said.

The architecture at Lot 10 has an organic science fiction look, as if designed by HR Giger or lifted from the set of Alien. I spasmed with self-doubt: I should have chosen Star Hill Centre, down the street, which looks more like something you'd see in Raleigh than a Star Trek episode. I enjoy Lot 10 but some people prefer a kinder, gentler retail ambience.

"You'll feel better inside Isetan," I said.

The shoe department had the tonic effect I had hoped for: Mom did the math, squealed when she saw what she could get for her tourist dollar (as diffracted through the British pound and the Malaysian ringgit), and soon had two sales clerks, a boy and a girl, neither more than 20, scurrying to bring her one pair of shoes after another. I had almost relaxed when Mom looked up in the middle of trying on a pair of low-heeled black pumps, seemed to realize I had caught her enjoying herself, and dropped her face into a pout. Mom sent the sales girl back for a size I knew she couldn't wear, and I decided I'd had enough for now. A brief trip upstairs to the men's department resulted in the purchase of a pair of trainers I'd been eyeing, and when I came back, Mom stood at the checkout counter with eight boxes of shoes stacked into two four-storey towers. My heart missed a beat from shock.

I grew up in clothes from the Salvation Army. *Why spend the money when you're going to outgrow them anyway*, was her stock response when I asked why she shopped there. *And I'm past the age where anybody cares what I look like.* Who was this woman impersonating my mother?

"Retirement's agreeing with you," I told her.

"I just can't believe the exchange rate here! It's all so cheap! When I was in England, good heavens, everything there costs a hat-arm and an overcoat when you go from American dollars to pounds, and it's just unbelievable, what people pay for things! When you see a value like this, you just have to go for it!" She turned to the blushing girl who was ringing her up. "Isn't that right? Goodness, listen to me, I sound like such a tourist. OK, get me out of here at once before I buy anything else."

I tried that, but we couldn't escape the gravitational pull of British India (think Eddie Bauer with jodhpurs), where she cooed over the inventory before settling on a pair of linen blouses and a lightweight dress.

"I went shopping in Scotland," she said as she surrendered a Visa card to make her purchases. "When I was up there checking out the family castle. One of them, anyway. You know there's another one down in Devonshire. Of course nobody lives in them any longer, but it's so exciting to think of that as our roots! I stayed in Edinburgh a couple of days, just doing the town up, and I wanted to go shopping but I was spending pounds, and I just didn't have the heart – it was all so expensive!" To the checkout girl, she said, "Hold on, I've decided on something else."

Mom dashed over to a nearby rack and grabbed a blouse like one she was already buying, only in a different color – blue this time, not green.

I didn't say a word.

At Tang's, in Star Hill Centre, Mom picked out a few dresses she liked. Even at a favorable exchange rate, these were not inexpensive items. I was not used to seeing her burn up money so freely, and made a mental note to find the right moment to swallow the lump in my throat and ask what had happened to her income. Some of her research had led to a modest history of eastern North Carolina being published, and I thought she had realized a small profit from that, but the way she spent money raised questions. As long as I could remember, she'd been a paragon of thrift.

"Scotland was lovely, and the castle was just amazing," she said, out of the blue, returning to the subject she had dropped when we left British

India. She handed me one of the garment bags containing two dresses to carry, then the other when I gestured to let me carry more. "I wanted to spend more time there, but I had to get back to England."

"I've never made it to Scotland. David and I have talked about a holiday in the UK but we've just never gotten around to it. We're probably going to buy a house down in Melbourne, so our last couple of trips have been to Australia."

"Well, I hope you don't mind that I'm talking about my family history project again, since it doesn't mean anything to you. I wouldn't want to put your nose out of joint," Mom said. She walked toward Dôme and asked if I felt like treating her to a cup of the finest coffee in the world. *Invasion of the Body Snatchers* had come true, and an affluent pod person had replaced my mother. The likeness was good, the guilt trip routine couldn't be beat, and she still completely lacked tact and timing, but I wasn't convinced: who was this woman and what did she want? I followed her into the café and suppressed a random death-wish as she yoo-hooed a waiter like a debutante.

From the lavatory I called David on my mobile.

"You can opt out," I told him after I said *I love you* and he said *I love you too* and I said *I love you more* and he said *I love you more than that* and I said *Oh bite me* and he said *Later.* "She's on the warpath, and it's all this covert passive – aggressive shit she's done all my life, and I'm going fucking nuts but unfortunately she's my mother and I do love her."

"Of course you do, darling. That's what she's for. I'll meet you at Balakong, just like we planned."

"You don't have to," I told him. "I can tell her you're stuck working on a last-minute proposal for a bazillion-ringgit project, and your job's on the line if you don't give 110 percent on this…"

"Don't," he said. "I'll be there. If she's being difficult, I can handle her. I'm Chinese, remember? We had difficult mothers and methods of dealing with them thousands of years before the Europeans landed in America. I'll be fine."

"You never cease to amaze me," I said. "Just don't say you weren't warned."

"Son, you're just not with it today, are you? Did you make another wrong turn?" Mom looked out the car window in obvious apprehension at the warehouses around us. "I thought we were going to a nice restaurant for dinner. We must be lost. This doesn't look like the restaurant district."

"You're right. It's the pothole district," I said, as the car jolted through one.

"It's a little out of the way, but it's there, believe me. This place is like that. Malaysia, I mean. Things aren't always where you'd expect them to be, but it all works anyway."

"Well." She looked around. "I guess I should shut up and let you do the driving, shouldn't I? You do live here, after all."

"Imagine that," I said.

When I pulled into a parking spot beside Balakong, I saw David at a table talking with our favorite waiter, a Chinese (of course – the restaurant was run by a Chinese family) guy of my own height, with shoulder-length hair and an exquisite face. From the intensity of David's facial expression and the animation of his gestures, I could tell they were discussing the menu. David is an unrepentant food snob. He has strong opinions on the various cuisines of Malaysia and how they should be prepared. I'm sure the wait staff at the restaurants we frequent either love him or want to dip his satay in cyanide. I killed the engine and set the parking brake.

"Quentin, this restaurant doesn't look… I mean, it doesn't have walls."

A quaver had crept into Mom's voice. She sounded old.

"Lots of restaurants here don't," I told her, climbing the low steps surrounding the restaurant to take a seat next to David at the table.

The waiter, Gershwin, smiled and said hello in English, and returned to the kitchen. Mom lagged several paces behind, and took her seat with a huff. Apprehension radiated out of her like factory exhaust.

To a Westerner visiting Southeast Asia for the first time, this style of restaurant may seem questionable: built into the corner of a building, there are only interior two walls. Instead of having two outer walls, the restaurant is open to the outside. Ceiling fans circulate air and tile floors keep the space reasonably cool. The chairs are often the cheap moulded plastic kind one might buy at Wal-Mart and park in front of one's double-wide, along with a glow-in-the-dark bird bath and some artificial flamingos.

What the Westerner who can't get past appearances fails to realize is that food here is a source of intense pride to both the kitchen staff and the patrons. Malaysians of whatever ethnicity take their food seriously.

After introductions, I tried to explain this to Mom. She didn't seem to want to hear it.

"Where's the ladies' room?" she asked.

David pointed the way.

"Poor thing," he said.

"Don't get me started," I told him. "What have you ordered?"

"You'll love it," he replied. "I hope she will. Gershwin said the steamed fish is not to be missed. He also said the eel is good but I decided to give that a pass. I doubt your mother would be happy if I ordered eels. There's a prawn dish – you said she likes seafood – and paper chicken."

"Did you order the shark's fin soup?"

He nodded. One of Balakong's specialties is a shark's fin soup made with tofu instead of Jaws. It tastes like the real thing and she wouldn't know the difference.

"Let's not tell her it's tofu," I suggested. "I think shark is inside her comfort zone. She can brag to her girlfriends back home about how she ate shark in Malaysia."

"Can't you get it in the States?"

I nodded. "Yes. That's the point. Oh, here she comes, and she doesn't look happy."

"The toilets here aren't the best part of the restaurant."

Mom took a seat. She looked a bit pale.

Before she could speak, Gershwin returned with our pot of tea and a bowl of teacups in steaming-hot water. He set these on the table, then took the cups out of the water, shook them off, and poured tea for the three of us. He then filled the customary extra cup, which he set before an empty chair.

"It's a tradition here," David explained, following Mom's gaze and anticipating her question. "I don't know who the extra cup is supposed to be for, but we do it anyway."

That *what have I gotten myself into* look slipped across her face again; you'd have thought the teacups had been brought out in a bowl of goat urine, and I felt my patience slipping. I was tempted to ask, *If you wanted everything to be exactly like North Carolina, then why did you come?* But I had sense enough to keep my mouth shut. She'd say something smarmy like *To see my only son; isn't that reason enough?* My goals were simple: for Mom, to have a pleasant visit, to see fascinating and lovely things, and to meet David and his family; and for myself, to keep her at arm's length, even when she was as close as the passenger's seat of my car. *I'm batting about 500 so far, at best,* I thought. *If that.* Mom sipped her tea and offered up a tiny smile that vanished the second she caught me looking.

The same thing happened with the food. First the soup: Mom ate as if she had just crawled starving out of the Sahara, blowing on spoonful after spoonful to cool it, then slurping the stuff down. She caught David and me exchanging a victorious look – She likes it! – and soured right away.

"What are these gristly things?" she asked, pointing with a chopstick.

"Tofu," David said. "There's some tofu in the soup, too."

"Not the shark? I thought it was cartilage."

Oops. "The shark is the tender part," I said.

The chicken provided more of a challenge: she didn't know what to make of the presentation: bits of meat in a rich, dark sauce, all wrapped in packets of baking paper, and tied with string. Impossible to eat without making a splendid mess. She tried. I always tried, too. No matter what you did, the sauce spattered, your fingers got slimed, and you had to remind yourself *This is fun* while you struggled to take your first bite.

She gave up on that dish, then asked in obvious relief when the prawns came, "You look like you've lost weight, Quentin. This must be why!" A titter. "The food's so complicated!"

She sobered up. A sip of tea, then: "So, David, how did you and Quentin meet? He's so cagey on that subject."

"On the Internet," David replied. "Several years ago, we subscribed to the same online newsgroup. I was still in grad school in Australia. He thought something I posted was funny, and he sent me an e-mail to say so."

"We were like pen pals for about nine months," I added. "Then I flew over here to visit."

"Well, that's sweet," Mom said. To David: "I thought it might be something like that, or a personals ad, or something. I'm sure Quentin would rather I didn't say this, but why not – you're family now." Her eyes sparkled, and she smiled my way. This was probably how it felt to realize you were one or two seconds away from being hit by a speeding bus. "He's always been such a loner, and I just – well, he's been through two or three failed relationships, really bad ones, and I know by the time he hit 30 he must have been wondering if he'd ever meet someone special. I think it's been very lonely for him. I just hope this works out for you both. You seem like a nice young man."

David's cultural advantage of becoming inscrutable to Westerners came in handy just then. I knew him well enough to recognize the millimeter narrowing of his eyes, but he didn't miss a beat: "I'm sure Quentin is very fortunate to have such a concerned mother. Would you like more prawns now? I can tell you like them. I can order more if you're still hungry."

Under the table, he moved his leg until his left foot touched my right one.

I watch Mom watch David resume eating. When she turned and saw me looking, I gave her the best smile I could manage – even as her own face slid back into its familiar pout.

I had another realization, just then: *She's lying.*

After dinner, I suggested picking up dessert at Alexis, our favorite coffee shop in Bangsar. I'd already be in the neighborhood, dropping Mom off.

"I am awfully tired," Mom said, exaggerating a yawn.

"I know how you love that tiramisu," I reminded David.

"Meet you at home, then," he said.

When I got home, he came into my arms and kissed my face and ears and mouth and neck.

"Don't say a word," he said.

Behind his back, I jiggled the box containing his tiramisu so he'd feel my arms move.

"Let me light the candles. I'll be right back."

In the kitchen, I mixed a tall gin and tonic. The swirling ice drew me in like a hypnotist's crystal pendant. David surprised me: I felt something behind me, started, then looked down to see two olive-tan arms wrapping themselves around my waist.

"I'm not sure how well gin mixes with tiramisu," I cautioned him, turning to follow him into the bathroom.

He was deliciously naked.

"I don't care. Come get into the tub with me."

He had transformed the bathroom into a candle-lit shrine. Flowers on the countertop and in the sink, a stick of champa incense burning, my favorite Enya CD adding sonic perfume to the air.

"You have your choice of three bath ballistics," he said, referring to the fizzy, scented spheres we bought at Lush on our last Australia trip. When dropped into bathwater, they zoomed around the tub as they dissolved, dispersing scent and providing great entertainment at the same time.

"Your call," I told him, not standing on ceremony but climbing in and taking another deep swallow of gin.

He unwrapped and chucked a blue one into the water.

"You know I'm trying," I said. "I mean, she makes me nuts, and you know she makes me nuts, but I'm trying to make this an enjoyable trip, and she's pulling out every covert sabotage technique she knows."

"Darling, you can't let it cause you stress. She'll be leaving in five days. You don't have to spend every waking minute with her." He stroked my hair. "I do have one question, though. Does she always divulge such personal things about you to people she has just met?"

I nodded.

"Proof that we don't change with age, we just become more completely ourselves," David said, kissing the back of my neck.

"So you see what I mean, now, yes?" I liked what he was doing with his hands.

"Of course I do, darling. No matter what you do for her, she always wants more. You've said it yourself: she doesn't know where she ends and you begin. Fortunately you do know. Now can we talk about other things?"

"Like what?"

"I don't know. Kiss me and one of us will think of something."

I called Mom at the guest house the next morning and proposed a road trip down to Malacca, a small city rich with history, about an hour and a half south of Kuala Lumpur. Malacca is the city where Europeans first colonized what is now Malaysia. Dutch and Portuguese settlers landed there centuries ago and built tidy churches and squares. In the old section of town, any number of cute shops, galleries, and restaurants vie for the contents of your wallet. Majestic temples and mosques coexist side-by-side. Mom listened for a few minutes before heaving a sigh, announcing she had horrific diarrhea, and asking if I'd be offended if we just stayed in KL and had some tea.

"Do you want me to bring over some medicine? You can buy Lomotil over the counter here. It's fantastic stuff," I offered. "If you're hungry, I'll pick up an order of chicken rice on the way. It's tasty, but it's very mild and kind to your system."

"No," she said. "I've taken something already, and the concierge told me about a place nearby that delivers. He ordered me some soup, and when it came, there was this nice bouquet of flowers on the tray with it! Such a sweetie, and I only had to tip him the equivalent of 50 cents! Can you believe that?"

"Welcome to Malaysia. Why don't I come over around lunchtime, then, to give you more time to rest?"

"Sure, honey. Anyway, I think I need to go spend some more time on the throne. I am just torn up!"

With that, she hung up.

Mom waited to assault me with guilt until after the film I took her to see that afternoon. She chugged enough medicine to feel confident leaving her hotel room. We saw a German techno-adventure-comedy at a new cinema. Mom laughed in the right places but I could tell something was wrong. I assumed the problem was intestinal in nature.

"I don't think you want me here," she said at a café afterward, as we sipped hot tea.

I instantly felt miserable on two levels: exasperated that she kept going round in circles like this, but also guilty as charged because she was right. Like America itself, my parents are easier to appreciate from a distance.

"I wanted you to have a nice time," I told her. "I was hoping you'd see why I like living here."

"But you're so... I just don't know. Distant. You act like having a relationship with me is the last thing on earth you want. I know it's been three years since we've seen each other, but I don't understand where you're coming from. Am I such a burden?" Without giving me time to answer, she plunged ahead, like she worried I might say *Yes*. "OK, then I'll just tell you why I'm really here. I want you to consider a move back to North Carolina."

All the blood drained out of my head.

"Just hear me out," she insisted. "I don't know how much I told you about the part-time job I took to supplement my income, after I retired from the state. It's a network marketing company – they're based in Dallas – and they specialize in utilities. Power, gas, Internet, paging, long distance. If you sign up through them, you can save 10 or 15 percent compared to what you normally pay. If you become a representative, well, the earning potential is unlimited. I'm going to become a Regional Sales Coordinator in two months, and my income – why, I bet I make more than you do! How do you think I could afford this trip?"

"I assumed your book had sold well," I said. Christ, my accent was coming back.

The blood hadn't returned to my head yet, and in a minute my brain was going to collapse like a failed soufflé.

"It did OK," she said. "But not well enough to turn me into a world traveller. Son, I'm getting older, and sooner or later I'm going to need care. I don't like to think about that eventuality, but I can't avoid it either. Have you thought about that much? What you're going to do when I'm..."

I interrupted: "You're not there yet."

"Sooner or later you're going to have to give up this globe-trotting lifestyle of yours and come home," she said.

"What's home?" I asked. "Where's that? The States? North Carolina? Which city? Or do you mean your house? Do you think my life is only a temporary detour, and I'm supposed to end up living with you again someday? That's how it sounds."

"You're not married," she said. "You don't have kids. Isn't that what homosexual bachelors do in the end? Move home to take care of their mothers?"

"I can't even count the number of ways that's offensive," I said. This discussion was going downhill fast. I couldn't look at her much longer if she kept this up. "You've met David," I said. "I'm not going anywhere without him, he's not going anywhere without me."

"Well, I'm not saying he has to stay behind," Mom started.

I interrupted her. "It's not for you to say where he goes or doesn't go. And we're not going to keep having this conversation. You obviously don't have a clue how insulting it is."

"You're all I've got left," she said. "Your sister hasn't talked to me in

10 years. I don't even know where she lives. I'm getting old all by myself. I need you."

"Insulting me and treating my relationship – my entire life – as if it's all just a passing phase is not the way to win me over," I said. "I think we need to pay the check now. If you want to go back to your hotel, I'll take you. You're welcome to have dinner with David's family tonight, because they were looking forward to meeting you, but give some thought to what you've said and why I'm upset about it."

"I'll take a cab back," she said. "They're cheap. You've said so yourself."

"I'll hail one for you."

When she was gone, I ordered a glass of Shiraz from the bar and sipped it, staring out the window at pedestrians and passing cars.

On my first trip to Malaysia, David took me to dinner at Tamarind Hill, an extravagant Thai restaurant nestled in the heart of the city. If you didn't know it was there, you'd never find it by accident: you leave a main road, turn up a gravel drive that looks like it's going to end up in a lot next to a disused building, park and follow the footpath, and end up in front of another of those grand colonial houses the British left behind. This one serves what David and I consider the best Thai food in Kuala Lumpur.

We were seven for dinner: David, his sister and parents, his grandmother (visiting from Sabah), Mom, and me. David and I had brought along three bottles of a South African Chardonnay. We finished the first two, pleasantly enough, over appetizers.

David's father and sister could speak excellent English. His mother knew enough to get by, but she was not ready for James Joyce. His grandmother could manage a few words, but with age, the less she spoke anything but Cantonese.

Mom had been pleasant all evening, smiling at everyone, speaking with exaggerated care (I caught David's sister's eyes glazing over once), not drinking too much. Maybe she really had reconsidered her approach.

Of course I was wrong. The horror show began when our waiter brought out my favorite dish, pandan chicken – bite-sized pieces of white meat tied in fragrant pandan leaves.

"I was telling Quentin that I think he has lost some weight since he's been here. Not that he had any to spare. The cuisine is so different from what we eat in America!"

"They don't have Thai food in America?" David's sister asked.

"Oh, that's not what I meant. I mean, it's very good." She untied a strip of pandan leaf, took a bite of the chicken, and made a rapturous face. "Delicious, but it's such a change for him. You know he has a sensitive stomach, and…"

"And that's not what we all came to dinner to hear about, now, is it?" I forced a laugh. The Chinese tend to be more sanguine about the squishier facts of life than us Amurricans, but this wasn't where the conversation needed to go. "So why don't you tell us about England and Scotland instead? I think it's great that you're travelling overseas, after all this time."

David and I had a telepathic moment just then. I knew he was thinking *Bravo*.

"England and Scotland." For the first time I realized that Mom was not sober. Her slushy pronunciation of Scotland gave her away. She had probably taken some Lomotil, an opiate derivative, before dinner. That, plus dehydration, plus a couple of glasses of wine… "England and Scotland are beautiful."

Smiles all around. I didn't think anyone else had caught on yet.

"I went to London last year for a convention," David's father said. "Unfortunately, I was too busy to see much. But I enjoyed the trip. Long plane flight."

"My ancestors left England 300 years ago," Mom announced. "They are descended from the British Royal Family, and there's a castle in the south of England that has been in my family ever since."

David's sister, in particular, looked surprised by this news. She murmured a quick explanation in Cantonese, for her mother and grandmother's benefit. They gave a very similar mother-daughter start, looked at each other, and began a side conversation of their own.

"They're very impressed," David's sister said. "That's very interesting."

"Quentin doesn't seem to think so," Mom said, selecting another bite of pandan chicken from the serving platter. "Quentin would rather I didn't talk about my family history at all, because it's not important to him. His family isn't important to him, and he demonstrates it by moving to a remote [she paused to take a dramatic look around] practically third-world country, and breaking off ties with all of us…"

"Mom, that's enough," told her.

"Do you feel well?" David asked. "I think you need to get to bed."

"Yes lah," David's mother said, addressing the group for the first time. "Hot tea. Maybe doctor."

"I don't need a doctor, I need for my son to stop living with a man and come back to his senses and come back to his family!" Mom shouted.

Heads turned.

I rose. "Please accept my apologies," I said to them all. "She's a little sick from her travels, and I think I should take her home…"

"That's for goddamn sure," Mom said. "*Home.* Christ, how can you people stand it? Our sons are living together?"

David's mother looked stricken. His father bowed his head, but not before I noticed a flash of anger. She knew; he didn't. Not officially, at least. These things were not spoken of. I didn't like the arrangement, nor did David, but when you butt heads with 5000 years of Chinese culture, you're not going to win the battle: his parents, while educated, were also ashamed. Deeply ashamed. With our two-bedroom apartment, we could maintain a charade of being roommates; even that step had been a big one for David to take. We were moving to Australia because in the long term, if we wanted there to be a long term, we had no choice.

His grandmother got in one question before I got Mom to her feet to propel her toward my car: *"Gay?"*

Mom had been gone a week and I hadn't heard from her. Didn't expect to, either. At least not until she got back to the States, after she concluded her stay in England, and perhaps not then.

I'm going to change your ticket, I told her in the car that night, leaving Tamarind Hill. David sat in the back, shell-shocked. *Whatever you were trying to accomplish tonight, it blew up in your face. You're not welcome here.*

I didn't mean… She sounded indignant, and I was past patience with her, past apologizing, past making excuses, past trying.

Save it. You know perfectly well what you meant. Now do you want to call British Airways? I can do it from my mobile, right now. In fact, why don't I?

I put her on a plane the next day. The only seat left was in first class, the telephone sales agent told me. I sacrificed a staggering number of frequent-flier miles to change the ticket.

David and I were on a flight to Melbourne, house-hunting. Our real estate agent had called, promising exciting leads in South Yarra, St Kilda, and Port Melbourne, three of our favorite suburbs.

"Promise me there won't be more visits like that," David said.

He looked gaunt after a week of family upheaval. His parents would barely speak to him. His grandmother refused to tell anyone else in the family, thank God, but she made it clear she wanted nothing further to do with me, since this whole gay thing was obviously my fault, an affliction

I brought from the States and infected David with, corrupting his Asian values, blah blah blah. Only his sister showed any sign of humanity.

I had been nauseated all week, myself. Malaysia isn't Denmark. You don't just casually out Chinese guys to their families and assume there will be no repercussions. You can't even assume they'll be safe. She had to have known that. All week, I had been coming back to the same question: did she plan it, or was it an accident? In the end, which was scarier, and did it matter?

David and I had a long talk and decided Australia couldn't wait.

"The next time I see her, if there's a next time, it'll be somewhere safe," I said. "Letting her visit Malaysia was one of the worst ideas anybody ever had. I should never have allowed it. Hell, I can't say I like the idea of bringing her to Melbourne. Not after this. The length of the flight, alone, would require her to spend a couple of weeks, just to get over the jet lag, and I'm not up to it."

"What will you do, then? She's not going away."

"You're right, but when I can't put it off any longer, and believe me I'm going to stall as long as possible, then we'll meet in London or something. We can take the train down to Paris, through the Chunnel. She'll dig that. Check out the tourist stuff there – the Eiffel Tower, the Louvre, Versailles, those places. Everybody loves the Musée d'Orsay." I reflected. "As long as I can keep her at a safe distance, I'll be fine."

"You're not going to leave me and move back to North Carolina, then?"

"When hell freezes over," I said, taking his hand.

SUNSET OVER BRITTANY

Sandrine threw me out this morning. She has done it before. Today I have on jeans and an old sweatshirt because I had to dress while Sandrine stood in the doorway screaming at me in a mixture of French, Breton, and English, and throwing things. When she threw cutlery, a knife struck the floor beside my foot. She left a constellation of bruises on me. Periodically, I mash my thumb into them to make the colors deepen.

I am determined to push all negativity and unpleasantness out of my mind. Sandrine will calm down soon enough, and when she does, she'll call me on my mobile, sobbing, near panic. She'll beg me to come home. She'll say she's terrified she has lost me forever. Maybe she has. I can't predict the future. Perhaps I'll set myself on fire and webcast my death over the Internet. Maybe I'll go to a supermarket and buy all the fruit from the produce section, return home, and pelt her into a coma with pears and apricots and tangerines. Or I may go to a gay bar and pick up a man, and run away with him. Sandrine has accused me of having that tendency often enough. Maybe she's right. Maybe she has lost me forever. Who can say? I drink cup after cup of black coffee, evil black lava from a place on Telegraph Avenue. With all this energy I have to do something creative.

I'm in Berkeley. The weather is warm and clear. And I have my camera.

Here in the East Bay, an updated version of the old streetcar network, the Key System, is to be resurrected. As part of the PR campaign, I'm photographing crowded streets, bored people slumped at bus stops, backed-up entrance and exit ramps to the freeways that crisscross the region. I also snap pictures of people in parks, at sidewalk cafés – urban scenes of the sort one sees in European cities. The message: we can keep things as they are (images of traffic-related misery), or we can run trams down busy corridors and make life better for all. Not subtle, but then neither is the Bay Bridge at rush hour.

Children play in the park down the street from me. Sandrine wants children, but she can't have them until she finishes her Ph.D. Too busy. I don't want kids, myself, but I think they're excellent subjects to photograph. Sandrine would always cry when I showed her the pictures I had taken, so I stopped. I do my job. When the trams come, we will have more parks. The air will smell better. Children won't be run over by cars as often. That ought to make her happy, but somehow it doesn't.

"Patrick, I cannot look at you today. Get out of here!" she spat, out of nowhere, twin pigtails bobbing up and down.

I sipped coffee and maintained my mildest expression.

"What's the problem, dear?"

She threw her half-empty cup of orange juice at me. The cup missed my head by an inch but drenched my shirt. Citric acid stung my right eye. I radiated peace and gentleness at her. I visualized doves.

"You are a terrible person! You are full of petty cruelties! I cannot stand you for another moment!"

"How am I cruel? Why am I terrible? I don't understand at all, Sandrine."

"I don't even want to talk about it! I am too upset! I want you to get out of this house now, or…" Sandrine's nostrils flared. I pictured a thoroughbred fresh off the track. A bright spot of pain began to glow behind my left eye, an infernal nuclear red. The side of my head throbbed. It still hurts. And my shirt smelled like Florida.

Nothing makes Sandrine happy. So I had to leave. Again.

I have taken a seat on a bench with a good view. This will be a good park for my photo essay: one of the tramlines will pass within three blocks. More people will come. The park will gain more picnic tables, more playground equipment, more flowers. It is my task to show all interested parties what this place could become.

To my right, an Asian family: Mom, I guess, with three kids, a girl and two boys. They have monopolized the swing set. I wonder whether the children have English names. Local folks, or visiting? The girl's legs are too short to reach the ground. Her little dress flies up when she swings. Her older brother, the middle child if height is any indicator, is showing off. *See how high I can go.* The oldest, also a boy, seems bored, but his mother has that *Have fun or I'll punish you* dragon-lady look about her. Very fierce.

Off to my left, sitting on the next park bench, one of those Berkeley women with faded ribbons in her faded hair, and faded political buttons on her faded vest. She's talking to the pigeons that warble at her feet.

Over here, a group of kids, the standard Berkeley mélange: all shapes and sizes, all colors, several languages audible in their babble. I pick out individual children to follow with my lens.

That sounds a bit depraved, I know.

I'm just taking pictures.

Sandrine hovers near, accusing. She's invisible, and at this particular moment I know she is at home gluing shards of china together, but I can sense her presence. She thinks I have illicit intentions. She hisses foul names, polyglot. *If you don't get out of this house within ten minutes I will break everything. Every object you own, I will smash it. If you are still here when I finish, I will then smash you. Understand?* Maybe I run against the grain, but I'm involved in a public works project, for God's sake. I am a public servant, not a pervert. Mostly.

Something from the hail of objects she sent my way this morning grazed my side. Perfect timing: my shirt was off, and she broke the skin. The wound stings. I touch it with a fingertip and feel shooting stars, comets, supernovas. A personal sunset just below my nipple. Why didn't I steal a packet of salt from the café? I'd have something other than soil to rub into the wound.

Here is a little girl who catches my eye. She looks like a younger version of Sandrine, to tell the truth. Her kindergartner's voice will have an accent when she speaks English. I'll call her Brittany, after Sandrine.

I abandon my bench seat to get closer.

Brittany wears a ruffled white sundress. She has a yellow ribbon in her perfect golden hair, and I'm reminded of a shampoo commercial. All the moment needs is gauzy soundtrack music instead of car horns and distant traffic. Brittany is talking intently to two other children, a black boy in corduroy pants and a T-shirt, and a tan girl in matching yellow shorts and T-shirt. They're pointing at something on the ground. A bug? Brittany stomps on it and claps her hands together in glee.

The little boy moves to a sandbox and joins an effort to build a sandcastle.

The girl in yellow begins picking flowers out of a wooden planter: petunias, jasmine, some pink things I don't know the name of.

Brittany climbs up the monkey bars.

One thing I love about Berkeley is the unexpected vistas. If you look west from certain places here, toward the Pacific down some of the latitudinal streets, you can see across the bay to the hills of Marin County. The Golden Gate Bridge can be seen if there's no fog. Today, as usual at this time of year, it is still possible to see the bridge. As the sun sets, the sky and clouds turn dramatic shades of pink and salmon. I'm surprised when I realize how late in the day it is.

At university in Rennes, Sandrine from a small town on the Breton coast, me studying abroad for a year. Marriage had seemed like a good idea: romantic, reckless, vaguely doomed. Now? Regrets.

Sandrine leapt up from her chair, seized her china plate where vegetarian sausages and perfect yellow circles of polenta cooled, and tossed it all at me. I fell sideways out of my chair and lay helpless. The floor tiles left their checkerboard pattern on my cheek.

"The vein at your temple looks like a pipe on the Pompidou Center," I told her. "It's very beautiful."

"*You are cold inside and I hate you! There is something badly wrong with you! When you fuck me it feels like I am being stabbed by an icicle!*"

Brittany thinks she is a gymnast and is trying to walk across the monkey bars, hands out at right angles, head held high. A perfect photo.

Someone screams: a woman, rushing through the cluster of children, a stricken look on her face. Also perfect.

You should do something, you miserable bastard! Sandrine is near. She is my conscience when I normally just have a camera. She smells like violets. Where would I be without her?

The woman screams for Brittany to come down, and when she turns to see what the commotion is about, she loses her balance. She wobbles back and forth on the monkey bars.

Why didn't you stop her, you useless prick? Why didn't you make her come down? Sandrine hovers like a wasp, following me everywhere, ever the critic. *You should have flown through the air to stop her!*

The wound in my side sings a glorious chorus of pain, no finger-jab needed. I hold my breath as the sweat cools my brow. Brittany is airborne. I take pictures.

Brittany's sundress rises like an angel's robe, revealing perfect white panties underneath, no socks, white sandals. The yellow ribbon comes undone and floats, weightless.

Screams shatter the air all around us: kids, adults, Brittany herself. Her mouth opens, a capital O ringed with pretty white teeth. In the distance, a car alarm joins the din. I hear a siren, but I doubt it's approaching.

Brittany falls, legs creating a 45-degree angle, toes pointed like a ballerina's. The sun is a brilliant red-orange ball between her left heel and the metal edge of the monkey bars. I steal this last shot and pray it turns out: sun, girl, playground equipment, all aligned just so, a combination unlikely to be seen again. I won't include this one in the photo essay. Brittany lands on her head with a loud THUNK, and the screaming intensifies.

It's over, Sandrine. It's really over.

I turn and leave.

FIXED

My name is Jasmine Melendez – Hill. I'm 16, and I live in Berkeley, California. I'm writing this because Jennifer, my social worker, said she wanted me to. The scientists and researchers all want to hear my side of the story. The psychologists want to hear it, too. In my own words.

I was adopted. That isn't what I'm writing about, well, it kind of is, but Jennifer said I should put in the background information so it'll all make sense. The scientists and the psychologists want to get the big picture. They may never meet me in person, so I have to make sure it's all very clear for them. She says I write well, too. I like her. So here it is.

I was adopted by Alison Hill and Maria Melendez when I was two years old. Alison and Maria are lesbians. They had been together like 10 years when they decided to adopt. I think Alison tried to have a baby via the turkey-baster method, with sperm donated by some gay guy friend of theirs, but she miscarried. They tried again. She miscarried again. They tried sperm from another gay guy, their friend Sam, who is like this gazillionaire travel writer. Alison's gynecologist said there were some kind of abnormalities. Her insides weren't up to the job of bringing babies to term, and Sam's baby was going to be deformed if it even lasted past the first trimester. Planned Parenthood took care of that one. Slurp. Maria didn't want to get pregnant, so they decided to do the third-world adoption thing like every other lesbo couple in the Bay Area who weren't conceiving babies on their own with borrowed sperm and a kitchen utensil.

Maria's from Cuba. She has very dark skin, and long hair in these beautiful braids. Because of her Latin origins and fluent Spanish, they decided that she would be the adoptive parent. I guess they got some agency to look for babies. Latin America is always having disasters that leave lots of babies without mothers. Unlucky for them, lucky for me. Maria went to Honduras and got me. The Honduras government officials made her stay there 30 days while all the paperwork went through. Maria showed pictures of Sam's lover Marco, who is from Brazil and looks Hispanic enough to pass off as the adoptive father. Maria said she and Marco were engaged. She fed them some bullshit about him going back to Rio to take care of his dying mother. They ate it up. Back to Lesbo-land we flew.

I have dark skin too but not as dark as Maria's. She has African ancestry. Cubans are often very beautiful that way: they are a blend of races, which is how I think everyone will look someday. Me, I am more Indian. My face is kind of broad, you know, but not like a dinner plate. Just enough to give me an exotic look. I have almond eyes and full lips. I think I'm probably pretty, but when your mothers sublimate the whole traditional female beauty thing, and you're not allowed to watch network TV or play with Barbie dolls (because if you do, you'll be convinced your ass is way too big but your boobs will never be big enough), you get kind of murky on what girls are supposed to look like.

They adopted Dmitri three years after they got me. Two kids was enough, they told me. Two was just right. We'd be a perfect little nontraditional family. Not that anyone in Berkeley would give us a second look.

This time, Alison did the traveling. She was born in England and it shows: very fair skin, freckles, reddish hair. She still has an accent. By similar logic to what they used when Maria went to Honduras, the moms decided Alison would have an easier time in Eastern Europe. The break-up of the Soviet Union put lots of babies on the market.

Alison flew to Moldova first. There was a baby there, according to the agency, but when Alison got there, this straight British couple had beaten her to it. She said Moldova was a beautiful country and she'd like to go back later.

Then she flew to Moscow. There were lots of babies in the orphanages there, and lots of little kids. Alison was overwhelmed. Nothing was in English, not the street signs or the restaurant menus or the information in the subway stations. It was hard to know which restroom was the right one. And when she did find the right one, it was like this hole in the floor. Too disgusting. She got really freaked out by the whole Moscow thing and took the train over to Nizhniy Novgorod.

There was this lady from an agency there in Nizhniy Novgorod, a social worker or something, and she acted as Alison's guide. She did translation and told Alison which officials to bribe, and how much to pay them, and everything. Dmitri had just been born. His mother was this poor peasant girl. She couldn't take care of him.

The State Department stuff took a couple of days. Maria handled a lot of it from back here in the US. Dmitri's mother had given him some mile-long Russian name like Sergei Snottoblottski, and of course Alison and Maria lesbianized it right away.

I guess Dmitri and I grew up in a more or less normal way, all things considered. I mean, there wasn't much normal about our lives, by the standards of the rest of America. Plenty of trashy right-wing religious people would faint if they could have seen Maria's goddess icons, or Alison's meditation room, or the box they kept their vibrators in. I wasn't supposed to know about those, but come on, kids get into everything. So our childhood was all very open and natural. Alison and Maria wanted to make sure their kids didn't get stuck with needless, unhealthy hang-ups.

They went through all kinds of trauma when they started to suspect something was wrong with Dmitri. He was two. At first they thought he was retarded. He wouldn't respond when they talked to him. Like if he was looking the other way, and one of us walked into the room, he wouldn't turn around to see who it was. He sort of jabbered and cooed, but they said his baby noises didn't sound right. I don't know what babies are supposed to sound like, and I don't think I ever want to have one, but that's what they said. They took him to a specialist at Children's Hospital over in Oakland. The specialist checked his hearing.

"He's just deaf," the audiologist said. "I doubt there's anything seriously wrong with him, other than that."

Alison fainted. Neither of them is really butch, you know, they're not those big burly women that ride motorcycles and look like football players, but Maria is the more durable of the two. After Alison had come to, and Maria had driven us all home from the hospital in her old Volvo station wagon, she called a friend of hers who was dating a teacher at the deaf school down in Fremont, which is close to San Jose. The teacher, this fortyish deaf guy, came over to visit us with his boyfriend, Maria's friend. The teacher could talk, even though he was deaf. When he talked, he also signed at the same time. His voice was pretty clear.

We had a Family Conference. The teacher, whose name is Jason, and his boyfriend Jeff, had tea with us in our living room. I remember it pretty well. I had just turned six, and I was already in school. They included me, which made me feel very important. I kept quiet and paid close attention to everything they said, although I couldn't understand all of it.

Jason, the teacher, said it was OK to grieve and worry about Dmitri for a little while, but not to spend too long on that because they had work to do. In other words, *get over it*. (If they only knew.) Jason said the moms should start learning sign language right away. Me too. Don't put off teaching him language, he said, unless we didn't want him to be able to think for the rest of his life.

So it was like this Dyke Power crusade after that. They went to classes. They taught me signs. Of course Dmitri was better at it than we were, and I picked it up faster than the moms, but you know, they did a pretty good job. When he got older, they let him go to school down in Fremont, which was kind of weird. Students live there. Even really young ones, like in the sixth grade. The school has dorms. Cottages, they call them. Some of the kids come from too far away to commute. And I found out a lot of their parents don't know sign language to begin with, so at home there isn't anybody for the kids to talk to. When they do go back to school again on Sunday nights, they're pissed off about having been left out all weekend. Do you blame them? The moms didn't want that to happen to Dmitri.

So that's the deaf thing. He went to school down there during the week, and on Friday afternoons, when he was a little older, he rode BART – the train – home. Alison or Maria would pick him up at the station.

Me, I was just like any other kid with interracial lesbian mothers at Berkeley High. My best friend was this Chinese girl named Elizabeth. Her moms had adopted her in Shanghai. We had all this stuff in common. Like Maria would speak Spanish to me so I would know my so-called native language. And Mei, one of Elizabeth's moms, would speak Cantonese and Mandarin to her.

Elizabeth and I were like, *whatever*.

One time, Elizabeth said, "Maybe we should be girlfriends." So we kissed each other some and didn't get anything out of it.

"Maybe we're straight," I said.

Elizabeth shrugged. "I guess so. So let's keep being best friends, then."

"OK."

So the Bible-bangers would probably think I was raised in this den of sin, but it all felt pretty normal at the time.

Turns out nothing was as normal as I thought, but it wasn't because

Dmitri and I were being raised by a pair of lezzies in Northern California. Alison had her job at the university, in the psych department. She was a full professor, and she wrote this book that sold a zillion copies, and that was cool. Maria opened a tai chi studio over in Oakland, and it did pretty well. I was on the yearbook staff in middle school, and by high school they appointed me to be the editor. I had a crush on this Filipino boy named Justin, but he was kind of a loser. Then I had a crush on this red-haired white girl named Candace. She looked like a boy and had a dirty mouth. We kissed once under the bleachers and then she got mad at me and wouldn't talk to me anymore. But this was all pretty normal compared to Dmitri.

For one thing, he never got sick. Never ever.

He was down there in Fremont at the residential school, and in a school like that where everybody lives in close quarters, if one person gets something, then everybody gets it. Of course all the kids were vaccinated for things like chicken pox and rubella and mumps, all the childhood shots you have to get. And they got the newer shots, hepatitis and E. coli. One kid in Dmitri's class got chicken pox anyway, and it was like the end of the world. Maria and Alison sent him all these worried e-mails: take care of yourself! Wash your hands! Don't touch your face!

He didn't get sick.

All the other kids got colds and he didn't. Sometimes Alison and Maria took me down there to see him, and cold season you'd see these kids with green snot coming out of their noses. Not Dmitri. He never got sick to his stomach, even though the food was pretty bad. The flu went around one year, and like everybody got it, even me. Alison had all the gross symptoms and spent a week lying around the house. Maria fought it off. I had to stay home from school for a week, myself, and take extra vitamins.

When Dmitri came home, Maria started fixing dinner in the kitchen.

Veggie lasagna, my favorite. Lots of fresh oregano and basil. Extra minced garlic to help our immune systems.

"Are you sick too?" he asked. He didn't actually ask it by talking to me, he used American Sign Language, which doesn't have a written form, but that's still what he asked. Does that make sense? Like, if he'd asked it in English, that's how he would have said it.

I nodded. Maria and Alison had rented a bunch of videos. I was watching the new Brad Pitt movie. It wasn't very good, but he took off his shirt a lot, which made it worth watching. I felt like shit.

"All the kids at school are sick," I signed back. "I have this headache that won't go away, and no energy, and I feel like shit."

He used this sign that means "Oh, I see" but with this sympathetic look on his face that added the idea "that really sucks" to what he was saying. Then he reached out and took hold of my wrist. My headache went away, just like that. I was used to the headache, so for a minute my system was confused. It's like I thought I still had the headache, and then I didn't, but it was supposed to be there, and then it wasn't. No headache. And I had energy again. I remember taking a deep breath.

"Did you do that?" I asked him in sign language.

He nodded. "Don't tell anyone. I'm going to fix Alison too, but it's a secret."

Have I mentioned we called the moms by their first names?

Dmitri wouldn't tell me how he fixed Alison, but the next morning, she looked healthier than she had all week.

"My fever's broken!" she announced.

We celebrated with a trip up to Marine World, in Vallejo.

I got nauseated from one of the rides, and Dmitri very carefully took hold of my wrist when Alison and Maria weren't looking. The nausea subsided just like I had taken some Rolaids or Tums or something, only better, because there wasn't that gross chalky aftertaste. Suddenly I didn't have to throw up. For about 10 minutes I had been feeling like I was about to blow chunks, and the sunlight was too bright and too hot, and I wanted to lie down, but then all at once I was fine.

"Fixed," Dmitri said, looking very satisfied with himself.

So, I mean, really – what are you supposed to do when your little deaf adopted brother heals you like one of those evangelists you see on TV late at night sometimes, but without all the Jesus crap and the big hair? If you tell your best friend, she'll think you're nuts. I didn't think Elizabeth would spread it around school that I'd gone psycho or whatever, but I just didn't think I should tell her. It wasn't like this awful Thing that kept me up all night worrying. I just kept it in mind for future reference. Next time I got really bad cramps with my period, I'd ask him to make them stop, and offer to do his math homework in return. I researched his social studies project for him, and he got rid of my acne. It was very convenient, and it didn't really bother us or anything.

Not long ago, Dmitri told me he fixed some kid's broken ankle on the playground. He had to do it before the teachers got there. Dmitri knelt down and held the little girl's hand. He said she was writhing in pain and crying. It was really hard to understand her signing. So he fixed her. It was like picturing a broken stick unbreaking itself. Her shoes and socks were on, and she was wearing jeans, so it wasn't like anybody could see what happened. The bone unbroke itself, and the pain went away. If the bone went crunch, or I guess anti-crunch, when it unbroke, nobody there could hear it anyway. The teachers carried her to the infirmary on campus, and they took her for an X-ray, and everything was fine. They decided the little girl had fallen and just gotten a bad shock. Aren't kids resilient. Blah blah blah. (If they only knew.)

That same school year, Dmitri came home one weekend missing the mole on his left cheek. He had this mole there, like Madonna's only not as pretty.

"What happened to your mole?" I asked him when we were alone.

"I peeled it off," he said. "Like a sticker."

Maria and Alison were fixing dinner. Ethiopian food. Lentils and things. We were going to sit around on the floor and eat the food with the big circles of bread, to make it seem more authentic.

"I could have sworn he had a mole," Alison said that night. "Why did I think you used to have a mole, Dmitri?"

Dmitri shrugged and scooped up more tangy Ethiopian vegetable stuff with a torn piece of circular bread.

"I know I haven't been sniffing paint fumes," Alison said, signing and talking at the same time.

Dmitri looked puzzled. Sometimes different things are funny for hearing people and deaf people, and I don't think he got the joke about paint fumes. He looked at me to explain. I tried, and after a while he either got it or pretended to. He responded with that same "oh I see" sign and a look on his face that suggested us hearing people were really weird sometimes.

Looking back, I think this kind of thing pissed him off. I mean, the moms did a good job compared to most of Dmitri's friends' parents, like they could actually communicate with him, but they left stuff out. He could get tantrummy.

He never has had much of a temper, you know, but I guess I should have thought about what I'd do if he lost it. Really lost it with somebody.

Maria didn't say a word the whole time. She kept looking at him. I think she knew there was something going on, deep down inside.

I have to say, Maria was (is, whatever) the smarter of the moms. Alison may have been the professor, with the Ph.D. and all, but Maria is sharp as a fucking tack. She does not miss a thing.

Later that weekend I asked him why he didn't fix himself. At first he didn't get it.

"You know, your deafness. You could make yourself hearing." I felt a little awkward for saying that, but it was the obvious thing. Maybe it was so obvious he'd overlooked it.

"Oh, that. I tried that." He made a face. "Awful. Too loud. I thought hearing people could close their ears, like closing your eyes. But I was wrong. You're stuck with all that noise. All the time, too much noise. It's awful. I didn't like it, so I fixed myself again. Deaf is better."

I had to take his word for it.

Then there was the roadkill. Gross, I know, but I can't leave anything out. I got a little nervous when Dmitri told me he tried bringing some roadkill back to life and it worked. That was like 6 months ago. It wasn't like this Stephen King *Pet Sematary* thing where the dead cat comes back to life and wants to eat you. The cat he brought back from the dead just got up, peed a little, and walked away. Dmitri followed it for a little while to see if it would keel over again, but it didn't. It groomed itself, then ran off into the bushes to catch a bird or something.

Dmitri tried a few experiments. His school is in this suburban area with lots of houses, near a couple of main roads. Fido and Fluffy sometimes get out, and try to cross the road at the wrong time of day. Splat! So anyway, if it was fresh roadkill, then he could bring it back. He just had to touch it (God that is so gross, I may not be able to finish the sandwich I'm eating) and concentrate for a second on making it well. Fixing it. And the dog or cat or rabbit or whatever would kind of twitch, and get up and go about its business. He said they always had to pee when they woke up. There's probably some explanation for that, but I don't think I want to know why. Maybe it's like when you wake up in the morning, you have to go. I don't know. Dmitri said his experiments on old roadkill, the mushy kind that's like bones and fur and surrounded by flies, those stayed dead. Now and then one would kind of twitch some, but it wouldn't come all the way back to life. He'd have to step on its head to make sure it was dead again.

When he told me that, I was eating then too. I spat out chunks of food to make it look like I was throwing up. I mean, does it *get* any more disgusting? I could just see him trying to bring the sushi back to life at the restaurant the next time Alison and Maria took us out. I pictured these pink cubes of fish jumping around on the wooden tray and knocking over the soy sauce. Ugh.

Two things started happening at the same time, and I guess everything worked out the way it did because I lived with Alison and Maria in Berkeley during the week, and Dmitri was down in Fremont at school. In literature, that's where a writer would say "unbeknownst to," or something like that.

Unbeknownst to us, Dmitri would sometimes play doctor with the other students. He was getting kind of, I don't know, *adventurous*. I don't mean pulling down other kids' pants to compare pee-pees, although he probably did that too. I mean like if somebody got sick or hurt, he would very quietly fix things in a way that hid who the real doctor was. He'd offer to walk them to the infirmary. One weekend when he was home, he made me promise to keep a secret.

"Of course, you dumbass," I told him. "Who would believe me, anyway?"

"You know my friend Juan?"

I nodded. Cute little guy from Nicaragua. I remembered him.

"I took his appendix out."

"*What?*" I didn't believe him at first. Silly me.

He nodded. "Honest!"

Juan was going to have to have an operation and was scared shitless.

He told Dmitri that the doctors said there was something wrong with his appendix. It wasn't an emergency but it had to come out pretty soon. Dmitri thought operations were a bad idea. Those doctors and their stupid knives and shots and stitches. He could do a better job. He got an encyclopedia from the library and looked up *appendix* so he'd know what to pull out.

One night when Juan was asleep, Dmitri snuck into his bedroom and fixed him so he wouldn't feel anything, or wake up. He reached in (don't ask how, I have no idea. I don't think he stuck his hand up Juan's butt or anything. I just don't know) and went *snip* and pulled it out. All better.

"I don't understand why you had to take it out," I said. "Why couldn't you just fix his appendix for him?"

Dmitri shrugged. "Because I was curious," he said. "The encyclopedia said he didn't need it. If I took it out it could never get infected again. And I wanted to see what it looked like. And it worked. Juan's healthy now. He doesn't have to go to the hospital."

"Cool."

Now for the unbeknownst to Dmitri part.

Maria and Alison were having problems. I lived with them, so I could see everything going to shit, but Dmitri was away during the week, and when he was home on weekends, they hid it from him. Or tried to. *Duh.* He's deaf but his eyes work. Any idiot could see the moms weren't getting along as well as they used to.

So this went on for a while. They wouldn't talk about it. Just kept going in circles, acting like the problem wasn't there, like nothing was wrong. They hardly touched each other. Dinner was getting to be more and more tense. I would ask one or the other what was going on, were they splitting up, and they wouldn't say. That was so not like them. So much for open and natural. I started finding reasons to get out of the house more often, because I couldn't stand to watch the disintegration.

On weekends, it was like they staged a play for Dmitri's benefit. Poor little deaf boy, can't handle reality, let's make like everything's just as sweet and nice as it ever was. I mean, come on, he's probably smarter than all three of us put together. Did they really think he wasn't going to see through their act?

And what about me? Why weren't they trying a little harder?

Finally, last weekend, when Dmitri came home from Fremont, we had a Family Conference. A really awful one.

Alison's face had this flushed look, like she'd been crying. Kind of puffy. Maria didn't say much, and I got the feeling she was mad and trying not to show it. But I couldn't be sure. Maybe I'd ask later. Much later. Talking and signing at the same time, Alison said that she and Maria had been having problems for a while now, and they didn't think they could work them out. They had been to see their counselor, and she thought Alison and Maria should consider a trial separation.

A trapdoor opened up underneath where I was sitting, and I fell through. That's what it felt like.

I looked over at Dmitri and could tell he didn't quite get what Alison had just told us. That happens sometimes, when you talk and sign at the same time. English grammar is different from ASL grammar. So I explained it to him again, more clearly: *They're breaking up.* Dmitri looked stunned for a second, then looked like all the pieces suddenly fit.

"Why didn't you tell us a long time ago?" he asked. "Why now, when it's already too late?"

Not bad for a 13-year-old.

"We thought the problem would go away, and we wouldn't need to burden you with it." Maria this time, finally opening her mouth. When she saw that the talking-and-signing thing wasn't working (again), she just signed. We could all understand that, anyway.

"So, like, is one of you going to move out? Are we going to have to find a new home?" I addressed them both. My hands were shaking so much I could hardly sign, but Dmitri seemed to follow me OK. "Alison adopted Dmitri, and Maria adopted me, so does that mean Dmitri and I have to split up too?"

Thunderstruck is the word to describe what Dmitri looked like then. He hadn't thought of that yet. Once that look passed, then you could tell he was really pissed off.

I was just crying.

These thoughts were running through my head: Did one of them have an affair? Was there another woman in the picture? Or did they just not like each other any more? Was it money? Was it us? It was all too horrible to deal with. I wanted to run upstairs to my bedroom, slam the door, and hide under the bed, but I told myself to be mature and set a good example for Dmitri. At least one member of the family needed to be sane.

Maria spoke up: they hadn't made final decisions yet, she said. But they had put off telling us as long as they could, and things between them just hadn't gotten any better, and please try to be brave and bear with them as they found their way through this.

After she said that, the Family Conference seemed to be over. This time, I did run upstairs to my room. I couldn't help it. I hid under the covers of my bed and cried myself silly.

I must have fallen asleep, because next thing I knew, Dmitri was waking me up. He was tapping me on the shoulder, a little too hard, like he was impatient.

"It's not fair. They should have told us a long time ago," he said.

"Maybe they were trying to help us," I answered. "I don't think they wanted us to be upset. What's wrong with that?"

Dmitri didn't answer. He sat on the bed next to me.

"You live here during the week. I'm away at school. Did you see this? Did you already know?"

I shook my head No. "If they were trying to hide it, they did a good job."

He thought about what I said. For a long time, he was quiet. After a long time, what seemed like forever, he said he believed me. "Go back to sleep," he said.

I didn't wake up again until the next morning, Saturday.

The house was unusually quiet, and the usual breakfast smells – the coffee Maria and Alison could not live without, the eggs and veggie sausages – weren't there. This already felt funny.

After I went to the bathroom, I went downstairs to see where everyone had gone. Had somebody already moved out overnight? The idea made me sick to my stomach, because it sort of made sense, at least for a little while. Alison and Maria weren't like that, but still. They say in a divorce people's personalities change. I hadn't seen this coming. So, like, who really knew what was going to happen next?

Downstairs in the kitchen: no Alison, no Maria. No sausages, no pot of Guatemala Antigua made from fresh-ground beans and smashed through a French press, no scrambled eggs or oranges or grapefruit halves because they have fewer calories or even a fucking bowl of Raisin Bran with vanilla soy milk. Nothing. The birds were tweeting outside. The jacarandas on the other side of the kitchen windows were as opulently purple as usual.

I had this feeling of *Something's really fucked up here* in my gut.

When I went to take a look in Maria and Alison's bedroom, I found out why.

At first I didn't know what I was looking at.

Dmitri sat in a chair by the bed, rocking and kind of talking to himself in sign language. I couldn't tell what he was saying, and anyway, the brownish thing on the bed, what the hell had he gone and dragged in here?

It was like this big lump of clay or something, with sheer gauzy patterned fabric covering parts of it and sort of pressed in between other parts, like the clay had been pushed together to make one solid thing, and the fabric was caught in the middle. One side of it was kind of pink, and the other side was brown, the exact same color as Maria's skin.

It moved. The lump moved. It was like a jellyfish or a sea anemone or something, like one of those creatures you see at the aquarium down in Monterey. It was breathing.

I looked closer and saw one blue eye looking at me.

The eye blinked. A tear slid out of one corner of it.

The lump was *breathing*. Half pink and half brown.

Dmitri smiled up at me.

"Fixed," he signed. "Now they won't break up."

I guess I fainted then, because I don't remember a goddamn thing after that.

There's only a little more to tell, and then I have to stop writing this. I just don't want to think about it any more right now.

Dmitri got stubborn. He refused to unfix Maria and Alison, even though I knew he could do it. I told him I was going to call 911 and the police, and they'd come and bring doctors and scientists, and they'd take the Maria/Alison thing (oh my God, I can't believe I said that, but as horrible as it sounds, it kind of fits) away, and they'd take him somewhere else, and that would be the end of us all. But he's a stubborn little shit, and he refused to do it.

So I called 911, and the police and the ambulance came, and, well, everything I said would happen, did.

The government is interested in how this all happened. We're all being

146

taken to Washington, DC, to the National Institutes of Health. I don't think any of the scientists and doctors are interested in me, because they've already said I have good grades in school, and for national security reasons they've made arrangements for me to attend an excellent university... in Chile. If I talk about this, like to the press or something, they will of course have to deny everything. They'll take steps to make it look like none of this ever happened. Did I understand?

Duh.

So I guess they were going to study Maria and Alison. Maybe convince Dmitri to separate them. Good luck. And they want to study Dmitri. He'd be good to keep around for shit like political assassinations and acts of terrorism. Preserving truth, democracy, and the American way. Whatever. I hope they feed their little deaf lab rat well. He likes Cheetos. Someone should tell them that. Dmitri probably won't mention it.

They'll never let him go.

It's like he said to me when I walked into Maria and Alison's bedroom that morning, Saturday morning a week ago: *Fixed.*

He hit the nail right on the fucking head. That's us, all right.

Fixed.

HARD TO PUT INTO WORDS (OR, THE WHITE GARDEN)

I remembered to shave Father this afternoon. In his prime, he shaved at least once a day, usually after his morning shower. His beard grew in fast – thick and black. If he and Mom had dinner plans or a social engagement, he'd take a second whack at his whiskers to keep himself looking tidy. He was always fastidious about his appearance, even as a lifelong gardener. At his grubbiest, he often looked cleaner than most men in suits. Since his illness began, he has lost that edge. The black has faded to a waxy, yellowish grey. I shave him every other day. It's enough.

Linden, he would tell me. I was five and standing on tiptoe next to him at the sink. The white mentholated mound of shaving foam in his palm filled me with strange longings. I wanted to take off my clothes and coat myself with the stuff from head to toe, then run circles in the backyard, trailing soapy blobs of mouthwash-scented fluff. *Watch closely. In a few years, you'll have to do this too. You hold the razor like this. Take it slow. Nice and easy. These little blades don't look like much but they're sharp. They'll cut you. Imagine a paper cut on your neck or your chin. You wouldn't like that, would you?*

All my life I have wanted to learn how to shave with a straight razor. The only thing stopping me was my skin. Then Dad became ill and I put my life in the freezer to move back to North Carolina and take care of him. He has helped me practice by doing nothing at all. My improved skill with the blade is the only benefit of his paralysis, as far as I know. I'm almost comfortable shaving my own neck these days. His nicks heal sooner or later, as long as I put Neosporin on them.

My sister Violet and my brother Ash call me sometimes. Violet moved to Chicago for college and never came back. She's married now, with two kids. Ash is gay and lives in Seattle with his partner of five years. Both of my siblings turned out more interesting than me. I live – or lived, I guess – in an anonymous townhouse in Front Royal, Virginia. Front Royal is Uranus in the expanding solar system of the Washington DC suburbs. I have a dog grooming business. I transform the poodles and shar peis of Virginia's Blue Ridge bluebloods into prize-winning canine bonsai. Washington ladies and gentlemen bring me their beasts. Some come from as far away as Richmond and Knoxville. I often drive into Georgetown – not at rush hour, though; never at rush hour – to trim exotic diplomatic dogs for exotic foreign ambassadors. For a hefty fee, which I'm worth, I'll even travel to the dog shows up in Philadelphia and Pittsburgh and New York to work on site, just before the competitions begin. I have a way with dogs, I'm told. A calming effect. Meanwhile, Violet and Ash travel the world with their families. They subscribe to obscure literary journals and speak foreign languages. Violet has written a novel, and her agent says he expects it to sell to a big publishing house. Any day now, he tells her. Any day now. And Ash owns a house on Washington's remote Olympic Peninsula with his boyfriend. They invite their well-heeled friends out to the boondocks for extravagant weekends, to eat food I've never heard of, have bitchy conversations full of words I'd have to look up in the dictionary, and probably swap partners for dessert. I am single, I haven't had a date in six months, all the women I meet already have husbands, and to make my living I trim the ass hair of expensive poodles. Sometimes when my siblings call me, I despise them.

When was the last time I bathed Father?

My nursing duties get to be too much, some days. Back here in Greenville, driving down the same streets I used to wish I'd never see again, taking in the way the town has grown and evolved and begun to resemble a city, I find myself thinking, *What am I doing here? How did this become my life?* Sometimes when I am grooming a dog, I think the same thing. One time I went to Long Island for a dog show. The owner lived in a mansion out in the remotest corner of the Hamptons.

"The house was featured in *Architectural Digest* last November. You might have seen it?" was my greeting when I arrived.

Nouveau riche twat, I thought. *Bet you only live here because you married well, or inherited well, or something. Lotto, maybe.*

Halfway through her Airedale, I found myself thinking, *What am I doing here? I'm not even a vet, I'm a doggie barber, and if this fucking mutt farts one more time I'm jamming my clippers up its butt.* I couldn't understand how I had arrived at that exact location and moment along the space-time continuum. A parallel sliver of understanding dogged me: this was also exactly where I was meant to be. I couldn't reconcile the two concepts. Maybe I didn't need to. Maybe my life was only meant to make sense in retrospect.

So, I thought. *Greenville again.*

Time to bathe Father.

Ash used to be a care buddy (I forget the exact term he used) for people with AIDS. He'd stop by with food once or twice a week and spend a few hours. His visits started out more as social events but as the disease progressed, included more intimate tasks like bathing. One of the guys he (there's a polite verb for this but I can't remember it, too many deathsome days here in semi-rural nowhere have dissolved some of my brain cells) was helping had developed an intestinal bug. Toward the end of his life, and without any warning at all, the poor bastard would double up with cramps and spray liquid diarrhea through the fabric of his pants. Ash told me a horror stories: adult diapers, Ivory soap, Clorox, rubber gloves. Thanks to advances in medication, Ash says, fewer people are dying or even becoming quite so sick these days. Just as well, because he washed one dirty butt too many and burned out once and for all.

I'm beginning to understand what that's like. Father has pancreatic cancer. Six months to live, the oncologist told him. Max. Father took the news hard. So hard he hanged himself less than a week later and, to everyone's mixed chagrin and surprise, lived.

Ash is in Seattle. Violet is in Chicago. They have families and lives and commitments. I buzz dogs. It's an earthy job, as Violet pointed out. Not to mention flexible as hell. I earn half my income under the table. Unencumbered by a wife and kids, not even a dog of my own despite what I do for a living, why shouldn't I be the one to care for him? *We support you, Linden*, Violet said earnestly in her last phone call. *We're here for you.* Here. Yes. I'm in Greenville, North Carolina, but somehow Seattle and Chicago are both Here.

I run the bathwater extra hot and pour some Clorox into the basin. Chlorine fumes sting my eyes. I keep a package of latex gloves in the bedroom on father's dresser, next to stacks of clean wash cloths and towels.

Bathing another person seems intuitive but isn't. Daphne, Father's home-care nurse, explained it to me the day before I fired her. It's different from bathing your kid or a lover because there's no joy in caring for a body that isn't dead yet but soon will be. Plus, there are details you cannot overlook. Bedridden people sometimes have accidents. In Father's case, with an inoperable tumor gradually closing off his digestive tract, and a good portion of his brain shut down from lack of oxygen, he can't take solid food. He has a feeding tube, which will soon be replaced by an IV.

Now and then he sort of coughs, which causes leakage. Important to wash his mouth out afterward, and clean the food matter away from his chin and neck, to minimize the corrosive effect of the acids.

"How much do you think he understands?" I'd just arrived. He'd just had the stroke, just hanged himself, still wore a livid necklace of bruises around his neck. "I can't tell."

Daphne shook her head.

"It's hard to say," she said. "He tried to take his own life and almost succeeded. That he survived at all... it's a miracle, really. I guess the Lord wasn't ready to take him, whether he was ready to go or not."

"Mysterious ways," I said.

She showed me how to clean beneath his nails with the narrow wooden sticks manicurists use. He'd stopped gardening weeks ago and was unable to move and thus couldn't scratch his own ass. I was at a loss to understand how he'd dirty his nails, but she was determined to teach me. First, I was to soak his hands in hot water. ("But not too hot," Daphne cautioned me.) Once this hypothetical caked matter beneath his nails softened, I could gently scrape it away. After that, I could wash his hands with a mild antibacterial soap. Finally, lotion.

"No Lysol?" I asked, just to see how she'd react.

"Lord have mercy, no! That stuff's harsh!"

"I was thinking for the stubborn caked-on stuff you were talking about..."

She looked up at me to see if I was kidding. I smiled down at her.

"Just trying to inject a little humor into the situation."

She whacked me with a towel.

"You! Well, it's probably healthier to find ways to laugh," she said. "Laughter is the best medicine, you know. Well... after prayer, that is."

From the look on her face (eyes downcast, head reverently tilted forward, hands clasped) I had no question she meant it. Inviting her to kneel and pray with me might have been more to her liking than cracking jokes about stubborn stains. When she showed me how to wash Father's privates, her face glowed with holy light.

"It's just so important to keep the potty area clean," she said. "For all kinds of reasons which I'm sure I don't need to tell you."

If she had kids, I felt sure they'd grow up to be Bible-banging serial killers, praise Jesus and pass me a serrated knife.

I fired her the next day.

"He was a devout atheist," I explained, as tears welled up in Daphne's eyes.

The garland of bruises around Father's neck has almost faded.

I stare down at him, inert in his tied-on hospital johnny, one of those flimsy blue things that fastens in the back and conceals nothing. I look from the basin of steaming bleach water to the inert form in the bed. I'm over my head and out of my league. He should be in a hospice. Violet and Ash should be here with me. I'd say the same of our mother but she went on to her reward five years ago, an accident.

Father used her ashes as fertilizer.

The garden has never looked better.

The climate of eastern North Carolina is almost subtropical but not quite. If you drive down to Wilmington, near the South Carolina border, you begin to see palmettos. If you drive east from Greenville toward the Outer Banks, you begin to see hibiscus. The temperature drops down to freezing during the winter often enough to stunt but not kill the palm trees and bananas some homeowners foolishly plant, but if you drive around and pay attention to foliage, you do see tropical foliage that doesn't belong here. *You'd think people would stick with crape myrtles and azaleas,* Father used to say in a voice rich with wonder and disgust. *You'd think they'd know better. Does that banana tree look like it's ever going to bear fruit?* As a kid, I just shook my head no and wondered how he could possibly know so much. As an adult, I drove by two days ago and was amazed to see the same banana tree (taller and still anemic) leaning against the same tract house.

Everything has its own climate. If you transplant a tropical flower to a state as cold as North Carolina, even down here by the coast, you're an idiot if you expect it to live out in the open. You need a greenhouse.

Which makes me a hardy perennial, I suppose, and my siblings a pair of rare orchids. Fine for them – everybody loves exotica – but I'm not sure I signed up to be the filial equivalent of a pine tree.

At best, Father has four months to live.

After his bath, his skin's looking ruddier than it has in months.

A thin reek of bleach wafts off him. In high school, I washed dishes at a diner on Greenville Boulevard a couple of nights a week for extra money. My hands always smelled like this – Clorox and detergent. My skin stayed chapped but I had enough money for beer and cigarettes.

I avert my eyes and dry Father off as quickly as possible. Best to get it over with. So important to keep the potty area clean, sure, but I don't have to *look* at it, do I? I don't want to see what old age has in store for me.

This is what my body is going to turn into. I push the thought out of my head. Yes, we're all going to return to the earth sooner or later, but I'm in no rush to take my own dirt nap.

When I cover him up again, my shoulders sag in spontaneous relief. When is this going to end? Sooner or later I'm going to go through his paperwork and his possessions. I'll have to call Ash and Violet to ask what they want. I'll have to call the funeral home and the church and the crematorium. Maybe I won't ask Violet and Ash what they want. They're not helping with the arrangements, are they? They're not washing his poopy ass. Before I deal with the attic and the office, I think I'll take a walk through the garden.

The closer to the house you are, the more orderly the gardens. As you move away from the structure, toward the surrounding woods, the straight lines and careful borders devolve toward a more natural look. Beyond that vague line of demarcation, Mother Nature takes over. Father's garden is draped like a living quilt over the contours of the land. Here are more tomatoes than I could ever eat, enough zucchini for a hundred tasteless casseroles, and a carpet of carrots and radishes. Basil grows among the tomatoes. I recognize rosemary and lavender. Low scrubby stuff appears to be two or three different kinds of thyme. A tangle of cantaloupes looks to be a couple of weeks away from ripeness. Azaleas and lilacs hug the perimeter of the property but I know that even among the trees, Father has made choices about what can grow there and what cannot. In the shade of the pines and the deciduous things I don't know the names of, I find the dogtooth violets and the intriguing green umbrellas of May apples.

The low chorus of crickets almost soothes me.

We're too far back from the highway to hear traffic.

Depinking is what he called his ritual in the white garden, the rough square of flowering plants and shrubs he built for Mom next to the house. When I was a kid, soon after we moved into the house, he screened in the porch that adjoined the kitchen and began the white garden: gardenias, dogwood, iris florentina, white azaleas and tulips and petunias and jonquils and hyacinths, and (closer to the house where it would be warm) jasmine. Roses, various lilies, the sinister-looking moonflowers I was always a little afraid of, even a potted night-blooming cereus for the porch. Whenever the time came for a species to produce buds, he would inspect each plant and cull out anything tinted red or pink. He told me, *Most of these plants weren't white in the wild, and Mother Nature wants them to revert back to the way she designed them. Any garden is always a struggle between man and Mother Nature, Linden. Man wants things to grow a certain way, and Mother Nature wants to do what she damn well pleases.*

He scattered Mother's ashes in the white garden on the one-year anniversary of her death. Within a day of the dispersal, the flowers took on an added luminosity. It was supernatural. They almost glowed in the dark. There's no way to measure something like that empirically, of course. It's something you know in your gut. Mother was in the garden. In a sense, she *was* the garden.

I was always Father's favorite and look where it got me. Ash wasn't masculine enough and Violet was a girl. He drove them both away by ignoring them. They both got into good schools and went on to lead exciting lives. Ash taught English in Taiwan for a few years, met his partner there, travelled all over Southeast Asia and Australia with him before they settled in Seattle. Violet had a short career as a runway model before marrying Bill and going back to grad school. I think both Ash and Violet feel sorry for me. I make more money than they realize, but I didn't turn out *interesting*. I'm not the kind of guy they'd invite to their parties. And Mom – they barely talked to each other. She only stayed because that's what couples of their generation did. I believe she expected his quiet contempt and in some ways even craved it; it served to confirm something for her, although what that was, specifically, she'd never say out loud. She did her thing and he did his. My siblings went on to become *interesting*, my mother went on to become fertilizer, and me? I give pedicures to poodles, I nurse my semi-corpse of a father, and I'm the kind of man who makes strangers think "he'll have funny-looking kids." On some level I must enjoy what I do – I must be getting something out of it – because I keep doing it. It isn't just about the money. But I keep thinking, *Is this all there is? Have I overlooked something? Did I miss a step?*

How satisfying would it be to seed the entire property with salt?

I read somewhere that two hours is the longest you can leave food out and uncovered without spoilage setting in. Meat needs refrigeration sooner than vegetables, according to the same guidelines. Where does that leave Father?

He'll keep, I tell myself, navigating the store with a cart that is either half-full or half-empty, depending on your perspective.

Nothing is more surreal than late-night shopping trips in small towns with limited entertainment options. I could have gone to a movie at the new multiplex, or I could have gone to one of the college-student bars downtown. I think a couple of the bars at the more upscale hotels on Greenville Boulevard cater to an older crowd, but my God, what would I do there? Drink too much and hold up a wall. Initiate a bored and desperate conversation with the bartender by asking "How's it going?" and seeing where it takes me. Pretend to watch whatever game is on the TV above the bar, and laugh at the closed-captioning mistakes. Flirt with women whose good-ole-boyfriends would kick the shit out of me outside, when I walk back to my car. *Now there's a thought to snap you back into the here-and-now.*

Low-sodium Triscuits, or the regular kind? How about those triangular onion-flavored ones? This is as rewarding as my Friday night is going to get. I add a second box to the cart, imagine I'm provisioning the house in advance of a hurricane or a winter storm, and move on to make more unhealthy carbohydrate choices.

Violet's words trail after me like a fart I thought I'd pinched off: *We're here with you.* I look around. I know the drinking age is still 21 but the kids buying booze seem younger and younger to me. Two girls wearing matching Greek sweatshirts giggle and clutch at each other, carrying a case of Budweiser between them. I remember being young enough to think it was cool to party 'til I puked. But I don't see Violet anywhere. I see another few college students out to get drunk and a couple of gayish guys about my age in the wine section comparing two bottles of red. Violet isn't here. If she were, she'd look around with her facial expression carefully whited out to mask the disdain. She shops in the sort of markets with hardwood floors and Vivaldi tinkling over the sound system. She'd survey the produce and sniff, "But it isn't organic!"

Sure, Violet. You're here with me. Wanna toss a second box of adult Depends into the cart? Careful not to squash my non-organic grapes.

By the time I check out, I'm in a foul mood. Look what I have to look forward to.

"Hang on just a sec, I forgot something."

The bored cashier blinks like a lizard on a rock. His eyes are bloodshot and I'm tempted to ask him where I can buy a bag. Pot would make this business with Father so much more tolerable. I wonder whether there are any painkillers in the house. Never thought about it until now. Seniors often have surprisingly good drugs, and when they kick off, well, it's a shame to put good pharmaceuticals to waste, isn't it?

"Sure, man. Take your time."

I don't know whether he's being ironic and don't care. There's no one in line behind me. Up-tempo Muzak wafts down from speakers I can't see. I dash back to the wine section. The two guys, both of whom look too coiffed for eastern North Carolina, are still there. I eavesdrop as I approach them:

"Marcus hates Pinot Noir. He says it's too light."

"We're watching Hitchcock movies and drinking, Alex. Who gives a fuck? Buy some wine in a box. Buy the cheapest shit they have. We're just going to piss it out in an hour, anyway."

"Did anybody ever tell you that you have a filthy mouth?"

"Yes, it has been pointed out before, usually after I've rimmed them."

OK, that part I didn't need to hear.

"Excuse me, I'm in a hurry and I don't know shit about wine and you look like you do and the cashier's already ringing me up…" I begin.

The guy on the left hands me the bottle he's holding. Alex. More pretty than handsome, blond hair, no highlights, looks natural. You can't do dog shows without being surrounded by gay men. His hair is gelled. His belt and his shoes match. His friend, a coppery redhead whose name I didn't overhear, looks me up and down as if I've puzzled him. What species must I be, to rush up to them like this and ask for a wine recommendation? I wonder why they are here. Whether they live here, and if so, why.

"Here, drink this Pinot Noir," Alex tells me. "It's from California's Central Coast. Not as good as Oregon's Willamette Valley or even the Okanogan, but it's one of the better ones in this store. I'm not going to get to drink it, so somebody might as well."

I don't have a clue what or where the Okanogan is, nor what advantage Oregon has over California, but this isn't a good time to ask. Alex might answer me and I don't have time for that. I'm going to take his word for it. He exhales in deep contempt and says to his friend, "Lead me to the cheap Cabernet." From the woebegone look on his face, you'd think he was on his way to the gas chamber.

"Thanks!" I call after them.

I hurry back to the cashier.

There's no change to Father's condition when I get home. After I put away the groceries and uncork the Pinot Noir, I spend five minutes in his room checking his vital signs and simply watching him. His eyes don't track when I pry the lids open and pass my index finger across his field of vision. When I squeeze his hands, they don't squeeze back. Not even a flicker of expression crosses his face. To see if he'll respond to sound, I fetch a metal cookie sheet and a heavy ladle from the kitchen. Not even a flutter of the eyelids when I bash the utensil against the cookie sheet. Nothing. I want to believe there's just a staticky organic hum going on between his ears, like the sound a TV makes after a local station signs off for the night. Back in the days before cable, that is. On the other hand there's a dim chance he's awake in there and aware of what's going on around him even though he can't respond. Now *that* would be a fate worse than death, wouldn't it? Knowing you're dying slowly but paralyzed and powerless to get it over with?

Maybe I had hoped he'd die while I was out, and simplify everything. I spend no more time than necessary in his room. Yes, I could stay and talk to him. Tell him how the garden looks. If he hears it's getting shaggy, he might snap out of it. He might come back to life just long enough to spend a couple of days frantically pruning and weeding, at which point he'd collapse, his work done. But I don't know what I'm hoping for. I want it to be over. He's suffering, which on some level even he must know he deserves, and by extension, so are the rest of us. Me, because I'm on the front lines. Somebody had to do it and nobody else stepped up to the plate. Violet and Ash suffer too, in their theoretical way. I'm sure they're processing their grief with their therapists for $120.00 per hour.

The house is overflowing with a shared lifetime's worth of crap: furniture two decades past its prime, a kitchen with every gizmo that ever caught my mother's eye, VHS tapes that haven't been watched in five years, closets that might not have been opened all summer. Father got rid of Mom's clothes when she passed on but he kept her old Mercedes sedan. I'm of half a mind to keep it too. Next to it in the garage is parked his pickup, a Ford of unknown vintage and unlimited appetite for gas. Guess I'll sell that.

I don't know how to do this. I don't know how to box up everything in an entire house. Father's oncologist told me the cancer would spread fast but nobody anticipated he'd hang himself. I still have time – I don't have to empty the house and sell it by next week – but *I can't do this.*

Not without alcohol, anyway.

And in the medicine cabinet, *voila*! Painkillers only a couple of months past their expiration date. I wash one down with a swallow of wine. After a moment's hesitation, I take a second. Happy trails.

I've read all the books and magazines that look interesting and watched all the movies I can sit through. My eye sockets feel like they've been lined with bird gravel. It's a Friday night and I can't go into town because there's nothing there, and there's nothing on TV. The idea of sorting through all the crap in this house makes me want to beat my head against the wall until my skull cracks and my brain fluid leaks out.

If the garden was Father's well-tended province, then the office was Mother's. The orderliness of her files and shelves had once mimicked the precision of his raised beds and rows of vegetables but in the five years since her death, Father had allowed weeds of receipts and bills and magazines to flourish unchecked.

The wine and the pills are dancing the tango in my head. The right angles between the walls and the floor seem more acute. When I blink, they're back to 90 degrees, but when I stare at the overflowing desk again, the geometry stretches again. It inhales and exhales. Houses are not supposed to pulsate. Not this one, anyway. The pharmaceuticals are making me feel tentative and detached, as if my soul is suspended from the inside of my brain by a Slinky instead of its usual sturdier shock absorbers.

I sit in Mother's high-backed wooden chair (she's been dead for years but it's still her chair) and let my head roll back.

Where's the will? That's what I want to know. I was always Father's favorite, even though I blame him for sucking the marrow out of my life. *Violet's going to turn her nose up at us one day,* he said once. I was twelve or thirteen. We were weeding the vegetable garden. The midsummer sun blazed down and the dense humidity was strangling me and I'd taken off my shirt because he said I needed to toughen up. He couldn't do anything with Ash, who wouldn't put down his books to come outside unless Father threatened to beat him, but he was determined I'd grow up to be his idea of a man. *Violet's too good for us. You watch. None of the colleges she's applying for are within a hundred miles of here.* When I complained about getting a sunburn, he struck me with the handle of his hoe. *You're the only one who's going to grow up and be worth a damn, Linden. Straighten up and fly right. It's just a little sun. You're tough; you're a man. Do the tomatoes next, and when you finish, you can go inside and call it a day.*

I got out of the house for 10 years and here I am, back again. Same walls stencilled with the patterns of bad history, same floors stamped with memories I'd just as soon forget. I'm sitting in my mother's chair, rummaging through the filing cabinets, wishing I didn't have to hear him say *I come down hard on you because you've got potential, Linden. You need discipline if you're going to amount to anything. Can you understand that?* over and over in my head. I got out of the house for a trip to the grocery store and here I am, back again, and Father's still a lump of breathing meat.

What does the will say? Mom was the morbid one, always full of instructions for us to carry out when she finally died. He never had much to say on the subject of his demise – *Just turn me off and burn me up* – but I know he remembered to update the will. It's not the kind of thing he'd forget. I assume he left me everything because of his contempt for Violet and Ash. The ones who would never amount to much. Contempt that profound is hard to put into words; it's best expressed through omission. It's all in what you don't say. Whom you don't mention. By the time Violet and Ash graduated from high school and went on to college, he barely spoke to them. He excused himself with, *I'm a man of few words*, and eventually the subject stopped coming up. Except in my siblings' therapy sessions, I guess. When they process their angst about how they saw me get beaten over and over again, but escaped from harm, themselves. Survivors' guilt. He didn't have much to say to them in life and in death, there's no reason why his disregard should be any different. With Mom gone, I'll inherit everything. With ridiculous restrictions on when I can have access to funds from the estate. For my own good, no doubt. Because I never did live up to his expectations. No law school, no executive job in Corporate America for him to brag about, no stunning wife and Gap Kids offspring. Just poodles and Airedales.

I can't find the will and all the words on these goddamn manila folders are blurring together, just like my thoughts, and I can't stay awake. For about two seconds I think *maybe I should brew some coffee* but fuck it, it's almost eleven, I should sleep...

Hangover will never be a popular flavor of toothpaste or gum. I wake up with a splitting headache and a mouth that tastes like hot sick ass. Someone lined my mouth with month-old cedar shavings from the bottom of a hamster cage in the night. While I'm brushing my teeth, I'm watching a mental movie: me, pulling out Father's feeding tube and dragging him out to lie in the sun. With his shirt off, because he's a man. I'll put him in the white garden with Mother. How long he'll live without nourishment, I don't know. In his condition, not too long, I don't think. A day or so. He can't swallow fluids, either, so water's out of the question, unless I turn the garden hose on him.

That's what this has all been building up to, isn't it?

The will doesn't matter. I already know what it says. I could even tear it up, and nothing would change.

I know all this. It is all clear to me, even through the smog and murk of an anesthetized mind. Won't I feel guilt? Where's my conscience? What separates me from those poodles whose butts I shave for a living? Depending on how you look at it, apparently not too much. Bow wow and pass me a Milk Bone. In the kitchen, I make myself a pot of coffee and look out over the gardens. On TV, the local weatherman drawls about another hot Carolina summer day. Temperatures in the high nineties, humidity that closes its fist around you like the ghost of King Kong.

If it sounds cruel, look at it this way: this isn't about revenge, I'm just planting a vegetable out in the garden where it belongs.

HURRICANE SEASON

Tony and I have a ritual. Each year, around the first of August, we open Hurricane Season with a pitcher of vodka martinis and a take-out Chinese feast. The exact date varies from year to year, because we have to wait until the government weather people (the ones I used to work for) announce that the first tropical storm has formed. In early years, we cooked the food ourselves, but the tedious nature of peeling dozens of shrimp and scaling all those fish has convinced us to start ordering in.

Once we're stuffed and drunk enough, I trudge upstairs to fetch the Ouija board. While I dig through the junk in the attic, Tony lights dozens of white candles. Sweet incense fumes permeate the house: wisteria and jasmine, geranium oil and sandalwood… lots of fragrant things, basically. Our own blend. Some people require their own coffees; for us, it's incense. We put soothing New Age CDs on the stereo to heighten the spiritual effect. While I retrieve the Ouija board, Tony also clears the kitchen table and unfolds a huge National Geographic map of the Caribbean, Central America, and southeastern United States. Eventually I return with the board in hand. We sit across from each other, say a prayer to whatever gods and deities might be listening, and rest our fingertips on the edges of the plastic planchette.

"Another year, Mr. Hagedorn," he says, as our final Hurricane Season commences.

"Another year, Mr. Xu," I reply.

We position the planchette over the letter A.

That is our ritual.

And now we're up to F, the worst letter in the alphabet.

Here in New Orleans, we are at Ground Zero for hurricanes. The risk that a storm might angle itself just right and churn its way through the Gulf of Mexico toward us has been keeping me up at night from August until the weather turns cold and the risk of watery, windy annihilation tapers off. No matter where you live, there is always some kind of risk. We've chosen to live in places we like. Most of Tony's relatives live in Taipei and Houston; he has a brother in San Francisco. My sister, the only surviving member of my biological family, lives in Savannah.

Mama probably isn't feeling benevolent this year, I reasoned, because she wasn't benevolent last year, nor the year before that. In fact, the longer she's dead, the worse she gets. I hope my own experience with the Hereafter will do more for my character.

Maybe this year I'll find out for myself.

But I told myself that every year, and had telling myself that since the age of eight.

"Louis, it's *your fault!*" Mama screamed at me. "You better straighten up, or I'm gonna drown you while your sisters watch, and both of them if they get in my way!"

Mama lined the three of us kids up in the bathroom. Strips of faded blue wallpaper hung from the walls, and two bugs scuttled across the floor at our feet. I dared not look at them for more than a second.

Some boys at school had beaten me up again. This time it was on account of my ineptitude at softball. In PE, I struck out at the end of the last inning lost the game for my team, and came home limping from where Thomas and Joey had sat on my chest while Julian and Greg had kicked my legs.

Naked, shivering, and crying, the three of us screamed and cried as she ranted and raved. Mama had already beaten Anna's backside black and blue, just for timidly saying she liked me like I was. Mama hadn't taken her medicine in a few days, and that night she was like some kind of unstoppable monster, some force of nature bent on destruction. Natalie's turn came next.

Mama slapped Natalie across her screaming mouth, leaving streaks across her cheeks. Natalie quieted down right away and withdrew into herself like she always did, whimpering quietly.

The tub had filled almost to overflowing. Mama never turned on the cold water, and I knew, even if the others didn't, that if she didn't succeed in drowning us like she threatened, she'd scald us to death. Nobody could stop her.

At ten, I was the oldest. Old enough to know this wasn't what happened in other kids' homes. Old enough to see that we were in a trap and weren't going to get out without losing blood first. We couldn't go anywhere, and none of my attempts to be *not different* had worked. I couldn't do anything, and there was nowhere for us to go. I wished at least one of our fathers was around to do something about this... but there was no chance of that happening. Anna's and my father died when we were still babies, and Natalie's father was in jail. Even if one or both were still around, who could say they wouldn't be as bad as Mama when I dropped the ball or talked funny or read too many books?

This time it was the back of Mama's hand that connected with Natalie's cheek, Mama's heavy knuckles bruising pale white little girl skin, the sound of the slap punctuated by screams that we could feel as well as hear, they were so loud. I wondered how long before the neighbors would call the police and tell them someone was getting cut to pieces over here. But of course no police would ever come.

167

Mama wiped a ribbon of saliva away from her mouth and stared blankly at the back of her hand. In her anger, Mama's face became smooth and taut. I imagined faces on corpses looked like this when rigor mortis set in. But her eyes. Sparks burned behind them. She raised her hand again, brandishing it at the three of us.

"That's it! I'm gonna drown every damn one of you, bury you in the back yard, and tell the social workers you ran away!"

Water sloshed over the sides of the tub. Some slopped across Anna's foot, and I saw her bite her lip and edge away from the steaming puddle.

I was afraid to focus on it, because I didn't want to give Mama any ideas. Not knowing where else to look, I stared into the glare of the lightbulb over the medicine cabinet. Electric purple-yellow ghosts swam behind my field of vision after that, and I felt a dark joy that I couldn't see Mama's face when I looked at her again. I'd seen enough. If she thrust one of us into that water, we'd die, for sure. Either she'd scald us, and our skin would come off like a cooked chicken's, or we'd drown. Or both.

Mama seized Natalie by the wrist.

"So what's it gonna be, sissyboy?" Mama hissed in my face. Her breath smelled like a sewer. I could picture slimy clots of fungus growing on her insides. "You gonna behave yourself?"

No words would come. I was paralyzed – couldn't even nod. With the effort I put into forcing some kind of assent out of myself, I started to gag, and had to swallow a stinging tendril of puke.

Mama thrust Natalie's arm into the scalding water.

Natalie's scream pushed my eardrums inward like a jet taking off, and the stench of her bowels letting go seemed to knock Mama out of whatever spell she was in. The fury left her eyes. Mama remembered herself. The rage gave way to surprise, shock... even sympathy. For a second I felt guilty for hating Mama and wishing she would die on the spot. Then I smelled what Mama had done, and the guilt evaporated. Shit cascaded down Natalie's leg as she writhed against Mama's leg, shrieking in agony.

"Oh honey, oh baby, let's get you cleaned up and take you to the doctor..." Mama cooed. Her abrupt switch from Psycho to Angel of Mercy left me dizzy and nauseated.

I wish nights like these had been the exception and not the rule.

Twelve years ago, Mama – Frances Smith Hagedorn – finally got her way. Natalie was living in Puerto Rico with her husband and kids, and Hurricane Florence cut a swath through the community where they kept a weekend house. Imagine a dense, overgrown lawn with one stripe mown across it, almost down to bare earth. That's what Puerto Rico looked like, with landfall right at the spot where Natalie and Esteban's house had been. I'll go to my own grave wondering what made my sister think she could survive the storm. Natalie, Esteban, and their three children drowned in the tidal surge. The bodies of two of the kids were never recovered, and what was left of baby Gloria the rescue workers found high in a tree, entangled among branches that had been stripped clean in the howling winds. I'd have killed Mama for that, but she was already dead.

Four years later, the sixth hurricane of the season bore down on Savannah, where Anna had settled. Mama underestimated the residents of that city. Stoically boarding up windows and dry-docking boats, they faced the storm with admirable fortitude. As one prune-faced dowager told the Weather Channel, "We outwitted General Sherman and got through the Civil War intact. We'll get through Hurricane Frances just fine." Anna drove to Atlanta to wait out the storm, and at the last minute Frances veered north and obliterated the southern suburbs of Charleston.

I called Anna afterward.

"There's a pattern here," I told her. "First Natalie and her family.

169

You know how she hated Esteban. Now, four years later, the next time a woman's name is assigned to Hurricane F, it hits Savannah."

"Louis, you are so full of shit," Anna said.

"So I'll go take some Metamucil. Then I'll call you back and tell you the same thing. There's a pattern."

"You're nuts if you believe Mama's trying to kill us by steering hurricanes toward the cities where we live," Anna scoffed.

I could hear her take a sip of something.

"So why are you drinking?" I asked her. "Let me guess: you've been pounding Merlot all afternoon."

"It's actually a very nice Cabernet Sauvignon," she said, gulping. "From Argentina."

Past that point, I couldn't say much. I told her I loved her, admonished her to be careful, and did my best to get on with my life.

Tony and I had been together about a year by that time. I feel a little squeamish confessing that we met via the Internet. Every week or so, when our mutual friend Corey found an editorial piece by one of his favorite writers, he'd e-mail a copy of it to a number of his more literary friends and acquaintances. I began to wonder who the other addresses in the "Send To" field belonged to, so I introduced myself with a generic reply-to-all message. Several of us began to correspond. Tony and I fascinated each other from afar for about six months; at the time, he lived in Chicago, but when he flew out to visit Corey, we all met for drinks at a tastefully hip little bistro in DC, where I lived at the time.

Corey sat back, gulped one Bass Ale after another, and tried not to get his eyebrows singed from all the sparks flying back and forth between Tony and me.

Tony put in for a transfer to the Washington office of the law firm where he worked, and was there within three months. Less than a year later – about the time Hurricane Frances was trying to drown Charleston – we'd decided to abandon the nation's overcrowded capital for New Orleans. We wanted neighbors with something other than the government and politics to talk about.

That year, Hurricane Season had started off quietly. Storms A through E had sputtered out over the Atlantic, except for Dawn, which had flooded Haiti. One Friday night, after Tony and I had been out drinking in the Quarter, a vision of Farrah Fawcett's face – superimposed over the fat and evil vortex the local news channel showed churning toward the Georgia coast – appeared before me. Her blonde hair blew straight back from her angry but perfectly made-up face and blended with the cyclonic winds emanating from a point between her nose and blood-red lipsticked mouth. Hurricane F. The face of evil.

"Oh my God, I've had too much tequila," I groaned.

This cracked him up.

The *Charlie's Angels* rerun blinked once, then vanished. For half a second, the screen of our television was dark; then a shot of the local newsroom appeared. Dramatic music throbbed. So did my stomach. I told myself lies and tried to believe them: *It's the just tequila; it's just the tequila; there's no crazy supernatural shit going on.*

"We interrupt this broadcast to bring you an update on Hurricane Frances," intoned the male talking head. 'The storm that caused such devastation in the Bahamas is now in the Atlantic and heading for Savannah. Let's go to our Storm Team weatherman, Marvin Gardner, for the full story on Hurricane Frances, the first storm of the season to threaten the US Gulf Coast."

"Fuck," I spluttered, leaning against Tony.

"Right now?" he asked.

"I don't think I could, but that's not the point. It's my mother. She..." Without a clue what to say next, I tried to swallow and found that my mouth had gone dry. "She has this thing about hurricanes."

Subtle emotions glimmered on Tony's face: puzzlement, concern, humor as dark as my own. "Is there something I've missed? Isn't she dead?"

"Oh. That. Yeah, I was meaning to tell you..." I couldn't continue for a second. My blood felt as sour as my mouth tasted, and my head reeled. "Yes, she's dead." Too late not to plunge ahead. "She died in a hurricane when we were kids, at her home in North Carolina."

"Your home, too, right?"

"No, that would be here. New Orleans. I may have grown up there, but I always hated North Carolina, and I don't consider it home."

Tony shook his head. "The more you're saying, the less I understand."

I mused over the whole bizarre mess for a moment.

"Do you believe in ghosts?" I asked.

Tony sipped his drink and peered over the rim of the glass at me.

"My parents are from a rural part of Taiwan," he said. "They live and breathe all that old-fashioned Chinese superstition... dragons, demons, ghosts, you name it. Of course I believe." After a second, he added, "At least a little," then crunched the last ice cube in his glass, looking at me with an expression that made me think there was a lot more he could say.

"I never used to," I said, "but I've had to rethink my position."

This time, everything will be different, I told myself this morning when I woke up and saw the sky already darkening to an ominous shade of steel. I spent most of the day telling myself that. I haven't convinced myself yet.

I always dread the ritual. I always know how it will turn out.

Ten days ago, when the tropical depression was upgraded to a storm and named Felicia, we went through it one more time. We already knew it would hit New Orleans.

"Louis, you realize you have to do something about this sooner or later," Tony said, covering his mouth to stifle a burp. We had both had too much to eat.

I could not bring myself to touch the planchette for a few minutes. Over time, I've come to despise the thing, but I have an evil symbiosis with it.

"Tony, what am I supposed to do? We can't keep running forever. We might as well stay where our lives are. What else can I do?"

That's the crux of it. The National Weather Service has been boasting for the last few years that its hurricane tracking systems have improved, and they're right: I work for them as a consultant. I also contract with several major insurance companies. Casualties are down. Profits are up. Tony and I live comfortably, except during the time of year when my mother uses supernatural means in an attempt to murder us. Everybody wins. Sort of.

"Maybe an exorcism?"

"On a hurricane? Oh yeah, I can see it now. I pilot a plane into the eye of the storm, launch bottles of holy water out of the cockpit with a slingshot, and shout *The power of Christ compels you!* through a bullhorn."

Like a five-year-old, I knuckled my eyes. I felt drained already.

Tony tapped a finger against the edge of the planchette.

"Felicia's already out there," he said. "Don't you think we ought to go ahead with this? Maybe she changed course."

"I doubt it. I need another martini."

"I'll fix it, then. Try to concentrate. We have work to do."

When he returned with my cocktail, we proceeded. The CD ended, and with a whir the system selected another disc. Ottmar Leibert played in the background, and Tony and I attempted to work our black magic.

"Natalie." I always invoked my sister's name quietly. "Natalie, are you there?"

The planchette twitched.

"Natalie, can you hear me?"

Another twitch.

"Natalie?"

The planchette slid over to YES. Our fingers followed its progress.

"Have you missed us?"

NO. One letter at a time: GO TO HELL.

"At least you haven't lost your sense of humor." I took a deep breath. No choice but to get on with it. "Felicia is out there. Can you see where she's going?

OF COURSE.

"Care to tell us?"

WHAT'S IN IT FOR ME?

"You always were the baby of the family, weren't you?"

I'M TIRED OF THIS.

"And we aren't?" I ask her. "Christ, Natalie. It's F. You know what that means. F. As in, Felicia. As in, Fucked. Do you really think this is the time to be dicking around with our lives, just because you're dead?"

NO.

"What, is the afterlife so much fun you think we should just hang it all up and join you? And let our psycho-killer bitch of a mother *win*?"

NO.

"Should we all just move to Denver, then? Or Phoenix? Someplace where nothing ever happens, and there's no water for thousands of miles?"

NO.

"How about... Winnipeg? Can you really see me living in Winnipeg?"

NO.

"Omaha, then. Or... I know! Peoria! Dubuque! BOZEMAN,

MONTANA!" I knew if I lost it now, I wouldn't be able to stop laughing. Not without Thorazine and restraints.

"Louis, I believe you've had a bit much to drink," Tony observed.

"Not enough, if anything."

The planchette remains above NO.

Calmer, I continue: "Where is Hurricane Felicia going to strike?"

Nothing.

"Natalie?"

Still nothing.

"It is still going to be upgraded to hurricane status, isn't it?"

YES.

"Do you know where the tropical storm will make landfall?"

YES.

"Where?"

The planchette didn't move.

"Want to use the map?" I asked Natalie.

YES.

Tony and I moved the Ouija board to one side. We each took advantage of the break in action to drain our glasses dry. Under the table, he moved his foot until it touched mine.

"Ready?" I asked her when I placed the planchette upon the spot where I thought the tropical storm in question ought to be.

The planchette twitched the second our fingers touched it, then proceeded in the general direction of New Orleans and Mobile slowly, inexorably. The storm would stall a couple of times over the warm waters of the gulf, gaining strength, before finally coming to a deadly stop… right here.

"Oh Christ." Tony got the words out before I could.

The sight of the slowly spinning planchette with New Orleans centered under its clear circular window nauseated us both. The smell of the incense Tony had lit made me think we were in a funeral home. I wanted to run outside – and keep running.

"Natalie, how bad is it going to be?" I asked, returning the planchette to the board, with trembling hands.

BAD.

"Should we leave now?"

No response.

"Natalie?"

Still no response.

"Louis, I think she's gone."

"Anna said the same thing to me once," I said. "Only she was talking about Mama. Natalie's not gone. Neither of them are. That's why this has to end."

Years ago, Anna and I told the social workers Mama had gone into one of her rages and rushed out into howling wind and rain of a whopping hurricane, at the very height of the storm. That wasn't even a lie. We didn't mention the three tabs of LSD Anna dropped into her Diet Pepsi that afternoon; nor did we mention that when Mama went raging out into the maelstrom, screaming almost as loud as the wind, I locked the door after her. For the first time I could remember, I saw hope in Anna's eyes that night.

Mama's body washed ashore three days later, several miles north of us on the beach next adjacent to Fort Macon.

The coroner wouldn't let me see her remains.

"I know who she is," he said. "If I let you see, you kids would be haunted by the sight of her for the rest of your lives. I'd rather spare you that."

Funny how things work out sometimes, isn't it?

"You can evacuate if you need to go," I told Tony. "I'm staying."

It stands to reason that Mama would come back for me after all this time. I killed her, and I suppose that means I started this.

By the time I turned fourteen the lashings had reached their miserable nadir and begun to taper off. We were too big for her to hit, and I had failed to exhibit symptoms of heterosexuality, despite Mama's best attempts. By then, we started to hit back. Mama lost her job, got on welfare, saw a new doctor, got different pills, and took them intermittently. Some days she drank. In the morning, she'd wake up, put on airs, and fix herself mimosas for breakfast. She'd watch the morning news with a pot of coffee, half a grapefruit, and two or three mimosas. She'd smoke one menthol cigarette after another, coughing her rattly dry cough, and bark at us until we fled the house to go to school.

By lunchtime her pretensions deflated; she switched to lite beer. The cans littered the floor every day when we got home from school.

"Less calories," she hissed several times. She had long since given up on dentures, and the gap in her upper teeth yawned like the Grand Canyon.

All afternoon she followed her "stories," with decreasing coherence. *Guiding Light* was her favorite, although *All My Children* ran a close second. She dismissed *The Bold and the Beautiful* as a Johnny-come-lately and wouldn't have given the actors the time of day if she'd passed them on the street, especially that "big fat harpy" who played the lead.

"Upstart crap," Mama slurred, a long cylinder of ash falling from her cigarette to leave a grey splotch across her distended belly.

If she was drinking that day, then later in the afternoon, around the same time the talk shows started – just Phil Donohue and Geraldo, then – she'd switch beverages.

Donohue interviewed several mustachioed men in dresses one day.

"Fuckin' pansies," Mama lisped. "Louis, don't you ever turn out like that. Livin with another man, wearin a dress, whatever. I'll wring your fuckin' neck if I have to come back from the dead to do it."

Anna and I stood there looking at her. Sometimes there just weren't any words. Even at fourteen, I had figured that out.

"What are you lookin at? Make yourself useful. Bring me a drink. No, wait, I gotta pee. Leave it on the coffee table. Go do your homework or something."

Anna and I looked at each other. We had learned to keep our faces blank at moments like this.

A swampy miasma followed Mama as she waddled to the stinking little bathroom. Almost telepathically, Anna and I looked away from her, to avoid seeing any stains or smudges on Mama's behind. She swore she didn't wear adult diapers but we had seen the boxes. And the sounds. I'd have happily rammed pencils through my eardrums had there been one in each hand, just then. Sudden painful permanent deafness was a much more attractive option than hearing Mama battle to get her poly-stretch pants down before her bladder and bowels began to empty... noisily.

"Well, she hasn't hit Natalie lately," Anna said under her breath.

Also *sotto voce*, I asked, "She's in after-school detention today, right?"

Anna nodded. "God, don't let her find out."

"She won't hear it from me."

A series of vile liquid gushes emanated from behind the bathroom door. Anna and I drifted out of earshot. Our house, a once-attractive bungalow in Salter Path, about halfway down the Outer Banks, hadn't caved in on itself because its original builders had done a good job. In our lifetime I couldn't remember Mama ever cleaning, much less having work done. Sounds traveled with sickening clarity at certain times of the day. Not to put too fine a point on it, I don't think our mother's digestive system had worked in years.

"I'd like not to hear anything from her."

Anna and I looked at each other.

"Enough to do something about it?"

Her mouth twitched as a smile tried to form there and was instantly banished. I knew my sister. Her eyes lit up with a dangerous, forbidden hope.

"Natalie's always going to have little scars on her face," Anna whispered. With a finger, she traced a line down her cheek in the same spot Mama had gashed Natalie with the broken neck of a liquor bottle three years before.

The toilet flushed. Anna and I retreated to a safe distance.

"We'll think of something," Anna said.

I looked out the window at the peculiarly blue sky and the spiral bands of clouds scudding into view. Hurricane Faith, heading our way, already packing hundred-mile-an-hour winds. The local newscasts had featured nothing else for the last few days, or so it seemed, and each new broadcast made the situation look more and more grim.

"You know, I think I already have."

In retrospect, if I had known this would have been only a temporary fix, I wonder if I would have done something different. Poison, maybe? Or waiting until she was passed-out drunk, and burning down the house with her still inside?

A dense fog of déjà vu surrounds me and, by extension, Tony: devastation roaring toward us, a sense of inevitability.

Natalie has already put in her opinion and disappeared, perhaps for good.

Tony and I decide we've had enough running from Mama and her stupid rages. Unfortunately, with a hurricane, you only have two options:

stay or flee. And this time we want to stand our ground.

The New Orleans Police, FEMA, and the National Hurricane Center in Miami have all issued warnings, each more dire than the last: leave now before the highways become totally gridlocked; head for high ground; take shelter at the highest point you can find; put your head between your legs and kiss your ass goodbye. This morning, FEMA disaster people and police officers started going door to door encouraging residents to evacuate the city. All the news channels have been showing live coverage of jammed highways and airports most of the day.

I tried to get Tony to leave but he refused.

"Not without you," he said, and that was the end of that.

When the FEMA volunteer nervously taps on our front door, we answer it, invite her in, offer her coffee, and let her use the bathroom. She's had a rough day, so we don't make it worse by telling her that this house is Ground Zero. She gives us an Emergency Measures kit and advises us that there's still time to make it out of the city.

"The storm surge is the deadliest part," she says earnestly.

I'd guess she is in her early thirties, a little younger than us.

"It'll be bad. This is a Category 5 hurricane, and this whole area will be underwater if the eye passes over. It's already raining, and things are only going to get worse from here."

"How deep?" Tony asks.

She eyes us both, and her look softens, passing from professional to personal: she is here doing this crazy sane beautiful thing – warning us – because she cares.

"If you insist on staying, go up into the attic. If you can find higher ground before this bitch hits, do it. But I have to say, there's still enough time to head north or west; you won't have to go too far to get out of the flood zone."

180

"We're not going anywhere," Tony says.

She looks askance at us both. Can she possibly be used to this by now?

"Sounds like you guys have made up your minds. I wish you luck. If you change your mind, they're turning the Superdome into a shelter." She looks at the both of us, probably wondering if she would be the last to see us alive. "May God be with you."

"And Natalie," I add under my breath, as we closed the door.

Tony kisses me hard after he locks the door behind the FEMA woman. "I love you," he says. "And we're going to get through this."

From the time Natalie gave us the warning that Hurricane Felicia would strike New Orleans, we have already done all the things the pamphlet advises: stockpiled food, water, and medicine; prepared kits with flashlights, battery-powered radios, and insect repellent. All these things we have sealed in waterproof containers and stowed in various high places in the house. Tony and I have life preservers and inflatable rafts with radio beacons and strobe lights, for the direst contingencies. We also have enough firearms to equip the police force for a small town, all stowed in watertight bins. Just in case. We've always believed in prior planning.

Let Mama do her worst. In a way, she already has, years ago, and everything since has been an attempt at playing catch-up. Hurricane Felicia will come, and with it Mama will bear down on this solid old house Tony and I love and call home, with all the fury she can muster. The floodwaters will rise and the winds will scream in gusts up to 200 miles per hour. Let them. We're ready. We have boarded up our windows and moved as much to the top floor as possible.

The thing that makes hurricanes lethal is the waiting. Even if you're in the safest place you can find, the excitement and danger wear on your nerves. You want to push the envelope, take chances. Tony and I find our tempers fraying within an hour of the FEMA woman's departure.

"Want coffee?" he asks.

I nod.

"You know," I tell him, "It's still not too late to get out of here."

"Right," he replies. "I'll just take the helicopter. I refueled it when you weren't looking. I'm so glad we had the landing pad built on top of the house. It didn't do much for our property value but I always knew it would come in handy." The expression on his face says, *You are such an asshole.*

Driven by a gust of wind, rain lashes the windows behind us. Tony and I both jump.

"You're going to get yourself killed," I insist. "You don't have to stay here."

"When are you going to get it through your goddamn thick skull that I love you and this is my house too, and that makes it my fight? What is this, some kind of white guy thing, you know, protect the delicate fragile Chinese guy who can't take care of himself?"

I wince. "You really think I deserved that?"

He admits to being scared to death.

Another sheet of rain slaps the shuttered window behind us, and another.

"I'll make the coffee," he says. "It'll give me something to do."

I follow him into the kitchen.

"The wind's picking up."

He nods. "Sounds like an animal outside howling."

A sharp gust blows open the shutters to the window nearest us.

"Shit!" We shout the word at the same time, both jumping away from the window as the rain lashed it like so much buckshot.

"I nailed that one shut," Tony said. "I did a thorough job. Think what the wind speed must have been, to do that?"

"Must have been coming from just the right angle. I'll go out and nail it shut again."

More howling from outside, a loud, eerie racket that throbs over and under the pellet-sound of the rain. Outside, all we can see was a solid wall of greenish-grey gloom. Rain pours from the sky, silvering the air.

"I have a better idea. You'll never be able to see in that, and the wind's already too strong. Nail some boards over the window inside, and we'll just replace the glass later."

"Assuming the house is still standing," I remark in dry tones.

"There is that," Tony says. "But then, if the house doesn't survive the storm, we probably won't, either. Think the garage will last long?"

I shake my head. "Not really."

"It'll give us an excuse to buy new cars."

Out of the corner of my eye I see something outside, a charcoal smudge in all that silver-green…

Green light. Grey-green light. Memories from growing up in eastern North Carolina flashed through my mind: death, destruction, flattened homes, trailers torn in half like so much paper and aluminum foil, trees snapped like toothpicks.

A rumble, dimly perceptible over the howling shrieking wind and torrents of rain.

"Oh fuck, Tony, that's a tornado!"

Tony freezes.

I bark, "Bathroom!" With no basement, that's the best we can do. I grab his arm and drag him to the downstairs bathroom, the one off the guest bedroom.

Whatever is out there rumbles toward us like an oncoming subway train. As Tony and I run for the bathroom, the rumble grows to a roar that drowns out all other sounds. The wind, the rain – these things are impossible to hear. Even our feet clomping over hardwood floors, and both of us yelling – we can't hear ourselves. We can't hear a thing over the tyrannosaurus roar coming from outside.

I push Tony into the bathtub first, and crawl in on top of him, sheltering him with my body. As an afterthought I reach up and pull the shower curtain over us, and at the last second, amid a deafening roar, I snatch a towel off a nearby rack and pull it over our heads. Flimsy protection, some nylon and an old white towel, but...

Something crashes against the house and rocks it to its foundations. Loud cracks snap through the air like gunshots.

Tony says something, and I can barely make out his words. Sounds like, "I love you." Then, a roar and a crash like the world ending. *The house,* I thought... *that's the house.*

The wall caves in and for a period of time, we are both knocked out.

"Louis! Louis!"

A finger pokes me in the ribs.

The air around me is hot and dank. I can barely breathe. Something stinks. Overhead, there are roars and rushing noises impossible to identify. Already curled in the fetal position, I tighten around myself and try not to move.

Every inch of my body either itches or hurts.

"We've got to get out of here. Louis, wake up, damn you!"

"I'm not sure I can move." Somehow I get the words out. "Not yet, at least."

"You have to," Tony says. "We have to get to the shelter. The outside wall is gone, and I don't know how much of the house is still standing. We're not safe."

Things become clearer. All our supplies. All that work. One tornado has rendered all of our preparations useless. At least we're alive. (But for how long?)

I squirm, and realize I'm still in the tub when I sit up and get a gash across the forehead from the tub faucet. Tony crouches over me.

"When did you come to?" I ask him, wiping a rivulet of blood away from the side of my face. I stare stupidly at the red smear on the back of my hand.

"Only a little bit before you did. You caught the worst of it. I had to crawl out from under you. It was scary when you didn't wake up right away. Now I'm going to get you out of here."

"If it's the last thing you do?" I smile up at him.

He nods. "If it's the last thing I do."

"Where will we go?"

"The shelter, I guess. The worst of the storm still hasn't hit. There may still be time."

We slosh through ankle-deep water – hunched over like old men as the wind threatens repeatedly to knock us off our feet – toward where the garage should be. In the gloom, we can barely make out a deadfall of timber and shingle, with colorful bits of car underneath. My Audi. Tony's Range Rover.

"*Now what?*" Tony screams into my ear.

I give an exaggerated shrug, knowing he'll feel it even if he can't see it. We turn and trudge back toward the house, hunched over even lower. The wind is still picking up. Once, I lose my footing and fell forward into the water. I land on my knees and pull Tony down with me.

"Get up!" he shouts. "We can't stay out here!"

I nod and struggle to get on my feet. Breathing is next to impossible, so heavy is the rain, so dense the humidity. We have to cup our hands over our noses to avoid inhaling water.

We slog back to the house, fighting the wind every step of the way. We cannot see the house, and have to rely on memory to guide us to where the side door ought to be.

That side of the house is still standing.

And then, just to spite us, the wind picks up.

We climb the steps, too exhausted to talk, and take shelter in the bathroom again. One wall of the house has been ripped away, but we are out of the rain, for the moment.

Ominous creaks and snapping noises emanate from the walls and the floor. With each gust of wind, the entire structure shakes.

We can't stay, but there aren't many places for us to go.

"We won't make it to the Superdome," I say.

Tony shakes his head in agreement. "Do we chance riding the storm out here?" he asks.

"We can't."

The house gives a loud GRONK to punctuate my reply. The wall at my back lists alarmingly, like a boat seconds away from being swamped by towering waves.

"The neighbors?" I ask. "They're all gone. All the other houses are empty. We can break in."

Tony nods. "Their windows are boarded up. We'll need to get out of the wind and rain as much as we can, if we're going to pry boards away and break the glass. We'll need tools."

"Maybe we should also check our supplies upstairs, if we can still get there. If we can salvage a few things, we can take them with us."

"I think the stairs are fine."

"I'll go," I say.

"No you won't. You're not as steady on your feet. Get the tools we'll need, and stay here. I'll go upstairs for supplies." With that, Tony leaves the room.

Various rooms were added to our house over the years, so that by the time we bought the place, it was an architectural crazy-quilt. Around back, we had a sunroom-slash-workshop space that we used mostly for storage. The jalousie windows hadn't lent themselves well to boarding up. With the power out and no flashlight, I have to grope around in the howling gloom to find my toolbox.

I have it in hand and am making my way back to the main part of the house when the walls emit a loud groan and start to crack. The bellowing wind and buckshot rain grew louder, more intense. Panic surges through me: *How can it keep getting louder? How is this possible? Won't it end?*

The house is not going to last, I realize. *It can't possibly.*

I back up against the wall, needing something solid to orient myself. Bad idea. The wall collapses, pitching me backward into loud wet darkness.

Wherever I am, I'm in the dark. Things have an *interior* quality, in the sense that regular concepts of time don't seem to apply. I don't know how long I've been here: seconds, eons, who can say? I am there and not there at the same time. Around me, the wind roars me in an enormous vortex. Rain lashes; tornadoes shoot out from the fringes, leaving mile-wide trails of complete destruction. Waters rise.

And Mama is with me.

She doesn't notice me at first, and I try to get away. I try to leave her to whatever she was doing – piloting this storm, I guess, although I can't tell how she is doing it. I have always imagined some kind of cockpit in the eye of one of these hurricanes, with Mama strapped in, wearing a fighter pilot's cap and goggles, psychotic and dashing, pressing a red button on a joystick to shoot tornadoes at us, gauges and meters to tell her how fast the wind was blowing and how deep the water was. The reality is this dark blank place. She is here. I am too. Things happen by force of will.

I can't leave, but I feel something new, a dim presence: Tony. I can't see him, but he is here too. With me. Inside me. Around me.

His message: *Eat her.*

It doesn't make sense. *Eat her? Be her?* I can't tell.

"You!" she shouts, when she spots me. "I got you this time, Louis, and ain't gonna stop with just killing you!"

Nothing happens.

Supernatural bellows ricochet off dark blank walls I sense but can't see. Mama roars like the winds in her hurricane, as the presence of Tony intensifies around me.

I'm here, he reassures me.

Then: *We're here.*

Natalie.

"I'm never going to get any peace until we're done with this bitch, will I?" she asks in a way that only we can hear.

Other voices join us, other presences: Anna, still alive, coming through due to – what? Whom? Tony? Yes, Tony, he was doing this somehow, through me and through Natalie and – Natalie's husband Esteban. Baby Gloria, no longer a baby, now something much older and wiser, sad, infinitely determined. The other two children, David and Joaquin, now older and not-older. Others whose names I would never know. Other casualties, not even related to us. This time I am the one at the eye of the storm, souls swirling around me, within, bolts of energy striking a lightning rod, our collective fury and resolve more than a match for one demented and damned woman with an unhealthy fondness for gale-force winds.

Mama tries again to do whatever she is trying to do to me, to us, and again, nothing happens.

More screams of rage from her.

"Looks like you've run out of options," I tell her.

"FUCK YOU! You're a goddamn faggot and you and your sister killed me and you're gonna pay for it until you're broken into a million pieces, and then some!"

"You deserved everything we did to you."

In supernature, just as in nature, bigger hurricanes can swallow smaller hurricanes. They merge. The identity of the smaller storm is subsumed. It vanishes without a trace. The larger storm does not always make landfall. Sometimes it stalls over a patch of cold ocean, the deadly vortex slowing, winding down, dwindling to nothing.

Nothing at all.

No Mama, then... we ate her. Swallowed her whole, digested her, absorbed her, left no trace. No dark blank place. No spirits of the living and the dead surrounding me. Nothing.

I wake up hurting everywhere. Overhead, a fluorescent light glares down at me. I recognize the pain in my arm as an IV needle. With effort I wiggle my fingers and toes, and sag with relief when I realize that everything still works.

"Louis?"

Tony.

"Are you awake? Can you hear me?"

"Yes," I croak.

"You were dead," Tony says, his voice breaking. "A wall collapsed on you, and you were dead."

"I know," I say. "Thanks for bringing me back."

Mama did her worst. She tried everything. She killed me. On the other side, I killed her again. Then I came back from the dead. Beyond that, what's the worst thing that can happen? Although I can't be sure, I don't think hurricanes will continue to target Anna and me.

Natalie doesn't respond when I try to contact her with the Ouija board. Let her rest in peace, or drink ectoplasm daiquiris on Jupiter with Esteban, or do whatever the dead do for fun. She deserves a break, after reporting the weather from the Great Beyond all these years. There have to be better ways to spend eternity. And Tony and I never have to work another day in our lives, if we don't feel like it.

Tony got out of the hurricane unscathed, a feat that earned him a couple of interviews and a blurb in *People*. I'm more in awe of him than ever. Me, I'm a little the worse for wear, but there's no permanent damage.

After just one visit from our claims adjustor, our insurance company cut us a huge check. "Live long and prosper," the adjustor said, wide-eyed and shaking his head in consternation at the heap of wreckage where our house had stood. He gave us a Star Trek Vulcan salute as he drove away. Tony and I took a total loss, and we're moving as far away from natural disasters as we can get. Somewhere free from forest fires, earthquakes, tsunamis, hurricanes, cyclones, El Niño, avalanches, the IRS, and practically everything else capable of being co-opted away from Mother Nature's control. Except for the outrageous cost of living, I expect we'll love London.

SIC GLORIA TRANSIT

When Julian Gray's mother first brought him home from the hospital, her own mother, Nadine, a rambling creature of thick ankles, mismatched eyes, and scarves that rustled with or without a breeze to inspire them, held the child in her arms and said, "He'll go far." Lisette Gray rolled her eyes and wondered if she could convince her mother to sit with baby Julian for an hour or so without anointing him with any oils more exotic than Johnson & Johnson. Long enough for Lisette to drink the tall cold gin and tonic she'd had spent the last nine months looking forward to. Grandma Nadine muttered in French over the little boy, then closed her eyes, crossed herself, and handed him back to Lisette. Lisette could hear her husband Gordon filling the tub with hot water; she wanted a hot bath almost as much as she wanted that glass of gin. Down there, she still hurt from the delivery.

"He'll go places," the old woman said. She kissed Julian on his forehead. "I see a bright future for him."

He gurgled, then wet his diaper.

Lisette wondered what had gotten into her, whether asking Nadine to come down from Canada had been a good idea. Gordon's parents would have been delighted to fly over from Newcastle to help with the newborn, but geography won out. Down came old muttering Nadine from Trois-Rivieres, crazier than she had been the last time Lisette had seen her. Her hair stuck out in all directions. When Lisette looked inside her mother's open purse, a litter of colorful Canadian banknotes left her blinking in surprise. A fair number of drab American greenbacks were interspersed with the Canadian currency. Little branches and packets of herb-scented things lay in there among all that money. Dried leaves. An entire desiccated jonquil.

"I'm going places, too," Lisette said. "To the washroom. Then to bed. Love you, *ma mere*, but I can barely stand up."

"Go far," said Nadine. "Yes he will."

As an adult Julian Gray remembered his mother's home-from-the-hospital story at odd times. He kept odd hours and had an odd profession, so the prediction his grandmother had wrapped around his life like one of her camphor-scented wool scarves seemed to have some merit.

The fascination with travel first manifested itself as a fascination with trains. In particular, subways. The idea that trains roared through tunnels below the surface of the earth intrigued the boy Julian beyond words. *Tunnels down there*, he'd tell his parents in the morning as they ate breakfast. *They're digging tunnels down there, and I can hear them at night.*

"We can hear them, too, darling," Lisette Gray said, holding her coffee mug with trembling hands. Without her makeup she looked a bit like a scarecrow.

"The Metro Authority promised the people in our neighborhood they'd be quiet. They said they were digging far enough underground that we wouldn't hear anything," said Gordon Gray, also sipping coffee.

"When will the trains come?"

"Not soon enough," said Lisette. Would this be a good day to tell Gordon she had started smoking again? And how soon could she sneak outside for a nicotine fix?

Gordon knew about his wife's tobacco habit and, being English, had no intention of confronting her. He ate a grapefruit section, then a spoonful of muesli, then another grapefruit section. Poor Lisette hadn't slept three hours last night. They all believed the Red Line tunnel was being blasted into the rock directly beneath their suburban Maryland house. For Julian, this was a source of endless fascination. The idea that in another year or two one might walk a few blocks to the station, board a sleek electric train, and zoom underground to the museums and monuments of Washington set him to jiggling. His parents had taken him to New York for a vacation when he was six, and the clatter and roar of the subways turned him into a pitcher full of excited jelly.

"I don't think they're using dynamite," eight-year-old Julian said. "I think it would be really loud if they were. I mean, really loud. I think the tunnels are just growing that way. Like blood vessels in the ground."

Gordon and Lisette exchanged a look.

"That's an interesting idea," Gordon said, to counteract the look of vague horror on Lisette's face. She looked as if she'd like to add a slug of vodka to her coffee.

"Well, it's true, isn't it? The train tunnels just grow down in the earth, like blood vessels? The trains are the blood. The people are the blood cells."

Lisette looked at her hands. Sniffed them. Julian knew they would smell like rosewater. She applied a floral lotion every morning when she woke up, in an attempt to ward off something she called liver spots. Julian couldn't understand how a pretty-smelling lotion on her hands would keep her liver from developing spots, but then, much of the world didn't make sense to him yet. Everything seemed to be governed by rule books everyone else had read but him.

"I assure you, Julian, they are blasting down there, and using a gigantic boring machine to dig the tunnel through the deep rock layers," said Gordon. This conversation was making his stomach feel sour. A glass of milk would be just the thing.

"The machine is boring?" Julian asked. He could just see it. The kind of thing Mrs. Brock droned on and on about in science class.

"No, it bores holes. It digs. We will have to visit the library and find you a picture."

Julian stared at the wall, contemplated the smooth expanse of white. He saw tiny capillary tunnels worming their way through the plaster, trains the size of baby caterpillars zipping through their little tubes, transporting micropassengers from floor to ceiling and back. Maybe the trains were magnetic. If he held a strong refrigerator magnet against the wall at the right time, the motion of the train would lift him up. He'd be pulled toward the ceiling as his parents looked on with their mouths open from shock.

Who could say where he might end up?

Julian saved his money through college and spent the year after graduation riding the rails across Europe. He'd settle for a month in some city picked more or less at random, then jump on a train every chance he got, exploring the surrounding area. In London, he rented a flat in Brixton and rode around on the Underground with a notebook, scribbling details about the faces he saw, the outlandish clothes, the rainbow hair, the previously unexplored cosmetic potential of safety pins and glitter. He chugged through green countryside on chronically delayed BritRail trains and got to wherever he was going later more often than sooner. As he would later see in America, suburbs were metastasizing their way out of city cores, beyond once-sacrosanct greenbelts. They were eating the landscape, digesting it, excreting little houses with two-car garages. He lived in Barcelona and took long walks through the overwhelming city, where buildings tended to look as if they were constructed out of cookie dough and sequins, designed by hallucinating architects who had washed down their acid tabs with shots of absinthe. Every corner he turned, his breath was taken away at some new vista, some oddity in tile and stone and brick. The Mediterranean Talgo took him along the coast, across the

French border into Montpellier. Down the coast he went to Alicante and Valencia. Late at night, the party trains made stops at the beach discos; crowds of drunk screaming university students climbed on, blissed out, threw up, wound down. He went to Zagreb and Naples, Berlin and Budapest, Zürich and Prague. And wrote a book about it all, more by accident than intent. Before Julian was 25 he found he had written the definitive guide to post-collegiate wandering: *Europeregrinations*.

There are advantages and disadvantages to doing something wildly successful by accident before the age of 25. Far more of the latter than the former. Julian's book sold out its first print run in three weeks, then sold out the second, the third… his publishers rejoiced, sent him a telegram in Malta instructing him to do whatever was necessary and *spend* whatever was necessary to repeat his success. In the meantime, how soon could he come back to the United States for a book tour? Student audiences in Berkeley and Ann Arbor, Austin and Boston, Chapel Hill and any number of other cities were clamoring for him.

Julian stepped off a plane from Heathrow to a three-ring media circus, organized by his publishers.

The speaking engagements at universities led to appearances on talk shows.

His chat with David Letterman led to an appearance in a couple of indie films, and then a big-budget, star-studded Hollywood bomb.

Between these projects, he quietly reclaimed both Canadian and British citizenship (his American passport being rather more of a hindrance than a help in some of the places he wanted to write about next) and travelled to South Africa and Australia. His goal: to turn his success upside down by exploring the bottom half of the planet.

The second book sold more copies than the first, and this time the college students accused Julian of being a sell-out. Sure, the auditoriums filled up, but as many professors showed up as students.

No matter where he went, at the back of his mind, he could hear his grandmother speaking to him: *You'll go far. You'll go far. You'll go far.*

An old woman approached Julian in an Amsterdam café. She wore a loud yellow raincoat and thick granny glasses. Like his grandmother, this woman's eyes tended to point in different directions. He couldn't decide which one to look at, so as much as possible he looked at the still dark water of the canal behind her. Passersby babbled in various European languages. One man stepped into one of Amsterdam's ubiquitous street-corner pissoirs and commenced to take a noisy leak.

"I read your book," the old woman said in an accent as thick as her ankles. "I'm a fan. And I know your grandmother Nadine."

She pressed a book of what looked like tickets into his hand.

"You said such funny things about Utrecht, where I live," she said. "You gave me a good laugh. I think you should have these."

Julian opened the booklet and looked at the tickets, careful to keep a good grip on them lest a breeze blow them into the Singelgracht or, worse, the effluent from the urinal across the street.

MULTI-PASS was printed in big capital letters, sans serif, on green paper. On the back of each ticket, Julian saw a magnetic stripe.

"They're something new, shall we say. They are a useful gift. They're widely acceptable, compatible with all ticket machines, and you can use them to go wherever you want."

Without waiting for thanks, she waved a hand at him, much she same gesture as if she were shooing a chicken, and waddled away.

MULTI-PASS.

What is this travel thing, anyway? Julian finished his espresso. He had been given various gifts – plane tickets, other travel books, clothing, the occasional plate of home-baked cookies – in the three years since his first book came out. Often these items were intended as a quid pro quo: endorse us and we'll do X, Y, and Z for you in return. Or: you're so cool, and if I give you this, then you'll be my friend. But this was the first time he had really questioned himself, why he travelled, how he got here.

It was also the last. He just didn't think the subject warranted that much self-talk. When you found your groove, you kept dancing as long as you could. If you had any sense at all.

Julian's first spectacular failure was the Antarctica book. He got the idea driving to the bottom of South America, through Patagonia. The farther south he went, as civilization seemed to be petering out, he expected to see the land burning, *gauchos* in high-heeled boots stepping on little blue jets of flame to put them out, scorched cattle and llamas everywhere. A permanent pall of smoke, eternal late fall. Why else did the place get the name Tierra del Fuego?

He booked a trip to the frozen continent. His ship sailed from New Zealand, dodging icebergs and chasing penguins. Corporate sponsors outfitted him in the latest subzero-wear, supplied him with a photographer instead of just turning him loose with a camera this time.

Julian imagined Antarctica colonized in an overpopulated future, subway tunnels carved in the ice, clear trains whisking white-clad urban Eskimos through the frozen South Pole metropolis. Silvery icicle rocket-turbo-jets taking off from glacier runways, their afterburn knocking over penguins like so many bowling pins in tuxedos. It would be like Sweden, only more so.

Antarctica is not a living entity; regardless, it single-mindedly attempts to kill anyone or anything not already equipped by nature to survive there.

And Julian's documentary efforts had taken on a patronizing tone, his critics pointed out. He was losing his focus, his fire, his relevance. His arrogance turned away the college students who had been his mainstay for the last several years, and the more affluent older travellers kept buying their trusty guides from Fodor's and Frommer's. Julian slipped through a crack in the publishing ice sheet. His niche closed.

When the Antarctica book sold half its already-low first print run (he hadn't said anything new about the place, and there was no nightlife), Julian's publisher suggested he take some time to think about what he wanted to do next, where he wanted to go.

Julian travelled back to Barcelona to collect his wits. Barcelona has always been a good place to recuperate. The sun shines all year (once the morning fog burns off). The locals are pleasant (if you can find them among all the tourists). Julian rented a flat in the Eixample, bought furniture, and tried to figure out how to put down roots. This was a new thing for him; he'd never stood still long enough to stick to one place.

A couple of weeks after arriving there, he found himself at a metro station without cash on hand. He'd left his wallet in his apartment, and he had no change in his pockets. Rather than turning back to rush home and retrieve the thing – he'd be late for a coffee date with a man he'd met a few days before – Julian stuck a MULTI-PASS ticket into the gate to see what would happen. He kept the booklet with him at all times, for luck he supposed. For the novelty of it.

A click.

He collected the ticket from the turnstile and walked through. A train pulled up to the platform just as he stepped into the concourse, and it must have been an express: it skipped several stations (other passengers protested, and one woman pounded on the doors) and dropped him off at the Port Olimpic station, where he was meeting Antonio.

Does the magic carpet have to be serviced every 3000 miles, like your Peugeot or Mercedes? Does the genie in that bottle you found demand paid sick leave, public holidays off, and regular training opportunities? Does the magic coin lose its power if the exchange rate is unfavorable?

Some questions cannot be answered. Julian did not stay up tossing at night, trying to guess at the truth behind his MULTI-PASS metro trip. The ticket had worked. It might work again, but if he was careless in his experimentation, he'd be likely to waste a trip. Just like the thing with Antonio could be said to be working, after a few months, as long as it worked, leave well enough alone. There was no telling what the future would bring. For now, things could be what they were. He kept the booklet of tickets in a strongbox with his passports, some emergency money in stable currencies, and his publication agreements. Now and then he'd take out the tickets and look at them, pensive, as if he could be putting them to better use if he'd just think, if he'd just see things from the right perspective.

Julian took a small part in a Spanish film and mostly escaped public notice. The director's boyfriend was a friend of Antonio's penultimate ex, and had lost an actor at the last minute. Time dragged by. Julian lived at the periphery of a dream, in a state of fringe celebrity, the sort of person café coffee-sippers ask each other about: where they've seen him, what he's done, why they should know his name. It's difficult to be miserable for long in Barcelona, which is not so much a city as a big and surreal confection of Play-Doh and jewellery, but Julian was suffering. The money from his first successes seemed to be dwindling, despite his financial manager's best efforts. Julian found himself teaching English with the distracted air of a professor twice his age, and desperate for another idea he could turn into a book.

I should be riding around New York and London in limousines.

I should be at the Oscars, walking across that red carpet holding hands with Antonio.

I should not be struggling with mediocrity.

Julian burned.

Miserable in Barcelona, a hybrid photo-essay and travel guide, aroused vague editorial interest on three continents. Julian's Spanish-language publisher in Madrid enjoyed the chance to poke fun at the capital's rival city and offered a contract with enough money to restore some of Julian's battered confidence.

"You really want to photograph the worst of the nightlife there?" Juan, a great gelatinous sphere of a man with a walrus moustache, clasped his belly and laughed like a Latin Santa Clause. "The underworld of Barcelona? I thought it was tossed into the Mediterranean before the Olympics came, and never allowed back within sight of Montjuïc!"

Julian nodded.

Vomiting club kids, fucked-out trannie hookers crawling the curbside at six in the morning, street urchins in the Gothic Quarter vandalizing cars, graffiti on the walls of toilets and metro stations.

Juan, a staunchly civic-minded *madrileño*, loved the idea.

Aaron, his British agent, who would also handle rights for Australia, New Zealand, Singapore, and South Africa if a publisher could be found, seemed reluctant but was at least willing to talk. Julian hopped on a plane to London and met Aaron, an effeminate, rail-thin Scot who smoked French cigarettes one after another, coughing as if a lung were about to come unstuck, at a dark pub in Kensington.

"You have to realise, you're on thin ice in the publishing world. After a few spectacular failures, it's more difficult for you to convince a publishing house to put out a new book than you'd have as a first-timer."

"Tell me something I don't already know."

Aaron named a large, reputable publishing house. "I called an editor there and pitched your project. Pitched? Listen to me, I sound like a bloody Yank."

"I am a bloody Yank," Julian said. "If you want to be technical about it."

"Well, yes, there is that." Aaron stared at the cigarette in his hand. Even in the pub's dim light, Julian could see that Aaron's skin carried a jaundiced hue. Aaron continued: "In any case, I think we'll be able to do it. Your photographs were strong, and the text you submitted was funny enough. The book will appeal to a certain readership. Maybe even the same ones who made you so popular in the first place."

An ember of hope glowed in the center of Julian all the way back to Barcelona. Antonio met him at the airport and, on hearing the news, surprised him with a weekend trip over to Ibiza.

Julian spent the next three months trolling the seediest places he could find in the coastal city, camera in hand, extra rolls of film in his pockets. Danger loomed: one night an angry man he'd photographed kneeling before a cop in the woods atop Montuïc, near the Palau Nacional, shouted and gave chase. The cop zipped up in a hurry and joined the pursuit. Julian dashed down the unmoving hillside escalators, frantic, camera banging against his side like a metal fist, and reached the Espanya metro station at the bottom of the hill just as the attendant was shutting the gates. About 20 paces behind, shouts and imprecations could be heard. Racing footsteps.

"We are closing," the attendant said.

"MULTI-PASS," Julian said, tearing off a ticket.

"Step inside."

The attendant shut the gate behind Julian, and when he descended to the platform, a train was waiting. The conductor asked Julian's destination.

201

Took him straight to Universitat, the closest Eixample station to Julian's home.

Most of the work necessary for the New York media behemoth to publish *Miserable in Barcelona* could be done via the telephone and the Internet, but Julian's US agent and editor wanted a face-to-face meeting when the time came to sign contracts. From New York, Julian would travel to Toronto, to complete a similar transaction with his Canadian publisher. Antonio kept Julian up late the night before the trip, celebrating in the best Spanish tradition, and as a result, Julian, sore in various places and woefully hung over, missed his plane to New York.

He disembarked from the train at the airport station and stared in horror at the clock, then out the window at an aircraft climbing toward the clouds. No way to know whether the flight was, in fact, his intended; it could have been bound for London or Berlin, Rome or Toulouse – anywhere, really. The moving walkway between the train station and the airport terminal stretched like elastic, elongating the distance to the Iberia check-in counter, where a Spanish girl was going to shake her head at him in disapproval.

"Please tell me my flight is delayed," he said, when he surrendered his suitcase and his tickets to the Iberia agent.

"No, señor, I cannot tell you that, because your flight departed on time."

"When is the next one to New York? I have to…" Julian stopped himself and shook his head. "But you must hear that all the time, when passengers arrive late. Of course I have to get to New York, or else I wouldn't be here and upset because I missed my flight."

"That was our only direct flight. We can route you through Madrid if you want to fly Iberia, or through Paris if you want to fly Air France. They

202

will honor your ticket, but there will be an additional charge."

"Are you sure this is the only direct flight?" Julian asked, surrendering another MULTI-PASS ticket.

He fully expected the Iberia agent to scorch him with a disdainful glare, but she nodded and picked up her phone to place a call. After a short exchange in Catalan, she rang off and smiled at Julian.

"Just one moment," she said.

Julian was led down a corridor he hadn't noticed before, in all the times he'd flown in and out of this airport. (BCN is not a sprawling metropolis like LAX or Heathrow.) The uniformed Iberia attendant explained, "There has been a change of schedule. One plane intended for to Havana will be rerouted through JFK. You're just in time to board. It will depart once you are safely on board."

Julian did not stop to ask questions, because he didn't care about the legal issues such a change might entail; nor did he want to know anything more than his estimated time of arrival at Kennedy. Let the American Immigrations people worry about the Cubans, their visas, and all the rest. He still had several MULTI-PASS tickets left, and a contract to sign in New York. He crossed the Atlantic trying to decide how he would follow *Miserable in Barcelona*, what his next project ought to be, what would be the next logical step.

The book landed on shelves in the Borders and Kinokuniya and Chapters stores of the world in than the critics began to pounce like hyaenas:

The New Orleans *Times – Picayune* called *Miserable in Barcelona* "Further proof that Julian Gray has passed his sell-by date."

According to the *Christian Science Monitor*, "While his first two books were minor masterpieces combining travel, wit, and social comment,

Gray's writing has deteriorated into tedious navel-gazing. Now struggling for relevance, Gray subjects his readers to close-up views of the dissipated and disgusting."

The *New York Times* said, "Slapdash and haphazard. Julian Gray writes as if he were in a state of arrested development, still holding onto his sophomore year of college, still writing as if unsure who his readers are. The quality of the photographs suggests they were taken with a generic drug-store disposable camera. Flip through this one in the bookstore – there are a few bright spots – but don't buy it."

The Toronto *Star*: "Utterly meretricious."

The entire English-speaking world seemed to unite against Julian's book. There were a few dissenting heretics: Vancouver, Sydney, and Dallas. Melbourne chimed in with a breath of faint praise. The book's sales were rather strong in the antipodes – God bless Australia and New Zealand, Julian thought, feeling otherwise as if a pack of vampires had been feasting on him for the last couple of weeks.

Outside of Madrid, the Spanish-language papers weren't much kinder. Positive remarks seemed only to be the editors in Mexico City, Buenos Aires, and Sevilla heaving sighs of relief: someone had finally shown that Barcelona, for all its glitter and polish, did in fact have a dirty underbelly. The book itself? "Unfinished." "Sophomoric." And, worst, from Caracas: "If you want to see antics like these, then you should watch an Almodóvar film. He knows how to make low-life lovable and interesting to look at. He knows how to make you care. Sr. Gray does not. He disdains his subjects. Yes, this is a book and not a movie, but the point remains, this is a pale and embarrassing imitation. If we are lucky, Sr. Gray will find something else to do."

Julian couldn't be sure whether the resulting public humiliation killed his parents, and, since they were dead, he couldn't ask them. He thought of consulting mediums or trying his hand with a Ouija board, but discarded both ideas. He flew back to Maryland for the joint funeral. The car rental agent at the Baltimore airport blushed when she recognized him and said, "Sorry about the book, man." Julian elected not to reply, "My parents died within three days of each other, and I know they subscribed to at least three of the periodicals that gave my book a drubbing. Write a fucking letter to the editor."

Antonio changed the message on his answering machine to indicate he would be in Naples for the next week. What the hell was that about? Naples? Antonio had an ex there, a man he had never quite gotten over. Julian opted to believe he had been dumped *in absentia*.

He celebrated his entire life going down the toilet by taking a cab from his parents' too-quiet house down 16th Street into Washington, getting drunk out of his mind in a Dupont Circle club, stumbling over to Georgetown to keep drinking, and tried to pick up a cute blond fraternity boy dressed head to toe in Ralph Lauren. The frat boy, whose name was Toby and who was a political science major and had a girlfriend named Lily and who was going to law school like his father and his grandfather had before him, and who was being groomed for a career in politics, and who had never ever ever touched another man sexually in his entire life (well, there was that time with that pledge John after initiation, but they were drunk and it didn't count because it was just mutual masturbation and anyway, no one would ever know), beat the shit out of him. Imagining the criminal charges Julian might press, Toby decided to make it look like a mugging. Julian lay in an alley on top of several boxes and bags of garbage. Toby emptied Julian's wallet and was looking at the booklet of MULTI-PASS tickets when Julian came to.

"Give me that!" Julian said in Spanish first. He remembered where he was and tried again in English.

The language choice might have helped. It at least confused the frat boy enough to buy Julian a little time. He grabbed at the book of tickets. It tore.

Toby took off as fast as he could run.

Julian was left holding one ticket, the last in the booklet.

His parents were good and properly buried, all prayers said, all tears shed. Relatives Julian barely knew had flown in from Canada and England, and had since returned.

Antonio did not return any of Julian's calls.

Copies of *Miserable in Barcelona* languished on bookshelves across the globe, being flipped through, their pages smudged with thumbprint oil and crumbs of food, but not bought. The book had cost a lot of money to produce, and it wasn't going to break even, at least not an any of its English-language editions. (Well, there was always hope for Australia and New Zealand.) The Spanish figures looked better, but then, it was hard to look worse. How long until his publishers remaindered it? How long before he found it lining somebody's cat box?

Julian made arrangements to sell his parents' house and do away with their belongings. After a week, his bruises from the mugging faded. They passed through an alarming spectrum of visible pain, first purplish-blue, then a bilious green, finally a terrible shade of deli-mustard yellow. Julian's spirits faded like his bruises. He could still pick up little roles in obscure Continental films, if he felt the need to remain in the public eye. At the very least, audiences in cinemas didn't hiss and storm out when he appeared on the screen. He could try his hand writing under a pen name, something modest in scope, something ultimately redeeming. There was always the teaching gig.

Julian was having these thoughts as he drank a coffee – despite the sauna-like weather of the American capital – on a sofa in a cozy caffeine bar in Adams Morgan. He watched the international bright young things around him chatting animatedly, in several languages. Some studied. Others read. Still others seemed to be waiting for someone to come, for something to happen.

He finished his coffee, stood, and walked outside. The humidity was like walking blindfolded into a brick wall. The breath was knocked out of him. But on the inside, despite the warming effects of his espresso, a deep interior chill remained.

Julian hurried home, then paid the cabbie an extra $20 to wait while he packed his bags. (Both cars were to be auctioned with the rest of the estate.) At the Baltimore airport, Julian presented his last MULTI-PASS ticket at the British Airways check-in counter. (He was changing planes at Gatwick. Or rather, that's what his tickets said. Without Antonio waiting for him in Barcelona, there seemed to be no point in going home, because where, after all, was home?)

"What is your destination, sir?" asked the girl in her handsome British Airways navy uniform.

Julian gave her the last MULTI-PASS ticket with a twinge of regret.

"That's in the hands of the gods, I guess," he said. "I just want to go somewhere I can roast in the sun, and not think at all. Alicante? Bermuda? Faro? It doesn't bloody matter."

The British Airways check-in girl gave him a polite nod, and directed him to his gate for boarding. Very unusual in its usualness, that. Julian waited with the rest of the passengers on his Gatwick-bound flight, boarded with them, endured the safety spiel, acceleration, lift-off.

The plane kept climbing, though, and the pilot never announced they had reached their cruising altitude of 39,000 feet. Julian's ears kept popping. Centrifugal force pressed him into his chair. Fortunately he was flying first class, so he wasn't suffering as much as the passengers back in Economy.

Night seemed to have fallen. Julian looked outside and saw the Earth receding, even as the plane gained speed.

"But I was supposed to transit through Gatwick," he thought stupidly, when he began to realize what he had done.

He'll go far, his grandmother Nadine had said.

For some reason the windows did not burst out of the plane; the aircraft held together as if protected by some exterior power, some kind of force field, travelling faster and faster through a black void Julian accepted, finally, as space. The 777 gave a great swerve, once, dodging Venus. *I need a drink*, Julian thought. Planes, trains, they're all the same thing. Rule Britannia. I need gin. He ordered a Bombay Sapphire and tonic from a strangely calm but very handsome flight attendant, and noticed that the rest of the passengers seemed to be asleep.

It was getting warmer in the cabin, much warmer, hot.

Julian had just a moment to sip his drink and think, *The sick glory of transit*, and then he arrived at his final destination.

IN THE CITY OF WARM RED LIGHT

Before:

I think a Japanese eggplant started all of this. There I stood in the produce section at Whole Foods, my favorite supermarket, trying to decide which vegetables to toss into my wok for dinner. I'd picked out a bunch of asparagus, a head of cauliflower, some baby bok choi. Bell peppers would taste good, yes, but what color? Red, yellow, green, orange? Decisions, decisions. Here in Berkeley, you find all these veggies us transplanted hicks from the South have never heard of. While I dithered over capsicums, an amazing shade of purple caught my eye. If you were picking out amethysts you'd want them to be this color. The vegetable in question looked kind of cucumber-esque, only more tapered and obviously not medium green. Nice heft, a little floppy but not too much give. The desperate could masturbate with them. I picked one up and turned it over several times. Should I attempt to cook the thing? What would it taste like? Would everything else in the wok turn violet?

"Ryan?"

I turned to look, and dropped the eggplant.

"Grace?"

"Oh my God, what the fuck are you doing here?" She gave me a big one-handed hug and sort of jumped up and down at the same time, mashing her breasts into me, which had to hurt.

Grace Tsang and I met as undergraduates at American University in Washington DC. We'd even roomed together for a couple of years before moving in with our respective boyfriends. After graduation, we lost track of each other.

"I live here," I told her. "Have for a few years. What are you doing here?"

"No way!" She let go of me and jumped up and down again. "I live over in the City."

We stared at each other for a moment. She seemed taller than I remembered but that might have been from her heels. She wore a rust-colored sweater thing and jeans, and had put her hair up in a loose bun. Her oval, black-rimmed glasses oozed nerdy chic. She'd gotten her nose pierced: *Twinkle, twinkle, little stud. When she got you, was there blood?*

"Tell me you're not going back East for Christmas," she said.

"Are you kidding? It's snowing in North Carolina. I'd rather go to Puerto Vallarta and lick Mexican boys." If I'd had my druthers, there would be someone to invite to her party: ideally, a boyfriend. My last one was long gone. Failing that, someone interesting and platonic from my circle (I'd even settle for an arc or a crescent) of friends. Thing was, the goddamn thesis had occluded most of my social prospects. Oh well. No point in bringing this up. Not here. "What about you?"

"My parents moved back to Singapore," she said. "They're pissed off at me because I wouldn't get married and have children. You remember Calvin, the guy from Ireland? My grandmother had hysterics when she found out I was seeing a white guy and even worse hysterics when I threw him out. So much drama." She shrugged and brushed a wisp of hair out of her face, then scratched the studless side of her nose.

"Do you have holiday plans?" I remembered the eggplant, stooped to pick it up. It didn't seem bruised from its fall, so I dusted it on my shirt and returned it to its bin. "I was going to meet some friends in Rome but the trip fell through. We need to catch up."

"I'm sort of having a party," Grace said. "You have to come. Oh my God. You so have to."

She rummaged in the leather bag she wore slung over one shoulder, produced paper and a pen, scribbled her address and phone numbers for me, then pulled out a tiny blue cell phone. Smallest one I'd seen yet. I hoped she wouldn't swallow it by accident while talking.

"Give me your numbers now," she said. "I'll program them in. Then, like, if you lose that slip of paper or flake out or something, I can call and give you hell. Promise you'll come over early so we can catch up. I've got to run now. I'm meeting a girlfriend in Oakland for dinner and we're cooking and then I'm driving her to the airport. I can't be late!"

Grace raced over to the express lane, turned and waved, her metallic green fingernails glittering like tinsel, then dumped the contents of her shopping basket in a heap on the counter. I wanted to follow her. The checkout girl tended to glare at customers who roused her out of her apathetic trance, and the look on her face must have been priceless. I watched Grace for a moment, then returned to the vegetables. Those eggplants. That purple. I put one in the cart and decided to try my luck. If it turned out to be too mushy inside to cube, or if my stir-fry came out the color of costume jewellery, then, well, so be it. I'd toss the whole mess into the trash and heat up a frozen pizza.

During:

Grace lived in a townhouse in the Sunset District, way out in the Avenues. The Sunset got its name from the fog that keeps the sky a Seattle-like grey at least half the year. Streetlights sometimes shine at noon. Motorists drive with their headlights on. It's clammy. The Avenues are, collectively, the northwestern quadrant of San Francisco. The street network forms a grid, and the north-south ones – the Avenues – are numbered in ascending order as one approaches the ocean. The area has a sort of suburban remoteness to it, while retaining that unique San Francisco vibe. Where else in the United States are you going to find interracial lesbian couples with matching nose piercings and magenta hair walking hand in hand, wearing shapeless alpaca wool sweaters and mittens in July?

In late December, because the weather here is a law unto itself, of course the sky had to be a heartbreaking blue. Not a cloud in sight. The temperature hovered in the high fifties. Flowers were in bloom.

I had no trouble finding a parking spot for my Volvo. On Grace's block, even.

OK, one benefit of the holidays, you can park in the City. Christmas isn't all bad. There are perks.

I thawed a little, even as a brisk breeze off the ocean gave me goosebumps. When I stepped out of my car I could smell salt on the wind. The Pacific lay only a dozen blocks to the west. I listened for the waves but couldn't hear them. Too far away.

Grace had painted her house three shades of blue, with pink and white trim, and all the flowers in hanging baskets and pots out front were white. The colors should have fought with each other like cats in a bag, but somehow Grace had imposed harmony. I admired the façade for a moment before ringing the bell. I heard a shriek after I buzzed. Three seconds later, she flung the door open. We hugged each other and jumped up and down again. I stepped into a hallway she'd lit with red neon.

"I already love your house," I told her, offering the bottle of wine I'd brought, a Montepulciano. I loved everyone's house. Everyone else's, that is. My own grad student's warren looked like an imploded library.

"So do I," she said. I noticed a tiny shift in her expression. "Let me show you around. Should we open this? No, wait, let's not, I've got a bottle open already. Let's finish that first. Don't tell me you've turned into one of those awful people who never drinks during the day. Or, like, you're sober or something. Everybody in this fucking city is either strung out on crystal or goes to like 80 AA meetings a week. I can't stand it."

"I know what you mean. Last week I went out on a date with this guy I met online, and after our appetizers he went to the men's room and stayed in there a long time. I didn't say anything about it – it's just not polite to comment on that kind of thing – but later, a bag of white powder fell out of his pocket. I just left. I got up and walked out of the restaurant. I was like, *Yes I really want to support you in detox after you hock my stereo and my computer and give me hepatitis C. Loser.*"

"You actually went on a date?" Grace escorted me to her kitchen and waved me to a chair at a bistro table by a bay window. "The view's not great but I never got around to landscaping the patch of dirt out back. So you went on a date? That is so retro. I love it."

She poured the last of her wine into two glasses and stirred the contents of a pot on the stove. *Needs more garlic*, she murmured. She quickly minced a clove and sprinkled the white shreds into whatever was simmering.

"We've got two hours before the rest of the guests arrive. What on earth have you been doing with yourself?" Grace asked, initiating a toast.

"Dotcom casualty," I said. "That's what I tell people. I was working at a startup. The owners sold it to Oracle during the height of the Internet craziness. I did really well when that happened. Good financial planner. He deserves all the credit. I was just in the right place at the right time. I diversified and got out before the market crashed. Now I'm back in school, at Cal. Not working, unless you count the thesis, in which case the children in Guatemalan sweatshops get more time off than I do. Hate me?"

"More than words can say," Grace said.

"What kind of party is this, anyway? Am I dressed OK? I didn't even think to ask."

"You're fine, Ryan. God, you're gay. You couldn't not be fine. Don't worry. It's like a get-together for Christmas orphans. I told three of my friends to each bring one friend of their own. Somebody who was in town for the holidays, you know, but not into the whole trees and presents and Jesus thing. And Asian food. It has to be Asian food. None of that Christmas turkey and black-eyed peas and that other stuff you Caucasians eat. It's Not Allowed."

The first guest arrived in the middle of Grace's story about breaking up with the Irishman: *He told me he didn't like my art, can you believe that? Fucker! I mean, I've only turned this whole house into a studio and gallery, and, you know, it's what I do.* Dramatic white sculptures made of some fibrous material stood sentinel around the dining table, for example. They resembled angels but I didn't want to tell Grace I thought so. She probably intended them to symbolize the Singaporean government's stranglehold over the local media, and would explain the significance in ten times as much detail as I needed. In her bedroom, she'd hung dramatic red tapestries on the walls, giving the space an updated harem ambience. *We'd been fighting for a couple of months, and one night when things were getting nasty, he told me he hated my art. That was it. I threw his ass out. I told him to find some other slut to marry for a green card. Fuck him, let the INS ship his skinny ass back to Dublin, see if I care...* The doorbell rang.

"Already? Fuck!" Grace jumped up and raced to the door, trailing clouds of a gardenia perfume she'd applied on a trip to the bathroom.

I followed her as far as the kitchen, took a seat, sipped my wine, and contemplated the slippery nature of time. After not seeing her for several years, here we were, sipping wine in her gloriously overdone house on the

West Coast; she'd be back with the guest in a second. Breathtaking. In college, she hadn't been so high-strung. Actually, we'd all been stoned most of the time. Maybe the weed had masked it. Who could say? Now that we lived close enough to hang out again, I could find out.

"Ryan? This is my friend Taro, he's from Osaka and you'll love him but not too much because he brought a date. Gabriel, right?" Grace led Taro and his date into the kitchen. While she struggled to open my Montepulciano, Taro and Gabriel gawked at the house like tourists seeing the Taj Mahal for the first time.

"You've redecorated," Taro said.

"You should have come by to visit sooner."

I introduced myself. Taro set a bottle of white wine on the counter to shake my hand. Gabriel handed Grace a covered dish to shake my hand next. Handsome guy – they both were. Gabriel looked kind of Latin: olive skin, brass eyes, short curly brown hair. Taro was the taller of the two, slightly. They gave off the sparks infatuated couples can't hide.

Taro wandered into the dining room and an exclamation could be heard seconds later. The angel sentinels, I guessed. Perhaps one had pinched him.

"Have you seen these things?" he asked, returning to the kitchen. "Gabriel, come look at these things Grace made."

The doorbell buzzed again. This elicited more screams from Grace. Delight, I supposed, or cocaine. The sounds a hostess makes when she's both happy and horrified to see her guests. No matter where people are from, hospitality is always an issue. The house will never be ready, the food will never be perfect, and there will always be a smudge on your cheek or your nostril when the doorbell commences to ring.

She ushered in a young Asian woman with dyed blond hair, Kate: *We went to kindergarten together in Hong Kong, and both ended up here, how funny is that?* Kate introduced an older white woman, Geraldine, who spoke with a Southern accent and surveyed the kitchen with her upper lip slightly curled, as if she'd spotted dog turds on the floor. She tended to look over the rims of her glasses with the disdain of the displaced Dixie blueblood. I had grown up with that disdain, actually. Hadn't missed it much, either. What didn't Geraldine approve of? She'd just gotten there.

Behind them trooped in two more: Warren, a pallid guy in darkly shapeless, paint-splashed clothing who might have been anywhere along the 25 – 40 continuum, and… Grace paused in her introductions.

"Straw?" She looked at this guest with doubt staining her expression.

The guy Warren had brought nodded. "That's right. Straw. Like, *hay?* Only that's not what it means."

"What does it mean?" Geraldine asked.

"Ask me again when we've had a few glasses of wine," Straw said.

"There can't be enough wine in this house to take me very far down *that* road, I'm sure," Geraldine said with a smile.

"Well!" Grace clapped her hands together, momentarily turned to arrange the food everyone had brought, seemed to be collecting herself, then turned to face the group again. "Merry Christmas. I'm so glad you all could make it! So, like, I can see we totally need to pour wine. Ryan, would you do the honors? I'm just going to run in the dining room to light all the candles."

As everyone took their seats, I watched Taro and Gabriel most. They made an attractive couple. They kept finding reasons to touch each other. I wanted to ask them how long they'd been together but preferred to do so in private. Warren, I noticed, was also staring at them. I couldn't read his face. He looked haunted one second, envious the next, bored the third. A strange carousel of emotions.

"I thought it was so delightful when Kate told me about this party, Grace. It's so pleasant to be invited," Geraldine said.

"Really?" Grace asked. I smiled inside: I could still read her emotional topography. She was doing a good job of masking her doubts. She hadn't always been so subtle. "I'm glad to hear it."

"Living here in San Francisco, one meets the most interesting people, don't you think? Such a variety. I was in LA for a couple of years, and I just couldn't stand it. At any given moment, no matter where I was, half the women in the room had bleached their hair the most unnatural blonde and had breast augmentation done. I never knew whether I was in the real world or a Barbie doll factory."

"I don't think anyone here has had work done," Grace said.

I stole a glance at the platinum-haired Kate, who had sunk an inch lower in her chair.

"Oh, of course darling, I can see that, it's perfectly obvious, and it's so refreshing! I have so much more respect for women who do their best with what Nature gave them. Do you suppose I could have a bit more wine? It looks like I have already drained my glass!"

Straw, who sat next to me, very discreetly snorted a half-moon of white powder off the web between his thumb and forefinger. I don't think anyone else saw. We exchanged a look. He winked. Then he rolled his eyes in Geraldine's direction and mouthed the word *Bitch*.

Grace brought out appetizers: gyoza from Taro, Kate's shrimp dumplings.

"I never really liked wine with Asian food until recently," Kate was saying. "We should have tea."

"Fuck!" said Grace. She set the two serving plates on trivets. "The tea! I forgot the tea." She raced to the kitchen. She called, "Oolong or green?"

"Lovely little dumpling things, Taro," Geraldine said. "Where did you buy them? I swear, I've never had this kind of luck with the frozen kind."

"I made them," Taro said. "Gabriel helped."

"Oh, well isn't that nice?" Another big smile from Geraldine as she doused two more gyoza with soy sauce. "Just like your mother used to make, I bet."

From the kitchen: "Oolong or green, anybody?"

"Probably not," Taro said. "She didn't like to cook. My aunt lived with us when I was growing up. She's the one who taught me how."

Taro took off his glasses and cleaned them with his napkin, not because they were smudged, I guessed, but to give himself a moment to reflect.

What a handsome guy, I was thinking, reminded of my own loneliness. *I wonder how he and Gabriel met.*

"But I bet your mother didn't make gyoza when you were a little boy," Geraldine said to Gabriel.

"No, she made sandwiches mostly."

"You're Mexican, right?"

Gabriel shook his head. "Mongrel."

Kate tittered. To my left, another snuffle: Straw had just inhaled another bump of his white powder. What was taking Grace so long in the kitchen?

"Whatever, Grace," I yelled. "Just throw in whatever's closest to your hand."

"Mongrel? That's not a nice word, is it Gabriel?" Geraldine asked.

She speared her gyoza with a fork, eschewing the carved chopsticks Grace had set out beside each plate, and chewed slowly, staring at Gabriel.

"I'm half Brazilian," Gabriel said. "That's what my mother said. My last name is Acosta, which is Portuguese. I doubt she made it up."

"Oooh, Brazilian," Geraldine said. "I've been there. I went to Rio for

Carnaval one year. Have you ever been to Rio, Gabriel?"

He nodded.

"And how about you, Ryan? Have you ever been to Rio?"

When I tried to answer before I'd fully swallowed, I aspirated some wine. After the spluttering fit subsided, I rasped *No.*

"I've been to a few islands in the Caribbean, and I've been to Venezuela, but never as far down as Brazil."

I tried to make my throat relax. Death by Montepulciano, what a bizarre way to go. I expected Geraldine to ask how far down I usually went but she confined herself to asking where I'd grown up.

"You've got an accent, you know," she said. "Not much of one, you'd hardly notice if you didn't know what to listen for, but it's there."

"North Carolina."

"Is that right? Which part? I'm from a little town outside of Roanoke, Virginia, myself. Where in North Carolina are you from, Ryan?"

"Greenville."

She furrowed her brow.

"North Carolina has a Greenville? There's one in South Carolina. It's a big city. But North Carolina? I don't believe I've ever heard of that."

"It's not big."

"Well of course it's not big. I'd have heard of it otherwise! So what happened to your accent, Ryan?"

"I've always wondered about that," Grace said, taking her seat again. The second the words came out of her mouth, a guilty look flashed across her face: collaboration with the enemy. "It'll take a little while for the water to boil. Sorry about that, everybody."

"So, Ryan, I can hear that little bit of the South in your voice," Geraldine said. "Was it deliberate, what you did to your accent? Did you get speech therapy to soften it?"

I shook my head. The bottle on the table stood empty, just a swirl of red dregs at the bottom. Like my glass. Nothing left to drink. God, where had Kate found this woman?

"I notice you kept yours," Warren said.

"But of course!" Geraldine said. "There's no better place on earth to grow up than the hills of western Virginia."

I tried to picture Grace growing up in Roanoke instead of Hong Kong and couldn't do it. She was a temples, incense, and IM Pei skyscrapers kind of girl. Myself, I couldn't see much difference between western Virginia and eastern North Carolina – same rednecks, different topography – but this didn't need pointing out at the table. Everyone fidgeted.

"I'm from Texas," Warren said. "Can you tell?"

"Really?" Straw asked, his mouth full of shrimp dumpling. Bits of pink showed when he talked. "I didn't know that. I grew up in Houston."

"El Paso."

"No way!" Straw stared at Warren, then sniffled like he had a runny nose. Which he probably did. In back, delivering the drug payload.

"After Ryan tells us why he erased this part of his heritage, I'm sure we'd love to hear all about Houston," Geraldine said. "Straw. And perhaps you can tell us about your name, then."

"It's not an interesting story," Straw said.

"Even better! Then you won't have to tell us, and we won't have to feign interest while you bore us with it! Or you can just tell us what you've been sniffing ever since we sat down at the table."

"Grace, where is your bathroom?" Straw asked.

"There's a little powder room down the hall that way." Grace pointed.

Straw rose and left the dining room. A moment later, through an awkward silence, the sound of him urinating could be heard. He seemed to be aiming at the deepest part of the bowl.

Ever heard your voice on tape? When I was five, my mother recorded me singing Christmas carols: "Away in a Manger," "Silent Night, "Here Comes Santa Claus." Those I recall. She had me recite "'The Night before Christmas." I remember the adoring look on her face. I remember how proud I felt to have caused it. When she played it back for me in my early teens – she'd been saving it for the moment when it would mortify me the most – everyone else at the Christmas party laughed. My friends from school. My cousins Lisa and Joey. *God, Ryan, you sound like a total fag,* Lisa had said. *Is your mother like deaf or something?* From that point on, I couldn't listen to my own voice on tape without hearing Lisa's remark.

"I never liked the sound of my voice on tape," I told Geraldine, hoping I'd spoken sharply enough to make her drop the subject.

"Is that because you're from the South? Is there something wrong with sounding like a Southerner?" I swear to God she beefed up her own accent as soon as she'd decided to grill me.

"Kate, will you help me serve dinner? I think it's time to eat the entrees," Grace said, jumping to her feet. "Geraldine, would you like more wine?"

Don't give her more wine, what are you thinking?

In my head I was screaming, but I didn't say another word.

Normally Grace would serve the soup as a second course. This I remembered from rooming with her. Her homemade hot and sour soup put every restaurant version I'd ever tasted to salty, bitter shame. I excused myself from Geraldine's alligator gaze and hurried into the kitchen after Grace.

"Will you think I've devolved if I don't answer her question?"

Kate stepped into the kitchen.

"I'm so sorry!" she whispered. "She's never like this at the office!"

"It's none of her business," Grace said. She rinsed spinach leaves in the sink.

"I'll do the spinach," Kate said. "Why don't you serve the soup?"

Gabriel and Taro walked in.

"Grace, we have to get going," Taro said. "We have a plane to catch."

Grace hugged him and said it was OK. She thanked him for coming, for bringing Gabriel.

Gabriel took me aside: "That guy Warren likes you or something. After you left the room, he told Geraldine he was going to set himself on fire with a votive candle if she didn't stop interrogating you."

Grace dashed upstairs to retrieve their jackets, one black leather and one brown leather, then gave them each a goodbye kiss. "Have a great time in San Diego, love you both, Merry Christmas, and I hope your plane crashes because you're leaving us in the lurch, you bastards!"

Gabriel put his arm around Taro's waist. Great view walking away, I couldn't help but notice. Both of them. The buttocks were what buttocks ought to look like.

"Maybe I should pretend there's an emergency," Kate said as she tossed spinach into sesame oil. "We can just leave."

"Only if you come back later," Grace said. "Look, I have to take the soup in there. In fact, let's take everything that's ready."

"Don't do anything special on my account," I said. "Look, it's not a problem. It's not the first time in my life I've been asked inappropriate questions and it won't be the last. Just drug her wine and we'll all live happily ever after."

"No, I didn't go to speech therapy," I told Geraldine, looking her in the eye. "When I was 15, my parents split up. I went to live with my mother. She wanted me to record the outgoing message on the answering machine,

222

because she thought a man's voice would be safer. And I refused to do it. I was fine in everyday conversation but when I heard my voice on tape… I just couldn't. Then I graduated from high school and picked a university in DC to get away from the accents and in time, I started to sound like this."

"You still sound gay," Geraldine said. "That's what you're trying to hide, isn't it?"

She blew on a spoonful of soup and I wondered whether Grace kept any arsenic in the house. The teapot whistled.

"No he doesn't!" Kate exclaimed. "I wouldn't know he was gay if… if I didn't already know him."

"English isn't your first language," Geraldine said. "You don't hear accents as well. Ryan, you sound gay. Is that or is that not what you were trying to hide?"

A flush from the powder room meant Straw was still in there. I'd already forgotten about him.

Deep breath, Ryan.

"It wasn't about sounding gay or not," I started to say.

Geraldine interrupted: "It was a straightforward question, if you'll forgive the pun. I think you're using your Southern accent as an excuse. It's really that you didn't want people to know you were gay."

"I don't fucking care," I said. "I don't. It's there. If you can tell from my voice that I'm gay, great. I'm a big fag. Is that what you wanted to hear, or exactly the opposite?"

"Geraldine, maybe we should leave," Kate broke in, from the doorway.

"It's Christmas, Kate. Where are we going to go?"

"Down to the beach for a nice walk." Kate disappeared into the kitchen again. The smell of garlic in oil wafted our way, arousing an appetite I thought I'd lost.

"You don't have to leave, but like, *chill out,*" Warren said.

223

"This is your house?" Geraldine asked. "You live here? Grace, does Warren live here?"

"No he doesn't," Grace said. "Is there something wrong, Geraldine?"

"No, nothing at all. It's Christmas and I came with my friend and colleague Kate to have a nice rousing festive meal among good people. All I'm trying to do is keep the conversation lively. Is there anything wrong with that?"

"I'd say you're succeeding," I said.

"It's the stressed vowels," Geraldine said, staring me in the eye.

"What?" said several voices at the same time.

"When Ryan said *I'd say you're succeeding* just now. If I hadn't met him, I would know he was gay from his voice because it gets kind of faggy on the stressed vowels. The *ay* in *say* and the *ee* in *succeeding*." She followed this with: "*I'd sAY you're succEEding*."

"Oh my God," said Kate.

"Cocaine," announced Straw from the side of the room.

"It figures," Geraldine snapped.

"It was cocaine and I got the nickname Straw because I used to be a dealer and I always had this gold-plated straw for doing lines." He took his seat. "Anyone want a bump?"

Grace said "I'd love one" and Geraldine said "How dare you!" at the same time.

The teapot screeched. In the kitchen, Kate turned the burner off.

"Geraldine, do you think you could take it easy on Ryan and the rest of us?" Warren spoke up.

Straw cut lines on an overturned saucer for himself and Grace.

"I just can't believe this," Geraldine said. "You're snorting cocaine off the dining room table in front of your Christmas guests!"

"Believe it," Grace said.

"This is all about Ryan being gay, isn't it? What is wrong with me asking questions? This is San Francisco, isn't it? If we can't discuss issues like adults here, then where can we?"

"I don't think me being gay has anything to do with anything," I said.

Kate entered the room bearing a tray of tiny cups and a turquoise fired-metal teapot just in time to see Grace vacuum up a line of coke. Wisps of jasmine wafted when Kate gasped and dropped the tray.

"What the fuck are you doing?" Kate screeched.

"Coke," Warren said. "Want some?"

"You're taking drugs because Ryan is gay. Jesus," Geraldine said. "Don't even try to blame me for this one."

"Why would anyone blame you for anything?" Straw said, as he leaned back and tapped the side of his nose.

"Geraldine, when I said I'd set myself on fire if you didn't lighten up, I wasn't kidding," Warren said.

Geraldine covered her face with her hands.

"My husband left me last year at Christmastime," she said.

Silence fell with the abruptness of night in the mountains.

"Our son Jason had committed suicide one week before. He hanged himself on a doorknob with one of my husband's neckties. I believe it was the Brooks Brothers one I'd just bought him. Jason left a note."

Nobody spoke. Grace sniffled and broke the silence.

"Ryan, have you ever tried to kill yourself?"

I opened my mouth but no words would come out.

"Have you ever wanted to? Tell me. It's Christmas. Please, I have to know. Did you lie in bed at night trying to make yourself die by force of will? Because that's what Jason said in his note. He said we were making him so miserable he couldn't go on living."

225

"I... I've never wanted to... I mean, maybe I went through a phase once but I never seriously..."

"Oh for fuck's sake," Warren said.

He plucked a taper out of the candelabrum on the table and held the flame to his shapeless jacket. Grace and Kate screamed the loudest, and Warren started yelling, himself, as if he'd just realized what he'd done. The flames raced over his clothing. He staggered back and collided with one of Grace's strange white angel sculptures, which ignited.

Geraldine had sprung out of her chair and, with a glazed expression on her face, threw the contents of her wine glass in Warren's direction. I raced to the kitchen and looked around for a fire extinguisher – under the sink I found two. More practical of Grace than I'd have thought. In the dining room, Straw had backed up against the wall. Bloody mucus dripped from his nose. Two more of Grace's angels burned. Warren had somehow gotten his jacket off but he was still in flames.

"Somebody call 911!" I screamed, dousing him with foam from the extinguisher.

Grace got the other fire extinguisher; we managed to put the fires out.

We stood outside and waited for the ambulance and the fire truck to come.

A warm reddish-orange glow engulfed the foggy sky: sunset suffused the city with the color of smouldering coals. I imagined Grace's whole block going up in flames, then the next block, then the entire neighborhood. Fire engulfing San Francisco's Les Invalides look-alike City Hall. Financial District skyscrapers with their windows exploding from the heat. Something flaming in the Castro other than the population.

"Will Warren be OK?" Grace asked, hugging herself and shivering in the chill.

"I think so," I said. "I hope so. He wasn't on fire too long. But I don't

226

know what the hell he was thinking."

"Merry fucking Christmas," Grace said.

After:

Taro e-mailed Grace from San Diego and asked her to invite me out to dinner. I reminded them of another friend of theirs, Grace told me, and they wanted to introduce us. A week later we were sitting barefoot on cushions around low tables at her favorite Thai place, sipping Singha.

She had filed an insurance claim on the damage to her dining room and repaired the walls as quickly as she could, herself, fixing the superficial damage, and bringing in a contractor friend to do the rest. Cheaper that way. She threw out the remaining angels, too, and put her house on the market. All in seven days' time.

"Bad feng shui," she said as we waited for Taro and Gabriel. Our little plates of larb and spring rolls came. "My grandmother told me not to buy that house and as much as I hate to say it, she was right."

Gabriel and Taro arrived, both bundled up in black coats against the dreary Bay Area winter weather: rain, rain, and more rain. The warm sunny spell hadn't lasted long but the elaborate carved teakwood walls of the restaurant left us all feeling cozy enough. That, or the beer.

How was Warren, they wanted to know. Recovering, Grace said. Recuperating. Enjoying his Vicodin. She'd been by to see him at San Francisco General, and the burns really weren't too severe. Nor were they extensive. The doctors thought he might have more of a need for mental health services than burn treatments.

Had I called him? Well, no, my tolerance for creepy excesses of attention got kind of maxed out at that party. Geraldine Warren and Straw, oh my. If he liked me, great, but what would happen when he changed his

227

mind? Would he set my car on fire? Or my house? Me?

Gabriel laughed to himself. I got the sense I'd landed on the sort of private joke that couldn't be shared or explained.

And Geraldine? Not seen or heard from since. Kate assumed she would show up at work after the holidays but there was no way to know; she wasn't answering the phone. Kate would call Grace with any news, of course.

I thought *Good riddance* but kept my mouth shut.

"So this guy Andrew," Gabriel said. "I don't know if he's your type but I think you're his. Got plans for the New Year's countdown? The correct answer is No."

"No," I said.

"Good answer," said Gabriel.

"I told them you spent too damn much time writing your thesis, and they had to drag you out of your apartment. Find some nice boy to fuck your brains out," Grace confessed. "I know you're farting cobwebs these days."

A smiling waitress in lovely royal blue garments came to take our order, and I found myself thinking perhaps I didn't have to like Christmas but I could at least warm up to New Year's, if this was any indication of how things would go. Taro and Gabriel's drinks came, and we toasted burn victims, real estate, San Diego, deranged Southerners, and everything else we could think of.

SIMON SAYS

Simon never looked ethereal. I'd expect someone who grew up seeing ghosts to dress in black every day. I'd expect him to be gaunt and to chain-smoke foreign cigarettes, Gauloises maybe. The kind wrapped in black paper. Strong. Two puffs and you've got throat cancer. I'd expect him to have… well, never mind what I would expect. Simon was none of those things.

He did see ghosts, however.

Starting almost at birth, he told me. They'd swirl around in the air above his crib, sometimes trailing ectoplasm, sometimes not. Supernatural mobiles. Baby Simon would stare at them, eyes wide, and gurgle. They'd gurgle back. Other people in the family had the ability, but to a lesser degree. Simon's mother told me she saved a bundle on baby toys, since the poltergeists amused him far more effectively than anything manufactured by Fisher Price.

The ghosts taught him to speak, to read, and to write. When Simon told me that, I had to raise an eyebrow. But by that point I was both convinced he really could see specters and head over heels in love with him, so who was I to argue? Before most other kids could write their names, Simon had developed a beautiful cursive. He could speak a few other languages: Italian (the language of his paternal forebears, some of whom kept him company cribside), German, French, some Russian. Simon's mother had sense enough not to call in priests or attempt exorcisms on her own. A practical woman, she concluded that there was nothing wrong with free education, regardless of its source.

Rather than fostering dependence, Simon's ability produced the opposite result: he charged through life determined to succeed on his own merit, as single-minded as a spermatozoon. Had he wanted them to, his ghosts could have done all sorts of errands for him, getting even with children who were mean to him (any gay child is fair game for his peers), providing answers to test questions that stumped him, and so on. Somehow, Simon sensed he'd never amount to anything if he allowed this to happen. In grade school, he gave himself headaches from studying as long as his parents permitted before sending him to bed. He took up the piano and practiced for hours, finally recognizing his lack of a gift for music in high school. He locked himself in his room in his spare time and wrote poems he'd burn in college. Everything he did, he did with a sort of abandon.

Here's where I come in.

Until recently I had never seen a ghost. Or, rather, I had never seen one and known what I was looking at. As a child the idea of ghosts fascinated me; I checked out all the books the library had and skulked around graveyards hoping to catch a glimpse of something supernatural. I expected transparency, shrouds and ectoplasm, tendrils of fog, moans and groans. I got nothing. Growing up in the South contributed to my outlandish expectations. Southerners take for granted things people from other parts of the country would never even consider. My own mother and grandmother, born and raised in coastal North Carolina, superstitious to their cores, scared the piss out of me time after time with their ghost stories: the Devil's tramping ground, a patch of sand where no grass would grow because Satan liked that spot to pace and think; the phantom engineer, decapitated by his own train, forever walking up and down the tracks on foggy nights, swinging his lantern, searching for his head; the hitchhiker in the darkest part of the Croatan National Forest, a girl who would ask for a ride home, arrive, wait in the car for the driver to knock on her parents' door, then disappear while the occupants of the house explained how she had been killed in a wreck years before. I believed every word and never saw a thing.

Simon thinks we met once, in junior high school, when he visited cousins in North Carolina, but I don't remember. I think I'd remember a boy with dark red hair and brown eyes. By that age I felt pangs of interest in other boys and would have had a crush on him at first sight. He swears we met. I disagree. In any case, when we allegedly met, Simon's ghosts were in attendance. I never knew. He says he was sitting in a park talking with two of them, a great-aunt who died in Ireland (the other half of his lineage was Irish) years before his birth, and some other man from Russia who liked to follow him around. I walked by, stopped to say hello, noticed nothing unusual about the boy on the park bench, and kept going. The Russian, who could see parts of the future, told him who I was and what my role in his life would be. Simon tried to run after me, but I had already disappeared around the corner.

We met again 13 years later.

Living in Baltimore, slogging through my 2-L year at Maryland Law, not entirely sure what I'd do when I graduated, or even next week, I managed to hold onto some kind of social life in my rare moments of spare time. My friend Mark Tucker from undergraduate days at Rutgers had moved to DC and gone to work for some agency that contracted with the federal government. His work involved computers. He earned obscene amounts of money. He told me what he did. I could never remember. When Mark and I were seniors, he met Jeremy Glass, a 1-L at Penn Law. Love at first sight. They spent all their extra time (Jeremy didn't have much) on the phone, swapping e-mail, or commuting first between Philly and New

Brunswick, then between DC and Philly. Jeremy finished Penn and took a job with DOJ. They bought an old rowhouse on Capitol Hill and restored it. Marital bliss.

At their housewarming party:

I knocked first, doubted whether anyone would hear me over the pounding techno music inside, then tried the doorbell. Both the knocker and the doorbell surround were shaped like gargoyles. I looked up the block, hoping nobody would break into my new Corolla.

Mark opened the door a crack, peeked out, recognized me, grabbed me by the arm, dragged me inside, slammed the door shut behind us.

"Drinks are in the kitchen," he said after we kissed hello. "Get a beer or a glass of wine, say Hi to everybody you know, and meet me on the deck around back as soon as you can, OK?"

Off to my right, in the kitchen I guessed, I could hear someone trying and failing to open a bottle of beer:

"Where is the fucking bottle opener? God damn it, where did that thing go? I just saw it here not three minutes ago, and these motherfucking imports do not have twist-off caps."

Mark propelled me in that direction and slipped into the crowd.

The music got louder. Somebody shrieked.

I found a Michelob Dry and gloated discreetly as I twisted off the cap and threw it into the trash next to the guy who was still swearing at his bottle of Amstel Light. Didn't even miss the garbage can. I felt so manly I scared myself.

Mark materialized again.

"Get your ass out here now!" he hissed in my ear.

I followed him outside.

"Is something wrong?"

"No, you just live in Baltimore, that's all. I never get to see you, so I'm being selfish. It's my prerogative because we're in my house." He kissed me again.

"Careful, bud, you've got a husband."

"John, come on. Jeremy's not insecure; he doesn't have self-esteem issues; he wouldn't keel over dead if he saw me kiss my best friend I used to sleep with at Rutgers."

"No?"

Mark swigged his beer and shook his head. "His head's screwed on too well for that. He likes you, John. He's not the jealous type."

"Things are going well, then?"

They were. Mark felt the jitters because he and Jeremy were the people everyone said had been born for each other. This led to a certain pressure to be "on" all the time, to be perfect… never argue, never fight, make wild love five times each night. Mark loved Jeremy and loved being half of a pair of bookends, but he felt a little puzzled at the same time. They had the house. They had a black Lab named Sam. They had year-old European cars (a Volkswagen GTI and a Saab). They made a lot of money and invested it well. What more could anyone want? Or rather, *Now what?* Mark didn't know which question to ask, much less what the answer might be.

"You worry about everything. If you were to relax and enjoy the ride, you wouldn't be Mark anymore, you'd be someone else. I'm not sure I'd know him if I passed him on the street," I said, nudging Mark in the ribs.

I shivered in my jacket and drank more beer. Sooner or later the alcohol would kick in and I wouldn't notice the chill. Mark caught my gaze wandering and changed the subject for a minute; he knew me well enough to know when I'd maxed out on something. Come spring, he and Jeremy intended to landscape their backyard plot. Their south 40 consisted of a paved slab where they parked their cars, a narrow strip of earth next to the fence on each side, and the deck off the kitchen where we stood leaning against the balcony. My nose kept threatening to run. I wanted to move the conversation to a quieter spot but Mark seemed to prefer talking outside.

Then Simon walked into view.

"Thank God you were finished with that," Mark said when the beer bottle slipped from my hand, bounced off the wooden deck, and shattered on the pavement under the front bumper of Mark's GTI.

"He's beautiful," I said. Maybe that's not exactly how I put it, but I know I said something just as inane. "Who is he?"

"Simon Rossi. He's not your average gym-toned Ken doll but you can't take your eyes off him, can you?"

"Italian? With red hair?" In the age of Caesar cuts and goatees, Simon wore his hair longish and tied back in a ponytail.

"Half Italian, half Irish. I'd call that auburn, not red. Jeremy knows him better than I do. He says it's not from a bottle."

I wanted more beer: another bottle to hold, something for my hands to do. Mark laughed when I grabbed his Kirin, still half-full, and drained it dry. He promised (or threatened) to get Simon and introduce us.

"He's single, you know."

More inanity: "With his looks?"

"If you're into guys with hard bodies and small brains, he's not for you. This is a brainy town, but most of the fags here still chase after gym clones."

Beyond belief.

"He's had an interesting life, John. You should talk to him. You might hit it off."

For some reason the idea terrified me. My heart raced. I fidgeted and, when I took a step away from the balcony I'd been leaning against, realized it had pressed a wet line across the seat of my pants.

"I should have mentioned it rained here this afternoon. I take it

Baltimore was dry?"

"Never noticed," I said, eyes on Simon, who, God help me, was making his way through the crowd in the kitchen. Looking back, I can't call what I felt that night love at first sight, but I knew I was intrigued. Knowing what I know about Simon now, I don't mind labeling this a premonition of the most basic kind. Destiny in Levis and a heavy wool sweater. Coming my way.

"I'll introduce you."

He did.

Like Bambi in the headlights I stared at Simon when he stepped toward me and offered his hand to shake. Mark gave me a mischievous wink and disappeared into the house for fresh bottles of beer. When Simon and I attempted conversation it limped along on crutches like "Nice place" and "Yeah, they've done a lot of work to it." "Where did you go to school?" "What do you do?" That kind of thing. I'm surprised he didn't think I was as boring an asshole as I thought I was at the time.

Mark returned with Jeremy and more beer.

Jeremy was already drunk.

"You're both tongue-tied," he announced.

Simon and I looked at each other and blushed. His face turned as red as his hair.

Jeremy continued: "So stick out your tongues and compare knots. If you're both into bondage we've got a guest bedroom."

He and Mark exchanged a glance this time, nodded at each other. They communicated on a level I couldn't access, although I could guess where their thoughts were going. Mark and I went back a long way and had our own private channels; when he and Jeremy talked on their secret frequency I could often get the gist but not the meat of the message. I knew what the skeleton of this animal looked like.

"You're not," I said.

Mark and I lived in the same dorm as freshmen. Although the honors dorm had been designed as a quiet, bookish sanctuary free from standard underclassmen's antics, we partied as hard as anyone else. One popular trick involved pennies: three or four of them, wedged between door and frame, no exit for the occupants of the room.

"C'mon, don't protest," Jeremy said. "You two look as good together as we do. Step inside and go upstairs or I'll get out my cattle prod."

"Cattle prod?"

"For the tourists," Mark hastened to explain. "And people in malls at Christmas. Now, go!"

Half the people at the party got involved. Simon and I were herded into the room and pennied in; the party-goers cheered when the deed was done.

When Mark and Jeremy returned two hours later Simon and I didn't want to be bothered. Somehow a real conversation happened. Simon told me he had seen ghosts. He could speak German. He warmed up to me when he found out I knew Latin. My Southern origins fascinated him; growing up in Manhattan and, later, Connecticut, he had read books about the South, trying hard to imagine the sultry weather and magnolia trees. For me, the South was more about mosquitoes and rednecks. Every day, I felt a twinge of relief not to be living there, but I didn't want to argue the point with this beautiful man. Especially when he had stretched out on the floor with his head in my lap.

I stayed at his place in Adams Morgan that night. He wouldn't hear of me driving back to Baltimore at 3.00 in the morning. The next night he drove to my place. That's how we got started.

We moved in together a year later. I had just graduated from law school and had the bar exam to prepare for and dread, plus the inevitable rounds of interviews. Simon and I found a little tract house to rent out in Aspen Hill, a suburb 10 miles north of DC, up Connecticut Avenue and accessible to nothing; we moved in during the narrow gap between the end of my finals and the beginning of those interviews. I would have taken the plunge sooner, but commuting between the District and Baltimore every day, keeping a law student's hours, is only for people who don't need sleep.

We got through the standard newlyweds' arguments about whose sofa to keep (mine) and whose to discard (his), where to shop for a coffee table (he didn't want to default to IKEA like every other homo from DC to Boston; I couldn't see why not), whether to buy groceries at Giant or Super Fresh (neither of us cared enough about the issue enough to continue bickering). We bought furniture. We filled in the empty spaces. We used one bedroom, had two left: an office apiece. We shopped together for an aquarium (hexagonal) and managed to agree on which fish should occupy it (the low-maintenance kind: a pair of kissing gouramis, some barbs, and a catfish we named George Bush). We lovingly Windexed birdshit off each other's car windows. When I passed the bar Simon surprised me with a chocolate cake. When I got my first job he surprised me with a week in Provincetown. At home, we woke up every morning, blearily made coffee, stumbled downstairs to Soloflex and NordicTrack ourselves into something like wakefulness, performed the morning rituals, kissed long good-byes at the door before leaving for our jobs, mine at the law firm downtown, his at the World Bank. I liked my life... our life together. Then dead people got our phone number from God knows where (I wouldn't have thought they had 411 in the afterlife) and started calling at all hours.

The first time, I didn't know anything odd was happening. The phone rang just as we had finished playing around on the sofa. I had gone to retrieve a towel from the linen closet. Simon lay still, to avoid creating a stubborn stain on the upholstery. The phone rang. Out of the corner of my eye I saw Simon reach carefully for the cordless handset.

"Hello? Oh, Hans." His voice hardened. "*Guten abend.*" That was the only part I understood. I recognize German when I hear it and can pick out words here and there but I couldn't follow a fluent speaker, especially when he is pissed off. Simon unleashed what sounded like a string of invective, then dropped the phone on the floor.

"Hurry up before the come runs off my chest," he said, voice still tight.

I tossed him the towel.

"Who was that? I didn't think anyone you know in Germany had this number yet."

"My, umm... that was Hans."

The phone rang again.

The aquarium aerator stopped bubbling. Power outage, I guessed... all the lights in the house switched off at the same time. The refrigerator's faint mechanical hum ceased; the blue-green numerals on our entertainment gadgetry disappeared. I looked out the window to see who else had been affected.

"The lights are on down the street," I said.

"I'm not surprised. I think Hans is having a tantrum."

"Are you going to answer it?" was all I could think of to say.

"I might as well."

Simon picked up the phone. More German. He absently toweled away our post-conjugal stickiness and scorched this Hans person's ears. Then something happened I couldn't quite follow: in the middle of what I assume was a sentence, Simon paused. "Oleg?" He switched to Russian, smiling now. The lights came on. I understood even less Russian than German but I knew Simon's vocal inflections well enough to pick up on a few things. Simon sounded like he was talking to a friend he hadn't seen in years.

After a few minutes he rang off.

We stared at each other, still nude.

"Oleg wanted to congratulate us for moving in together. I haven't heard from him in ages. Well, once in a while, but not lately."

"Who is Oleg, again?"

"He's Russian. He was with me the first time I saw you."

"At Mark and Jeremy's housewarming party?"

"Before that, in North Carolina, when we were both in the eighth grade."

"I love you but you're a nut sometimes. An adorable nut, but still kind of a nut. Have I told you that before?"

He nodded.

"Oleg was born in a village near Tashkent. He's Uzbek but speaks – spoke – verb tenses get so complicated when you're talking about the dead – Russian. During World War II he was conscripted…"

"Wait a minute, Simon."

"Believe me," he said, looking me straight dead in the eye. "The ethnic Russian officers conducted their own ethnic cleansing long before the former Yugoslavs got around to it. They'd march regiments of boys from the Central Asian republics across minefields, to clear them, to keep their precious Russian and Ukrainian soldiers from being blown up. Oleg stepped on a mine in what is now part of Belarus."

"That's a hell of a long-distance call," I said. It was the first thing I could think of.

Simon nodded.

"Hans is from the same time period. I don't like him as much, but he has his uses."

"His uses?"

Simon sat up now, noticing (I guess) for the first time we were having this completely whacked conversation while sitting stark naked in our living room after sex. He pulled on his boxer briefs and stared into the aquarium, where our gouramis wrestled in a passionate liplock.

"Oleg can see the future, up to a point. Mostly he gives me stock quotes. With his help my investments have completely surpassed the market average in the last ten years. He warned me to get out before the crash in 1987, and he told me there'll be another one at the very end of the Nineties. I didn't inherit as much from my grandmother as I allow people to think."

I searched the pile of clothes by the sofa for my own underwear. It's one thing to say you believe in ghosts when you're a kid. Kids also believe in Tinkerbell in order to keep her from winking out like a candle flame. Kids believe in Santa Claus, the tooth fairy, and happy endings. It's expected. It's quite another thing to be a rational adult (a lawyer, for God's sakes) and be asked to accept that a dead Russian, excuse me, a dead Uzbek, gives you great stock tips from the hereafter. Especially when the news is shared while you're covered in come after sex on the sofa. This is more or less what I said to Simon.

He blinked at me. I had never seen him look more haunted.

"I haven't seen any ghosts up close since we moved in together. Most of them are respectful enough to allow me some space. Unlike Hans. Hans was on the crew of a U-boat. He was a Nazi. Claims he sank the Lusitania. I think he has a lech for me."

"Then I'll call him back and tell him if he lays an ectoplasmic finger on my boyfriend I'll come after his ass, dead or not."

"What?" Simon actually looked alarmed.

"Star 69," I said.

The phone rang a couple of times on the other end. I expected but did not get the taped recording: *We're sorry. This service is not available for the number of your last incoming call.* The ringing stopped, but instead of an answer I got silence. Dead air. I pressed the phone closer to my ear and strained to hear anything in that void. I seemed to pick up voices in the background, very faint, speaking in languages I didn't recognize.

"Hello?" I asked. I didn't like this. Too real. "Is anyone there?"

Simon reached up and took the phone away from me. He turned it off, then crossed the room and turned off the ringer. His normally olive skin had gone a shade of pale whiter than I had ever seen. His eyes were huge, and sweat shone on his brow.

"It's real, John. I'm not making this up. Remember the first night we met? I told you I had seen ghosts. I just didn't mention that I had seen them more than once, or that it was a regular thing."

How could I doubt a man whose face looked like that? Simon looked scared. I knelt on the carpet next to the sofa where he had stretched out, and cupped his face in my hands. I kissed him.

"I don't know what I heard, and I don't remember seeing you in the park, but I don't think you're crazy." I hugged him. "What do we do now?"

"We get dressed and fix something to eat, we brew a pot of coffee, and I tell you the rest of the story."

We talked late into the night. He did most of the talking, to tell the truth. As I listened I felt increasingly uneasy, not out of doubts about his sanity but out of (this shocked me) belief. Our kitchen with its cheerfully dowdy yellow wallpaper, its refrigerator covered with magnets shaped like farm animals (cows amused Simon to no end), the smell of the vegetables I stir-fried, was no place for a story like this. My chair creaked a little when I leaned back in it. If someone wanted to talk about growing up haunted, the place for that was a big spooky old house with suits of armor in each room, battle axes decorating the walls, white dustcloths draped over all the furniture, and one black rotary phone in a cubicle under the stairs. Not here.

I know more now than I did then.

This weekend Jeremy, Mark, Simon, and I decided to drive up to Philadelphia for a change of scene. After that phone call from Hans and Oleg, a certain equilibrium returned to Simon's and my life. Simon's ghosts flocked back but kept a fairly low profile, or so he told me. I could sometimes tell when he saw something I couldn't: he'd just stare fixedly at a point in space. I never heard him talking to thin air, to his credit. A fractured sort of peace reigned, but I had a sense of something being about to happen. And I'm as psychic as your average two-by-four. Simon's ghosts (Oleg, I assumed) weighed in with the occasional forecast about which stocks to buy or unload, which roads to avoid, and the like. Benignly unobtrusive. Simon and I grew a bit wealthier. He traded his Saturn for a blue BMW. We got a cat and named her Bicker because that's what we did for two days, trying to settle on a name. Simon rarely mentioned ghosts, and if any poltergeist activity was taking place it was too discreet for me to see. I suppose this is what it's like to live with HIV: you get on with your daily life but in the back of your mind you remain vigilant.

South Street is Philadelphia's urban hip strip. Funky shops proliferate. Pierced twentysomethings browse in thrift shops or buy CDs next to buff gay boys and middle-aged tourists. Lines form at the cheesesteak restaurants. None of us had been there since Jeremy graduated from Penn Law. Simon had never been at all.

"You'll never find a parking spot in this crowd," Jeremy said.

He thought Simon was either naïve or crazy to drive into the one-way congestion on South Street and expect to find a place to leave his car and had said so twice already.

"Oh, I think I will. I'm lucky that way."

Simon winked at me.

I mouthed, "Oleg?"

He nodded.

True to form, Simon found the perfect spot in front of Tower Records. A blue Mitsubishi 4x4 left the space just ahead of us and to the right. Simon claimed the spot and graciously did not gloat over it to Jeremy.

We spent the next few hours browsing, relieved to be away from Washington for the day. The plan was to spend the afternoon on South Street, have a late dinner, then go out dancing, close the place down, then find a hotel afterward to crash for a few hours. Of course it didn't happen that way.

In the depths of an antique store, where Jeremy and Mark had dragged us to look at fixtures for their house, my cell phone rang. This wouldn't have raised any red flags, but I always kept it turned off until I had to make outgoing calls. Always. Oblivious, Mark picked up a stained-glass window and held it up for Jeremy's approval. Simon looked at me instead.

"This is probably for you," I said, holding the phone at arm's length.

His eyes widened and he looked over my shoulder, not at Jeremy, Mark, or their window, but at something only he could see. His face darkened.

"Oh shit." He took the phone.

"What is it?" With a grunt, Mark put the window down.

Simon's voice broke: "My mother and sister were killed about an hour ago." I moved to put my arms around him. "It was a car wreck… I saw them just now. Before your phone rang."

"They were here?"

He nodded. His chest hitched; he was trying not to cry.

"We need to go home right away," I said, trying to take charge of the situation before it slipped irretrievably into the Twilight Zone. Jeremy and Mark did not ask Simon to clarify what he meant by seeing his mother and his sister.

Walking back to the car, Simon leaned over to me and whispered, "It's worse than you know. Hans did it."

"What?"

Simon nodded. His eyes welled with tears; one broke free and ran down his cheek.

"You think I'm insane," he said.

I shook my head No. "My cell phone was off when it rang, Simon."

He nodded.

"This isn't easy. This isn't how we're taught the world works."

"Surprise, surprise." He barked a short laugh. "Ever wonder which other basic truths aren't really true?"

"Every day. Here's the car. Give me your keys; I don't want you to drive back."

He agreed he shouldn't drive. Jeremy and Mark huddled together, saying nothing, obviously sensing something wrong beyond what they already knew. I promised myself I'd find some explanation by the time we got home. Driving would help clear my mind.

Simon's car permitted me to make much better time than I would have in my practical little Toyota. I had us home in two and a half hours, most of which passed in silence. I noticed Simon seeing things whose nature I could only guess. My stomach and bowels lurched and knotted in fear of what revelations he'd have for me after Mark and Jeremy left our house. They offered to stay for moral support if Simon wanted that, but he declined, and kissed them goodbye. We promised to keep them posted.

Finally we were alone.

"It's a lot worse than I thought. Some of this won't make sense because you can't see Hans and the others, but trust me on this one, okay?"

I started brewing a cup of coffee to keep my hands busy.

"I told you I thought he had some kind of lech for me?"

I nodded.

"I guess I was right. My mother came back to warn me: he'll come after me now. She and my sister were like an experiment. He scared the driver of an oncoming truck; he lost control and hit them head-on. Now they're in the same place Hans is. I don't know how or why, but they are. I thought they'd be somewhere else, but…"

I sat on the kitchen floor and traced the patterns in the linoleum. I didn't want to be having this conversation. My stomach writhed like a vat of eels; I wanted to vomit, to run outside where the cold air would shock me back into the real world where ghosts didn't exist at all. My head started to pound, a baby migraine taking its first faltering steps; I figured I had half an hour before it reached full gallop.

"Hans has always said he wanted me to be with him forever, but I basically dismissed that. I never though he'd be able to do anything about it."

"What can you do now?"

Simon looked bleak. "I don't have a clue. As much as possible, I've always pushed the ghosts away. You know that. I mean, I've always known I'd never have a normal life like everybody else, but I've tried to minimize the impact the ghosts would have on me. Maybe I should have been paying attention."

"You have to do something," I said.

"I know."

We sat at the table drinking coffee laced with Bailey's, waiting for the phone to ring. Over the next few hours Simon's father and brother called from Hartford and Chicago. Relatives were already on planes from Ireland

245

and Italy. Arrangements were being made. Simon decided he'd leave first thing in the morning. He jotted down phone numbers for me. I'd join him two days later.

"I think I need to spend a few hours in the office with Oleg and a few of the others," Simon said after the last call from his family.

I nodded.

I kissed him.

I followed him through the house and watched him close the door to his office. He shut off the light. I heard a match being struck: candles. This was the last time I saw him alive.

I fell asleep channel-surfing. When I awoke a talk show was blaring from the TV, some asinine story about trailer park dwellers who kept large pets. A big-haired woman named Gert from west Texas lived with two goats in her mobile home. I tried to imagine the smell during an El Paso summer and almost puked at the thought. The coffee and Irish cream roiled like lava in my stomach. I switched to the Weather Channel, my favorite soporific, and wondered whether I should knock on the door to Simon's office.

He didn't answer when I tried.

I opened the door, saw him on the floor, not breathing, and started to scream. I'm not really sure what happened next. 911. At some point I must have called Mark and Jeremy, because they were there. And the EMTs, the ambulance, defibrillators…

Last night I saw my first ghost. I expected my first sighting to seem alien and bizarre, but that's not how it happened. The experience felt so normal. The ghost was Simon, of course. I was so glad to see him I forgot he was dead.

"You're here," I said, reaching for him.

He lay next to me in bed. He felt solid and warm as real life.

"I'm here."

I started crying again. "I can't live without you. I don't want to."

He held me. "John, don't."

For a long time we lay like that, his arms around me, him dead, me alive, until I had cried myself out.

"Why now? Why are you back?"

"I took care of Hans. Hell doesn't exist – not the way the Baptists would have people believe – but Hans is in the closest thing there is. He'll never be a problem again, not for me or anyone. I wanted you to know."

"Why did you leave me?"

"It was the only way we could think of to stop him. Oleg, the aunts, a few others. We made plans for hours while he laughed at us. He didn't think it would work, but I surprised him."

"Can't you come back? That's the only part that matters now."

"I wish I could. But it doesn't work that way. You know that."

"I don't know anything anymore. You saw to that."

Simon said nothing in response to that. Finally: "I miss you too."

Eventually, late that night, I fell asleep. Simon and I talked for hours. I had an idea and convinced him of its merit. He cried this time, and I did, but we couldn't find any other way out of our predicament. I didn't want to spend the rest of my life sleeping with a dead guy, basically, and I didn't like the idea of waiting for him to reincarnate and becoming a pedophile or, worse, him coming back straight. That left only one option.

I called in sick at work today.

I put my affairs in order.

Remember high school, when you read Poe? "We loved with a love that was more than a love." Only I'm not going to dig Simon up to be reunited with him.

He'll be back for me at midnight. He said he can do it for me the way Oleg did it for him: I'll just close my eyes. There won't be any pain.

My ashes will be scattered in the same place as his.

Together forever.

Marital bliss.

THE GLUE FACTORY

1.

Clouds stain the horizon: an ice storm, according to the television. Starting late this afternoon, at the height of rush hour, the northern suburbs can expect to be coated with freezing slush. The people here drive like clowns on cocaine. Since I am far to the north of the city, an hour from where suburbs give way to farms and forests, it's probably sleeting already. I'm being kept deep underground in a room warm enough to make most clothing too hot to wear. Despite the heat, these images of the storm-darkened sky send chills rippling through me. Stifling in here, Antarctica outside, and I am naked. I am naked.

2.

Who's crazier?

Me, or him?

Him, because he runs this inferno? This Factory? Profits are up, demand can't be met, the machines roar and the vats boil day and night. Garish blue labels are applied to the bottles, which are then packed into cardboard cartons. Conveyor belts convey an endless stream of product (that's what the Emperor calls it, *product*) to a fleet of trucks. The trucks dispatch the cartons to points around the country. Orders are pouring in from all over! And he barely sleeps. Only when he thinks nobody is looking. There are so many demands on his time. Always, some problem takes him away from his rooms. From me.

Or me? Am I the one who's nuts? Probably so, because I despise him and I am infatuated with him in equal measure. He keeps me here. He is my heroin and I am addicted to him, I cannot get enough of him, I want my mouth to be salty with the taste of him. I want the smell of him on my body. If it means I have to stop showering and brushing my teeth then so be it. The blood he comes to me smeared with, I will preserve it like sacred oil; I will anoint myself every morning and night. I want him on my tongue. I want him to leak from my pores. I want him to crawl inside my skin and become one with me. I cannot be filled up with him enough to become content. If I become him, then there will be no more me, and I will not have to hate myself. I can hate him instead.

3.

Blind slaves labor on machines. All of them can see and all of them are employees on a payroll but they hold their heads down, gluing labels pushing buttons pulling levers, not free to leave until the Emperor sounds the whistle, not free to quit without his permission, not free to eat or piss or place a telephone call unless he allows it: *slaves*. I cannot tell them apart by the end of the day. They are filthy. Sweat sluices through the grime that cakes their bodies. The first time I saw the Factory floor

I swooned. I was unsteady on my feet, recovering from grievous injuries, and the smell overpowered me. Locker-room abattoir urinal stink. I could feel greasy molecules of stench coating my sinuses when I inhaled. Great dark machines loom, roaring monoliths. When I passed over the floor on a catwalk I felt myself becoming slimy. The Emperor saw the gleam in my eye, saw the blush rising through my pallor, and smiled.

"All this is mine," he said in a voice as rich as rotting meat, barely audible over the din below.

He took my hand and led me back to his quarters. He had sewn my stitches himself, by hand, daring me to cry out when the thick needle penetrated my flesh. He had pulled coarse thread though a deep wound in my leg, then coated the area with salve. With *glue*. I had lain in a dark room for days, fed chunks of roasted meat and dry bread, with metallic water to drink from a battered tin mug. Primitive, I know, but I'm not in the world any longer. I'm here. When the gash had closed up, the Emperor cut the stitches with a pair of scissors too dainty for his ham-hock hands, showing a rough delicacy as he snipped. I winced when he jerked the stitches free. He used his teeth. I got an erection. *I will show you the Factory*, he'd said. *Come.* I followed. I surprised him. He hadn't expected me to like what I saw.

4.

We drove out to the Factory, made our way over the fences at the perimeter of the property, and broke in: Joshua, Erich, Reynaldo, and me. Was it curiosity? Stupidity? Has anyone ever found a way to tell them apart?

Rey had heard rumors: "They use meat."

Josh was scornful: "Well, yeah, of course. That's what kids always say about glue. It's made of horse meat. They put horses in an enormous vat and boil them down until there's nothing left but mush and a few teeth."

"That's disgusting," Erich said.

"It's protein, isn't it?" What had made Josh fixate on the Factory? It had been open a year. This corner of the state had been prosperous once… but not recently. The Factory irrigated a withering region with jobs and cash. So people spread sinister rumors to make life seem more exciting than it really was. This is the story of the human condition. Josh cared, because… ? "That's why it works so well. If that's what they use. I bet it is."

"People say that about Chinese food, too," said Erich. "It's not really pork and beef you're getting, it's Fido and Fluffy. What a load of crap."

Rey protested. "But I've heard it's not horses. I've heard they send out trucks to the morgues and the graveyards. It's bodies. It's people."

"Bullshit. I heard that the Factory buys up the… I don't know what to call them, *leftovers* from stockyards and slaughterhouses, but no corpses. No body parts. That's morbid," I said.

"So we should go look," Joshua said. "We can take my car."

His father had bought him a new Citroën for his birthday: sinuous, black, very fast. After our token resistance ("We'll get caught" and "What about school?") faded, we couldn't say No. Students are like that.

5.

I shouldn't have fallen asleep in the car as we drove out of the city and into the vast green expanse of nothingness beyond the suburbs. Then I might have had a better idea how to get home. This is what I thought when we were attacked. But I couldn't help it at the time. Erich and I took the back seat. I dozed off with my in his lap, his cock stiff against my cheek. Rey and Josh wouldn't have cared about me unzipping Erich's jeans, taking him in my mouth; they'd have been happy to watch. I thought about it. I wanted to. Erich stroked my hair. They didn't know we'd been up late feasting on each other the night before, tasting each other here, licking this, swallowing that. I sucked honey off his cock and he poured white wine down the length of mine to catch the Chardonnay stream in his mouth. He came with my two fingers deep inside him, his salt spilling over my tongue and mixing with the sweetness of the honey. We hadn't gotten much sleep. It couldn't be helped.

6 .

"Lions!" Josh, who had taken the lead, screamed.

It had been too easy to break in: no alarms, no sentries with rifles, just a high chain-link fence, easily climbed. No strand of barbed wire at the top, even. The Factory loomed beyond, a featureless grey monolith. Dense smoke, the same color grey as the building's façade, billowed from a pair of smokestacks. We stopped and stared, then caught sight of something rushing toward us. The approaching shapes looked like tremendous dogs at first, and dogs would have been bad enough. Then I recognized the matte golden color of their coats. Joshua turned and sprinted back the way we had come. He was the tallest, with long cross-country legs; he moved fast. The fence lay only a hundred yards behind us. Rey seemed frozen to the spot where he stood, a dozen feet ahead of Erich and me.

In the split-second we had, I made a fast choice: "Run!"

I gave Erich a shove. We raced behind Josh toward the fence, screaming Rey's name but knowing there wouldn't be enough time to reach him before the lions did. With the agility of a squirrel, Joshua scaled the fence. Erich stumbled. I pushed him upward against the fence, away from me, hesitated long enough to see him climbing, then started up, myself.

I almost made it: three-quarters of the way up, high enough to be feeling sure of myself, and then came the swipe of a tremendous paw. The world went red. In a moment of weightless blankness, I tottered. I almost lost my grip on the fence.

Erich, at the top, grabbed my flailing arm and hauled me up before the lions made a dessert of my bowels.

We almost got away.

Even now, when I sleep in the Emperor's cell, I grieve my losses. In my nightmares I still hear the sounds of the animals, eating.

7.

Men in dark blue uniforms caught us climbing down the fence on the other side, and led us at gunpoint into the monolith. The lions, mysteriously, stopped eating Rey after taking several bites out of him. They padded back toward the building. Maybe he tasted bad. I'd never noticed, myself. Or maybe they were remote-controlled and someone had pressed a button. A black bank of clouds sun had eaten the sun, and cold rain started to fall. I think the men led us by Rey's mangled remains out of sadism. The lions had torn out his throat and ripped open his belly. Rain washed his blood into the grass. Organs gleamed. Dead brown eyes stared at a point in space above and behind our heads.

"How can you look?" Joshua asked, his voice breaking.

"I want to remember what they did to him," I said.

8 .

"One of you will die, one of you will stay here, alive, and one of you will leave."

"What do you mean?" Josh protested. "You can't do that!"

"Look at me," the man in the raw meat coat said. "Look closely. Think about what you see."

I saw a tall, dark man, hugely muscled, in a cloak assembled from cuts of raw meat. Thick steaks somehow attached, still bleeding, still shiny with the fluids of whatever beast they'd been carved out of, marbled with white fat. This expanse of sartorial carnage extended to the floor. His collar, the breasts of some kind of fowl. His belt, intestines I assumed, tied around a single white bone. He wore no shirt, only boots and some kind of leather pants, as rough-hewn as he himself was.

"I am the law here. What I say goes. The four of you broke in. One has already died. His remains are going to be boiled down. One more of you will join him. One of you will stay with me, here. The other will go home and tell people not to break into to the Glue Factory."

"But that's murder!" Josh said.

"Your local authorities are paid to look the other way," said the man in the raw meat coat. "And the judges here are the best money can buy. We are the largest contributor to the local economy. You know as well as I do how fond the local people are of the students at your college. This is a public service."

"It's still murder, and it's wrong. You should let us go," Josh said.

I marvelled at Josh's boldness: he stood only as high as the raw man's nose, but he didn't back down.

The raw man nodded at two other men, who stood behind him.

"Vat 3-B," he said.

They descended on Josh. Erich tried to stop them. They shoved him aside. I could not move without fresh thunderbolts of pain ripping my leg apart, so I lay helpless and watched the two men hold Joshua down. One of them produced a large scissors from his dark blue robe-like garments. He cut away Josh's clothing like a nurse in an emergency room might have done in a different crisis. Josh's screams and struggles amounted to nothing.

"Don't overlook the piercings," the man with the raw meat coat said.

One of the thugs caught the stud at the corner of Josh's eyebrow between thumb and forefinger, tore it out, then did the same thing with the hoops in his earlobes.

"The remains of his friend are still fresh. Put them in the same vat. That's where this afternoon's shipment from… I don't remember where it's from, just add them to the new batch."

Joshua screamed himself hoarse as the thugs dragged him out of the room, naked, writhing, pissing in terror. They dragged him through a puddle of his own urine. Erich and I clutched at each other. I felt cold all over, and would have thrown up if there had been anything in my stomach.

"You will leave because you are unhurt," the man in the raw meat coat told Erich. "This one is going into shock. I'll keep him. You have exactly four minutes to make it back to your car and drive away. The keys should be in your friend's clothes here. If I see you again, I will have you rendered down to a stew of protein and bones. Is that clear?"

"Go," I told Erich.

"I'll send help."

"Just be safe."

I think his parting kiss told the raw man everything he needed to know.

9.

"The product we make here has revolutionized the field of adhesives technology," said the Emperor, carrying me in his arms like a virginal bride on her wedding night. Fluids from his cloak of flesh soaked through my clothes but warmed me up instead of leaving me colder. The world felt far and wee. "The demand is unparalleled. Wounds close in half the time. Only the deepest, like yours, need stitches."

"I thought this was a Factory that made glue for paper dollhouses and flowers," I said, delirious.

"Our lesser product goes to that purpose, but the highest-grade adhesive we make is of surgical quality. Look down."

Below, I saw a conveyor belt delivering gigantic, gutted carcasses into a vat the size of a garage. Clouds of bloody steam issued from vats farther down the production line. Meat, melting. Bones, being boiled. Images blurred together: one tremendous maw to pulverize the living and the newly-deceased (I thought I saw Josh down there, dry-heaved, then offered a feeble farewell wave), vats to melt the flesh down to its component proteins and amino acids, tubes and pipes and belts. There were some kind of chemicals involved. It all ran together into one overwhelming, erotic nightmare of the flesh. HR Giger himself had probably been commissioned to design the Factory floor.

The Emperor stroked my hair. The smell of him overwhelmed me, engulfed me. He could not have failed to notice my jutting cock.

"Are you going to boil me alive and make me into Elmer's School Glue?" I asked him.

"If you die, yes, I probably will," he said.

"Then I won't die."

10.

I healed in my cell.

The Emperor (this is what the raw man had instructed me to call him, and that is truly the best word for his role here: Emperor) cut out my stitches in his quarters, then lay me down on his coat of flesh. By some miracle, there were no flies. Only candles and incense, and butcher's diagrams on every wall.

"What keeps it from spoiling?" I asked him, luxuriating.

I had never known I'd find the idea of lying naked on a steak the size of a dining room table arousing, but there it was. I did. The steak was warm to the touch: skin. Meat. When I pressed down with my fingertips, juices collected in the little indentations I made. Little pools of blood. The crescents of my fingernails browned.

"Nothing. It rots. We throw it into a vat, and two weeks later schoolchildren glue bits of paper together with it. When the time comes, I have a new one made. There are people here who do that for me."

"You take whatever you want, don't you?" I asked.

He nodded. Looking down at me, he seemed eight feet tall, solid muscle. This is how Ares, the Greek god of war, must have looked after battle. Bloody, built, beautiful. I detested him. I craved him. I wanted to abase myself in a defeat that ached like victory.

"We take the homeless. We heal wounds. We accept the newly dead from hospitals to avoid filling cemeteries. We are rebuilding the economy in this part of the state. I see this as good," he said, undoing the leather pants.

"My leg has healed quickly," I said. "That's indisputable."

"I'm going to keep you here." His voice, rich as the blood in the jar by this bed, smooth as the rendered fat he smeared over my body, was an aphrodisiac. Naked, he knelt next to me, ladling the fat over me, spreading it. "This came from your friends, you know."

There just weren't words.

"But I let you live." He coated his cock with the stuff, then turned me over and lubricated the opening of my ass. Both Josh and Rey had been inside me before, but not like this. "Remember that. I chose you, and I let you live."

And then he followed Rey and Josh.

11.

This went on for weeks.

12.

I learned the workings of the Factory: trucks brought in loads of bodies and body parts all day and all night. The highest-quality surgical glue came from flesh fed to the vats still living. The kindergarten stuff came from slaughterhouse offal. Intruders could wind up in either product. We'd send the lions to intercept them. On a monitor in his rooms, the Emperor would watch the feast for a time. Very entertaining. Then he would press a button and signal the lions to stop. He would dispatch men with tongs and carts.

I learned the shifts and the routines, the names of the machines.

I learned the working of the Emperor's body as days turned into weeks. He would untie the bone from the coil of flesh around his waist, dip it into a pot of rendered fat, and pleasure me with it. He showed me which spots to touch, where to put my fingers or my tongue, when to hold my breath, how to lose myself – and find myself – in him. I stayed drunk on his bloody come; there seemed to be no end to the supply.

And in the back of my mind, a single thought lingered: Erich?

13.

I've decided that seizing power is like having sex: timing is crucial when you spot the right opening. The Emperor had bent me over the handrail of one of the catwalks above the Factory floor. He'd buried himself up to the hilt in me, not caring if one of the sweat-grimed drones down below should happen to look up. He held absolute sway over them all. Did they want their kids to eat? Did they want their lights to stay on? Then they would do what they were told.

So big, I thought. Huge. He'd stretched me wider than I thought humanly possible. I knew how Vlad the Impaler's victims felt, dying on their spikes.

The semen spurted out of me and landed on one of the workers below. He didn't look up. He absently wiped the droplets off his upper arm without giving them a second thought.

That night, the Emperor made the permanent mistake of not locking me away in a cell when he slept. He'd grown complacent. I choked him on his belt of intestines, then snapped the bone he'd pleasured me with (it was still wet) and speared his jugular vein with it. Blood fountained. He marinated his coat of raw flesh in his own juices. When I summoned his attendants, I'd have the spot that tasted most like him grilled medium well and served up with a glass of Cabernet Sauvignon. I watched the Emperor thrash, clutching the bone jutting out of his neck. His eyes glazed over, fixed the same point in space Rey's had, some uncountable time before.

His attendants came when I called.

"Vat 3-B," I told them, pointing at the tremendous corpse.

I stood before them as bloodied as the Emperor's corpse on its dais of meat, unabashed, challenging them with my own nudity. I didn't blink, didn't look down.

"Keep the bloodiest part of his cloak for the cooks," I told them. "You know what to do with the rest of it. I won't be needing another."

I hesitated.

"Actually, something in linen, I think, if anyone here has a tape measure. And have someone send a car for my friend Erich."

14.

Dark clouds stain the horizon above, and a winter storm threatens.

The Factory produces glue 24 hours a day, 7 days a week. We take the homeless. We heal wounds. We accept the newly dead from hospitals to avoid filling cemeteries. We are rebuilding the economy in this part of the state.

And Erich is with me, deep underground in this warren of rooms.

We eat well, and we are useful.

I see this as good.

THERE AND BACK

Anyone who has ever read a literary journal or seen a subtitled movie knows that people who live at the periphery of civilization have more meaningful lives than us schmucks from the American suburbs. Had I been born in Dubrovnik instead of Frederick, Maryland, I could have been a plucky peasant lad carted off to the killing fields when President Tudjman expelled the Serbs from the Krajina in an offensive that elicited nothing more than a certain amount of hand-wringing from the Western European and North American media. I could have had adventures, stared death in the face, and returned home (missing an earlobe and part of my nose) to the rubble that had been my family's apartment. In the aftermath, I'd loiter in cafés drinking pitch-black coffee and waiting for Reuters to feature me an article about the resilience of youth in the postwar Former Yugoslavia. At least when my parents got killed (by mortar fire instead of the Metroliner) I wouldn't have learned I'd been written out of the will because they disapproved of my loathsome homosexual lifestyle, praise Jesus and pass me a snake. They wouldn't have known.

As an American, I didn't stare death in the face but I did catch a glimpse of the reaper in profile. He zoomed by me fast, low, looking kind of stately (picture a nun on a broomstick); his robe brushed against my left thigh, just below my crotch. The same afternoon a train wreck conjugated my immediate family from the present tense into the past perfect, messily, I sprouted an otherwise inexplicable rash. My dermatologist called it jock itch and prescribed a tube of goo to smear on the affected region. The goo made a decent lubricant, so I masturbated with it twice and probably caused the pharmacist to raise an eyebrow when I called back the same afternoon for a refill. The following day, both my family and my rash were gone, just like that. All I had left were the estate and some residual itching and redness.

In college on the West Coast, somewhat guilty on account of all the grief I should have felt but didn't, I weighed options. I turned them over like eggs in the grocery store, checking for breakage and bad odors. Interesting: the 'rental units had intended to leave everything to my sister. Conveniently, she was on the way to New York with them when the train derailed. The will didn't address the chance all three might die together. Oops. The estate, valued at a number ending in lots of zeroes, defaulted back to me.

Can you tell I didn't have much regard for my sister, either? And that it was mutual?

If I sound like a ghoul, well, then, I guess that makes it official: I'm a ghoul. I'm a heartless bastard. Run. And I intended to revel in my ghastliness. First, I resolved to imitate Liberace (before he died) and cry all the way to the bank. I could have afforded to fly back East for the funeral, but assuming I could have found a nonstop, that would still have required me to spend five and a half hours in flight. All that, or God forbid, a red-eye, just to yawn my way through the exequies? *So* not worth it. The 'rentals wouldn't have cabbed across town for mine.

The attorneys and I sent each other faxes. There were a couple of phone calls. I told them to liquidate everything as soon as possible, and FedEx me a check.

Why not just do the disaffected student thing, I thought, travelling hither and yon with a laptop (the purists in the audience may insist on writing longhand with their blotchy fountain pens in their leather-bound journals. Let them. As far as I'm concerned, the Middle Ages ended a few centuries ago, and I'll keep my Toshiba), a backpack, and an endless supply of French cigarettes? I could afford an extended spring break. There was nothing else going on in my life.

My friend Robert's motto: *Fake it 'til you feel it.* As an alternative to proclaiming that I was, in fact, torn up over this, just to shut people up, I considered checking myself into a psychiatric hospital. Why not? It sounded more interesting than the midterms I hadn't studied for. I called my friend Jessica's shrink, talked to him for a few minutes, found myself on the psych ward by sundown. Within two hours I knew it had been a bad idea. I was stuck there another 70. Picture a military school run by Mr. Rogers, with catering by K-Mart. *OK, fuck it, I'll just get out of here and spend the money*, I thought. My friend Julian's girlfriend's girlfriend Babette had gone to Israel to clear her head after her father got pulverized in a car wreck one year before. Babette lingered in Tel Aviv smoking a pack of Gauloises a day, drinking vodka straight from the bottle, and dodging Palestinian nail bombs. An art major, Babette returned to school, painted a series of canvases using a mixture of creosote, cigarette ashes, and cobalt blue, cut off all her hair, and, bald, jetted off to the Scottish Highlands to continue trying to find herself. She hasn't been heard from since, unless you count one letter containing a bit of something spongy and grey: *This is a piece of my lung – I've started coughing them up, but my head is clearer now, Love, Babette.* If you want to take a leave of absence from society and can choose between the Wonder Bread Lite version of *One Flew Over the Cuckoo's Nest* and, for example, Malta, opt for the Mediterranean. If one more dumpy woman in mismatched athletic gear, with a dyed black bird's nest of hair, mushroom-underbelly complexion, and enough scars on her wrists for a platoon of schoolchildren to play Tic Tac Toe on ever comes into my room wailing that people in the Morning Check-In Group think her feelings aren't valid, I'm buying an AK-47 and visiting the nearest mall.

At my apartment, I threw underwear into a duffel bag, added a pair of jeans and a couple of sweaters, and ran. Hadn't changed the oil in my old Volkswagen in months. For some reason the engine still started when I turned the key. Clouds of blue smoke farted out of the exhaust pipe when the engine rattled to life. Did it matter now? When I got back I'd buy something new. Between flights at JFK, I called my landlord and asked him to pick up my mail. Left a couple of voice mail messages telling people I had taken off and to hang out until I got home.

People I didn't call:

My boss, Hugo Perez. I worked at the library part time for extra money. Shelving books agreed with me because I got to read, but the library's HVAC system had to be a biological warfare experiment gone awry, what with all the sinus infections I developed. I resented my job. When you're boiling ramen noodles for dinner your third night in a row, and your father has just bought a weekend house on the Outer Banks of North Carolina, something's not right. While alive, the parents were monsters with me when it came to finances. Dead, they'd come in handy. As for Hugo, fuck him, the library could hire another clerk for $7.00 per hour. Given the stratospheric cost of living in the Bay Area, plenty of students would suck the canker sores off a homeless man's dick for extra cash to make rent. Library work was a much more palatable option. Me? I had to get to... somewhere.

My boyfriend, Peter Yuen. Handsome brilliant Chinese guy. Should I mention that he's uncircumcised? It wasn't working out. The relationship, that is, not the foreskin; I kind of grooved on that. Peter studied 25 hours a day. I sort of looked at my books sometimes, on alternate Wednesdays, every other month, if there was a full moon. Peter wanted to plan for a

266

future together. I liked the idea, up to a point, but I also craved the French guy in the apartment across the hall from mine. Jean-Marc had made his lecherous intentions crystal-clear, albeit with an accent. *I want to know what your dick tastes like*, he remarked one afternoon when we were collecting our mail. *Come upstairs with me?* I had promised him a rain check. He kept reminding me, pointedly but politely. By contrast, Peter exuded a sort of endearing puppy-dog-like earnestness, especially when he told me what a terrific guy I was. I could only squirm, say *Thank You*, and pull up his shirt to lick his nipples again because I knew that totally turned him on and would, therefore, shut him up.

My instructors. Please. I'm a student, not an indentured servant. They could figure it out for themselves when I didn't turn up.

I'm out of here.

As airports go, Frankfurt's isn't so bad. Of course, by the time you have flown there from California, you are too anesthetized from the flight to give much of a shit. You're no longer on the plane. That's what counts. But the train station – the Hauptbahnhof – is another issue altogether. I got turned around, changing between the S-Bahn and the area where the trains were. Looking for the men's room, I had to step over blue-tinged junkies shooting up in a dim stairwell. A constellation of broken glass glittered on the floor around them. The air had a pervasive smell of beer farts. When I found the restroom I had to count to 30 before I could pee. Few experiences are less pleasant than standing dick-out at a urinal counting the seconds until your piss comes, all the while wondering how long until some diseased piece of German street trash wanders in and stabs you in the back with his hypodermic.

Just then, at that precise moment, standing there with my shrunken dick in my hand, I experienced one of the darker forms of epiphany: *This is why I'm here. Yes, by all means, bring on the syringes.* I turned away from the urinal and pissed a sour yellow arc on the floor, then had to hop over it to avoid getting my shoes wet. A sallow blue-haired man in faded black clothes saw what I was doing, raised a fist in mock salute, then followed my example. People who look like zombies just exhumed from fetid earth should not have penises as big as that; it's not fair. The thing hung five or six inches, flaccid – I couldn't exactly fail to notice. The yellow puddle on the floor widened. *Bring on the syringes.*

I had heard dark rumors about Gypsies on the trains between Budapest and Zagreb. They lock your sleeping berth and pump in some sort of gas to keep you unconscious while they rob you blind. Maybe they molest you if you're cute enough. That sounded like an authentic experience to me. Off to Zagreb I would go, then.

Zagreb ought to be interesting. The former Yugoslavia was teeming with misery. Shit that would give Clive Barker nightmares: buckets of testicles hacked off of Croat and Muslim prisoners, men taken out behind their own houses and shot, a beauty pageant whose contestants strutted up and down the catwalk wearing livid shrapnel scars and not much else, tanks ornamented with sliced-off human breasts (no, wait a minute, that was Ingushetia, wrong war, never mind), no beef to make Big Macs at the Belgrade McDonald's. (Perhaps those severed testicles could be put to use. Who would know the difference?) It was essential that I take a train into the thick of it all and soak in horror through my pores. Anything to set the crispy mortal remains of my parents spinning in their graves.

I went by way of Budapest, to improve the odds of something untoward happening on the train. Nothing did, but the sex clubs would have been something to write home about, had I come from the kind of home where one could discuss such things. (Does anyone?) I was having a splendid time until the ghosts of my ancestors appeared. I was spread-eagled in an orgy room having my ass eaten out by a tall blond hunk who looked like a

268

younger Val Kilmer while also blowing some other guy whose face, to be honest, I couldn't see. The ghosts said, *This is depraved and wrong, and you should not be here.* I thought I was drunk, and ignored them. The ghosts said, *Our souls are not able to find peace because you have profaned our peace with your disregard.* Telepathically (this all made sense after seven or eight beers and a joint I think was laced with opium) I told them that was the idea. The ghosts vanished. *You should eat more,* I told myself, mouth now full of someone else. *Seeing ghosts in back rooms isn't a good sign. Major dick-shrinker.* I spent three more days in Budapest, mostly undressed, then took the train south, feeling pleasantly soiled.

Unless you are or have at some point in your life been a disaffected college student smoking cigarettes rolled in black paper on a noisy train in Eastern Europe, you haven't lived. On the train, you eavesdrop on conversations in foreign languages, understanding little of what you hear but feeling pleased with yourself all the same. You're supposed to peer over your copy of _____ (supply name of foreign newspaper – *Stern, Paris Match,* whatever) from time to time, imagining what your fellow passengers must be yapping about, blowing stray ashes off the back of your hand.

Are you dressed in black? Bonus points if you answer Yes. Before I left Budapest I realized I didn't like my clothes, so I threw them away and bought new ones. Black, of course. To match the cigarettes I was smoking. To match my lungs, by the end of this trip. To match my *outlook.*

On trips like this you're supposed to meet a French couple of murky sexual orientation, have an affair with one of them, perhaps both, and abandon your previous plans (however vague they may have been) in order to join them in Ibiza or Sitges, never leaving their cottage until your cock and/or your asshole ache from all the sex. You are *not* supposed to travel to an uncharted island off the coast of Thailand with them, to take up residence in an enclave of photogenic international outcasts who look great despite the utter lack of shampoo and toothpaste. Things like that just do not happen.

In my case I met and joined a French couple of the clearly homosexual persuasion for a couple of days on the well-charted island of Krk, off the coast of Croatia, in the upper Adriatic. Bizarre place. Pretty. Croatian is hard to decipher. Not that we came into much contact with the language. We took walks along the beach, ate rustic food from a couple of quaint restaurants, burned lots of candles, almost set the cottage on fire, and... well, by then, it had been long enough since the sexathon in Budapest that I had the energy for full-time slutness. The ghosts I saw in Hungary didn't put in an appearance, but the candles kept blowing out when somebody's dick was in my mouth. What the hell. It wasn't Thailand, and nobody involved looked like Leonardo DiCaprio (well, Yves kind of resembled a less muscular Ben Affleck when I squinted), but it passed the time.

On trips like this, you're also supposed to send a couple of sketchy postcards to friends back in the States. The rule of thumb: write no more than two lines. State nothing. Imply everything. Exaggerate.

I skipped the postcards.

It is also advisable that somewhere along the way you befriend a local boy your own age, a fellow university student. He should live at home with his mother and his grandmother. They know he's gay, because Eastern Europeans are like that, because it's less of an issue to them than the epileptic fits contorting the economy ever since democracy was imposed, and because the story would fall into disagreeable cliché if it turned into an overwrought coming-out drama with accents. You and we'll-call-him-B. drink coffee in a plaza near a Metro station in Sofia (Bucharest, Athens, Bratislava, whatever) and stare meaningfully at each other while pigeons warble and passersby jabber into their mobile phones. He takes you to a movie way out-of-date by Hollywood standards, something dubbed into Bulgarian (Romanian, Greek, Slovak, whatever) or, worse, subtitled, and you share a Coke and gently jack each other off as Bruce Willis blows up a building full of drug-lord mafia goons. You and the building explode as one. Later, at his house, his parents tell you they think it's wonderful he has befriended a nice American tourist. Someone speaks pretty good English and gets stuck interpreting the conversation all night. Everyone gets drunk on the bottle of slivovitz the family was saving for a special occasion. Talk of B. going to grad school in England or, if he can get grant money, the States. After a few days you exchange e-mail addresses, say wistful goodbyes, and talk about hooking up again at some unspecified time and place. You part. There's a lump in your throat.

In my case, I didn't meet anyone like this in Zagreb, because they kept coming up to me and speaking German. Do I look German? I *so* do not look German. I don't even know how to say *I don't speak German* in German. Even if I were to look up the phrase and rehearse with a native, it would still come out of my mouth sounding like *I want to fuck your sister's pet rabbit*. A couple of Swedish guys tried to strike up a conversation with me in one bar I found after spending an entire afternoon riding around on trams with no real destination in mind. The Swedes spoke excellent English with a cute ABBA accent but, strapping blondness notwithstanding, after a few minutes they had bored me to tears. When they invited me back to their room so they could tie me up and piss on me in the shower I declined, drained my drink, and hurried back to my pension. I'm a slut, not a mentholated urinal cake.

After Zagreb I wanted to head south to Athens.

Of course I didn't make it. It's a bitch to get there directly – you have to pass through Bosnia and Macedonia, and who wants to go *there*? – so I thought I'd head north again, enter Italy, go down on the eastern coast, and catch a ferry from Bari. It would take time. I had time. The catch: my train derailed in Slovenia. How circular. I wasn't killed, but other people were, rather grisly I heard, severed body parts flying through the air, corpses burning, vultures, photographers. I got a little banged up by flying debris, and was taken to the hospital by people who seemed to know I was American just by looking at me. (Demerits.)

Ask yourself: what is the worst thing in the world?

I suppose having your balls sliced off and tossed into a bucket with those of your male relatives, friends, and neighbors, just before you're all shot and thrown into a mass grave, would have to be at the top of the list. However, being harassed for two days by two chunky Slovenian nurses because I wouldn't take a dump in the bedpan they kept shoving under my butt was at least third runner-up. I didn't have to go. They spoke English. How many times did I have to say it before they'd understand, I didn't have to go? *Let me out of here, I'll get a room at the Hilton in Ljubljana, eat a couple of nice fattening meals, drink some wine, and I promise, I'll save the byproduct for you in whatever containment device you provide.*

In Ljubljana everything began to come apart at the seams. I took a room, decided to spend several days chilling out after the train wreck, catching my breath, you know, getting it together. Eating. Taking walks in parks – the Slovene capital is good for that. The entire country is the size of a postcard, so you can see a lot without trying too hard. However, it's hard to feel refreshed when one sees the image of one's dead martyred (she thinks) mother wagging a finger in disapproval and intoning *You have brought shame upon our family* every time one looks in the mirror or passes a storefront with reflective windows. I hooked up with this Sardinian businessman attorney banker type who picked me up in the hotel bar. I was sitting at a table drinking a glass of Perrier, chilled, no ice, and looking at the pictures in a copy of *Stern* when this beautiful olive-complected guy

272

in an Italian suit took a seat across from me, speared me with a look, and asked if I had the time.

I have plenty of time, *I told him.* I have all the time in the world, and a new Rolex watch to prove it.

Excellent, he replied. *I have a room upstairs.*

It was that simple. Then my father materialized beside the bed while I had my legs wrapped around Carlo getting jackhammered like a natural woman. *Shame*, my father intoned. *The fires of hell are going to burn hotter for the likes of you. I wish you had been born dead.*

It's hard to keep your mind on your lover's rhythm when you're having a telepathic conversation with your dead, disapproving father. You tend to get distracted. Is your father really there? Or is this an hallucination brought on by several weeks of meal-skipping, late nights, carnal excess, and mind-altering substances interacting poisonously with your antidepressants?

There is a problem? Carlo asked, pausing, his hyper-infra-green eyes lasering into mine.

When I looked back at the space where my father had been, I saw nothing but sunlight slanting into the room through the gap in the curtains. Motes of dust. A stain on the wall I hadn't noticed before.

Nothing a different position wouldn't fix, I replied, straddling him.

In the shower with Carlo after our encounter, the soap kept sliding out of its holder. One of us kept having to bend over and pick it up. Each time I retrieved it, a different word (SHAME, FILTH, SINNER) was carved into it, visible to me but not him. I've seen enough horror movies to know how these things work, so I didn't waste my breath asking if the soap looked funny. With my luck he'd decide he'd hooked up with a dangerous freak and dash out of the room still dripping. At the café I found down the street from my hotel my glass of Pinot Grigio turned into what looked like blood, with clotted things matting the rim of the glass. I sent back my drink and asked for a Coke, an unspoken challenge to whatever was trying to frighten me: *Sure, you can change wine into blood, great trick, but let's see what you can do with all these synthetic carcinogenic chemicals.* If this was how it had to be, then I'd fly to New Orleans first thing in the morning and hire voodoo priestesses to tackle my problem.

That I might have gone nuts never crossed my mind.

I left Ljubljana the next morning on a flight to London, not a train bound for the Italian border. At Heathrow I'd catch another plane to New York; on to New Orleans from there. Like the Zagreb to Athens trip, getting there directly is a bitch.

Somewhere over the Atlantic, ghosts of *other* people's ancestors started to pop up. In the dead of airplane night, the specter of an elderly Asian man appeared in the seat next to me. A faint scent of spring rolls wafted my way. I groaned. He scowled and shook his head in disapproval. I telepathed, *Aren't you supposed to be in an Amy Tan story? Why are you here? My parents put you up to this, didn't they? You're wasting your time, if this is going to be another one of those Change Your Ways lectures. Honest.* He muttered something in a language I didn't understand, wagged a finger, and disappeared, presumably to show up in a novella about someone's coming-of-age experiences in Beijing.

A sense of preternatural foreboding crept over me as I unpacked my luggage. New Orleans is the kind of city best described with adjectives like *preternatural* and *crepuscular*. The guest house where I had rented a room seemed lavish but a touch seedy at the same time, as if years of humidity and scandal had caused the very matter of the walls and furniture to unravel, to suggest a state of near-collapse while still appearing solid and intact. The rooms with their gilt mouldings and rich white bedspreads and canopy beds and water-stained ceilings evinced a sense of ancient murders, dramas unfolding even now in alternate time-spaces. *New Orleans, I decided, is going to agree with me.* Right away I saw why no writer who has ever even mentioned the place could avoid ultraviolet prose. The place was like that. Purple, purple, everywhere you looked, even when things were other colors.

Separating the legitimate voodoo priests and priestesses from the ones who do nothing but wave rattly sticks in the air, jabber meaningless incantations, burn incense, and live like minor nobility on tourist dollars isn't easy. There aren't credentials. It's not like you can watch a Martha Stewart special to learn how she found her own personal hexmistress to cram more hours into the day, to give Her Tastefulness time enough to thatch the front of her house, assemble an exquisite arrangement of late-spring flowers in a Czech glass vase she designed herself, organize a stock split, and whip up a succulent meat pie containing the entrails of everyone who has uttered a cross word to her in public, all before lunch. Instead, you go into the first voodoo shop, slink up to the person behind the counter, and ask whom you should talk to about ghosts. Then you visit the next shop and compare answers. This was the method I employed, and it led me to Zazie Richelieu.

I found Mme. Richelieu, a dusky-skinned polyhedroon (or whatever the polite word is for people with more mixed blood than the Red Cross) with one long braid hanging down to her behind, in a small house between the French Quarter and the less tame area just to the northeast. Walking was possible but inadvisable, sources told me. I took a cab and got there slower, thanks to the hordes of slack-jawed tourists with alcoholic drinks in hand, than I would have on foot. Mme. Richelieu was outside cutting lilies in her garden when I arrived. She had on a flowery dress, a straw hat into which fake flowers had been woven, and little pumps with fake flowers on them. I expected her to smell like a flower when I got close enough to take a whiff, but the only scent I caught was some kind of deodorant.

You're the boy that wants to talk to me about ghosts, she stated, once I had introduced myself.

You are a clairvoyant, I marvelled.

No, I just got a fax from Lucretia at the store on Dauphine. Come inside. Would you like tea?

I guess I was expecting a decoction of rose hips and wild nettle in a brittle cup of bone china, but Mme. Richelieu served Celestial Seasonings. Tension Tamer, to be exact. I drink gallons of it at home. And I had seen her mugs at Crate and Barrel.

Clear your mind, she told me. *Gaze into my crystal ball and tell me what you see.*

The little wooden base thing the ball is resting on. Is that rosewood? I should buy one before I leave New Orleans. I like it.

Mme. Richelieu glared at me. *What else do you see?*

A faint reflection of my face, very distorted. The ghost of my mother, standing right behind you, with that "my hemorrhoids hurt" look on her face.

My hands shook as I lifted the cup of tea to my mouth.

I can see your last few weeks have been very difficult, said the voodoo priestess, looking through me with her X-ray eyes. Was she doing a brain scan? Could she see terrible things inside my skull, craziness and big clotted tumors festering in there? Was it obvious to her that I was a ghoul who was actually kind of getting off on the fact his parents had bought the farm? *The exhaustion and horror are up there like a neon sign on your forehead. You have to take some time off, rest – drop out of sight for a few weeks and just bum around.*

I protested: *I tried that. Look where it got me.*

In the end she gave me an off-white candle to burn over my parents' grave. I sniffed it: kind of sweet, a bit salty, familiar. The name of that aroma was right on the tip of my tongue. I had hoped to avoid a trip back to Maryland but if it had to be done, then it had to be done. I also accepted a small brown bottle of something that made my eyes and sinuses sting when I sniffed.

Mme. Richelieu said: *If I were still a psychiatrist in private practice over in Metairie, I'd tell you I've diagnosed you with a brief reactive-type psychosis brought on by extreme stress, grief, and heavy use of drugs. I'd write you a scrip for one of the anti-psychotics, Risperdol maybe. Possibly one of the anti-anxiety meds like Paxil, if you were to ask me nicely. And I'd follow up in 30 days to monitor your progress. I don't think you have a long-term need for medication, but I could be wrong. Have been before, but that's not the point. I got out of that line of work a few years ago. Promised myself I wouldn't go back to that office park in the suburbs, and I'm sticking with it.*

I asked, *How does one go from being a psychiatrist to being a… what's your job title, anyway?*

You quit, she said. *You transfer your patients to your colleagues, who can't decide whether to have you committed or to congratulate you. They're certainly not complaining about the extra business. You cash in your retirement plan. You hang out a different shingle. It's not too difficult. It's just a matter of deciding you've had enough of the status quo, and working to make things different. Better.*

So now what? That was what I had flown to New Orleans and tracked her supernatural ass down to ask, wasn't it?

Mme. Richelieu rose to see me to the door. *Take the preparation I've given you, a few drops a time in a glass of water, a few times a day. Burn the candle over your parents' grave. Go back to wherever you call home and be quiet for a while. Figure out who your friends are, and spend time with them.*

I balked. *Wait a minute: you never mentioned whether you believe I'm seeing ghosts or not!*

277

You're absolutely right, and I don't intend to. She smiled as she opened the door to her parlor, causing me to blink and squint in the sun.

Bitter disappointment coursed through me. No magic wand, no gasp of *Oh great goddess I can see the evil presences now, this is going take my strongest spells and incantations but if I get to work now I will prevail.* I had flown from Slovenia for this? Pithy keep-a-stiff-upper-lip advice from a lapsed psychiatrist who probably got her degree in the mail? I attempted to keep my face blank. I stood and turned to leave.

My grandmother was a Brazilian Candomble priestess, said Mme. Richelieu as I stepped across the threshold. *So was my mother, when she moved to this country. I grew up in that world, then went away to Cornell and came back with an MD.* She smiled at me again. *Trust me. Go to the airport, get on a plane, fly off to wherever your parents are buried. Burn the candle over their grave at midnight. Once it burns down, tell them what it's made of, then go on your merry way. They won't trouble you again.*

Last question: *Are you going to tell me what the candle is made of?*

Last smile from her, wider than ever. A wink, a gleeful grin that suggested she understood things much better than I could know. She wiped her hands on her skirt as if they were sticky.

Think about your travels. Think back. Take another sniff or two. You'll figure it out. It's certainly a substance you've come into contact with often enough.

And finally:

I wish I could say that all this has made me a better person.

I wish I could say I never saw apparitions again – at least none since this happened – because I flew back to Maryland, burned the white candle over my parents' grave at midnight, as instructed, and announced *It's sperm* as the stuff ran down my parents' garish marble obelisk. I doubt that's why it happened. I don't know what the hell to attribute it to. The sour bitter herbal crap in the bottle Zazie Richelieu gave me in New Orleans? Yesterday I stopped at Whole Foods and bought a little St. John's Wort extract, on a hunch. Same stuff. I don't think she ever left the psychiatric profession. She just dresses differently and has a crystal ball on her desk instead of a copy of the DSM. And I think I know BS when it's being shoveled at me. I'd like to think I'm too sophisticated (or cynical) to be susceptible to the power of suggestion. But In the end, I don't know what to say.

I'm not a better person. Hell, I'm not even a very *nice* person.

I didn't wake up my first morning back in California bubbling over with newfound zest for living. The only bubbling over was done by Peter when he picked me up at the airport, happy to see me for reasons I cannot and will never be able to fathom, and again, more literally, that morning when I went down on him before we got out of bed.

I ran around Europe but didn't soak up the kind of horrors I was hoping to soak up. No mortars. No robberies at all, not even a pickpocketing by scruffy street urchins in a metro station. No testicles that weren't still attached to their owners. One train wreck, but it didn't amount to much. No strangely gristly Big Macs in Belgrade. Some ghosts, but they probably weren't real. Bottom line: to be honest, I ended up more or less back where I started. Like I said when I started writing all this down, anyone who has ever read a literary journal or seen a subtitled movie knows that people who live at the periphery of civilization have more meaningful lives than us schmucks from the American suburbs. Had I been born in Dubrovnik instead of Frederick, Maryland, I could have been a plucky peasant lad carted off to the killing fields of the Krajina… but that's somebody else's story.

THE NIGHT TATTOO

Quinn stood barefoot in wet sand, staring out at the luminous black Atlantic. A strong wind off the ocean stung his face. His hair, brown but greying at the temples and sticky from the salt spray, whipped his cheeks and jaw – he was months past the point of needing a trim. He needed a lawnmower.

Traces of phosphorus lent the seawater a faint glow. Whitecaps gleamed. Sand covered his feet as the dregs of a wave drained back out to sea; lingering foam gave off a dim and dirty luminosity. The constant pounding of the waves against the shore: this faded to a dull but comforting roar. He found he could tune it out like the rhythm of his heartbeat or the quiet susurrus of his breath.

Quinn felt laden, heavy, like a statue of himself made of compressed black ashes. Grief gave him hope for permeability. He wanted the wind to blow right through and scatter his ashes across the dunes, leaving just the outline of a man.

He'd driven down from his townhouse in the suburbs of Baltimore to his father's vacation home in Emerald Isle, on North Carolina's Outer Banks. Quinn had stood on the landing a moment, considering whether to lock the door. Let someone walk in and steal every stick of furniture, every scrap of clothing. Empty the place down to the floors. Good riddance. In fact, let someone douse the living room in gasoline and toss a match. But in the end, and with a twinge of regret, he bolted the door. The service light on the instrument binnacle of his Accord glared red at him when he turned the ignition key, reminding him the car was long overdue for an oil change.

He ignored its diode accusation and drove on, hoping the engine wouldn't seize up in some sneeze of a town like Emporia.

"Are you sure you don't want me to fly out there?" his father had asked, long distance from Houston. Quinn had called from the road to say he was on his way.

"No, I'll be fine."

"Are you sure?"

"No, but I don't want anyone around right now. I just want to get out of that house."

The stale air in the beach house smelled like a mix of salt spray, the paint Quinn's father applied at the end of the summer, and new furniture. His father summered there and wouldn't return until April or May, when Texas turned into a humid, blazing hell.

Quinn dropped his duffel bag inside the door as soon as he arrived, took a piss, headed straight for the beach. He couldn't endure another empty house.

While the sun was still setting behind him, he planted himself in the sand and stared out to sea. Bermuda lay out there, due east. Beyond that, north Africa. The Mediterranean. The Persian Gulf. His eyes stung, and the moisture leaking out of them could have been tears, or maybe it was just an accumulation of moisture from the late-fall wind. Deep in the off-season, Quinn had the beach to himself: just him and the gulls, no other tourists.

The row of houses at his back stood dark, lights on in only a few. When the sun crossed below the horizon, gloom descended – a palpable sense of the day having given up and gone in search of something better to do.

"Cut it out, this gloom and doom shit," his friend Bryan said, two days earlier, when Quinn announced his plans to stay at the beach for an unspecified while. "Give it a rest, already."

"I think the phrase is *doom and gloom*," Quinn had said.

"Whatever, man. It's been three months. You have to move on."

"I am."

After promising to stop by for a copy of the house keys, Bryan had hung up on him in exasperation.

Appetite finally forced Quinn off the beach. He put it off as long as he could. His stomach was going to digest itself if he didn't find something to eat, or his head would snap off at the neck and float away. Turning his back on the waves felt like betraying them. He telepathed a low note of respect toward the ocean as he walked up the sand toward the steps of his father's pier.

I'll be back tomorrow, he promised.

The kitchen showed no sign of recent use: no Hefty bag in the garbage can, stove pilot light out, layer of dust on the countertops. The refrigerator contained a box of baking soda, several jars of crusty condiments, and a sour, plasticky odor; the pantry had nothing more tantalizing to offer than some stale Saltines and one can of tuna. Quinn wondered, *Am I hungry or desperate?* Quinn hadn't been here in years but the Outer Banks wasn't the kind of place where things changed much – new houses went up, condos and timeshares, but the deli 10 minutes down the road would probably still be around. *Berry's Carolina Deli – Sandwiches, Beer, Bait.* A fingerprint-smudged magnet on the fridge displayed the number. Quinn called ahead and ordered a pastrami on rye, hold the crickets.

The girl behind the counter at the deli had checkerboard forearms. A pattern of black and white crossword puzzle squares started at her wrists. If the squares continued all the way up to her shoulders, her sleeves hid their ascent. How far up did the pattern extend? Could she play chess against herself upon her breasts?

"So do you want your sandwich?" she asked.

She waggled it like a gift she doubted he deserved. The white paper crunkled in her grip.

"Don't squash it," he said. "I haven't eaten since noon, and that was in Baltimore."

"Then you'd better stop looking at my tattoos and pay me," she said.

Quinn fumbled for his wallet. He couldn't take his eyes off the girl's arms.

"Those new?" he asked. "The ink is so black. You haven't had those very long, right?"

"Few years." The girl accepted his ten-dollar bill and shrugged. "The tattoo guy does good work. His ink doesn't fade."

"I was thinking about getting mine touched up," Quinn said. "Too much time in the sun. You know. Ruins the ink."

"Are you hitting on me?" asked the girl.

If there had been anyone else in the deli, Quinn would have been embarrassed.

If his wife hadn't been blown up in a helicopter accident in the Middle East, Quinn would have been more inclined to banter.

"No," he said. "Can I have my sandwich now?"

She handed it over.

"So, like, if you want to know who does my tattoos, I'll give you his number. He only takes referrals. Can't have the phone ringing off the hook all the time, you know?"

Quinn didn't know. His phone had stopped ringing a couple of weeks after Anna's closed-casket service. He didn't want company but he didn't want to be alone, either. His friends had forged an unspoken pact to treat him like an egg: *Don't pick him up – he might crack, and his guts will spill all over the floor.* Nobody wanted sticky fingers.

"Are you in there?" The girl mimed knocking on a door. "Hello?"

"Sorry. I'm starved. Catch you later, OK?"

Quinn knew by the prickle between his shoulders that she was watching him exit the deli. He felt like a stork or a flamingo, some ridiculous long-legged tropical bird. Not fully sure he trusted himself to drive, he finished his sandwich in the car and waited until the light-headed sensation subsided. If it had been a longer drive back to the house, he didn't think he could have made it. He'd have lost his way among the island's dark streets and ended up in Norfolk or Wilmington or Cuba or Brazil.

Quinn dragged his duffel bag upstairs. In his exhaustion, the thing seemed to have doubled in weight. His eyes wouldn't stay open for long. But before he went to bed, he needed a shower to scrub off the layer of glue the salt spray had turned into.

"What are the odds there are sheets on this bed?"

Quinn was tired enough to collapse atop the bedspread but didn't want to wake halfway up at 2.00 AM, pull back the duvet, and find a bare mattress underneath. He lifted the worn blue comforter for a look.

"Sheets. Beautiful. Thank you, Dad."

The icy blast in the shower slapped him back to his senses – he'd have to turn on the hot water heater before he went to bed. To reduce utility costs while the house stood vacant, his father left the water heater off. Unable to adjust, Quinn jumped out of the water after a couple of minutes, blue and shivering. He supposed he'd sluiced enough salt and sweat away so as not to foul the linens.

I've lost a wife too, his father had said. *I'll fly out there. We don't have to talk about anything if you don't want to. I just want you to know I'll be there.*

This, for Quinn's father, was a speech of legendary proportions.

I know you have, but I don't want company. Not now. Not yet. Not until I'm ready. But thank you.

Quinn flipped the switch in the fuse box. Tomorrow morning he'd go for a run on the beach, unless it was pissing rain outside. When he got home, he'd have a decent shower. Maybe by then, new food and drink would have magically appeared in the fridge, and breakfast would be possible: a mushroom omelet, some Canadian bacon, a couple of oranges. Was there any coffee in the house? If his father had coffee, it would be either instant or the canned stuff that tasted like dark-roasted kitty litter. A trip to the store, then, first thing.

Quinn, too tired to sleep, tossed and turned like a goldfish on a tile floor. His dreams were a roller-coaster ride through hell. At five, he gave up, put on shorts and a pair of sneakers, and went for a run. He didn't bother with sunscreen – the sun wouldn't rise for another couple of hours, and it was the wrong time of year to worry about a burn.

He'd lost weight in the months since Anna's death – he now had a couple of folds of loose skin where he'd once had a bit of a belly. Ever since he'd turned 30, he'd been losing the battle to keep his stomach flat, and after 35 everything he ate turned into love handles, but all that had changed when Anna's helicopter went down. The muscles in his arms had gone slack. He'd never been developed or defined – Anna had called him her brooding Lord Byron in the castle – but now he looked like a scarecrow.

The run on the beach accomplished two things: it got Quinn's mind off his grief, and it whetted his appetite. When he returned to the house, legs and lungs burning, two impressions hit him at the same time: *It's too quiet in here*, and *I'm starving*. He turned on the TV in the living room, cranked up the volume until he could hear CNN while he rummaged in the kitchen. More attacks in the Middle East. A ferry disaster in the

Philippines, hundreds of casualties. Stock market malaise. Nothing unusual.

"On second thought," Quinn said.

He switched over to VH1.

There was still nothing in the refrigerator. No coffee in the freezer. Not even the instant stuff. At least when he took a shower this time, he had hot water.

At the store, a few surfers pushed a cart full of beer, sandwich fixings, and bottled water. Two black-clad club kids wandered up and down the aisles – still hallucinating, Quinn assumed; one cradled a bag of chips like an infant, and the other cradled a bottle of Dr. Pepper. On every aisle, at least one bleary clerk was restocking shelves.

Shopping hungry makes every item in the store seem necessary. Quinn filled his cart even though he didn't know how long he wanted to stay or even what he wanted for breakfast. Apples and pears and Pop Tarts. Coke or Pepsi? Same difference. He compromised: six-pack of one, half a dozen of the other. The Cheerios and the Froot Loops presented the same problem: he had a craving for round cereal, but which one? Why not both? And on and on. The shopping cart groaned under its load. Like his Honda when the tires needed to be rotated, it developed a pull to the right.

At first glance, the bag boy seemed to be wearing a long-sleeved shirt. Then Quinn saw the tattoos – Snakes? Paisley? Vines? All of the above? Indigo serpents sprouted livid lavender leaves. Vivid red carp swam among morning glory blossoms. Psychedelic kelp stared with paisley eyes.

"They're tattoos," the bag boy said, as if Quinn hadn't figured this out for himself.

"Sir, will that be debit or credit?" the checkout girl asked.

"Plastic," Quinn said. "The paper ones always tear."

"No, I'm sorry, I said debit or credit? Do you want to pay with your ATM card?"

She looked like Anna, but fifteen years younger: curly brown hair tied back in a loose ponytail; same high cheekbones and dark eyes; same build. Quinn's throat went dry.

There was a black star tattooed on the left side of her neck, below the ear. The eye inside the star seemed to be looking at him. When it winked, Quinn jumped back and dropped his wallet. *That wasn't real!* The tattoo brought to mind those menacing Goyas in the Prado, in Madrid – when you walked through the gallery, you got the impression of painted eyes tracking your every move.

"Yes," Quinn croaked.

He picked up his wallet, opened it without looking inside, and with an unsteady hand, handed the girl cash.

"You're staring," the bag boy said.

"Debit," Quinn said. "No. I mean, plastic. Did you give me plastic?"

"Are you OK, mister?" the girl said, accepting the money with raised eyebrows. "You're not sick are you?"

"You look like my wife," Quinn said.

"You gave me too much money," the girl said.

"I'm sorry. Will you give me the change back?"

"No, I'm going to keep it."

"I don't think you're supposed to do that."

Quinn swallowed saliva. It went down like a mouthful of rocks.

"Did you guys get your tattoos done in the same place?"

"Yes, but he's pretty exclusive," the checkout girl said. "You get more choice if you drive over to Jacksonville. There's a tattoo place on every block. It's like 30 minutes from here."

"I know where it is," Quinn croaked.

He picked up the pieces of his composure and put them in the bag with his receipt and the last of the groceries. Not staring at the girl took effort. Looking at her took a different sort of effort – choosing to be reminded of what he had lost.

"But there's this guy who does it by referral," the bag boy said. "He's the best. He's a fucking god. You gonna get inked?"

"Maybe," Quinn said.

"Come back if you decide you want the guy's number."

Quinn wolfed a bowl of cereal and guzzled two cups of coffee for breakfast but passed out on the sofa despite the sugar and caffeine roaring through his system. He covered up with an old quilt and nodded off watching game shows. Why did Bob Barker get to be immortal and not Anna? How had Vanna White remained lifelike for so long when Anna was burned too badly for her body parts to be identifiable? No remains had been shipped home. Nobody could tell which cinders had been which crew members.

Brooding Lord Byron in the castle. Brooding, Quinn tended to hide in his upstairs office with a beer and a stack of books. Anna would ask, *Is Lord Byron writing a new poem? If she asks nicely, will the lady get to see the fruit of his genius? What if she shows the moody genius her tits?*

Quinn slept most of the day away and, like a vampire, began to feel conscious again around sunset. Overcast as the days tended to be, it was hard to tell the difference between noon and dusk. With the curtains closed, he lost all sense of time. He and Anna had honeymooned in Spain: their first few days in Madrid had been a jet-lagged horror of 8-hour naps at 2.00 PM, and pre-dawn lunches at an all-night restaurant near their hotel. This temporal disconnect felt similar.

Coming to, he stumbled downstairs to brew more coffee and rummage for something to eat. Outside, the wind howled. A scum of clouds obscured the moon. The waves would be huge. He had to see them.

What am I doing here?

Quinn closed the refrigerator door and sat on the floor. He stared at the crumbs of food and the dust bunnies his father had overlooked before leaving a couple of months ago. A few grains of rice, some brown stuff that looked like fossilized bread crust, one Cheerio.

I think the point is that I came here to do nothing. When does the act of doing nothing become a thing unto itself? Behold, the void. Nietzsche was right. Sort of.

Brooding Lord Byron stretched out on the kitchen floor. He lay on his back and looked at the ceiling.

One of Anna's last acts before her deployment to the Gulf was to get a tattoo.

"Are you nuts?" Quinn had asked, when she told him her intentions.

"Maybe," she said.

They were in the kitchen fixing breakfast. Two squirrels perched on the windowsill, chattering. Coffee percolated. Anna could never decide whether she wanted her eggs scrambled or fried. They went through this sort of thing more mornings than not. She could cleanse and suture a bleeding wound, she could speak three languages (English, Norwegian, German) fluently, and the shelves she hung were always straighter than Quinn's. Food was just beyond her, though: her omelets always crunched with eggshell fragments and she tended to boil pasta down to an oatmeal-like mush.

"You've never talked about this before," Quinn said.

"You have seven tattoos, Quinn. Why can't I have one of my own?" She cracked an egg against the edge of a mixing bowl and looked distractedly down at it. "I've been thinking about it for a long time."

"Where do you want it? What do you want? When?"

"You're against the idea already. I can tell."

Quinn raised his hands in a truce gesture: "No I'm not. I'm not against it at all. After all, like you said, I've got seven. Who am I to talk?"

"I want to get something from Norwegian folklore. Have you heard of the tree Yggdrasil?"

"I'm Brooding Lord Byron in the castle," Quinn said, with a grin and a nod. "I even know what it looks like. The World Oak."

She separated the two halves of the egg. "I guess we're having scrambled," she murmured, breaking a second and a third in quick succession.

"Are we out of tarragon yet? You want to get a World Oak tattooed on your back?"

"No. I mean, yes. Why did you ask two questions like that? I mean – you know what I mean!"

"No, I don't. I'm sorry. I don't care whether we have tarragon or not. Sage will be fine. When are you going to get the tattoo?"

"Next week. We're shipping out on the 23rd, so I figure it'll have enough time to heal... before." She broke a fourth egg, then a fifth. "I'm not sure how hungry I am."

There it was again, the ugliness in the Middle East and her role in it. The war itself had ended but American forces wouldn't be leaving any time soon. Quinn didn't want her to go but her unit had been mobilized and that was all there was to it. He didn't get to make these decisions. Uncle Sam did. The prick.

"I'm not either. Just scramble them and we'll either eat them or stare at them until they turn into yellow blobs of rubber."

Anna shrugged. As usual, her omelet turned out crunchy. Quinn grimaced inwardly but didn't complain – her nerves were shot, and a little extra calcium in the diet wasn't a bad thing. Yggdrasil on her back, then. She wanted to reconnect with her parents' culture in a tangible way before being shipped off to risk her life for a country in which she had not been born. Quinn had heard of worse reasons for tattoos.

She claimed the tattoo, which occupied a substantial piece of the real estate on her back, hurt like flame from a blowtorch going on. She cried when the tattooist inked the sensitive skin directly over her spine. True to her prediction, her Yggdrasil healed before her deployment. When she left, it was an itchy mess of flaking white skin.

"It'll look better when I get home," she promised him, when he dropped her off at the base.

Quinn never got to find out for himself. Three weeks later, she was dead.

Quinn picked himself up off the floor and looked outside at the night sky. With no light on the beach, he couldn't see the horizon. The grey expanse of the back deck disappeared into the dark. He couldn't see the footbridge leading over the dunes. Quinn imagined the boundaries of the real world lay at the edge of his vision. Beyond that, he'd find a sheer black void, a howling darkness that would swallow him whole if he came too close.

This is what nothing looks like.

A chill zinged through him. The dark surf could wait. It would still be there later. Quinn decided to drive back to the market to ask where the clerks got their tattoos.

Returning to the store gave Quinn the excuse to buy a frozen pizza and a bottle of red wine. Purchasing something, he felt less conspicuous than he would have, just walking up to the check-out girl and asking where she got her ink.

"Why don't you drive over to Jacksonville?" she asked. "Look around at the designs on the walls. You know, take your time."

"But the guy here on the island, the one who's so good... what about him?"

"You should ask George over there." She gave Quinn his receipt. "*Hey George!*"

George looked up.

Quinn walked over.

"So you wanna go see this guy?"

Quinn nodded. "Is he hard to get in touch with?"

"No, but he's picky, you know? You serious about this?"

"It's just a tattoo," Quinn said.

"It's never *just a tattoo*," the guy said. "It's always about something."

"What, do I have to give a secret password before I can make an appointment?"

"No, but he doesn't see just any asshole who walks in off the street."

"Glad to know you think so much of me."

"It's not that. He's just good, you know. Really fucking good. Look at my arms, man." The bag boy held them up for Quinn's approval. The vines seemed different, as if they were another shade of green now, or were twining along a new course up the kid's arms. The fish – hadn't they been more *paisley* last night? Now they looked like a school of sharp-toothed piranha among the morning glory tangles, vicious instead of benign orandas from a third-grade classroom. "He's like a god when it comes to skin and ink."

"What makes him divine?" Quinn asked. He wondered how long until the store manager waddled up to them and huffed orders for the bag boy to get back to work. The manager would look like a walrus in a stained white shirt and would have teeth like a dead coral reef. "What makes him God?"

"I dunno. It comes from inside. Like, his own talent. He just knows what you want."

292

"So he tattoos you and then you win the lottery and you get this great house and a Mercedes and a beautiful wife who doesn't get killed in a stupid war in the Middle East and everyone lives happily ever after?"

"No, man. He just knows the right tattoo. Don't ask me how. He just knows."

"You got his number?"

The bag boy fished out a surprisingly thick wallet. *Grocery stores must pay better than I thought.* Then he saw the contents of the wallet: bits of paper, photos, only a few bills.

"Here, keep it until next time, OK? I gotta get back to work."

Quinn pocketed the card and drove back to his father's house.

He probably doesn't go to sleep before 5.00 AM.

While the pizza baked, Quinn took his first sip of wine and made a face. He regretted his choice – a cheap California red, the oenological equivalent of Kool-Aid – but had to have at least a glass in his system before he could make the call.

Joe the tattoo guy lived at the north end of the island, near Fort Macon. Driving up NC Highway 58, memories returned in a tidal flow: road trips from college, two or three cars at a time, to drink, chase girls, and get sunburns. Traffic on the two-lane highway up the island crawled like the Baltimore Beltway at rush hour. Further proof that everywhere in the world was turning into the same place. Even in the dark, everything on the island looked just as it had, his last trip down: more wood-frame houses on stilts, fewer scrubby trees hugging the dunes, more fast-food restaurants and surf shops, a few quaint mom 'n' pop shell shops and soda fountains. Nothing surprised him. The commercial section of Atlantic Beach thumped and blared as it had when he'd been a 20-year-old college kid drinking with fake ID. The same mix of military guys and their big-haired girlfriends, wide-eyed college kids from the mainland, a few weather-beaten locals. Here were the bumper cars. There was that T-shirt place that's been around since the earth cooled. And finally, a green light. Traffic petered out as he drove north, toward the fort.

Joe lived in a decaying bungalow down a short dirt road. Quinn missed the turn, had to turn around at the fort's front gate – now closed – and double back. A mailbox without numbers was the only indication anyone lived out this far. Quinn had thought residential development stopped another mile or so back, but perhaps this house predated current zoning laws. The sense of time passing by speared him through. How many years had elapsed since he'd last climbed through the Civil War-era fort?

Quinn parked in front of Joe's house and got out of the car.

Joe answered, shirtless, the third time Quinn knocked.

They shook hands.

"I thought you were going to say *I've been expecting you*, like in a horror movie," Quinn joked.

"Well, you called, didn't you?" Joe's voice sounded as if he'd swallowed a pine cone before opening the door. "Mind if I smoke?"

"So long as you don't exhale on my fresh ink," Quinn said.

"I'm a professional." That seemed to be the end of that subject.

The room smelled of dust and salt. Joe's furniture, junk not yet old enough to be called antiques, gave off the scent of rotting upholstery. Ashtrays overflowed on every flat surface but the open windows kept the stink from being unbearable.

"Mind if I sit down?"

"Go right ahead. Tell me what you want," Joe said, clearing himself a space on the sofa opposite Quinn's armchair.

Quinn studied him: no tattoos, that was the odd thing. In fact, Joe had to be the most nondescript human he'd seen in years. Brown hair the

294

color of a mouse in a sink full of dishwater, symmetrical features, deep-set eyes either blue or green or some shade in between. The two floor lamps in Joe's living room illuminated the space about as well as the dome light in Quinn's car would have – from outside. Quinn squinted.

"You're trying to figure out where my tattoos are," Joe said.

"If they're all on your ass and nowhere else, it's OK, you don't have to show me," Quinn said.

"I can tell you need a beer," Joe said.

No tattoos on his back, either. What did he use, then – invisible ink? What would Joe look like under black light? Would his skin blaze up like a carnival attraction? Quinn looked around the room and wondered what kind of situation he'd gotten himself into. On the heels of that thought followed another, *Does it matter? When you've lost a wife, the worst has already happened. Everything after that is just denouement.* Maybe Joe had gone to the kitchen to load a gun. When he returned to the living room and pointed it, Quinn decided to say *Just be accurate.*

If one shot would do the job... why not?

Joe returned with two cans of Bud. Quinn walked a tightrope between relief and disappointment.

"So I just wanted you to touch up the band around my upper arm," Quinn said. "It's not black enough."

"Maybe, but that's not all you're here for."

"It isn't?"

"You want something black but that barbed wire around your arm isn't it," Joe said, popping his beer open. As he drank, he looked straight at Quinn.

"What is it, then? That guy at the grocery store called you the god of skin and ink. Do you have some kind of telepathic powers I need to know about?"

"No. I'm just good at what I do," Joe said. "People who come to me want the kind of tattoos nobody else can give them."

"OK, fine. I lost my wife. I want her back. But you can't tattoo her back into existence, can you?"

"Nope. Sorry about your loss, man." Joe took a respectful gulp of beer. "I can't do that for you."

"Or you can use a dirty needle and give me hepatitis, and I'll die and be reunited with her," Quinn said. "There's an idea for you."

"I've got standards," Joe said.

Quinn drank his beer and looked at the floor. Still looking down, he said, "She got killed over in the Middle East. Clean-up operation after the war, helicopter went down. She should never have gone over there in the first place." He looked up again. His eyes stung. "She got a tattoo before she went."

"Thought it might be something like that," Joe said. "Tell me what it looked like, where it was. You want the same one yourself, right?"

Quinn nodded. "I guess so." He thought for a second. "And I want it black. The kind that won't fade. I keep hearing that's a specialty of yours – your black doesn't fade."

"Depends," Joe said. "It won't if you don't want it to. It's really all up to you. What do you want it to be a tattoo of? What do you want it to do? Draw me the best picture you can. And come back tomorrow night. Meet me at the beach at the base of the breakwater off Fort Macon. Know where I'm talking about?"

"Good night for black tattoos," Joe said, the next night.

Behind him, dark surf roared. No moon hung overhead to illuminate the sky, and the stars hid behind a scrim of haze. Up at the point of land where the island ended, the dark ruin of Fort Macon loomed, its stone walls still guarding against long-gone Union forces.

"Did you already know it was the new moon?" Quinn asked.

"Yeah. I keep track of that. I'm almost ready, here. Want to take off your shirt?"

Quinn complied. "Can you see well enough? It's fucking dark out here."

"You wanted absolute black," Joe said. "This is the only way to obtain it."

"As long as my back doesn't look like a kid's first coloring book when you're done."

"No comment."

Quinn sat on a small but sturdy chair inside a light metal frame that had resembled the skeleton of a tent. At each corner of the four-sided structure, a silver cable rose as high into the night as he could see. There seemed to be dark things up high, maybe fifty or a hundred feet above the ground: *Feathers?* Quinn didn't know where the thought came from, but there it was. The feathers from some gigantic raven, attached to those cables. Gigantic black wings? *Nevermore.*

"Are you going to explain any of this?"

"No, not really," Joe said. "You wanted your wife's tattoo, and I'm going to give it to you. The only place to get a black that pure is from the space between the stars, and deep underground. There are no caves around here. This is the best we can do."

"You want me to believe you're going to tattoo the night itself into my back?"

"You're free to get up and leave at any time," Joe said.

Quinn shrugged. Giving in seemed easier than pressing the point. Joe would either talk sense or he wouldn't. Quinn would either get a tattoo or he wouldn't. Would he get some kind of infection from the open air? Were diseases borne on the wind? He doubted it. The salt spray had to be a natural antiseptic.

Joe's tattoo equipment looked like surgical implements from Mars. An apparatus resembling the child of a squid and a lawn mower engine connected the tattoo needle-gun with the creaking cables. Quinn thought of the gondola in a balloon ride he and Anna had taken over Napa County on a trip to California. These cables creaked in much the same way as the balloon, straining toward the limitless immensity overhead.

Some other gizmo – half umbrella, half camera tripod – acted to stabilize the equipment. Telescoping legs ended in the claws of an old-fashioned bathtub. Quinn wondered if he'd taken a wrong turn somewhere and fallen into a David Lynch film.

"Just do it," he said.

Anna was right: going on, the tattoo hurt like the mean end of an angry blowtorch. Tears leaked from Quinn's eyes after the first ten minutes and in that Mozart symphony of pain, he didn't care. Afterward, he drove home in a sweat-soaked daze, shivering, not remembering much. He sat up all night drinking wine and staring out to sea, the tree on his back smoldering like dark embers. Waves crashed. What would it be like to dash out into the surf, ignoring the sting of saltwater against the raw tattoo, and swim east until his lungs and his muscles gave out? *Anna, I'm on my way.*

Were those things up there really feathers? Something like a weather vane? Some kind of filter to draw black out of the nighttime sky by a capillary action Quinn couldn't even begin to get his mind around? Cables like wicks delivering night-black ink in a steady trickle, as Joe tattooed the Old Norse tree into Quinn's back?

Quinn was of two minds about this: *Impossible* and *But what else could it be?*

In his father's master bathroom, Quinn surveyed his back in the mirror, with the aid of a second mirror. Tiny beads of red dotted the glistening black tree. The World Oak gleamed with blood and wet ink. Yggdrasil, with ornaments. It was almost the holiday season, so why not? On closer inspection, Joe missed had a spot here and there. Or was it just grit from the beach?

"Christ, that can't be hygienic," Quinn muttered, craning his neck to see better.

Tiny white spots scattered through the fresh dark of the tattoo made Quinn wonder how thorough Joe had been.

"But then, I've never heard of a tattoo this big that didn't require a little touching up after the first session."

A yawn interrupted the flow of Quinn's thoughts. His back hurt. His eyes hurt. Everything blurred. Dawn couldn't be more than an hour away. It had been a long night.

Quinn slept the day away and, lying on his stomach sometime in the gloom of early evening, decided he'd done what he had to do. It was time to drive back to Baltimore. One more walk down to the beach, and he'd hit the road. He'd get home no earlier than 3.00AM, but so what? He'd been keeping a vampire's hours lately.

The skin on Quinn's back felt stapled on, as if it were false or had belonged to someone else until last night. Yggdrasil stung, a World Oak of low persistent pain. Tense and sore all over, he felt as if he'd just crawled off a long flight with half a dozen babies screaming and a fat lady overflowing the seat next to him and crushing his leg.

He pulled on a pair of jeans and a loose sweatshirt. Barefoot, he walked down to the beach, and broke into goosebumps as he stared at the sliver of moon and the surf.

"Time to go," he said out loud. The grief coursing through him had not diminished but something about getting tattooed had changed his perspective – he couldn't see the point in staying.

In the bathroom mirror, Quinn inspected his new tattoo. Last thing before hitting the road. He held a hand mirror in front of him and kept pressing it closer and closer to his face, to get a better look at the thing on his back. When he bumped the little mirror against his nose, leaving a dime-sized smudge of sebaceous oil in the center of his visual field, he recognized a simmering wave of panic for what it was.

The Yggdrasil on his back glistened, already well on its way to healing. He saw none of the usual bloody-black crust above the fresh tattoo. He should have already started to slough off a layer of dead surface skin, thin scabs, and excess ink. But this skin seemed intact, healthy, new.

"What the fuck?"

And the white flecks in the tattoo, they hadn't faded as the ink settled into his skin. Nor did they look accidental. When Quinn squinted at one such spot, a disquieting thought crossed his mind: *they're stars.* Quinn stood there blinking. He thought, *If a comet flies from one branch to another I am going to lose my goddamn mind. Assuming I haven't already lost it.*

He drove back to Baltimore consciously *not thinking about it.*

Burglars hadn't done him the favor of stealing his house. At 3.35 by the clock on the dashboard, wired to the point of jittering from three Cokes and an entire canister of Pringles, Quinn had turned off the main road into his development – *townhouse canyons,* the real estate columnists called neighborhoods like these – in vague hopes of finding an empty black square where his home should have been. He parked in front of the house, Anna's Nissan in the space next to his, and contemplated the structure.

Brooding Lord Byron in the starter home that's already finished. Might as well go inside. His back itched after the nine-hour trek back from North Carolina but otherwise wasn't calling much attention to itself. He'd begun to convince himself the spots in the ink were nothing but flaws, places Joe hadn't filled in. What else could be the outcome of getting your tattoo done on the beach in the middle of the night? Of course there would be flaws. Quinn let himself in, satisfied himself all the furniture and valuables hadn't been pilfered, and stretched out on the sofa.

The answering machine, when he checked, contained ten new messages. He pressed Delete ten times. Anyone who mattered would have sense enough to call back.

Quinn couldn't sleep. He gave up on his bed (too big now that he was the only one in it) and tried the sofa, a big overstuffed thing his older brother had handed down. The cushions smelled like shampoo and history. Quinn's eyes would not stay closed. His eyeballs had turned into sandpaper and every part of him itched. He wanted to wake up in the morning (or afternoon, it didn't matter, nothing did) feeling if not refreshed, at least *reset*, but after a squirmy hour on the couch, failing to relax, he said "fuck it" and went to the bathroom.

He took a leak.

He almost convinced himself not to look at his back.

Pussy, a voice inside his head taunted him.

Quinn took a deep breath and drew the shirt over his head.

He took another deep breath, turned around, and looked.

Several branches on the tree had fused together. In the night black sky between his shoulder blades, he could almost make out constellations. If the gleaming spots back there were mistakes, why did the mistakes look like Orion?

He couldn't look more closely because his legs wouldn't hold him up. "Stars," he said, sitting heavily on the toilet. "Fuck."

Joe answered the phone on the fifth ring.

"Do you know what time it is?" he croaked.

"I'm sorry I woke you up," Quinn said.

"You didn't," Joe said. "I don't sleep much. What's up? That tattoo working out for you?" He laughed. His bark of a laugh turned into a cough. "I always ask that. Like there's anything you can do, once you got a tattoo, you know? Like they make White Out for tattoos?"

"I can see the stars in the dark parts," Quinn said. He took deep breaths and forced himself to speak in a reasonable tone of voice. If he let the panic come capering in, Joe would hang up.

"Isn't that usually where stars can be seen?"

"But not on my *back*," Quinn said.

"Oh, that. Yeah. That's one of my better jobs. That's what you wanted, right?"

"The branches are fusing together."

"Are you sure you really wanted a big tree on your back?"

Quinn started to say something but the thought slipped out of his grasp before he could express it. He stopped to think. The words *just be accurate* came to mind.

"Or did you want to see your wife again?"

"I... uhh..." Quinn wanted to break the connection, to make this conversation not be happening.

"Remember when you got to the beach a couple of days ago? There was something about grief and permeability? You've got a piece of the night inside you now. It'll get bigger. You could have used a gun or tried to swim to Bermuda, but you came to me instead. You got what you want."

Quinn slumped down in his chair.

"How long do I have?"

"Couple of nights, I don't know."

"Will it hurt?"

"Depends on how you define pain."

Quinn hung up on him.

When Quinn checked the mirror again, Yggdrasil's roots had already grown across his lower back, down to the curve of his buttocks. The branches spread wider, around his sides. Darkness gleamed. What were the next couple of nights going to be like?

"There can't be enough vodka in the world to get me through tomorrow," Quinn said, pulling off his clothes. He walked downstairs to the kitchen naked for a drink.

Would he freeze to death if he lay down outside, in the tiny patch of yard behind the townhouse, surrounded by a six-foot-high fence? How long did it take to succumb to exposure in late-fall conditions? The temperature had to be in the low 40s. And would the neighbors see?

Quinn decided clothes would be the better idea and dressed warmly. Might as well do this right. He unfolded a deck chair unused since Indian summer and stretched out, drink in hand, to wait for the coming of the night.

PUBLICATION CREDITS

Black Shapes in a Darkened Room: *Queer Fear 2* (Arsenal Pulp Press, 2002). Michael Rowe, Ed.; *Velvet Mafia*, November 2004.

The Right Way to Eat a Bagel: *Outsider Ink*, December 2002; *The Insomniac Reader: Stories of the Night* (Manic D Press, 2005). Kevin Sampsell, Ed.

Sex and Dragons: *Suspect Thoughts Journal*, July 2001.

For Your Own Good: *Lodestar Quarterly*, December 2003.

Notes on a Disappearance: *Of the Flesh: Dangerous New Fiction*, Greg Wharton, ed. (Suspect Thoughts Press, 2001).

Enough Oxygen: *Velvet Mafia*, November 2001.

Everybody Loves the Musée d'Orsay: *Rebel Yell 2* (Haworth Press, 2002). Jay Quinn, Ed.

Sunset over Brittany: *The Barcelona Review*, January 2002.

Fixed: *Suspect Thoughts Journal*, February 2003.

Hurricane Season: *Space & Time*, July 2001.

Sic Gloria Transit: *Shadows of the Night* (Haworth Press, 2004). Greg Herren, Ed.

In the City of Warm Red Light: *Upon a Midnight Clear* (Haworth Press, 2004). Greg Herren, Ed.

Simon Says: *The Ghost of Carmen Miranda* (Alyson, 1998). Julie Trevelyan and Scott Brassart, Eds.

The Glue Factory: *The Best of the Best Meat Erotica* (Suspect Thoughts Press, 2002). Greg Wharton, Ed.

There and Back: *Harrington Gay Men's Fiction Quarterly*, Spring 2002 (Vol. 3, No. 2).

AUTHOR'S INDULGENCE

Thanks:

The editors who accepted these stories in one form or another.

And for encouragement, inspiration, moral support, and miscellaneous good deeds: Rubén Alatorre, Noël Alumit, Dan Boyle, Poppy Z Brite, Ellen Cotter, Mitch Cullin, Ghalib Dhalla, Julie Do, Linda Drew, Neal Drinnan, Warren Dunford, Douglas Ferguson, Gemma Files, Jim Gladstone, Brent Hartinger and Michael Jensen, Wil Hawk, Trebor Healey, James Johnstone, Bryan Jones, Collin Kelley, Bob Kerr, Gary Kramer, T'jie Kwie, Richard LaBonté, BJ Lim and June Whey, Eve Lopez, Jason Luciano, Anthony Ly, Rodger Marks, Sean Meriwether and Jack Slomovits, Elizabeth Shuey Morgan, Felice Picano, Andy Quan, Jay Quinn, Michael Rowe, Vikram Seshadri, Geoffrey Steinberg, Jeff Teh, Jim Tushinski, Andrew Xu, Dav Yaginuma, and Orsino Yeung.

.

www.ingramcontent.com/pod-product-compliance
Lightning Source LLC
Chambersburg PA
CBHW031154050726
47495CB00019B/1739

* 9 7 8 1 6 0 8 6 4 3 7 3 8 *